Ambersley

Amy Atwell

Ambersley is a work of fiction. Names, characters, places and incidents either are the product of the author's imagination or are used fictitiously. Any resemblance to actual persons, living or dead, events, or locales, is entirely coincidental.

Copyright © 2011 Amy Atwell

Cover Design by Laura Morrigan

Published by Amy Atwell
ISBN-13: 978-0-9849682-1-3
ISBN-10: 09849682-1-0

Acknowledgments

Bringing this book to publication has been a twenty-year journey. Really. I began jotting random scenes for what became *Ambersley* in the early 1990s. My heartfelt thanks to the talented and tenacious Debbi Michiko Florence, a fellow author whose friendship and support encouraged me to finish the first draft back in 2000. More thanks are owed to authors P.J. Alderman, Dale Mayer and Therese Walsh, all of whom slogged through the massive revision (and cutting of 20,000 words) in 2008.

To my writing groups—Writing GIAM, Pixie Chicks, LaLaLa Sisters—you've been there for me during the dark times when I might have abandoned my writing. Thanks for all the encouragement and support.

A note of thanks to literary agent Kevan Lyon, who championed this book to the New York publishers. I owe thanks for your conviction in my writing and your prodding me to dig more deeply into my hero. It's a better book because of your input.

To the terrific ladies of the Publishing Underground, thanks for all the guidance and advice in bringing this story to readers. Special thanks to Laura Morrigan for the breathtaking cover art. It's just what I wanted.

I'm grateful to my family for bearing with my unyielding desire to write and to my husband who always encourages me to follow my dreams.

In loving memory of my mother,
Nancy Ann Johnson Atwell,
who shared her passion for reading with everyone
—especially me.

The wait is over, Mom. I know you're smiling.

Ambersley

The Lords of London, Book 1

Part One:

Johnny

1

He'd simply done what any good man would do.

Thomas Bendicks repeated that to himself as he carried the small child along the forest path. Overhead, birdsong heralded the approaching dawn. He swore silently, afraid the bright light of day would bring regrets. Best not to think too closely upon the previous night's tragic events or the possible repercussions of his actions.

He adjusted his burden to gently shoulder his way into the cottage. "Martha?" She would know what to do next.

His wife bent over the stove in the dim light. "Is that you, dear? Go out and wash up. Eat something, then you can sleep your fill. You must be tired after last night." She turned toward the door and promptly dropped the loaf of bread she carried. "Tom, what's that you've got?"

He craned his neck and managed to whisper past the child's chokehold. "I found her just this side of the stream. I heard whimpering and there she was, all curled up under a rhododendron. When I pulled her out, she climbed into my arms. Now she won't let go." Awe tinged his voice, for he still couldn't believe this little being had trusted him. She clung to him like a vine to a sturdy oak.

He lowered himself into a chair as Martha approached to

peer at the child. The little girl could be no more than four years old. Cuts and scrapes reddened her chubby arms and legs beneath the torn and filthy nightdress. Sooty smudges marred a pale round face framed by a disheveled mass of long dark curls knotted with brambles. Her blue-green eyes overflowed with unspoken terror.

"Tom, why did you bring her here? You know she must be His Grace's daughter. Everyone will be searching for her."

He pulled the child from his shoulder and adjusted her across his lap. She nuzzled her head against his chest and closed her eyes, one tiny hand clutching his sweat-stained shirt. The smell of ash bound them as one.

"I was almost home when I found her." A poor excuse, he knew. "Besides, it's a right mess up at the Hall—the fire destroyed half the roof, the west wing is gutted, and I hear most of the inside is damaged." His voice dropped to a whisper. "The duke and duchess are dead, as is half the house staff."

Martha's eyes filled with tears, and she swept away the moisture with hasty fingers.

"I was told the child was dead, too," Tom continued. "Some daft story about her ghost sailing through the smoke last night. Nobody seems to know who's in charge or what to do next." His arm tightened about the child. "Look at her. She's so scared, I thought it better to bring her here for a day or two. I don't think she should see the Hall like it is now."

The little girl had fallen asleep against his chest. Gingerly, Martha reached over to smooth a stray curl from her face, bracing against old memories that swamped her. Poor little orphan, what was to become of her now? The title and the property would go to some male relative. Maybe he'd have a family—that would be best. It might be days before he arrived, and meanwhile...

She smiled. "Tom, you did the right thing. She needs peace, and she won't get it at the Hall. We'll keep her here with us until her relatives arrive. That shouldn't be nigh long, right?"

When he didn't answer, she realized he'd drifted to sleep,

his grizzled cheek slumped upon the child's head.

❧

The child awoke screaming.

Her soprano shrieks brought Martha running to her makeshift bed. Violent nightmares had assailed the little girl these past four nights, and once again she sat erect amidst rumpled blankets. She made no further sound, merely trembled while tears trickled down her face. The terror within her huge eyes ripped at Martha's heart.

She reached down to offer comfort, but the girl raised her arms to Tom who gathered her close. He crooned a wordless melody in her ear until her trembling subsided. Martha retreated to the hearth and tried to ignore the pang that came each time the little girl turned to him for solace.

She stirred last night's embers in the fireplace. "Come, Tom. I'll make a pot of tea and some porridge. It's no use trying to sleep more." Fetching her woolen shawl and a pail, she went to the well.

When she returned, she found Tom and the child seated on the chilly floor, where the little girl played silently with two cornhusk dolls he'd fashioned. Setting the kettle to boil, Martha's eyes stung as she recalled her first husband and little son, both lost to the pox years ago. Her son had been just this age when... She busied herself. Tom had offered her marriage, provided her solace for her loss, and asked for naught in return but that she prove a good wife. How she wished she could have given him a child—he was so obviously smitten with the little girl.

"She smiled at me," Tom said in a church whisper.

Martha raised her brows at him.

"She speaks not a word, and her eyes carry that haunted look still. Do you think she'll ever forget the fire?"

Martha knelt on the floor with them, although getting back on her feet would be no easy task. She stroked the little girl's shorn curls—cropping them close had been the only way to remove the briars.

The child responded with an upturned face and solemn

eyes. Martha barely dared breathe. Then, with an exhalation of breath, the girl returned her attention to the dolls.

Martha closed her eyes in a watery blink.

Tom stood and bent to help Martha to her feet. He followed her to the hearth and watched as she prepared the porridge for their breakfast. "I'm sorry she—" he began.

"No need apologizing for her. She is what she is and no harm done."

"I think she only turns to me because I found her." Tom swallowed. "I could take her up to the Hall, if you think that's best."

"I'm glad you found her, Tom, and I'm glad you brought her here. She's frightened and she's hurting, poor dear." She handed him a bowl of porridge. "'Twill do her no good to go traipsing up to the Hall. I saw the place yesterday, and it's a sorry sight. And who would look after her? Her nursemaid's dead. The poor child would be nothing but a burden to the butler or the housekeeper."

"I hear the duke's solicitor has left to find the heir."

Martha nodded. "Very well. She stays with us until the new duke arrives. She trusts you. You cannot betray that."

She went to the child and led her to the table. The girl sat docile as a lamb while Martha fed her small spoonfuls of porridge.

"Her appetite's improving," Tom said.

"Aye, 'tis. And yes, I think someday she'll forget. But the pain is deep and may take time to heal. We need to be patient."

As the weeks passed, the child's nightmares became less violent. She still clung to Tom for comfort, but whenever he left the cottage, she followed Martha about dog-like, silent and watchful. Martha laid her own ghosts to rest by clothing the little girl in her son's old shirt and breeches. The clothes fit well and even Tom approved, for it made her look less like an invalid. They spoke to no one of keeping the child—after all, they had no right to make themselves her guardians. Yet they believed they did what they did for the best.

One night at the table, Martha pushed her spoon through her stew. "Do they say anything about Miss Amber?"

It was the first time either of them had spoken the child's name in her presence, but she showed no sign that she recognized it as she ate her bread and honey.

Tom leaned forward on his elbows. "Only to say they cannot find a trace of her. But Mr. Pritchard told me the duke's solicitor planned to visit Bow Street while he was in London. There's tales someone may have set the fire deliberately."

"Why?"

Tom shrugged.

Ill at ease, Martha climbed to her feet. "Come, Johnny, help me with the dishes." The girl obediently rose and followed Martha with her plate.

Tom reached for his pipe. "I'm not sure it's right to call the child that."

"We must call her something." Martha added gruffly, for it had been her son's name, "It brings me peace, and she doesn't mind, do you, Johnny?"

The child looked up at once.

"See? I can't get her to look at me when I call her Amber."

The child cleared the table with no regard to her own name.

"Tom, is it possible she doesn't remember?"

He rubbed his nose in thought. "I suppose even though she doesn't have any burns, Miss Amber may hurt inside. Stokes said he's heard of cases where people who have bad experiences sometimes forget all about them—they even forget everything about themselves."

Martha snorted. "What does Stokes know? He's a footman."

"Ah, but he once worked for a physician in London."

This silenced Martha. She scrubbed plates while the child rinsed them with a pitcher of clean water. With a sigh, Tom rose from his chair to dry the plates and place them on the shelf. Preoccupied with their thoughts, silence hung like a thick fog while they worked.

While wiping down the table with a sodden rag, Martha paused. "Tom, are you telling me she might not know who she is?"

He watched the little girl on the floor with her dolls. "'Tis possible. No way to know until she starts to speak. And Martha, if she has forgotten, Stokes said that this, *amnesia* I think he called it, isn't always permanent. Sometimes people wake up one day, and they remember everything again."

As summer waned and one autumn moon proceeded to the next, Martha tried not to dwell too much on this conversation. Yet, while she watched orange colored leaves float free from the trees, she couldn't help but wish that Miss Amber would likewise magically fall free from her family. More than anything, though, she wished little Johnny would speak to her.

On a chilly November morning, Tom announced his intention to go hunting. He grinned widely as he checked his musket, which only made Martha laugh.

"Bloodthirsty man that you are. Bring us back a fat goose or a brace of doves."

"Aye, 'twill be my luck to shoot a big goose right into the lake, and me without a dog to fetch it. Remember that when I come home sopping wet and shivering." With a tip of his hat, he marched off.

Hoping for a rabbit or fowl to grace their table that night, Martha led Johnny to the arbor to gather chestnuts for dressing the meat. "I'm either getting too old or too fat for this," she said as she stooped to pick up a chestnut. No doubt her back would ache something fierce at the end of the day.

With pride she watched her little Johnny, in breeches, shirt and tricorne, dart about as quick as a squirrel. The child barely resembled the cherub they'd rescued—she'd grown taller and lost her chubbiness, while sunshine had browned her once porcelain skin and streaked her short dark curls with reddish gold. Johnny gathered handfuls of chestnuts and dumped them loudly into the pail they'd brought. Soon the tinny sound of nutshells against metal turned to the softer thud of nutshell against nutshell.

"This won't take us long at all, will it?" Martha kneeled on the ground and spread her shawl to fill it. It would be much easier to get up once than bend over a dozen times.

It was a full minute before she sensed that silence had

replaced the thud of nutshells, and she looked around to discover what might have caught Johnny's attention. Martha found herself alone in the arbor. With a grunt, she hefted herself up, stepping on her hem and spilling chestnuts in her wake.

"Johnny!" she called. *Remain calm. She cannot be far.* "Johnny!" The sound of crackling underbrush from behind made Martha turn with a start.

A tall, round man dressed in riding clothes and long cape stepped from the trees, the little girl in his arms. The sight of a stranger come to Ambersley made a shiver course up her spine.

"Johnny," she huffed. "Give me my Johnny."

The man looked down his snub nose at her. "Is this your little boy, Madam? Perhaps before I hand him over, you can help me. You see, I'm searching for a little girl about this same age."

Martha felt lightheaded as she realized the man wore a red coat beneath his cape. *A Bow Street Runner.* It had to be. And he'd already guessed the truth.

"Ah, you've gone pale. Don't tell me you believe this nonsense of the little girl's ghost? We have every hope that Miss Amber Vaughan is alive. Now tell me, do you know of any family in the area that may be harboring a little girl?"

Martha couldn't have answered his question had her life depended on it. But suddenly, Johnny, her eyes huge and round, reached out her arms. Her lips moved silently, and her throat bobbed until finally she managed to utter, "Ma!"

Instinctively, Martha charged forward while Johnny continued to bleat, "MaMaMa!"

The man surrendered the child to her. "Your boy seems to fear strangers."

"He's not accustomed to them, is all," she answered guardedly. The girl clung to her, and Martha, who had waited months to hold Johnny in her arms, wouldn't let the Devil himself pry this child away without a fight.

But the man seemed to believe the child was truly a boy. "I didn't mean to frighten your son. Tell me your name, boy. My name's Jackson," he coaxed with a friendly wink.

Slowly, the child smiled back. "Johnny."

Martha feared she might faint. While the child responded to the name, she'd never guessed the child *thought* of herself as Johnny.

After answering questions about the tragic fire and discussing the Ambersley staff and tenants, Martha felt brave enough to invite Mr. Jackson to look in at the cottage whenever he was by. She even wished him well with his search. "Although, I doubt you'll find Miss Amber living with anyone else around here."

"You may be right. Whoever set the fire, may have kidnapped her. If that be the case, I'll wager they took her away from the area. Even so, we'll find them, and if there's foul play, we'll send them to jail. Good day." With that, Mr. Jackson melted back into the trees.

Martha hugged the child closely to her bosom before setting her on the ground. "Johnny, let's go home. Quick, fetch the chestnuts."

The child ran to the pail, but it took both her arms and all her strength to heft it up and carry it to Martha.

"Good boy," she said, consciously training herself. Their very lives depended on everyone believing that she and Tom had taken in a little boy. Mr. Jackson might share this information with anyone—and everyone—he met. Her pulse steadying, Martha accepted that she and Tom would have to lay careful plans.

She led the way home. While they walked, Johnny tugged on her hand.

"I love you, Martha."

"I love you, too, Johnny." Thankfully, the path to the cottage was well-marked, because her eyes were clouded with tears the remainder of the way.

While the child slept that night, Martha poured forth her story of the Bow Street Runner to Tom. Though knowing they should hand the child over to the law, they worried for her safety. If someone had meant the Vaughan family harm, announcing the child's miraculous survival could endanger her. And so, Martha contrived a distant cousin who'd passed away, leaving a young son. She embellished the story by making her cousin unwed, so when she died, none of her immediate family wanted the child.

"Everyone knows you've wanted a lad to apprentice with you and learn the gardens, so they won't be surprised that we took in a little boy. We'll tell them he's been living with us since spring, but he was so sad about losing his mum, we didn't want to draw attention to him."

Tom watched her, sympathy tingeing his eyes. "You cannot grow too fond of the child. Remember, we must restore her to her family."

"To her family, yes, but we cannot let anyone else take her."

"Agreed." Tom took her hand in both his own. Long into the night, they sat awake in bed but spoke not another word on the painful topic.

And thus, Amber Johanna Vaughan disappeared, and Johnny became the foster son of a gardener.

෨৵

Johnny blossomed during her first year with Tom and Martha. The nightmares were forgotten, and the bright, happy child was accepted by all at Ambersley. One evening, after receiving the child's token of battered daffodils, Martha asked Tom if he thought Johnny would ever remember her past and tragic loss. Tom shrugged and lit his pipe. They both tried to remain detached, but as another spring progressed to summer and the second anniversary of the fire passed with no sign of the Ambersley heir, they realized Johnny had become an integral part of their family. They loved her as their own, and she loved them as any child would her parents.

Johnny adored the gardens and the conservatory that were Tom's domain—especially the rose garden. He let her play in the churned up dirt, only warning her to mind the precious roses and their protective thorns. Her other favorite spot was the stables; it was a special treat when Tom would suggest they pluck some clover for the coach horses.

One day, after they'd fed and petted the nose of one of the dappled grays, Rory the groom asked Tom if Johnny wanted to see a litter of kittens only two weeks old. The kittens were soft mewling balls of orange striped fur, and the mother watched with tail twitching as Johnny stroked them. Rory showed her the difference between the little boys and girls, let her touch their tiny but sharp claws and explained that their uniform blue eyes had only opened two days before.

As they walked back to the cottage, Johnny asked, "Tom, am I boy or a girl?"

Tom longed for his pipe as he sought an answer. He looked down into Johnny's troubled face with its firm chin and trusting blue-green eyes. He'd grown accustomed to her wavy chestnut curls pulled back into a shoulder-length queue, and it no longer seemed odd to him that she dressed in boys' clothes.

"You're a girl, Johnny." He said it gently, as if somehow he had to soften the blow.

She looked at him earnestly. "But I'm dressed as a boy. You always call me your foster son."

"I know. 'Tis the only way you can stay with Martha and me. Come home, and I'll explain everything." Tom offered his hand and Johnny grasped two of his fingers.

Tom explained the situation to Martha as soon as they arrived. She pulled the stewpot away from the fire and went to Johnny seated on the table's bench.

"Johnny?" Martha's voice was little more than a whisper. When the girl looked up, Martha recognized fear in her eyes— fear like she hadn't seen since the first few weeks the child had come to live with them. Not but six years old, how could they make her understand?

With great care, Tom started to explain. "You know we're not your true parents."

Johnny nodded slowly.

"You were not meant to live with us. But something happened to your family, and I found you. Do you remember the morning I found you?"

Johnny shook her head.

Tom and Martha exchanged a look. Tom added, "I found

you, and we've kept you with us, but someday you must return to your family."

"No. I don't want to leave you. Don't send me away." Her wide eyes pleaded for mercy.

"We'll never send you away, sweetheart." Martha wiped her sweaty palms on her apron. "We want you to stay with us always, but you should be with your family. If they return, we'll have to give you up."

"Even if I don't want to go? Even if my parents left me?" Johnny's voice cracked.

Tom cleared his throat. "I'm sure your parents didn't want to leave you. Someday, I hope you'll understand, but for now, we can't tell anyone who your parents are until your family is found." Tom leaned forward for emphasis. "'Tis not a good thing to lie, Johnny, but in this case, we chose to do what we did to keep you with us and to keep you safe."

Martha nodded in agreement. "Do you remember the Bow Street Runner we met in the chestnut grove? He was looking for a little girl just your age." She watched the child for any flicker of recognition.

"But he was looking for Miss Amber." Johnny's brows knit together, and she touched her head as if it ached. But within moments, her brow cleared again, and she added blithely, "Rory once told me he saw Miss Amber's ghost fly by him on the night of the fire."

Tom opened his mouth then shut it again. With a shake of his head, he walked to the fireplace for his pipe.

Martha sat next to Johnny. "We believe Miss Amber is still alive. What do you think?"

"I don't know."

She studied the child for some moments. "If the Bow Street Runner had discovered you were a little girl, I feared he'd take you from us. That's why I told him you were a boy. Now, if we told everyone you're a girl, there could be trouble. Someone might decide we were wrong to lie and take you in. They might take you away from us and send us to jail."

"Don't frighten the child," Tom said from the fireplace.

Martha took Johnny's hand. "You must understand 'tis no

game we play pretending you're a boy. Our lives depend on it now. All of our lives."

"If I pretend I'm a boy, can I stay with you and Tom?" Desperation tinged the childish voice. "Please?"

Martha nodded, tears in her eyes.

Tom set his pipe on the table and scooped Johnny into his arms for a tight hug. "Aye, lad. You can stay with us forever. That's what we want."

2

Nigel Minton tried to appreciate the irony that his search for the Ambersley heir had led him, after three years of traversing the length of the country, to a man owning a London house that stood not more than a mile from his own solicitor's office. Tracing the late duke's lineage had proven more difficult than Minton had anticipated, but he'd finally revealed a seventh cousin who was a direct descendent of Ambersley's original Vaughan male line.

"And, God willing, may this be the end," he said as he opened the wrought iron gate.

A gloomy dusk did little to enhance the townhouse's features, its marble grimy and chipped. The backlit windows with curtains drawn reminded him of the awkwardness of the hour, but like any good hound, he was eager to tree his quarry. Perhaps he could leave his card and arrange to call properly the next morning. He knocked and waited, anticipation growing.

The door opened to reveal a lad with black hair and icy blue eyes that quickly narrowed in scrutiny. Minton pegged the lad at perhaps a dozen years, clearly too young to be the butler or even a footman.

"Do you have business with us, sir?" The boy marred his

neutral tone by jutting out his chin in an obstinate manner.

Minton cleared his throat. "Indeed. I wish to speak with Reginald Vaughan."

"Father's dead," the boy answered flatly. "Been dead nigh three months now. Did he owe you money, too?"

Disappointment struck Minton, but he rallied with the hope that before him stood a male heir. Much too young to take active control of the dukedom, but given time—

"Curtis, whatever are you doing?" From the shadows, an elegant woman clothed in mourning approached to stand behind the lad, her hands on his shoulders. The two shared a striking resemblance, not the least of which was the unfriendly look mirrored in both their eyes.

Minton smiled. "Lady Vaughan? Forgive my intrusion at this hour. My name is Nigel Minton. I'm a solicitor, and I have business to discuss with the heirs of Reginald Vaughan."

"He wants money just like all the rest," Curtis said, clearly bored by Minton's brief speech.

"Hush," his mother hissed. She took hold of the lad's ear and pulled him backward. "Return to the schoolroom, and if you run off on Miss Trent again, I will be very displeased." She released him, and the boy fled deeper into the house, swallowed by the dark interior until only his footsteps could be heard clomping up the stairs.

Lady Vaughan turned back to Minton. She was a tall, handsome woman, mature but not old. He estimated her age to be ten years shy of his own five-and-forty. Unpowdered raven curls haloed her face in the latest style while the dark clothing she wore accentuated her pale face and angular features. A half-smile curved her lips, but her pale blue eyes remained aloof. "Forgive the boy. He's still distraught from Reginald's death."

She tossed off the comment as though her son's emotions were an unpleasant weakness. If he were to hazard a guess, Minton would say the lady before him had never been distraught about anything in her life.

"It's understandable."

She inclined her head briefly. "Do come in." The black

bombazine of her gown rustled as she bade him follow her into a spacious and well-lit parlor.

"I am sorry to hear of Lord Vaughan's death." Taking the chair she offered, he laid his hat atop the cherry side table.

Lady Vaughan seated herself on the divan. "Yes, everyone is sorry, yet they all want their due." Meeting his gaze, she became suddenly businesslike. "Tell me, Mr. Minton, what it is you want from us."

Her demeanor encouraged him to exercise caution with his information. "Reginald Vaughan was bequeathed something from a client of mine."

Her brow furrowed. "He never mentioned a bequest."

"I doubt he knew of it. Nevertheless, with Lord Vaughan's death, this bequest would pass to his eldest son. Would that be Master Curtis?"

Lady Vaughan leaned forward in her chair. Minton may have imagined the predatory gleam that flickered in her eyes, but couldn't deny the uneasiness that washed over him. She opened her mouth as if to speak, but instead released an audible sigh.

"No." She gave the single word emphasis by rising, agitation clear in the twitch of her skirts.

He started to stand, but she stopped him with a gesture. "Curtis is the second son, though, I must say we have every reason to believe his elder half brother is dead."

Her words dashed Minton's hopes. "Dead?"

"Ha!" Lady Vaughan's bark of bitter laughter caught him off-guard. "*If* we are lucky. Derek is the offspring of Reggie's first wife—Alicia Coatsworth Vaughan. I'm sure you know *her* notorious story."

Though Minton didn't often follow gossip of the *ton*, he remembered the scandal surrounding Alicia Vaughan thirteen years before. The woman had murdered her lover during a secluded tryst. Arrested, she'd accused her husband of the murder, but he'd never been charged. During her trial in the House of Lords, the young baroness had named many of her lovers, thereby besmirching the reputations of many top families and making her husband an infamous cuckold. The most notorious murderess all London could recall, her life had ended tragically by a public hanging.

Clearly, the current Lady Vaughan held little affection for her predecessor. But her acidity toward her stepson puzzled him. Best to know the worst. "I'm sure her death affected this young man."

With raised chin she peered down her nose at him. "I cannot say, for his mother was dead a year before I married his father and moved into this house. Not that Derek ever spared her a tear. The boy has no feelings for anyone. He abandoned his father, left home and we've neither seen nor heard from him since. I honestly believe he's dead." She sank gracefully back onto the divan, withdrew a handkerchief from her cuff and dabbed at her eyes, though they still appeared dry to Minton.

But now he understood. She resented the prodigal who, even absent, prevented her own son from inheriting anything from Reginald Vaughan. "Have you any notion where I might find Derek Vaughan?"

"India," she said with a sniff. "At least, that was his intended destination when he left here seven years ago."

Exercising great control, Minton pinched the bridge of his nose and readjusted his spectacles. It would take months to send a message across the world. But at least he had a name, and with luck, his task of finding the rightful Ambersley heir would end soon.

Ambersley, May 1804

A fortnight later, Rosalie Vaughan reclined against the plush squabs of the ducal coach and barely repressed a satisfied purr. All her toil, her infinite patience, was to be rewarded, and by the Duke of Ambersley, no less. If only Reggie had lived to see this day and make her a duchess.

Like so many things in her life, she had dealt with her

disappointment privately. Turning her head, she watched as Curtis steadied little Olivia, who pressed her nose to the coach window. As much as Rosalie loved her daughter, her hopes were pinned on her first-born. Curtis would secure their future at Ambersley without question. Her son had inherited a dukedom.

If only she could convince this solicitor of that. He insisted on initiating a search for Derek and refused to publicly announce her family's claim to the title, despite having a valid heir in his grasp. Minton's timely invitation to reside at Ambersley saved her from the embarrassment of creditors dunning her, but if Derek returned, she and her children would be subject to his whims. It irked her to think of Derek inheriting this prize he so little deserved.

But then, they'd had no word from him in the past seven years. She rather hoped he'd died out there in the wilds of India after the way he'd abandoned them all. With great care she'd urged Reggie to look upon Curtis as his true heir. Everything had been progressing nicely until Reggie learned that Derek had become a highly prized officer with Wellesley.

Glancing sidelong at Minton, Rosalie pursed her lips. The solicitor need not know *that* little tidbit. Let him search the globe for Derek—it would take months. Meanwhile, she would lay her own plans while she and her children remained at Ambersley. Rosalie closed her eyes, imagining herself as chatelaine of the ducal estate.

"Ah, here's Ambersham," Minton said.

Rosalie opened her eyes with a blink, unsure if she'd drifted to sleep or closed her eyes only moments before.

Curtis, his lip curled in dissatisfaction, turned his attention from the window to Minton. "The town is little more than a hovel."

"Aye, it's a small village," the solicitor replied, unperturbed.

Rosalie peered out the window to see thatched-roof cottages, what appeared to be a cooperage and a girl not much older than Olivia herding a flock of geese. The agitated birds gave voice to unmelodic honking as the carriage rolled past. A putrid odor warning of cattle nearby made her withdraw a perfumed handkerchief to cover her nose.

"How very...rustic," she said after they'd cleared the town.

Minton's lips curved in a gentle smile. "We prefer pastoral, but I'll admit it's a far cry from London."

To say the least. A bounce jostled her, and she barely had time to steady Olivia. Apparently, the quality of the roads was *pastoral* as well. They continued on in silence.

"Look at the pretty house, Mama." Olivia clapped her hands in delight. "Let's live there!"

Minton chuckled as he pushed his spectacles higher on his nose. "How clairvoyant of you, Miss Vaughan, for that's exactly where you will live."

The coach drew to a halt before a whitewashed stone building, and Rosalie helped Olivia down from the seat. Someone opened the coach door and lowered the step.

"Ah, Paget, there you are." Minton hopped to the ground then offered his arm as Rosalie shook out her dark blue silk skirts and stepped carefully down. The children followed her, Olivia gripping Curtis's hand.

Rosalie smoothed her daughter's wayward black curls and smiled at her son. "This will all be yours one day soon, Curtis."

The boy looked nervous, but she'd train that out of him soon enough.

Minton regained her attention. "My lady, may I present Paget, the butler and head of staff?"

"Welcome to Ambersley, my lady."

She considered the stiff-backed, beak-nosed butler as he bowed and decided he would do.

"If you'll allow me, I'll gather the rest of the staff for introductions."

With a nod, she excused him, and he strode up the shallow steps and through the front door. Her brow furrowed as she inspected the façade of her new home.

"Is anything amiss, Lady Vaughan?

"I confess I expected the Hall to be larger." She tried to

hide her disappointment. This house wasn't any larger than their home in London.

"Dear me," Minton said with a chuckle. "This is the Dower House. I thought I'd explained the Hall is unfit for habitation until the repairs are completed. "

"Mr. Minton, we are the duke's immediate family. My son is the heir. I hardly think it's appropriate for us to be forced to live *here*."

"I think it's a pretty cottage, Mama. I *want* to live here!" Olivia sniffed, clearly overtired.

"Hush, Livvie," Curtis admonished.

Minton accepted Rosalie's criticism without umbrage. "No one except a handful of servants has lived in the Hall for three years. With most of it uninhabitable, we temporarily bricked up a majority of the windows to reduce the property tax."

Rosalie touched a hand to her breast. Heavens, who had been making these decisions? A rustic solicitor and a shabby set of servants? Her gaze followed Paget as he ushered a handful of men and women down the steps toward her. "Then unbrick them immediately. I assume the furniture has been under Holland covers. We must have the maids set to work at once to make the Hall fit for proper people again."

"I'm afraid that won't be possible, my lady," Minton responded with irritating patience. "As I've told you before, I cannot make substantial repairs to the Hall until the duke claims possession of the property. Until that time, I recommend you take up residence here."

Paget stepped forward. "My lady, while the Dower House has been closed for some time, the staff has prepared it for your arrival."

Apparently, she had little choice but to accept their plans with grace. Minton continued to prove implacable in his belief that Derek was the true heir. "Very well," she sighed.

"May I present the staff to your ladyship?"

At least the butler showed her the proper deference. Minton would have to learn he was no longer running things around Ambersley.

For the next quarter hour she stood beneath a blazing May

sun while Paget introduced her to the matronly gray-haired housekeeper, the flat-chested cook, the Duke's thin-shouldered secretary, the bald-headed bailiff, and two young footmen and two maids.

"Ah, Bendicks," Minton called out. "This is the gardener and his apprentice, my lady. The Ambersley gardens have been the envy of kings and queens for generations."

Rosalie doubted that, but she nodded to the weathered face of the wiry man who worried his hat. A half step behind him stood a grimy urchin with huge eyes. She'd have to remind Miss Trent to keep Olivia and Curtis away from any of the children around here.

"Can we go inside, Mama?" Olivia pulled on her skirt to gain her attention. "I want to see my room."

"Very well, dear, let's go in." She swallowed her disappointment. Instead of the duke's home, she and her children were already being shuffled into the Dower House. Instead of the army of servants in shining liveries she'd imagined, she was faced with a ramshackle crew of aging retainers who eyed her as if she were the usurper. Rosalie ushered her children inside, already laying plans for a more satisfactory outcome.

Clearly, a number of things needed to change at Ambersley.

ৎ৵৶

Johnny's excitement over the arrival of the Vaughan heirs was quickly doused by the tumult surrounding their first week at Ambersley. Though she didn't understand it, she sensed the undercurrents of change rippling through the staff. Tension and formality replaced the casual camaraderie around the massive servants' table during Sunday supper in the Hall kitchens.

"Mrs. Chalmers, I hope you didn't find this meal too taxing for you," the housekeeper said as they took their seats.

"Not a bit, Mrs. North," the cook replied. "'Tis indeed a pleasure to prepare a meal for people who know my name."

Mrs. North leaned across Johnny to whisper loudly in

Martha's ear. "Lady Vaughan has taken to calling her 'Cook' to her face."

"And she's entitled to do and say as she pleases," said Mrs. Chalmers as she set down a platter of roasted hares. "But I was retained here long before she married into the family and birthed any heirs. The late duchess accorded me a certain level of respect. It was very ladylike of her."

Johnny watched heads around the table nod in understanding.

"She's not truly the dowager." Mr. Pritchard said before swallowing a forkful of peas.

Everyone stopped eating to look at the late duke's secretary.

"Didn't you know? Mr. Minton explained to me that Lady Vaughan is the heir's stepmother. Master Curtis and Miss Olivia are the duke's half-brother and half-sister."

Mrs. North shook her head sadly. "Oh, the duke lost his mother, poor lamb."

"Miss Trent, the governess, mentioned the duke's mother was hanged as a murderess."

"Good heavens." Paget drew his napkin to his lips. "Baroness Vaughan. What a notorious scandal. She was such a distant relation, I never thought it would taint Ambersley." Briefly, he recounted the facts of the trial and her hanging.

His story sent a shiver up Johnny's back.

Beside her, Tom sipped his ale then broke the silence. "When will the new duke arrive?"

"He's in India," Paget announced in his deep voice.

Not to be outdone, Pritchard offered more details. "At least, those were his last known whereabouts. He left London years ago. Lady Vaughan claims he *abandoned* his father."

"It could be months before he returns," Tom said. "The voyage is so long, he might not make it home at all."

"Then keep him in your prayers," Pritchard said. "For if he dies, young Master Curtis will inherit."

Johnny wanted to ask a dozen questions. *Where was India? What was the new duke like? What did Mr. Pritchard mean the duke had abandoned his father?* She squirmed with the effort to keep silent for it wasn't her place to talk at table.

Martha chewed a bite of rabbit. "The boy is so young. Lady Vaughan would control Ambersley."

"Humph, she already acts as though she owns the whole estate." Mrs. North buttered a piece of bread.

"What makes you say that?" Martha asked.

Mrs. North set aside her bread untasted. "After one night at the Dower House, she demanded the keys to all the storage closets."

"As is her prerogative," Paget said.

Mrs. North lifted her chin. "Indeed, and is it her prerogative to demand all the spare linens be given to her maid for safe keeping? I fear the china will disappear next."

"Then there's this matter of dining late." Mrs. Chalmers settled her hands on her broad hips. "She never eats supper before eight. I've burned more candles in the kitchen this week than in the past year."

Mrs. North nodded vigorously. "Not to mention the dining room, the drawing rooms, why, the whole house is lit up at night. She ordered a hundred candles from the chandler and had me forward the bill to Mr. Broadmoor."

"Ladies—" Paget dabbed at his lips with a napkin before bringing reason to the table. "May I remind you that her ladyship is entitled to every service we can provide her."

Mrs. North eyed him coolly. "And, I suppose, you'll be turning the keys to the pantry over to her then?"

Paget scanned the table like a hawk examining the terrain. "While Lady Vaughan may use the Dower House and its contents as her own, the table silver at the Hall is the property of the Duke of Ambersley. Like the late duchess's jewelry, I have secured the duke's property against his return, at which time I will relinquish it to him and to no other."

Tom coughed into his hand, and Johnny smiled. She and Tom had helped the butler bury a wooden crate at the edge of his vegetable garden the day before.

Door hinges creaked and a warm breeze swept into the kitchen as Rory and Mr. Broadmoor joined them.

"My apologies, Mrs. Chalmers."

"None needed, Mr. Broadmoor," she said to the bailiff. "'Tis three years since we stood on ceremony when it comes to meals. We all have our work to do. I'll do my best to keep you all fed."

"Thank you, ma'am, but I'm not sure I can eat a bite." The head groom, Rory, paced the length of the room. "Lady Vaughan has just ordered me to sell all but four of the horses. Mr. Broadmoor, I appeal to you, does she have any right to issue such directives?"

Broadmoor accepted a plate from Mrs. Chalmers and sat in his chair at the foot of the table. "It's regrettable, Rory, but I must agree with Lady Vaughan. The horses cost a fortune to feed. We've been mad to hold onto them this long."

"They've been earning their keep."

"Aye, but if we sell them, they'll earn all of our keep for a year or more." Broadmoor shook his head at the dejected groom. "It's a shame, but we can always buy new horses."

"'Tis the end of the finest stable in England." Rory pushed a hand through his hair, though it did nothing to tame the unruly silver waves.

Paget laid down his knife and fork. "It will take time for us to grow accustomed to Lady Vaughan's ways. She is undeniably different from the late duke and duchess, but I have no doubt, if we persevere, we will be able to anticipate her needs and serve her well."

"God help us all," Rory muttered.

The butler looked sternly down his hooked nose at the groom who flushed and offered a quick apology.

"I'm sure you're right, Mr. Paget," Martha said. "Lady Vaughan must have a good side. Family seems to be important to her. Her children are very well-behaved."

"That's Miss Trent's doing," Mr. Pritchard replied. "For a governess, may I say, she exhibits a great deal of common sense."

Martha stole a glance at Tom before turning back to the table. "But what of Lady Vaughan? Has she expressed any interest in the Vaughan family?"

"The day she arrived, I was given the task of showing her

around." Mr. Pritchard pushed back his chair, squaring his thin shoulders as he warmed to his story. "I told Lady Vaughan the history of Lord and Lady Ambersley, the many children they had lost in infancy, and then she asked about the fire. I told her what I could and shared with her our devout hope that young Miss Amber is somewhere still alive, and that one day she'll return to us."

Johnny felt a knot form in her stomach. Talk of Miss Amber always made her feel sick, though she didn't know why it should bother her.

Tom scratched his chin. "What did she say to that?"

Mr. Pritchard looked around the table at each and every face. "I'm afraid she's more interested in the money and the title than the family. She said it was just as well that no one had found Miss Amber, for it would be just one more mouth to feed, one more child to raise."

Johnny watched Tom and Martha grip hands while everyone else stared at Mr. Pritchard.

ॐ

Martha always helped Mrs. Chalmers with the baking, but curious to see the Lady of Quality first-hand, she offered to help prepare luncheon the following day for Lady Vaughan and the children.

"She don't keep country hours," Mrs. Chalmers said as she put a cover over the platter of stuffed chicken. "Luncheon never before two. As if any of those London dandies are going to pay a morning call."

Martha considered the luncheon platters. "Only three plates? What about the governess?"

"Lady Vaughan never shares meals with *the help*," said Mrs. Chalmers. "After I serve in the dining room, I take a tray to Miss Trent and the maid."

Nodding, Martha hefted a tray and followed Mrs. Chalmers to the dining room where Lady Vaughan and the children were already seated. Martha set her platter down and lifted the cover in unison with Mrs. Chalmers.

Instead of acknowledging their services and the appetizing

aroma, Lady Vaughan's lip curled. "Cook, you cannot expect the children to eat only poultry in the middle of the day. There should be a pudding or at least a ham or some beef."

"Begging your pardon, my lady, but we're very limited on meats. Most of the livestock is owned by the tenants, and we would need to barter a pig or a cow from them." Mrs. Chalmers grew flushed during her speech.

"Then tell Broadmoor to do something about it. I am accustomed to having veal on Fridays, so find a way to slaughter a calf by then."

"But, we'd have no way to cure and store the leftover meat—"

"Dispose of it, if you must. Lud, you cannot convince me the former duke and duchess lived in anything but top style. I expect no less. I left London to take possession of this property, and I must say I'm constantly disappointed at the staff's inability to resolve even the most minor problem. I fear I must discuss staffing with Minton."

"Yes, my lady," Mrs. Chalmers said with a nod.

Lady Vaughan seemed to notice Martha for the first time. "You, you're not the new serving maid, are you?"

"Me? No, ma'am, I'm Mrs. Bendicks, the gardener's wife." Martha dropped a knee-creaking curtsy.

"Thank heavens. You wouldn't do at all." Lady Vaughan turned back to Mrs. Chalmers as if Martha ceased to exist. "Cook, remind Paget that I want another six servants hired. There's far too much to do around here for any of you to manage."

Martha delivered the other luncheon tray upstairs and returned to the kitchen to find Mrs. Chalmers chopping vegetables for supper with a large knife and a strong arm.

The cook vented her spleen along with her energy. "She's always like that. There's no convincing her we're all living hand to mouth. Did you know she's going to London to buy new gowns? Wants to have all the latest styles when she comes out of mourning. I only hope Mr. Minton can talk some sense into her."

"Would she truly replace the staff?" Martha asked quietly.

"No," Mrs. Chalmers said. "Mr. Minton has already assured Paget that we work for the Duke of Ambersley, and no one but the duke may dismiss us. I'll not be leaving Ambersley while she's here. Heaven knows what she'll do if we don't keep a close watch on her."

Martha tried to imagine Johnny under the guardianship of Lady Vaughan. In less than a heartbeat, she decided she'd rather face the constable than hand her child over to *that* woman.

That night, after Johnny fell asleep, Martha shared her revelations with Tom. "The woman's mean and calculating. I'd worry so, if Johnny were in her clutches."

Tom tilted his head to watch the sleeping child as he drew on his pipe. "'Tis best for her to be returned to her family," he said gently, knowing the words would cause his wife pain. "It only gets harder each day we keep her."

"But her ladyship is not a Vaughan by blood." She kneeled by his chair. "Please, Tom, let us wait upon the duke's arrival. I fear what kind of man he'll be—his mother was a murderess."

Firelight played across his weathered face. "I'll think on it." Which he did, most of the night and well into the next day while Johnny helped him at his labors.

Finished weeding the kitchen herbs, the two headed toward the rose garden on their way home. Rounding the corner of the Hall, Tom stopped with a gasp.

Someone had cut and removed more than half of the bright blooms. In the soft breeze, bushes waved freshly chopped stems where vibrant petals had been that morning. Strewn on the ground lay evidence of the culprit's work—discarded blossoms in red and pink littered the grass like bodies on a battlefield.

Johnny stood like a pillar, unsure what to make of such a scene. "What happened?" she asked Tom in a whisper.

Unshed tears glistened at the corners of his eyes. "I don't know, child."

"Lady Vaughan wanted roses throughout the Dower House," Paget answered from behind them. "She cut them herself."

The normally stern butler shook his head sadly at the destruction. "I'm sorry, Tom."

Tom bent over one of his beloved bushes. Nearly all the flowers had been cut from it. "She's destroyed this plant. I'll have to prune it back so far, 'twill take a year or more to recover."

His gaze swept the garden. "I'm glad the duchess is dead. I couldn't bear to see her face were she to witness this. She spent hours tending this garden." He turned and held out his hand. "Come, Johnny." Nodding to Paget, they left.

Johnny hurried to keep up with Tom's strides. She spied his clenched jaw and a fire gleaming in his eyes. She'd never before seen Tom angry. "Will the roses die?" she asked in a small voice.

Tom's expression softened. "No, we won't let them die. I'm too upset to do them any good tonight, but tomorrow's a new day. I'll teach you how to save bushes even after they've been abused like that."

"You'll let me help save the rose garden?" It seemed an awfully important task to trust to her.

Tom chuckled and squeezed her hand. "I think you would be the perfect person." As they walked home, Tom battled his conscience, Martha's tales from last night still fresh.

"I don't like Lady Vaughan," Johnny announced, as if she'd read his thoughts. "She's not at all nice."

With a struggle, Tom's conscience surrendered to a laugh. "No, she ain't. Not at all."

❧

Over the following week, Johnny learned to prune the delicate rose bushes. Tom taught her to define the plant's shape while not pruning back so far as to stunt its growth. Together they collected the rotting carcasses of the forgotten blooms and watered the plants that had withstood Lady Vaughan's pillaging.

Tom gave Johnny the added responsibility of continuing their care. "I must return to my other tasks, but I want you to look after the roses every day. Can you do that?"

Johnny agreed with all the gravity of her seven years.

Daily she visited the rose garden, if only to watch the bees lazily hover above the blossoms. After her chores one afternoon, she lay upon the grass to listen to the insects and birds, and inhaled the scent of the roses she'd rescued. The sun warmed her, and the grass tickled the back of her neck. She pulled down her tricorne to shade her eyes as she squinted at the clouds.

"Hello."

The little voice made Johnny sit up so fast her vision swam.

Standing a few feet away, a little girl almost Johnny's age wore a yellow dress with a white pinafore. A matching bonnet covered her raven curls. "What's your name?" the girl asked.

"Johnny."

"I'm Olivia."

"I know." Johnny scanned the garden, but they were alone. "Where's your governess?"

Olivia giggled. "I don't know. Curtis is always giving her the slip, and today I snuck away, too. She was reading to us about how Spain declared war on us. Do *you* know where Spain is?"

Johnny shook her head. In truth, she didn't know *what* Spain was, much less where it was or why it would want to declare war on Ambersley. Fortunately, the subject seemed unimportant to Olivia.

"I see you up here with the roses sometimes. Mama brought back armloads of them for our house. They smelled so pretty, but then they all died." Olivia reached out to pull a stem toward her and sniff at the pink rose.

"Mind the thorns." Johnny scrambled to her feet and showed Olivia how to feel along the stem to avoid a painful pricking.

"Miss Trent said you're the gardener's apprentice, and that I shouldn't talk with you because my older brother's the duke. I think that's silly, but she said it would make Mama mad." Olivia's nose wrinkled in disdain of her elders' opinions, then she sighed. "There's no one to play with here. It's boring."

Johnny recognized sadness in the girl's voice and cast about for something that might entertain her. "Would you care to see the kittens at the stables?"

Olivia brightened immediately. "There are kittens?"

Johnny laughed. "Always. Rory likes a stable without rats. Come along." There was no sign of Rory in the stable, but Johnny went unerringly to the harness room and showed Olivia where the cat and her latest litter lay wedged behind a barrel in the corner.

Olivia cooed over the gray and white balls of fur. The kittens were floppy on their feet, but more than willing to pounce upon the leather tassel of the coach whip Johnny dragged along the floor. Olivia laughed, and Johnny smiled, pleased she'd been able to make the girl forget her boredom.

"What's going on in here?"

Johnny was startled by the unfamiliar voice, but Olivia greeted her older brother with a giggle. "Look at the kittens. Aren't they cute? Do you think Mama would let me have one?"

Curtis gave a heartless laugh. "She wouldn't let me keep the puppy I found. She made Paget take it away and drown it."

Johnny kept silent but knew Paget had given the puppy to the village smithy.

Curtis poked a kitten with his finger until the kitten retaliated with tiny but razor sharp claws. "Ouch! You little demon." He shoved the kitten, and it rolled across the floor in an undignified heap. The boy stepped forward, a grimace on his face. Afraid he meant to kick the helpless creature, Johnny pushed the boy aside while the kitten found its footing and scampered to the safety of its mother.

Curtis stumbled then glared at her. "How dare you?" He pushed her against the barrel. The mother cat hissed angrily at being so disturbed.

Red-faced, Curtis stood half a foot taller than she, and Johnny knew she'd never be able to best him in a fight. Though she held the coach whip in her hand, she didn't dare raise it. Instead, she tried desperately to make peace.

"I'm sorry. I didn't want the kitten to get hurt."

"Kitten!" Curtis spat. "Who cares about a kitten? They should probably all be drowned. Just more mouths to feed around here. I hear you're an orphan, and the Bendickses let you live with them. Maybe I should talk to my mother and have you sent to an orphanage so there's one less mouth to feed." His gaze lighted on the whip. "Are you threatening me with that? Give it to me."

Johnny lifted her shaking hand to comply when Rory entered the harness room.

He stopped short and smoothed back his wild white hair. "What's this? Have we all come to visit the kittens, then?"

Curtis sneered at Johnny before turning. "This boy was threatening my sister and me with this whip. I demand that you punish him." His clipped tone reminded Johnny of Paget when he issued commands.

Rory quickly surveyed the room before clearing his throat. "Aye, Master Curtis. I'll see to it, but I'll have to speak to his guardian first. You take your sister home now, sir, so she can recover from this shock, and I'll see to Johnny."

Curtis's eyes narrowed as if he'd argue, but then he turned on Johnny. "Stay away from me and my sister." He stalked past Rory and grabbed hold of Olivia's arm. She barely managed to dump the kitten into Rory's hands before being whisked out the door. Johnny could hear her crying as Curtis dragged her from the stable.

Swallowing hard, she raised wide eyes to Rory. "I'm sorry, sir. Will I get a whipping?" She was prepared for whatever punishment Rory might mete out.

"Heavens no." Rory took the whip from her. "The day I let an untried boy like Master Curtis issue me orders is the day I leave Ambersley. I don't know what happened here, but it looks as though you were about to land into a peck of trouble."

"I thought he was going to hurt the kittens. I wanted to protect them."

Rory handed her the kitten. "Good for you. But you shouldn't have crossed Master Curtis. I'd give him a wide berth if I were you."

"I was only trying to be friendly with Olivia," Johnny said as she let the kitten hop to the floor.

"That's *Miss* Olivia to you and me, Johnny. One day you'll understand, boy, that the likes of them and the likes of us don't mix. Everyone has their place on this earth, and we must each stick to it."

Rory's words echoed in Johnny's ears as she slowly walked home. She had never thought about the differences between the servants and their masters before. She was accustomed to Paget's word being law at Ambersley, but now even he had to bow before Lady Vaughan and her children.

She sensed a shifting in the balance of her world, and though she didn't completely understand everything that went on around her, of one thing she was certain—she had made an enemy.

3

London, March 1805

On deck of the East India ship, Derek Vaughan drank in his first bittersweet sight of London in eight years. From the throng on the docks—more active than an ant colony—to the chimneys belching smoke into the gray sky, he'd once thought London the most exciting city in the world. But after living in the panorama that was India, his homeland appeared dingy and overcrowded.

He turned to the burly giant beside him. "Home again, Cushing. Are you eager to return to dry land?"

His servant shuddered at the gentle gibe. "To be sure. I've never been so seasick in my life. May we never again make such a harrowing journey."

"Aye," Derek agreed absently as he gripped the rail and stared out over London again, besieged by long-buried memories more turbulent than the stormy seas they'd traversed. "It's time for us to forge ahead with our lives."

They continued to stand their watch over the hive of activity on the dock while the ship was safely moored. Even without words, the older man's presence buoyed Derek. Slightly past his prime, Cushing stood strong of limb and broad of girth. Though he laughed readily and was always the first to join in song, creases etched in his leathery face hinted at personal loss. At five-and-twenty, Derek understood loss too well, and so had never pressed for details.

"Two more morose men I shall never hope to see."

Derek glanced over his shoulder at tow-headed Harry Coatsworth. Tall and lean with arms akimbo, his cousin radiated the happiness of a man about to debark on his native soil—a man assured of the open-armed welcome of his family. Where Derek found it difficult to uproot the joy in life, Harry tended to trip over it.

"Two more morose men you shall never find," he responded. He waved Harry to join him at the rail where Cushing, silent, flanked his other side. These two men were all the family and friends he had—or needed. He would always remember they'd both been by his side when Harry delivered his painful tidings.

'Tis your father. He's dead.

The memory of those simple words sent a swift searing pain through Derek's belly, much like a gunshot. Though he'd left London convinced he would never again see the man he'd called father, the finality of those five words had caught him unprepared. That Harry, with little more than a score of years to his name, had taken it upon himself to travel halfway around the world to deliver the news still astonished him.

His cousin leaned on the railing and held his peace for fully a minute—half a minute more than Derek would have thought possible. "Are you yet sorry you returned?"

He turned to lean against the rail. "No. 'Tis my filial duty."

"Duty?" Harry snorted. "It's your inheritance."

Derek remained silent. Any bequest meant little, but he couldn't as casually discard the notion of repaying a debt of honor. Reginald Vaughan had raised him, though Derek had been no more than a cuckoo in the nest. Despite a notorious wife whose public and outrageous liaisons had culminated in murder, the man he called father had always treated Derek with the utmost respect and paternal love. Always—until that final day when Derek had confronted him with the truth.

To refuse to return to England would have been churlish,

and Reginald Vaughan's memory deserved better than that. Derek had returned to fulfill his obligations as head of the Vaughan family, regardless of what it might cost him personally.

An elbow poked him in the ribs. "You're still pining for the lovely ladies you left behind," Harry said.

Cushing chuckled.

Derek frowned, but that only urged Harry on with his foolery. "Do you think I didn't hear the feminine sighs over your silky dark locks, your penetrating blue eyes, your fine leg in the saddle, your penchant for stealing a kiss?"

"Did you also hear what they whispered behind their fans? Their furtive questions about my prospects or sad laments over my mother's behavior?" Derek laughed darkly, the memory of Helena Thorne haunting him. "No, if I miss anyone, it's my men."

"And what did the cavalry think of our fair captain?" Harry looked pointedly at Cushing. "Did *they* admire his fine leg in the saddle?"

The giant scratched his nose. "His leg? No, but I did hear tell he had an excellent seat, and they were confident he'd keep his head when facing the bayonets. They were proud to follow him."

"High praise indeed," Harry said with sincerity.

"Oh, and there was a tailor in Jaipur who swore the Master's shoulders were the finest in all of India for showing off a well-cut coat."

"Cushing—"

"What? You still own that coat."

Derek tried to curtail Harry's infectious laughter with narrowed eyes but failed to repress his own twitching lips. In truth, he wasn't one to preen before a mirror, for contemplating his own reflection only reminded him of unanswered questions.

"With a barony and a well-cut coat, you shall find yourself an heiress and make your fortune," Harry said.

Derek's own dark laugh joined theirs.

"What? Don't want an heiress? I'll wed her."

"Harry, you don't need to wed an heiress. You already have a small fortune."

"Ah, but I'll need a bride with breeding and connections. Now that I've seen the world, I think I'll work for the Foreign Office."

"Lucky girl," Derek said. "She can wed you and be rid of you immediately."

With a grin, Harry turned to the servant. "Cushing, what will you do now that we're back home?"

Cushing scratched his chin. "Don't have what you'd call a home here, exactly, so—"

"So he tells me he plans to continue to work for me with no pay," Derek finished.

Cushing straightened and folded his arms. "The Master's concerned we won't be able to feed ourselves, but I've told him time and again that whether his fortune be good or ill, I'll stick by him the same way he stuck by me."

"Did he now?" Harry said to Cushing while contemplating his cousin. "He's not known for an overly generous spirit. The one time he tried to help me, I wound up with a black eye."

His gaze rolling up to the clouds, Derek pushed away from the rail.

Encouraged by Cushing's questioning brow, Harry unfurled his story. "I was eleven, and Derek, at the ripe old age of fifteen announced he would teach me to box. Apparently, I was a poor student, for he got right past my guard and popped me in the eye. His father tanned his hide."

His father. Like a festering wound, the topic was best left untouched. Derek drew the conversation to safer ground. "Cushing had much the same luck with me, Harry. He got into trouble, I tried to help him, and he got sacked. The least I could do was offer him a position with me."

"And I've never regretted it," said Cushing.

"Nor have I," Derek said with a genuine smile. "I've no idea what tasks to set him in London and even less how I shall pay him."

Cushing gently clapped him on the shoulder. "You just leave that horse to me, sir. Sabu will make our fortunes."

"Indeed, I hope so, Cushing. I truly hope so." Derek had borrowed a small ransom from Harry to buy the desert-bred stallion's passage back to England.

"You still plan to breed your little horse and start a racing stable?" Harry asked.

"I like horses. If studied, they're more reliable than cards."

"And less fickle than women," Cushing said with a wink.

Derek frowned. "Indeed."

A quarter hour later, the cousins descended the gangway. Harry sent up a joyful shout when his feet touched the quay then shrugged at Derek's lifted brows. As they shouldered their way through the crowd, a lusty woman approached. Older than he, and a little the worse for her painted lips and eyes—she tugged her tight dress down to better reveal her bountiful bosom.

"'Allo, Guv'nor," she greeted in a saucy tone, "let Millie give you a welcome home kiss." Her breath smelled of stale gin, and Derek repulsed her with no remorse.

She turned to Harry, who stopped her with mock horror. "Oh, no, Millie, you look old enough to be me mum!"

With a snort of contempt, Millie marched grandly away.

Derek looked at his grinning cousin. "Must you treat everything as a lark?"

"Life *is* a lark, Derek, if only you'd let it be so."

They hailed a hack and rode to Harley Street to find Vaughan House silent and shuttered. Derek paid off the driver and stood with Harry on the cobblestones.

"Odd that they'd leave before the end of the Season," Harry said. "They'd be out of mourning by now. Wherever do you suppose they could be?" He barely paused before adding, "Let us visit your father's clubs tonight to see if there's any news of Rosalie Vaughan's whereabouts."

With a resigned sigh, Derek assented. He hadn't expected much from his homecoming, but finding no sign of them at all was disconcerting at best. As the two men walked south on Harley Street toward Cavendish Square and ultimately Claridge's Hotel, he contemplated how demeaning this situation would be if he'd arrived here with Helena Thorne as his bride.

But then, her rejection had been demeaning enough.

ବ୍ଦ୍ୟ

As dusk descended, Harry and Derek handed their hats to a porter at White's. The addition of a tip that amounted to pure bribery prompted the servant to usher them directly to the gaming room where, despite the early hour, the top tier of Society drank and gambled in earnest. A few gentlemen conversing in groups or lounging in chairs heeded their entrance with little interest before returning to their own pursuits.

With relief, Derek noted that while some of the older men wore wigs or powder in their hair, the younger generation had adopted the fashion of the simple queue. His "well-cut coat" might not be the latest in style, but he need not feel inferior.

"Vaughan, is that you?" A gentleman detached himself from a group at one of the gaming tables and came forward. Though older and grayer, Derek immediately recognized the Earl of Montrose, his father's closest friend.

Derek made a brief bow. "Lord Montrose, you're very kind to acknowledge me after all these years."

Montrose waved away formalities by clapping him on the arm. "Nonsense my boy, I'm glad you're here. Hasn't been the same without your father around. It's good to see a Vaughan in the place again."

"Thank you, sir, though I confess I'm here under pretense. My cousin and I are just returned from India, and neither of us are members."

"Consider yourselves my guests," said Lord Montrose. "You've heard about your father then?"

"My cousin brought me word."

Montrose nodded with understanding. "Reggie missed you. Not that he spoke of it, but I could tell by the way he read every word the papers printed about India. He hungered for word of you but was too proud to write." Montrose perused him. "I suspect the apple falls not far from the tree, eh?"

Derek tensed as his face flushed with warmth. "Never far."

The benevolent approval in Montrose's eyes made it clear the older man had no idea Derek had fallen from a different family tree altogether.

"Lord Montrose, do you know where my father's wife is?"

"Rosalie?" Montrose frowned. "She left London some time last year. Reggie fell deep into debt before he died. The gossips say she's living at Ambersley and that the duke shall make good all of her family's debts. The duke hasn't stepped forward to dispute her claim, and so her creditors wait."

"The Duke of Ambersley?" Derek had never held much faith in gossipmongers, perhaps because they'd hovered around his family like hungry vultures.

"Your family's related to Ambersley, is it not?"

"Yes," Derek answered. "But the kinship is so distant, I would never dare presume upon it."

"Ah, but Rosalie's been widowed twice and has two children to raise." Montrose gestured toward the nearest card table. "Will you join me?"

"Another time, sir," Derek answered. "But thank you for the news of my stepmother."

Montrose's eyes narrowed shrewdly. "Your father and I were friends for many years. Now that he's gone, I'd like to extend that friendship to you. I'll propose you here for membership."

He felt like a thief accepting, but to refuse would cause the sort of stir he wished to avoid. Derek gripped Montrose's outstretched hand. "I'm honored, sir." With due courtesy, he excused himself and sought out his cousin.

Harry handed him six wafered letters. "The porter told me these were addressed to your father here but were never picked up by anyone in the family."

The sympathy in his cousin's eyes, did little to dispel Derek's dread.

"You'll want to read them," Harry urged. "I'll have a look around the tables." With no further preamble, he drifted toward the noisier games.

Derek seated himself in a well-lit corner, broke the first seal and settled himself to read the missives.

The first five were from merchants requesting, imploring then demanding payment for long overdue credit they'd issued. But the final letter's tone differed. The sender must have learned of Reginald Vaughan's death, for it was addressed to "The Right Honorable Derek Vaughan, heir to Reginald Vaughan." *Please contact me at your earliest convenience...* Undoubtedly, he'd be asked to settle a debt or answer for some business venture of his father's that had gone wrong, but the marked courtesy of the letter made it the first he would answer.

"Nowadays, they'll let anyone enter White's."

Derek lifted his gaze at the sarcastic tone to see a dark-haired gentleman flanked by two others staring down upon him. The first gentleman wore buckled shoes, stockings and satin knee breeches with a black coat impaled by numerous silver buttons that bespoke wealth and station. But it was the familiar jaw and blue eyes that triggered recognition.

He rose stiffly and bowed, too wary of offering a hand that might be refused. "Trevarthan."

"Oh, it's Worthing now. Buried dear *pater* over two years ago now. You must be back to do the same for *your father*." The emphasis on the final words was not lost on Derek, nor was the omission of introductions to Worthing's friends.

St. John Trevarthan—now the Marquess of Worthing—had been a fellow student at Eton. Once friends, the two boys had turned enemies when they learned Derek's mother numbered St. John's father amongst her many paramours. Derek found himself shunned by any boy who agreed with St. John's taunts that Alicia Coatsworth Vaughan was little better than a whore. Derek had quickly tired of the insurmountable task of defending her. She'd never shown him any love, and if he could have drained her blood from his veins without killing himself, he would have done so long ago.

But the resemblance he and St. John bore troubled them both.

"I've come home to settle his affairs and take my place in Society," Derek said neutrally.

Worthing gave a sinister chuckle. "Don't be a fool,

Vaughan. You don't belong in good society."

Harry bumbled into their midst, oblivious to the tension. "I say, Derek, let's seek supper. I've improved none at hazard—regardless of your hours of instruction. More importantly, I'm famished." He pulled up short at sight of the men and sketched a bow. "Lord Worthing, your servant."

Worthing looked down his aquiline nose at Harry. "Another Coatsworth. Indeed, seek your supper elsewhere, gentlemen, for White's is not the place for *either* of you."

Derek's fingers curled around the letters, but his military training firmed his resolve. Petty injustices were better ignored when larger battles could erupt at any moment. "We'll bid you good night, gentlemen." He steered Harry toward the entry where they collected their hats and stepped outside to the summer night.

Harry hesitated only a moment before heading down Regent Street. Fitting his hat atop his head, he glanced back toward the club. "Never liked Worthing. Too stilted by half. Mark my words, one day, his family will suffer a scandal, and I, for one, shall enjoy watching him ride out the tide of ridicule."

"I wouldn't wish that on anyone."

"Not even your worst enemy?"

Derek didn't answer. St. John was right—Derek no more belonged in this world of alliances and manners than his mother had. And the whole *ton* had been witness to that disaster. Still, he refused to be routed while he had debts to pay. He would suffer Society's barbs and do what he could to provide for Reginald Vaughan's children, especially now that he knew how destitute his father had been upon his death.

"Derek, do you intend to be silent and inattentive all evening?"

Derek looked up. "I'm sorry, what did you say?"

Harry laughed good-naturedly. "That's precisely what I meant. We've just arrived in London, and I plan to embrace the city and celebrate my freedom from that ship. Think of it—tonight we'll sleep in beds that don't rock with waves. There's fresh water by the gallon, not that I'd drink it if you paid me, but I did enjoy an excellent hot bath this afternoon. We have so much to be thankful for—"

Derek's brows knit. "Harry, have I ever told you that you jabber like a magpie?"

"Daily," Harry replied, unabashed.

"And have I ever expressed that I find it irritating?"

"Almost hourly."

"Yet you persist."

"Because I often find your conversation lacking. Just now, you were a thousand miles away—why, you may as well be still in India."

Derek was glad for the mask of darkness as Harry contemplated him.

"Derek, we're *home*, and I sense neither elation, nor grief, nor anything from you." Harry continued to watch him. "When we were boys, we kept no secrets from each other."

They walked in silence for a few moments before Derek responded with a sigh. "I shall try to be better company."

"You need family," Harry said quietly. "Join me and Mother for supper tomorrow in Bath. She'd love to see you. We shall enjoy a few concerts, perhaps an Assembly or two, and soak away our cares. It may be just the remedy for this sudden melancholy of yours."

"It might at that," Derek agreed with a fleeting smile. "But I cannot go tomorrow, Harry. Will you grant me another day?"

"Certainly."

Derek acknowledged the prodding of his cousin's uncharacteristic silence. "Those letters were from creditors and a solicitor here in London. Whatever business must be conducted for my father's estate, I'd like to put it behind me as quickly as possible."

ৎৄ৶

Despite the following day's heavy mist, Derek threaded the streets around the Chancery and Temple Church before successfully locating Tallis Street to contemplate the shingle, "N. Minton, Esq." Glancing once again at the signature scrawled in the mysterious note, he opened the door to the solicitor's office.

A bell heralded his entrance with a tinny clamor. As Derek's eyes adjusted to the dark interior, he detected a figure hunched over a desk at the far corner of the long room and made his way toward it.

A young clerk, lit by the sputtering remains of a single candle, stopped scratching out words with quill and ink. "How may I help you, sir?"

"I'm here to see Mr. Nigel Minton."

"Mr. Minton's away from Town," the clerk replied.

Derek accepted this latest delay with fatalistic calm. As if to punctuate his thoughts, the lone candle died with a wisp of smoke and the strong scent of beeswax.

"One moment." The clerk unfolded his limbs and reached atop a high shelf for a fresh candle, which he inserted into the melted remains of its predecessor. "Perhaps I may be of assistance?" He struck a match, casting welcome light about the dark wood walls and desk.

"Yes." Derek held forth the note. "I'm Derek Vaughan. I received this from Mr. Minton requesting I introduce myself at the earliest opportunity as he has urgent business to discuss with me. I arrived in London yesterday, and—sir, take heed, you'll *burn* yourself." Derek grabbed the young man's skinny wrist and shook the match from it. It fell to the desk where it scorched the edges of some papers before dying.

The clerk stared at Derek, mouth agape, until he finally regained his voice. "You're Derek Vaughan? From India?" To Derek's answering nod, the clerk flushed to the roots of his hair, swept a deep bow and murmured, "Your Grace."

Derek stood for a moment, confused, then glanced over his shoulder to be sure no one had entered the office behind him. Turning back to the red-faced youth, he could think of nothing to say. "I beg your pardon? I think there's been some mistake."

"No mistake, Your Grace," the young man's head bobbed in earnestness. "Father was very thorough in his search, and you're definitely the heir."

Derek's stomach knotted. "The heir? To what?"

"The Dukedom of Ambersley."

క్ల♥

"You're *what?*" cried Harry, back at the hotel.

Still trying to accept the news himself, Derek said nothing as he crab-stepped past his cousin's trunk and portmanteau to reach the sideboard and uncork the wine.

Harry coursed his heels. "Derek, you're not shamming me, are you? He called you the Duke of Ambersley? It's—it's—extraordinary. This calls for a toast."

Derek tossed off a meager portion of Madeira then poured a more liberal splash without offering his cousin any.

With entire good humor, Harry waited his turn at the bottle. Lifting his glass, he proclaimed, "To my cousin, the duke!"

Derek stopped his agitated strides to stare down at the drink pressed between his palms. A title, a home, an income—this was a future beyond his reach. How many in London recalled his mother's scandalous behavior, her notorious crime? Even as a youth he'd not escaped the whispered rumors surrounding his paternity. Whether or not anyone had *proof*, he knew he carried no Vaughan blood. No, he had no right to contemplate, even for a breath, accepting the Ambersley peerage. But the dukedom could provide for the children, and that was key.

He recalled his mother. Blonde, lovely, heartless. She'd had all the golden good looks of the Coatsworth clan, but none of their warmth, certainly none of their honor.

"What was I thinking getting saddled with a child?" she'd said to him one day. She'd studied him as though he were a hat she might buy. Or not.

He'd been no more than six at the time.

She'd never held him, never comforted him, never engaged in conversation directly with him. If not for Father taking an interest in his upbringing, Derek might have rotted away in the nursery on Harley Street.

He hadn't shed a tear for her when his father sat him down to explain that she'd been imprisoned and charged with murder.

"Did she truly kill a man, Father?" he'd asked. At the age of ten, he'd understood enough about death to fear it.

"I don't know. But Derek, you must always remember this—she's a good woman. She sacrificed for both of us. You must always remember that and always love her." Father had left the room, his tears barely suppressed.

Derek sat for a long time and contemplated his mother, but no matter how he tried, he couldn't find a reason to love her.

Father remained steadfast, even when she tried to accuse him of murdering her lover. No one believed her. Her trial was the talk of London, especially when she publicly named every man she'd ever bedded in an attempt to exonerate herself. In the end, they'd hanged her.

No, he refused to pass along her blood to future generations of Vaughan peers.

"Derek, you're wool-gathering again." Harry sounded amused. "I've proposed a toast, and you won't even drink your own health."

"I was thinking of my mother."

Harry sobered at once. "Don't torture yourself."

"I grew to hate her, you know."

"So did my father," said Harry. "And he was her brother. He believed a fit of madness took her."

Derek wished he could believe that, but she'd always been too cold, too calculating. Still preoccupied, he allowed Harry to push him into a chair.

"Tell me your tale," Harry said. Gathering the wine bottle, he refilled their glasses, removed his coat, tossed a log on the fire and stretched himself comfortably in the chair opposite. Impatiently, he kicked Derek's chair as a final prompt. "When did the old duke die?"

"A fire swept through Ambersley Hall, killing the whole family, in 1801."

Harry sputtered his wine. "1801? That was four years ago. You mean to tell me they couldn't get you word before now?"

Derek shrugged. "No one traced the lineage to Reginald Vaughan until last year. I'm told some poor soul was dispatched to India. He may still be out there beating the bushes for me."

Harry whistled. "Must have left soon after me. I didn't hear a thing about your father inheriting a dukedom." He loosened his neck cloth. "So what are the holdings? What are you worth?"

"I have no idea." Seeing his cousin's raised brows, Derek continued. "The duke's solicitor, one Mr. Nigel Minton, has gone to Ambersley. I met his son, young Percy, who acts as junior clerk for his father, but he wasn't prepared to answer many of my questions. If I travel to Ambersley now, I should still find Mr. Minton there. Harry, I know you planned to leave for Bath tomorrow, and I've already delayed you—"

With a snort, Harry dismissed the concerned words. "As if I'd let you leave London alone. I'll be happy to accompany you, Cousin. I'll even fund the journey."

"I'll repay you—"

"Tush. Mother and I have plenty of money."

"You must let me do something," Derek said in earnest.

"You may introduce me to the first circles of polite society." Harry grinned like a schoolboy and refilled their glasses. "Think of the horrified Mamas— 'There goes the duke's cousin. Handsome and witty fellow, but poor soul, his mother married a tradesman, you know.'" He heaved a melodramatic sigh. "'Pity the duke allows him to come around.'"

Derek's tensions eased beneath his cousin's inanity. "Not only will you be allowed, you will be encouraged to bear me company."

"Careful. Once word gets out, every long-lost relation you've *never* known will appear on your doorstep." Harry wagged his brows.

A terse expletive escaped Derek as he sat forward.

"What's amiss?" Harry asked.

"Lord Montrose told me last night that my stepmother is living at Ambersley with her children and plans to lay her debts at the duke's feet." Derek stared into the fire. Rosalie Vaughan could reveal him as a fraud, but if she'd done so, Minton would hardly be seeking him. He would have to go to

Ambersley and confront her if he wanted to set things right.

4

The trip into Gloucestershire took the better part of a day by mail coach. Arriving at a noisy inn yard in the late afternoon, Harry suggested they get a good night's sleep before turning Ambersley on its ear with Derek's arrival.

Long after the inn quieted, Derek lay awake anticipating the next day's meetings. By morning, his nerves were taut with indecision—a state of mind he hated—but 'twas impossible for him to know what was best to do until he understood the situation more clearly. A dukedom should provide well for Reginald Vaughan's children, but not if mismanaged. He could hand it all to his half-brother, but Curtis was hardly more than a boy, and if gossips were to be believed, Rosalie had buried two bankrupt husbands.

His concerns mounted as he and Harry trotted their hired hacks along the winding drive flanked by pruned trees not yet in blossom. Derek noted vast meadows stretching to forest, a small lake and rolling slopes dotted with ornamental hedgerows and pockets of trees and shrubbery. As they rounded a bend in the drive, he took in his first view of Ambersley Hall situated atop a hill as imposing as any monarch on his throne.

Derek drew rein to study the four-story façade while his

pulse settled. There was no denying the magnificence of the structure, though its once golden stone exterior was blackened with soot, while its gabled roof—or what remained of it—met the clouds at a defiant, if broken, angle. Windows that once beckoned weary travelers were bricked over, turning what should have been a home into a mausoleum. Nestled amid carefully manicured lawns and gardens, the flagstones before it swept clean, the Hall reminded him of a slow-healing wound that required time and tender care to restore it to its former glory.

The cool morning breeze buffeted him as he continued to stare, the noble home's silent plea tugging at him until a whistling falcon overhead cut into his thoughts. Brushing off the tremor that traveled down his spine, he set his heel to his mount and drew abreast Harry.

"You've inherited a giant wreck," his cousin quipped.

Derek remained silent, unwilling to give voice to his thoughts. Ambersley had rooted the Vaughan family for generations. How ironic that he'd been forced to come here and witness Reginald Vaughan's heritage first-hand.

A blackbird's warble welcomed them as they approached the Hall. Seeing no one but a scrawny lad as they dismounted, Derek pulled the reins over his horse's head and tossed them to the child.

Harry did likewise. "Look alive there, boy."

Derek raised a brow when the child missed grasping the second set. "Hold onto those horses 'til we return."

Upon skirting the structure, Derek and Harry found Ambersley Hall as it had been left years earlier, a burned-out shell of a building abandoned by its occupants. Confused, they returned to the drive to find both horses grazing at the child's feet.

"Boy!" Derek's shout flushed a rabbit into a skittery dash across the lawn. One horse threw its head up in alarm, and the lad, unprepared, was literally yanked off his feet as he tried valiantly to hold onto the reins. The other horse shied at this further commotion, backing away as the boy's feet struck the ground again and buckled.

With an oath, Derek dove into the chaos. He grabbed the rearing horse's reins with one hand and, with the other, lifted the child by the scruff before he got trampled. The second horse, snorting his contempt of the whole scene, jerked free from the boy's grasp. Harry made a lunge for it, but the animal avoided him neatly and was last seen clearing a hedge.

Holding the first horse on a tight rein, Derek shook the boy's shoulder. "Now see what you've done? What kind of a stable boy are you?"

The boy ducked his head as if he expected a blow. Not one to beat children, Derek loosened his grip. The child raised eyes as wide as any frightened animal. His clothes and face were dusted with dirt and grime, and this close, he smelled of manure.

"I'm not a stable boy, and it wasn't all my fault."

Derek's brows knit. "Well, of all the impertinent—" His cousin's burst of laughter drew his fire. "What do you find so amusing?"

"You, sir," Harry replied, unabashed. "You can hardly call a child out because he's honest. Besides, I don't think the cursed beast suited you. You were too long in the leg for him."

"And how do you propose we return to the inn? Ride double?" He'd all but forgotten the boy before him.

"I'm sure once we explain who you are, we'll be able to find another horse. It's a ducal estate, *milord*—you can't convince me there are no horses here."

Derek bit back the sharp set down he would have liked to give his younger cousin, deeming it inappropriate before the boy. He turned to interrogate the youngster, but Harry was quicker.

"What's your name, lad?" he asked affably.

The boy studied Harry. "I'm Johnny. I'm apprenticed to Tom, the gardener."

"Ah, a gardener's lad, not a stable boy at all. I'll wager you were mulching this morning."

The boy nodded at this clever deduction as Harry tossed a look at Derek.

With a sigh, he redirected the conversation to important

matters. "We believe some relatives may be staying here, a woman and her two children. Do you know them?"

"You mean the duke's family? Oh yes, they live in the Dower House."

"And where is that?" Derek asked.

Johnny pointed. "It's that way, about a ten minute walk. I could show you the way if you like."

"Thank you, but no." Derek raised a brow at his cousin. "Are you coming?"

"You'll want your privacy for such a reunion."

Derek acknowledged the sense of this, though he doubted there would be any overflow of emotion at his return. With a curt nod, he marched off in the direction the boy had pointed, the horse following docilely in his wake.

Johnny watched him go, her own curiosity growing. *Was it possible?* "Is he the new duke, then?" she asked the blonde man.

With a startled laugh, the man replied, "He's Baron Vaughan for the moment. Beyond that, we'll see what the duke's solicitor has to say."

"Mr. Minton, you mean?"

"Yes, do you know him?"

"Aye, sir. Mr. Minton is in charge of Ambersley while the duke is away. He should be at the Dower House today. He comes every month for a few days."

"Good to know." The gentleman fished in his pocket until he withdrew two coins and held them out.

She'd never had money of her own, and she watched enthralled while he laid the pieces of silver in her palm.

"Here's for your trouble, lad. Now, would you like to earn a bit more?"

Johnny nodded.

"While my cousin speaks with his family, I plan to catch that horse we lost. If you'll lend me a hand, there's another crown in it for you."

Johnny grinned, and led the gentleman toward the east meadow.

꘏

Derek stared at the Dower House. Stone and trellised, the quaint cottage rose a mere three stories and could be considered small only by the very rich. While the burnt shell of the Hall had caused him grave doubts, the Dower House held much promise. The estate could be refurbished as a fitting home for the Vaughan children.

He climbed the wide stone steps and rapped on the varnished oak. In moments, the door opened on soundless hinges, and Derek found himself being perused by the hawk-like eyes—and nose to match—of an older stiff-backed gentleman.

"Mr. Minton?" Derek faltered when he noticed the other man wore gloves.

"No, sir. I would be Paget." Derek detected a note of disdain in the response. And then Paget clarified. "The butler."

"Ah." Derek cleared his throat. "Would you tell her ladyship that Derek Vaughan has returned from India?"

With an almost imperceptible twitch of his brows, Paget bowed. "Welcome home, Your Grace. Please, follow me."

Removing his hat, Derek allowed the butler's deference to sink in. Despite the dignified reception, the butler had appraised Derek with caution. No doubt the butler knew of his murky parentage and feared the peerage's reputation would suffer.

The butler led the way to a drawing room decorated in pale gold and cream. "I'll inform Lady Vaughan of Your Grace's arrival." Paget bowed and quit the room.

Left alone, Derek scanned his surroundings with the care he'd give a battlefield. He presumed the two men depicted in portraits on the north wall were scions of the Vaughan ancestry. Judging by their clothes, they represented vastly different generations. Other paintings featured landscapes and a still life of a fruit bowl. The divan was upholstered in cream brocade, the floors looked recently waxed, and the Aubusson carpet was an extravagance to walk upon. Despite a limited knowledge of furniture, Derek recognized the spindle and finish work on the secretary in the corner as the hallmark of a master.

The room bespoke an elegance entirely casual with the wealth that made it possible. But a closer inspection revealed water stains on the east wall and a threadbare section of carpet artfully concealed by a small table. Turning to the fireplace, he leaned on the mantle to study the detailed mahogany carvings surrounding it. A rustling at the door made him lift his head.

Paget stopped at the open doorway to announce grandly, "Lady Vaughan, Your Grace."

Rosalie swept into the room, still reeling from the news of Derek's arrival. Seeing him posed by the fireplace, a hand on the mantle and one shiny Hessian resting on the fender as if he owned the place, made her nerves coil with frustration. He stood taller, stronger, fully a man now, and one about to gain untold power over her, unless she could prevent it.

Knowing Paget watched closely, she continued forward and embraced her stepson, pressing her cheek to his chest. "Oh, Derek, thank heavens you've returned safe. We were so worried."

With a sidelong glance, she watched the butler back from the room. The moment the door clicked, she pushed away from Derek's embrace. "I wondered if you would ever dare show."

Derek spread his hands. "Ah, so the reunion was for the butler's sake. I doubted my return would endear me to you." He no longer sounded like the youth who'd retreated from her candor like a beaten cur. No, here stood a nobleman, set to embark on a new life with property, position and wealth on his side.

His return spelled ruin for her and for *her* son. But for Curtis's sake—and Olivia's—she would play the distasteful role of dowager. The situation demanded finesse, but she was accustomed to such difficulties.

"I am surprised to see you is all. We had no notion of what had become of you, whether you were even alive."

"Harry traveled to India to bring me word." A glimmer of the unsure boy quivered in his voice.

So, he still had an Achilles heel if she could expose it.

"I'm glad you've come."

He gave a sardonic laugh. "You surprise me. I thought you would be pleased to see me out on my ear. I didn't exactly fit your notion of the ideal family."

Rosalie sank into her favorite chair, a Queen Anne style fitted in gold damask. "Derek, I know you were hurt by what happened, but I was equally wounded by it. I braved your mother's scandal when I married Reggie, but to learn that she'd foisted you upon him when you were no more than a...a—"

"A bastard?"

"I would never say such a thing, but you are the son of a murderess." She drew a handkerchief from her cuff and pressed it to her lips while she measured his reaction.

Frowning, Derek perched on the back of the divan and folded his arms.

Reggie never told him the whole truth. Triumph surged through her veins, though she kept her voice low. "Reggie was too generous to ever disown you. I understood that. But he deserved a new start, a new family."

"I would never have driven a wedge between Father and Curtis."

Guilt tinged his words, and she pounced on it. "Remember, you were the one who determined to leave. No one asked you to go."

"And none asked me to stay."

"My son is Reggie's true heir. Do you blame me for wishing you elsewhere?" *How often, in truth, had she wished him to perdition?*

Derek shook his head slowly. "No, I grant him happy to have a mother's love."

"And what of a brother's love, Derek? Will you now deny Curtis his due?"

"That's not my intent." He stood and adjusted his coat of superfine as if he found it uncomfortable. "Reginald Vaughan was always good to me. The least I can do is see that his debts are paid and his children's futures secured."

She rose and shook out her skirts. "Curtis and Olivia will

secure only condemnation and notoriety if you return to Society and remind everyone of a scandal better forgotten."

"I'm well aware what my return will mean. But until I'm certain they are provided for, here's where I shall remain. I must talk to this Mr. Minton and discover how matters stand."

Tamping down her agitation, she tried once more to reason with him. "Derek, you cannot mean to sully a peerage in this way. If anyone proves you're not Reggie's son—"

"That's not likely, is it?" He turned on her, bitterness darkening his eyes. "After all, you've no proof. If you did, the butler would have shown me the door, and Curtis would have been proclaimed the new duke by now." The rigid line of his jaw relaxed some. "Depend on me to do what is best for everyone's interests."

"*Depend* on you?" Despite her good intentions, her patience snapped. "You disrupt our lives with your sudden return, you threaten our family's good name, yet I'm to trust you will provide for us?"

Derek frowned at her heated argument. This was the Rosalie he remembered from his youth. Her mercurial moods had frightened him then, but now he withstood her outburst with no outward sign of emotion. He knew not how long he'd need to remain here, but he'd be damned if he'd do so at a disadvantage. "If you like not the terms, I suggest you return to Vaughan House."

Her lips clamped shut, and he saw the effort it cost her to calm herself. One elegant hand smoothed her dark locks as she released a shallow breath. "Forgive me, Your Grace. Your sudden return has surprised and unnerved me." She dipped him a small curtsey.

He nodded. "It's understandable, but bear in mind, I mean no one harm."

"Of course not. The children are my chief concern. Olivia knows nothing about your regrettable parentage, and I'd prefer she not learn of it until she's much older."

"Agreed."

"Then let us set aside our differences and cry truce."

"Truce," he conceded. "Lady Vaughan."

A feline smile dusted her lips. "For the children's sake, I think you should call me Mother."

Mother? Derek hoped he wouldn't choke on the word.

He was spared answering by voices in the hall. The drawing room door opened as if on its own, until Derek's gaze lowered to find Johnny peering around its edge. Spying him, the boy pushed the door open further.

"Well!" Rosalie wheeled with a swish of skirts as if a grubby lad in her drawing room were the worst sin.

"They're in here!" Johnny called over his shoulder, oblivious to her judgment. He turned back to give Derek a cheeky grin. "Mr. Harry said I might have another coin if I ran you to ground, sir."

"Mr—oh, lud," Rosalie sighed as Harry and a spare man, small and wiry with spectacles perched high on his nose, entered.

"Here they are, Mr. Minton," Harry all but crowed. "Told you the boy could find them." He added with uncharacteristic decorum, "Nigel Minton, my cousin, Derek Vaughan. I believe you've been searching for him."

"Indeed, I have." Minton swept a graceful bow. "'Tis an honor to meet you at last, Your Grace."

"The honor is mine, Mr. Minton." Uncomfortable with courtly gestures, Derek offered his hand to the solicitor and did his best to ignore the older man's scrutiny as he turned back to Rosalie. "You remember my cousin Harry?"

"How could I forget?" She inclined her head in brief acknowledgment. "You and Derek were forever getting into scrapes together. I wasn't sure you'd ever grow up."

Harry's eyes lit with anticipation as they did whenever he sensed opposition of any kind. "I stand proof that I *have* grown up. But then none of us can avoid growing *older*, can we?"

Rosalie cleared her throat. "May I offer refreshments, gentlemen?"

Minton's eyes sparkled. "While this is a moment worth celebrating, I fear the hour is a bit early, and there are many things I'm eager to discuss with His Grace."

"Then perhaps I should leave you gentlemen to your

business." Though politely worded, Rosalie's lips tightened into a thin line.

"No need." Derek stopped her as she walked toward the door. "Our business encompasses this whole estate, and I am eager to see Ambersley Hall."

Harry grinned. "Then by all means, let's not infringe on the lady's generosity."

"I'm more than happy to do what I can for my family, Mr. Coatsworth."

Belatedly, Derek recalled his stepmother had never liked his cousin nor, for that matter, anyone named Coatsworth.

Minton either didn't recognize the veiled animosity between the two, or purposefully ignored it. "My lady, if we might then impose upon you for luncheon?"

"Of course, Mr. Minton. Shall we say half past twelve?" Rosalie managed to look down her nose at all of them, finishing with the boy, Johnny. "And, Your Grace, I'll tell Curtis and Olivia of your return."

"I look forward to meeting them," Derek said. He ushered the others out to Minton's waiting carriage, where Harry paid off the lad. Johnny stared at the gold sovereign with awe, gave a whoop of delight and dashed away, leaving the men to chuckle as they climbed into the coach.

Churning gray clouds hung low as they pulled up before the Hall once more. The turbulent sky darkened the already sooty façade as if to blot it out completely. Derek couldn't help but worry for the estate's welfare if Rosalie became its chatelaine. She wouldn't worry about restoring its former glory—she'd want to use it to glorify herself.

"The original Hall was Tudor, but the eighth duke undertook to refurbish it in the Baroque style over a century ago," Minton explained as they descended from the coach. "As you can see, the fire burned through the main hall and damaged most of the upper floors, destroying many of the servants' quarters."

"How did the fire start?" Derek asked.

"I'm afraid we don't know. At the time, the staff expressed concern that the fire had been set deliberately, but I employed

Bow Street, and they could find no proof of the claims. It appears it was naught but a tragic accident." Minton led the way around the right flank of the house. "I had the roof repaired to protect what was left of the interior, but it wasn't meant to be a permanent remedy. You see it hasn't weathered the elements well."

The solicitor's words were readily evidenced. "Why weren't more extensive repairs done?" Derek studied the bricked-up windows as they passed.

"The estate was rather tied up while we tried to find the rightful heir," Minton replied. "You'd not believe how many Vaughan men have died young and left no sons. I've acted as the executor of the estate for the past four years, but my powers are limited."

"Looks as if someone's been maintaining the roses, anyway." Harry stopped to inhale one blossom's sweet fragrance.

Derek studied the rear of the Hall, the worst of its damage hidden at this angle. The golden stone projected a warmth that beckoned him with promise.

"Shall we?" Minton opened one of the French doors that gave access to the gardens and entered the Hall.

Derek hesitated on the threshold of the dimly lit interior while Harry peered over his shoulder.

"Ten to one the place is haunted," Harry whispered in his ear.

Derek shushed him as Minton began the tour.

"This part of the Hall weathered the worst part of the fire." Mr. Minton led them down a wide corridor where charred walls were beginning to crumble. Ashes, dust and cobwebs dotted the black soot that covered everything like a cracked skin. "This was the newest wing of the house. Much more timber than stone work here." He led them into a large room where the startled scurry of rodent feet greeted them.

"This was the late Duke's study." Mr. Minton pulled back the heavy draperies masking the nearest window, allowing gray light to filter in through the airborne dust and reveal a rotted rug with large holes and burned edges. Two leather chairs were piled in the nearest corner, their hides scorched beyond repair. Mr. Minton crossed behind a large square desk to pull the drapes back from the second window.

Derek surveyed the room with a critical eye. "Most of what's here will need to be discarded."

"You might consider keeping the desk. It suffered some damage but could be refinished. It's been in the family for five generations."

Derek ran a hand along the heavy piece of wood. Generations of Vaughan men had used this desk. *Real* Vaughans.

"Mind if I let some fresh air into this tomb?" Harry crossed to the far window. A floorboard issued an eerie creak beneath his weight, and Harry, nimble as any deer, sprang forward only to have the boards collapse with a sharp crack. He clawed the air as he fell into a black void.

Derek immediately rushed forward with his cousin's name on his lips.

Minton grabbed his shoulder. "Take care, Your Grace. More of the floor might give way."

Derek went down on hands and knees, crawling toward the black cavern. "Harry! Harry!" he shouted into the hole.

"I'm here. You haven't got rid of me, yet." Harry's familiar voice sounded from below.

Derek's initial wave of fear receded. "Here—take my hand," he instructed, leaning further into the hole.

"Your Grace!" Minton grabbed his ankles. "What if you fall?"

But Derek strained to hear Harry. "Derek, I can't see a thing, and I don't think I can stand. I've injured my knee."

"Is it broken? Are you bleeding?" asked Derek.

A laugh drifted up. "I don't know. I can't see a bloody thing."

Derek looked at Minton. "What kind of a room is he in? If I jump down there, is there another way out?"

Minton looked embarrassed. "I'm sorry to say, I don't know, my lord. I never had cause to tour the underground rooms. However, I would not advise jumping down that hole in any case."

"The drop isn't all that dangerous if you're expecting to do it."

"Not for you, but you could easily injure Mr. Coatsworth by landing on him." Minton retrieved a heavy sash cord from the nearby drapes. "Here, see if this will help."

Derek smiled. "Well done." He lowered one end over the edge of the precipice. "Harry, we've got a rope. Can you reach it?"

"Wait." Within the hole, something fell with a clatter and Harry cursed under his breath. "Yes, I've got it now."

It took a little patience—though Harry muttered a few more colorful curses—but with Derek and Minton working together, they managed to pull him up until Derek could reach Harry's coat and pull him over the edge of the broken boards.

Silent for now, Harry lay on the floor, pain etched on his face.

Derek kneeled over his cousin, panting from the exertion of lifting him out. "I believe you've put on some weight."

His cousin smiled gamely at the quip. "It's that damn lack of exercise on board the ship," he said through partially clenched teeth.

"Which I've more than compensated for. Maybe you should pull me from a hole."

"Yes, I'll do that—as soon as you are obliging enough to fall through one."

Derek's eyes widened to see blood seeping through the cloth of Harry's breeches. "Harry, lie still. You may have hurt yourself more than you think."

Harry looked down at his leg and then his hands, which were smeared with blood. "That explains why my knee felt sticky. Can you tell how badly damaged it is?"

"Not without more light." Derek removed his neck cloth and tied it around Harry's thigh just above the injured knee. "This will help stop the bleeding, but we'll need a surgeon. Minton, is there someone local?"

Minton suggested they retire to the Dower House and fetch the local barber to look at Harry's leg. Derek heartily seconded the motion, and between them, they managed to help Harry limp to the carriage.

5

Derek continued to fret over Harry's wound in the coach. He'd seen enough leg injuries in the cavalry to recognize that prompt treatment would do Harry the most good.

Clucking over the injured guest, Paget ushered the three men into the familiar cream and gold drawing room.

"Thank you, Paget," Minton said. "Send Rory for the barber immediately."

Paget stood back as Harry was settled onto the divan. "Yes, Mr. Minton. May I do anything else?"

"Yes, I'll need a knife and a bottle of brandy," said Derek, preoccupied with removing Harry's boot from his swollen leg. "Harry, I hope you won't mind, but I'm going to cut the leg off your breeches."

"So long as you don't cut off my leg," Harry bit out from his seat on the ivory brocade.

"No, I'll save that task for the barber." Successful with the boot, Derek looked up to find the butler hadn't moved. "Was I unclear, Paget?" It didn't bode well if the staff wouldn't carry out his commands.

"I'm sorry, sir, there is no brandy. The duty and all. If necessary, there is a bottle of cognac the late duke laid aside for—"

Derek waved off the details. "Cognac will do. Fetch it."

Paget bowed his head. "Yes, Your Grace. I should point

out that the cognac is meant to be aged for another ten years to reach its full potential."

"What do I care what it tastes like? I'm going to pour it into the wound." With care, Derek placed a small pillow under Harry's knee.

"P-Pour it into the wound? My lord, surely there's something else in the wine cellar."

Derek's head snapped around at this further hesitation. The men in his cavalry unit had never questioned him. "Enough shilly-shallying, Paget. When I issue an order, I expect it obeyed. Knife. Cognac. Now, go!"

Paget retreated, his face flushed.

Derek released the tourniquet's pressure and watched the wound seep slowly through the torn fabric. He monitored it while he massaged Harry's ankle and lower calf. "Do you feel your whole leg, Harry?"

"Yes, thank you, I do, and I rather wish I didn't." Harry grunted when Derek's hand moved too close to the bruised knee.

"No, believe me, the pain is a good sign." He studied the wound as best he could, noting the tiny wood slivers still piercing the skin. "I can clean the cut, but I think it will need to be sewn up. Shame Cushing isn't here. He sets a pretty stitch." Derek looked shrewdly at his cousin's perspiring face. "Does it hurt much?"

"Like the devil," Harry admitted.

Paget returned bearing a tray with a large knife and a dust-coated bottle still sealed. He set the tray next to where Derek knelt by the divan and retreated from the room before Derek could thank him. Concerned he'd been too abrupt with the retainer, Derek started to call him back only to have the words catch in his throat as Rosalie entered the room with her children and a drab woman in tow.

"Oh!" She stopped at the sight of Harry bleeding on the divan.

Derek's only greeting was to raise the large knife and test its blade, before he returned his attention to Harry. No one spoke as he sliced through the breeches and removed the blood-soaked shred of cloth.

"What is all of this?" Rosalie demanded.

Mr. Minton stepped forward and explained the situation quietly while the duke uncorked the cognac. "This will likely sting, Harry," he warned and then quickly doused the knee.

Harry's face paled, and his fingers clenched the cushion of the divan until his knuckles turned the same ivory color.

Rosalie's eyes narrowed as she surveyed the carnage at the divan, and she shuddered as if in sympathy to Mr. Harry's pain. "Lud, Derek, could you not have chosen another room? This divan is ruined."

Derek glanced at the cognac and blood stained brocade. In truth, he hadn't given a thought to anything beyond Harry's welfare. "It was expedient. I'm sorry if the piece is ruined, but there's no object here I value more than my cousin."

"Of course not. You haven't lived here for nearly a year as I have. You don't consider this your home, or these your belongings."

"As you do," interpreted Derek.

Rosalie looked down at him proudly, if a trifle coldly. "As I do. Someone must look after the Vaughan interests."

Derek's back stiffened. "I'm sure I can count on you for that, *Mother*."

With a huff, Rosalie seemed to acknowledge a stalemate. "Derek, can you not spare a moment to greet your brother and sister?"

Ill at ease with this lie, Derek rose to look past the divan at the young faces of his supposed siblings. They flanked a tall austere woman he surmised was their governess. The woman didn't look unkind, simply unimaginative. Curtis, Reginald Vaughan's true son, would be eleven now. He was an awkward colt with a long neck, black hair and icy blue eyes that appraised Derek and then swept dispassionately over the room. Olivia was a tiny replica of her mother with raven hair and blue eyes. She would be seven, Harry had told him.

He'd interrupted his life to return and ensure the welfare of these two youngsters, and their distrustful eyes followed him as though he were a bear intent on devouring them.

"How do you do." Derek inclined his head before offering his hand to the boy. "Curtis, I doubt you remember me."

Curtis stood frozen, until his mother sniffed loudly in some unspoken command. Finally, he took Derek's hand with a frown. "Your Grace, I am honored as is my sister," he said in grand tones befitting the lord of the manor.

My sister. The lad used a proprietary tone. At least little Olivia had a champion. "You must call me Derek, for we are one family. Will you introduce me to your sister?"

Curtis seemed to consider this a just request, and with only a brief glance at his mother, he motioned to his young sister who stepped forward. "Derek, this is Olivia Vaughan."

Fear painted Olivia's face until it nearly matched the white pinafore she wore over her green dress. Blue eyes widened as she said, "Mama said the new duke might send us away from Ambersley. Will you send us away?"

Derek stole a glance to see his stepmother blush and purse her lips. So, she'd painted him the ogre. He kneeled before the delicate girl who backed into the comforting arms of her brother as if Derek might breathe fire upon her. "Olivia, I'm the new duke but I'll not send you away. We're family and we belong together."

"Prettily said, Derek," Rosalie said from his left. "You see, Olivia? I told you we lived here at the duke's will."

"You said we were at the duke's mercy," Olivia corrected ingenuously.

Derek noted the dark look shared between Rosalie and Curtis, the boy's mouth tight.

Paget reappeared at the open doorway. A small shadow lurking behind him materialized into that gardener's boy, Johnny.

"My lady, luncheon is prepared. We shall serve it at your leisure." Paget's simple statement spoke volumes on how his stepmother ran the household.

"Derek, will your party join us for luncheon now, or shall we wait upon your convenience?"

"Thank you, but I'll await the barber here with Harry. Mr. Minton, please dine with them. I'm sure you'll be more comfortable than camped in here."

The solicitor seemed only mildly flustered by this. "Since Your Grace and I shall have leisure this afternoon to speak, I'll happily join Lady Vaughan for lunch."

"Paget, whisk that urchin back to the kitchens where he belongs." Lady Vaughan nodded toward Johnny.

Johnny's eyes widened at being caught. She never should have snuck in here, but she'd been concerned for Mr. Harry. She glanced from Olivia's smiling face to Curtis's glare, which dared her to speak. And Paget looked down his hooked nose as though he'd eat her in two bites.

But Mr. Harry came to her rescue. "Leave the boy here, will you? I still owe him a crown."

She beamed at her benefactor and ran to his side. "Truly, sir, 'tis not necessary."

"Come, children. We shall leave your brother and his party." Lady Vaughan exited with a rustle of silk, leaving Miss Trent to lead Olivia from the room. Johnny's triumphant smile dimmed before the menacing look Curtis shot her as he left. Why should he be angry with her?

Mr. Minton conferred with the duke. "After luncheon, you'll grant me a few hours?"

"Once the barber has seen Harry, you may have my whole afternoon."

Harry held his peace until the door closed softly behind Paget. "You should have dined with them."

"Nonsense. You cannot sit at table, and I'll not leave you while you're in pain. Paget will fetch us something when he gets a moment."

"I can fetch you something from the kitchen if you're hungry," Johnny said eagerly. "Tom always says I should make myself useful. Being Tuesday, Mrs. Chalmers will have baked steak and kidney pies. Lady Vaughan doesn't like them, but Mrs. Chalmers makes them every week anyway. Rory says the late duke enjoyed them with ale."

Mr. Harry cocked a brow at his cousin. "Then by all means, go tell Mrs. Chalmers that the new duke would like to taste her pies and ale."

Johnny needed no further encouragement, but left the room in a trice.

Entering the kitchen, she heard Paget speaking. "He must have poured half the bottle over his cousin's injured knee. I remember the day the old duke put aside that cognac. It was the day Miss Amber was christened, and he said he'd toast her wedding with it. He was so happy that day. Somehow, I always believed we'd find Miss Amber, and I'd be able to carry out her father's wishes and give her that bottle for her wedding."

Mrs. Chalmers wiped her floury hands on her apron. "Is he so impetuous then to not let you finish a sentence in his presence?"

"Wouldn't let me complete a thought before issuing another command. He likes a tightly run household."

"Then he's no better than her ladyship?" Mrs. Chalmers asked doubtfully.

Paget shook his head. "No better. I hate to think what will become of Ambersley."

Johnny stepped from the shadows to ask Mrs. Chalmers for pies for the duke and his cousin. Mrs. Chalmers and Paget shared a look, but neither asked if she'd heard their conversation. She hadn't meant to eavesdrop, but she knew she would share what she'd heard with Tom. He was always interested in what Paget thought about the Vaughans.

❦

Following luncheon, Minton returned to the drawing room in time to hear the barber's encouraging prognosis that nothing appeared broken. As the practitioner repacked his bag, he recommended the gentleman stay off of the leg for a week and then have the stitches removed.

After Paget ushered the visitor out, Minton cleared his throat. "Your Grace, the library is at our disposal. We can meet at your convenience."

The young nobleman looked back, reluctant to leave his cousin.

Mr. Coatsworth laughed, only a trifle worse for a small

dose of laudanum. "Go conduct your business with Minton. Johnny will bear me company and fetch anything I might need."

Johnny smiled with evident delight and seemed to relieve the duke's concerns. Without further ado, Minton led his new employer to the library.

He couldn't have asked for a finer specimen of youth and vigor to take the reins at Ambersley. At five-and-twenty, his lordship stood tall and straight, kept his head in an emergency and took command when the situation demanded. He'd been abrupt with some of the staff, but Minton felt his military training would work to his advantage. Here, at last, was a man worthy of inheriting a dukedom.

"Perhaps I should begin at the beginning." Minton waited for the duke to take a chair before beginning his narrative. "Minton & Son has proudly served the Duke of Ambersley for three generations. At all times, our goal is to protect our clients' interests. I myself have acted on the duke's behalf for twenty years."

Lord Ambersley nodded his understanding.

For the next hour, Minton disclosed the history of the tragic fire, Miss Amber's mysterious disappearance, and his lengthy search for the heir. "I traced the lineage to Reginald Vaughan and you over a year ago. When I sought you in London, your mother—"

"My stepmother," Lord Ambersley corrected, his tone unbending.

"Indeed. Lady Vaughan told me they'd received no word from you since you'd left your father's household years ago."

"I've returned to fulfill my familial obligations. I'm not surprised there are debts to settle." Despite the averted eyes, Minton felt the younger man's tension. Something had driven a wedge between father and son, that much was obvious.

"I have a full accounting of them, but we'll handle those another day." Minton pushed his spectacles higher on his nose and stood. "Since a blood tie exists between you and your half-siblings, I suggested Lady Vaughan remove her family here to the Dower House. If I acted incorrectly, I humbly beg your pardon."

"Not at all. There has been some dissension between my stepmother and me, but they are family. I could not put them out on the streets."

"Precisely so, Your Grace."

Lord Ambersley leaned against the mantle, resting one foot on the fender, a hand on his hip. "Mr. Minton, are you sure you have the right man?"

The solicitor suppressed a smile. "Yes, I rather believe I do."

He turned his head to stare into the unlit fireplace. "But when you say the title must be passed down to the closest male heir—"

"My research has been quite thorough, I assure you. It led me eventually to Reginald Vaughan and to you." He waited, unsure what had prompted these concerns.

"And if I were to pass this title along now to my half-brother, Curtis, could I do that?"

A cold gloom permeated him. "You may, but why would you wish to do such a thing?"

Lord Ambersley turned to face him. "I'm a soldier, Minton, and rather a black sheep."

Minton inspected the younger man for a moment before answering. "You refer to the scandal surrounding your mother."

"She was convicted of murder and hanged. Hardly the blood to introduce to a peerage." The young man watched him with hooded eyes and a frown.

He'd rather sacrifice the title than bring shame to the dukedom. Minton was impressed. "A peer is not only blood, but behavior."

"I left home and my family. I've led men into battle intent upon killing the enemy."

"And yet, when you learned your father had died, your first instinct was to return and provide for your siblings. Was it not?"

"But a barony and a dukedom are quite different matters."

Minton removed his spectacles and rubbed the bridge of

his nose. "Your Grace, I doubt you comprehend the powers you now wield. As the duke you're not only head of the Vaughan family, you hold a seat in the House of Lords. You own this estate, four smaller estates, and a house in London. This power carries certain responsibilities to your family, your tenants and staff, and your country. It's my devout hope you'll rule Ambersley with a firm and just hand, and that you'll take your place in London society and evoke pride in the Vaughan name."

Still unconvinced, Lord Ambersley's lips set in an uncompromising line. "Pride, eh? More likely whispers behind gloved hands. After all, my father was a notorious cuckold, so what must that make me?"

Minton's blood heated at the thought of people casting such aspersions on any member of the Vaughan family, much less his lordship. "The rumor mill is an endless, meaningless wheel, so don't allow what is said behind gloves to trouble you. You will have the power to make and destroy reputations with a smile or frown. Remember that."

The duke pushed away from the fireplace and took a few agitated strides across the room. "Fret not about me. The dukedom should provide sufficient funds for both children, but my presence here will only reignite gossip best left among the ashes. In the end, I want to do what's best for the peerage and the Vaughan family."

"Agreed," Minton said. "Your Grace, let me outline the particulars of your inheritance. You may then judge for yourself what's best for all concerned."

With a nod, Lord Ambersley rejoined him to sit in the two chairs near the hearth. Without further delay, Minton unfolded the intricacies of the former duke's personal fortune.

Derek returned to the gold drawing room, preoccupied with the information Minton had disclosed. He forced a smile for his cousin, reclining on the divan. "I'm sorry I was gone so long, Harry. I hope you found something to occupy you."

"As a matter of fact I spent the time teaching our protégé

his letters."

"Who?" asked Derek, momentarily at a loss.

"The boy. Johnny." Harry readjusted the pillow under his knee.

"Oh, yes," Derek murmured. He rubbed his eyes, aware of the ache behind them, before looking about the room. "Where is he?"

"Gone home. Thought someone might worry about his whereabouts."

Derek nodded and raised the dusty bottle with its remains. "Cognac for you?" Harry nodded assent with a yawn, and Derek poured a splash into a glass for the patient and a larger portion for himself.

I could still walk away from all of this.

When he'd first entered the library with Minton, he'd been prepared to tell him the truth: he was a usurper, denying a true Vaughan from inheriting what should remain in the family through the pure, unsullied, male bloodline. He hadn't found the right words to express his thoughts before the solicitor had unfolded the many details of the inheritance.

"Was your discussion fruitful?" Harry asked.

Derek handed him the cognac, and the two raised their glasses in a mutual toast. Derek savored the warming touch of liquid while he considered Harry's question. "There are a few difficulties I didn't foresee." Least expected had been the blossoming desire to stay, despite the hazards, and rebuild Ambersley. The Hall had all but spoken to him, beseeching him for help.

"Name one."

The most pressing was that Minton seemed unconcerned whether Derek was truly a Vaughan or not. The solicitor clearly wanted Derek to accept the title, and once Derek gleaned the true financial situation, he could understand why.

Derek lowered himself into a chair opposite his cousin and stared at the water stains on the wall. "I've become the Duke of Ambersley, but I've only been given the income the property earns. The late duke's personal fortune was left to his daughter."

"But the daughter is dead," Harry said.

"Missing, presumed dead. No one's ever found a trace of her. According to Minton, if you don't present a body for the inquest, you have to wait seven years to pronounce someone dead."

"But that would be three more years," Harry interjected. "You don't mean to tell me you can't lay hands on any money until then."

"Small sums. The last duke obviously thought his heir would have a certain amount of money already. The cash sum he left me will pay off my father's debts. Rosalie incurred more debts when she arrived here, and I'll have to pay those."

And there lay the crux of his dilemma. The staff hadn't been paid in years, and the Hall was a shamble. If he left Ambersley now and Minton settled the title on Curtis, he feared Rosalie would drain her son's resources just as she'd ruined the finances of both her husbands. Minton had reviewed her spending since her arrival at the estate, and Derek heard the unspoken plea in the solicitor's voice for someone to help him curb her expensive habits.

It would be nearly ten years until Curtis came of age. Could Derek accept the title, face Society's recriminations, and protect the Vaughan assets until then? Once Curtis could be relied on to look after his—and Olivia's—interests, Derek could hand the title down to him. He hated the idea of living closely with Rosalie for such a long period, but he owed a duty to Reginald Vaughan to provide for the children's future.

The only remaining hazard would be if someone in London unveiled the identity of his real father.

Harry interrupted his thoughts. "So, when the daughter is declared dead…"

"I inherit a sizeable fortune." A large portion of which he would invest for his siblings.

"And if she's alive?"

"Then Minton and I would become co-executors of her estate, and she'd continue living here with my family."

"But you still couldn't touch her money."

Derek shook his head and drained his glass.

Harry toyed with the empty glass. "You don't *need* a place as large as the Hall. Do you own another property?"

"Some smaller estates, and a house in London, but it would cost a small ransom to open it and outfit with a staff. I don't want it known in London just how tight things are."

"You could sell—"

"No." Derek's response was immediate, visceral, and surprised him. More softly, he reasoned, "The holdings are entailed. I feel it's my duty to rebuild the Hall. I just don't know how I'll finance it." The pair sat in silence for some time.

"You must marry an heiress," Harry said flatly.

Derek choked out a harsh laugh. "I doubt any woman wants to live with me in that burned out shell."

"I have it, cousin." Mischief lightened Harry's tone. "Find the missing daughter and marry *her*. She has impeccable breeding and a fortune to boot."

Derek responded to the ribbing with a shudder, but Harry's humor had dispelled his low spirits. "Impeccable breeding usually means freckled and short-sighted with teeth like a horse. She would be far too young to marry anyway, better to wring her neck and be rid of her. Then I'd have all the money I—"

A gasp sounded from the doorway. Frowning, he turned in his chair to see the housekeeper holding her hand over her mouth, dismay evident in her eyes.

"What is it?" Embarrassed at being caught making an unkind jest, Derek spoke more sharply than he intended.

"I beg pardon, Your Grace. Paget thought you might like to join Lady Vaughan and the children for tea and cakes." Mrs. North's voice trailed off as he stared at her.

"Thank Paget for me, but we'll be leaving shortly with Mr. Minton."

"Yes, Your Grace." Mrs. North hastily retreated from the room leaving silence in her wake.

Derek massaged his forehead ruefully. "And now the staff believes I murder children."

Harry chuckled. "Give yourself time. You need to get to

know the staff and let them get to know you. In the meantime, perhaps you should…" He paused, searching for words.

"Watch my step?" suggested Derek with a raised brow.

Harry nodded. "And maybe your back as well."

6

Derek and Harry with his makeshift crutch took a coach to Bath the following day as Harry was anxious to apprise his mother of his return. After gaining Harry's promise to visit Ambersley soon, Derek left for London to finalize his inheritance. Here, Minton took him to view the residence on Grosvenor Square—which boasted twelve bedrooms and its own mews—and it began to seep in that he truly was the twelfth Duke of Ambersley. Minton asked if His Grace wished to open the residence for the remainder of the Season. Without regret, Derek declined and announced he would return forthwith to Ambersley and start repairs on the Hall.

On a bright April afternoon, Derek and his burly servant Cushing rode up the long drive to Ambersley Hall. As they rounded the final bend, Derek experienced that same eye-stinging sense of homecoming. Cushing let out a low whistle that made Sabu prick his ears and prance in delight. Derek controlled the desert-bred stallion with a steady hand on the rein and a stroke along his arched neck. He looked sidelong at the servant. "It makes an impression, doesn't it."

"It's as big as a bloody palace, beggin' your pardon, Master—I mean, Milord." Cushing tapped a heel to move his newly purchased gelding apace.

"Don't let it fluster you, Cushing. You know I don't stand on ceremony."

"To think you went all the way to India to seek your fortune when this was waiting right here for you the whole time."

Derek shook his head. "The irony is, I have inherited one giant expense and not nearly enough coin to support it." Regardless, he had no regrets. Not about this.

"That will come in time, Master."

In time. The question was, how much time did he have? There remained the possibility that somewhere lived a man who could offer up proof that Derek was not truly a Vaughan. If his stepmother found such a man, she wouldn't hesitate to rid the place of Derek and put Curtis in his stead. Though drawn to Ambersely, he needed to remember his time here was temporary.

"We need to start training Sabu," Cushing said. "I'm sure he could win at the races. Look how quickly he's recovered from being aboard the ship."

It was true. Sabu had finished the leisurely two-day journey from London as fresh as he'd started. "There will be racing at Goodwood in late summer. I don't know whether they'll allow a foreign-bred horse."

Cushing scratched his rather bulbous nose. "The Duke of Richmond might bend the rules to allow the Duke of Ambersley to race his best horse. You could write to him."

"Or have my secretary write him." Neither spoke another word, but they wore broad smiles as they drew rein at the stables.

The head groom trotted out on bowed legs to take their horses as they dismounted. "Welcome back, Your Grace," he said with a nod.

"Thank you, er—"

"Rory, my lord."

Derek turned to Cushing. "Bed the horses down. Rory can help you find a loose box for Sabu." Over the horse's shoulder, he saw the groom's mouth gape and tensed.

"I'm sorry Your Grace is displeased with my work. I'll help your new man find his way around then pack my things." Rory's voice shook with emotion.

Belatedly, Derek realized his error. Gruffly, he said, "Good God, man, he's not replacing you. This is Cushing—he'll be supervising Sabu's training for the races." As Harry had suggested, he would need to learn the rank and file of every staff member or risk offending them.

Rory's mouth closed, and he stepped back to consider the two horses before pointing to Sabu. "You plan to race *this* horse?"

The little stallion arched his neck and pricked his ears in reply.

Cushing laughed. "He's a might on the smallish side, but wait 'til you see him run." He took Sabu's reins and allowed Rory and the gelding to precede him into the stable.

Derek would have followed, but he spied Paget. The butler—without his coat—wiped his hands on a large white linen handkerchief as he approached.

"Forgive me, Your Grace. We weren't expecting your return."

"And where else should I be?"

"Lady Vaughan has been preparing to withdraw to London for the Season. We assumed the family was joining you there."

How like Rosalie to take immediate advantage of his return. She'd waited nearly a year for Minton to publicly acknowledge her immediate family's claim to the title. Now out of mourning, she would be eager to open the ducal residence and throw lavish soirees. It would hardly matter to her whether Derek was there or not.

"My fault for not discussing it with her. The family will remain here for the summer."

"Very good, my lord." He started to turn away but Derek stopped him.

"Paget, what duties brought you to the stables?"

The older man squared his shoulders. "I was planting vegetables."

Derek's lips twitched at the butler's discomfiture. "Do you have a penchant to be a farmer?"

"No, sir. Merely to help provide for the household. Will that be all, my lord?"

"One last thing. I've brought my manservant from India with me. I'll need a suitable position for him on our staff."

"It so happens, my lord, the late duke's valet accepted employment elsewhere long ago."

"Excellent." Derek was relieved to know he wouldn't have to face some fop who would try to turn him into a courtier. At least Cushing would know better than to try and dress him.

"Send him to me, and I'll have Mrs. North arrange a room for him."

Derek recalled many of the servants were quartered in the least damaged wing of the Hall. "Let's do it now. Cushing!" he shouted then turned back to the butler. "If there's a spare room, I'd like to use it as my own."

Paget's hooded eyes widened. "My lord, there are plenty of rooms at the Dower House—"

"Better suited to a duke," finished Derek as Cushing approached them. "But, I'll be more dedicated to repairing the Hall if I'm living under its roof." Derek still read concern on the butler's face. "Remember I've lived much of the last three years in an army tent in India."

"This will be high living compared to that, eh Master?" Cushing's boisterous laugh turned to an embarrassed cough under Paget's disapproving regard.

෨৵ৎ

Upon hearing of Derek's return, Rosalie told the butler she wanted a word with the duke.

"I'll inform His Grace that you've requested an audience, my lady."

This reinterpretation of her directive did not please her, and she barely managed to bite back an angry retort. How irritating that Derek not only had reappeared in their lives, but he'd had the gall to accept the title. She'd much preferred having full command of Ambersley in the duke's absence. Honestly, he'd been living in India all these years, couldn't he have returned sick, wounded—*dying*?

She collected herself when Paget announced the duke would see her in his study. *His* study. Already he was laying claim to rooms. Then Rosalie realized the advantage and smiled. She would play on his eagerness to be rid of her and the children. Smoothing her green silk gown, she entered the study prepared to be an agreeable, perhaps even loving, mother.

"Welcome home, Derek."

He kept his back to her as he ran his index finger along a row of books on the shelves. "Thank you."

"I'll ask Mrs. North to prepare a room for you."

"No need." Derek selected a book and turned to her. "Paget has found room for me at the Hall."

She clasped her hands before her. "How good of him. Will you be comfortable there?"

"Tolerably."

"If you don't wish to share the house here, I can easily take the children to Grosvenor Square. Curtis is of an age where he could use a little town polish. Even Olivia might enjoy a museum."

"Yes, Paget mentioned you were planning to open the London house, but I fear that's out of the question. There's precious little money at hand and a mountain of debt. We cannot afford to staff two homes."

Rosalie flexed her fingers as she tried to remain calm over Derek's ploy to control her. "Surely Minton can loosen the purse strings now that he's found you."

"They're not Minton's to control. Not to bore you with my financial woes, but…" In brief, Derek shared with her the details of their limited funds and that the bulk of the late duke's fortune could not be touched for years.

Once more, Rosalie saw her hopes dashed. Despite her patience, she now had to wait three more years until her family could have the money they deserved. She resented that Minton hadn't shared these important details with her before now.

"So you see, we'll have to live very simply for awhile."

"Why? The money is there."

"Minton still has investigators seeking Miss Amber."

"Miss Amber," Rosalie spat. "Have Minton call off his hounds. He'll never find her."

"Though I agree with you, he thinks otherwise. Since it's legally still her money, I cannot stop him."

Rosalie took an agitated turn of the room. "I'm heartily sick of that girl. She's dead—you cannot convince me otherwise. Eventually we'll be able to settle all the accounts, so why can we not live as we should?"

"I'd rather not be burdened with more debt. I intend to start repairs on the Hall."

She bit back a laugh. "With such limited funds, how will you pay for that?"

"We'll do the work ourselves. I'm afraid I'll need to borrow the staff during the day. I hope that won't inconvenience you." With that, he sat on a chaise and opened the book. "Oh, I've already told Paget you and the children will be remaining at Ambersley throughout the summer."

"How dare you!"

He closed the book with a snap. "I dare because it's my duty to make the decisions now. You see, Mother, I've had time to think this through as well. Curtis is too young to handle the responsibilities here."

"I can see to them—"

"Ambersley is already at rack and ruin, so I'll not leave the finances in your hands. I feel it's my duty to support the children, but I'll not be blackmailed into footing outlandish bills. You dare not expose me when you have no proof. For now, we're at an impasse."

She hated that he was right. As long as he was the acknowledged duke, she'd be forced to wheedle what she could from him. "Curtis is the true duke, and that's *his* money. I want it set aside for him."

"When I inherit the money, I shall set up funds for both children."

"And you'll grant the title to Curtis? And *leave?*"

"We can discuss that in three years. Now, if you'll excuse me." He set the book aside and rose. "I need to talk to the bailiff."

She allowed him to walk past her, but if he thought she would allow him to order her life, she would ensure he learned otherwise. Derek Vaughan had become the devil, and for now, she consigned him to hell.

෯෬

Johnny expected the new duke's arrival to make everyone at Ambersley happy. Instead, Lady Vaughan became more demanding and Curtis more short-tempered. Olivia cried more, though she never could say what was wrong. The duke always seemed preoccupied and spent much of his time with Mr. Broadmoor, the bailiff.

Remembering how tense the staff had been when Lady Vaughan first arrived, Johnny wasn't as surprised by the worries she heard them express. Mr. Pritchard retold the story of the duke's murderous mother and how she was hanged, but Johnny wasn't clear why that made the duke a bad person. Most troubling to her was the sadness and worry she saw reflected in Tom and Martha's eyes, as if they feared the duke would do something awful to them. She'd hear them whispering deep into the night, but the one time she'd dared ask, Martha had wiped away a tear and said with her matter-of-fact tone that naught was amiss.

Johnny nodded at the lie and did her best not to upset anyone.

As the initial turmoil of the duke's arrival eased, Johnny was allowed to join the swarm of activity at Ambersley Hall. Tom had told her how the staff had been pressed into service to clean out the Hall and start repairs. To contribute to the cause was an honor.

Her first task was to scrub the soot from the main staircase so the duke could decide whether the treads could be sanded and preserved. At the top of the stairs, the duke rasped burn marks from the banister. Stokes and Mr. Pritchard worked behind him, sanding the wood that had been cleaned and dried. Throughout the main floor, other small parties were similarly employed.

Tom set a bucket of clean water at the bottom of the stairs, and she trailed his gaze as he watched the duke work. "Can't make heads nor tails of him," Tom muttered. "Doesn't seem to know his own importance." He was still shaking his head as he carried away her dirty water.

Johnny hid her smile as she bowed her head and returned to work.

Late in the morning, Paget carefully stepped past her as he climbed the stairs to bring the duke a salver piled high with letters.

The duke paused, the rasp still in his hand. "What's this?"

"The mail, my lord," Paget responded. "I suspect you have received a number of congratulations on your inheritance." As the duke didn't seem inclined to take the salver, Paget retrieved the top letter and held it out. "This one bears the Royal seal, my lord."

Johnny watched the duke wipe his hand along his breeches before taking the envelope and turning it over. He broke open the seal and his eyes scanned back and forth across the paper. Then he sat down on the stairs with a thump. "I've been invited to dine with Prince George the next time I'm in London."

Paget nodded gravely. "The Crown has always held the Duke of Ambersley in the highest regard."

To everyone's shock, the duke burst out laughing.

Johnny tugged on his sleeve. "Is the Prince funny?"

"No, I am." Derek's gaze sought his thin-shouldered secretary. "Mr. Pritchard, remind me to send his Royal Highness a thank you for his kind invitation."

"When will you be leaving for London, my lord, if I might be so bold?" Paget asked.

"Oh, not for some time. There's far too much work to do around here. Gentlemen, let's get back to it." He returned the missive to Paget. "I'll read those later. Oh, and if you could drum up some cold ale for everyone, it would be much appreciated."

Paget nodded and strode down the stairs. In the kitchen, he relayed what he'd just seen to Tom. "My first impression of His Grace may have been a trifle hasty." He added darkly, "Lady Vaughan would have had her bags packed within the hour of receiving such a note."

Tom had to agree. Listening to Johnny's tales of the new duke, he could tell she thought he was a paragon. Still, he reserved his own judgment.

But the next afternoon, Tom whistled a joyous tune as Johnny raced ahead of him into the cottage.

"Look, Martha, look!" Johnny jumped up and down and pointed to him.

Tom held out a silken purse that was heavy with coin.

Martha stared at it. "Whatever in the world—?"

"Four years' wages," Tom said simply and watched Martha's eyes overflow. "Mr. Minton brought the money from London, and every one of the staff got paid. His Grace said he wanted to do right by us, and that's why we're doing the repairs on the Hall ourselves." His eyes rested on Johnny's shining face. She'd made the duke a hero, he knew. Had the time come to tell her the truth and restore her to her family? A picture of Lady Vaughan came to his mind, and he realized His Grace would never be responsible for raising a little girl—that charge would fall to Lady Vaughan.

Besides, would Johnny even remember—or accept—that she was Miss Amber? With a heavy heart, Tom resolved to hold their secret fast.

ॐॐ

Restoring life to Ambersley Hall brought meaning to Derek's days. He welcomed the hard work and the growing camaraderie with the staff. It helped him bear the stilted, mostly silent meals he shared with Rosalie and her children. He would have liked to befriend his siblings, but Rosalie guarded them as though he might poison them in her absence.

His evenings were filled with quiet hours. He used his time reading, or occasionally, like tonight, calculating the sums it would take to repay all his debts. In lighter moments, he could appreciate the irony of inheriting a prestigious title and no means to provide for himself, much less those around him. But this evening, seized with disappointment, he went to the stables for solace.

As he strolled through the honeysuckle-scented evening,

he reminded himself why he was masquerading as a duke. Repairing the Hall had become a Herculean task, one he was determined to see completed. Providing for Curtis and Olivia's future, that was far more important than any personal wishes Derek had.

Inside the darkening barn, he discovered Johnny. "You're out late."

Johnny motioned toward the harness room. "I brought the cat supper."

"Everyone looks after everyone else here at Ambersley."

"Yes, Your Grace. Tom says we all have to stick together during hard times."

Derek sighed. What a simple world this boy lived in. Not easy, but simple.

"Cushing says Sabu is going to race against other horses and win a lot of money for you." Johnny went to Sabu's stall and held out his hand.

"Careful, he bites."

"He knows I don't play those games. See?" Johnny turned his back to Sabu who snuffled his hair until the boy giggled.

"I fear Sabu won't be racing this season. There's no money left at the moment to pay for the entry fees, so we'll have to wait until next year."

Johnny's happiness collapsed into a frown as he considered Derek's words. "You paid the staff their wages instead of taking Sabu to the races."

Surprised the boy had gleaned the facts so quickly, Derek shrugged. "A gentleman must always pay his debts, Johnny. Remember that."

The boy thought about this. "How does a duke make money?"

Derek laughed darkly. "Normally, a duke is born with money. He invests it, gambles it, earns rents on his property, he marries a rich wife—"

"Are you going to marry a rich wife?" Johnny interrupted.

A vision of Helena Thorne flashed in his mind. *Marry you? You have nothing to offer.*

He'd been stung by her response, for he had believed she

loved him. *Nothing but myself,* he'd told her.

Who will marry you on those terms? she'd responded coldly.

Focusing on Johnny's face, Derek shook himself from the unpleasant reverie. "No. You see, most dukes aren't saddled with a home that practically burned down or a staff who hasn't been paid in four years. I cannot make money fast enough to pay my debts, and no woman wants to marry me while I'm camped out in the servants' wing."

"Would Sabu win lots of money at the races?"

"If he won, there would be lots of money."

"Oh." With no more than that, Johnny kissed Sabu's nose and left with a nod. Derek shook his head over the little boy who seemed so wise.

The next morning, he sipped his tea at the kitchen table while scanning the latest issue of *The Times.* As Mrs. Chalmers removed his plate, he heard the distinctive sound of Paget clearing his throat. Derek lowered his paper to find Paget, Mr. Pritchard, Rory, Stokes, Mrs. North and Tom Bendicks standing before him. Johnny hovered in the shadows.

"Did I request an assembly this morning?" Derek asked, setting the paper aside.

Paget looked back at his compatriots, who all nodded.

Tom gently elbowed the butler in the ribs. "Go on. Give it him."

The old hawk hesitated before placing a familiar silk purse on the table.

Derek's brows knit. "What does this mean, Paget?"

"Your Grace, the staff has unanimously voted to return two years' wages to you so that you may enter Sabu in the Goodwood races." He nodded to the purse and bowed slightly. "With our compliments, sir."

Derek looked again at the purse, then back to the sea of serious faces. "How did you—?"

"Johnny told us you didn't have the entry fee." Tom Bendicks worried his hat in his hand.

"Johnny." Derek pointed to the floor before him until Johnny stepped forward timidly. "I told you that in confidence." Unsure whether the boy knew what that meant, he added, "As when a friend tells another friend a secret."

The boy glanced over his shoulder at Paget and the rest before turning to Derek again. "They're your friends, too."

Silence hung in the kitchen while he gazed at the little boy then up to his nervous benefactors. He wanted to laugh but couldn't get a deep enough breath past the constriction in his throat. Surely he wasn't getting sentimental over a bag of coins given to him by a handful of servants. He barely knew these people.

He cleared his throat. "Very well, I will accept this on Sabu's behalf. But, this is a loan, and even if Sabu loses, I will pay you back in time. If he wins, you will each earn a bonus. Now I expect most of us have work to do."

The staff scattered with smiles on their lips leaving only Johnny behind. The boy held out a single crown to him.

"What's this?"

"I wanted to give some money, too. I earned this from Mr. Harry."

Derek took the coin without a word and surrendered the field to sentimentality.

7

London, July 1805

Derek returned from Goodwood with a winning horse, a heavier purse and the Prince's personal invitation to join him at Carlton House at the end of the Season. His Highness was in the throes of redecorating and eager to display his latest additions to an intimate gathering of cronies. The invitation surprised Derek, but the Prince ignored his protestations.

"Nonsense, of course you'll come. Always counted Ambersley as a friend. Besides, Richmond pointed out that little stallion of yours. Wouldn't be putting him out to stud any time soon, would you?"

"I hope to race him another year."

"Good, good. Bring him to Ascot. If he does well there, I may have some mares for him."

"Your Highness is too kind." Derek bowed and accepted the invitation.

"Not married, are you Ambersley?"

"No, sir."

"Good. No wives at this gathering. Bring a guest if you like."

Upon his return to Ambersley, Rosalie voiced her outrage. "You cannot afford to send me and the children to Grosvenor Square, but you can come and go as you please."

"I go at the summons of Prince George," he corrected. "And I won't open the house with only a fortnight left to the Season. I'll stay with Aunt Bess and Harry."

This made the situation more palatable to her. "You must make a good impression on His Highness. Invite him here—"

"With the Hall like it is? Not to mention I couldn't afford to feed him." Derek snorted and walked out.

He was a bit unnerved when he and Harry arrived at Carlton House. He'd expected a formal supper, where the merits of the new furnishings and décor were discussed, followed by quiet music and cards. Instead, they were ushered to the main ballroom where a rousing event with an extended buffet, an orchestra and dancing was already underway. Belatedly, Derek realized every other gentleman invited had brought his mistress.

His initial embarrassment was quickly doused when Harry burst into laughter so loud it drew attention their way.

"Hush, you fool," Derek whispered fiercely while he tried to control his own mirth. "Maybe we should bow out of here quietly."

"Never." Harry dabbed at his damp eyes. "There's far too much potential here. You outrank most of these men, you're half the age of some of them and you've no lady on your arm. Let us see how many of these little birds will willingly feed themselves to a new cat."

Sobering, Derek scanned the sea of young beauties in their daringly low-cut gowns. "A faithless mistress is less worthy even than a faithless wife." Spying the Prince, he squared his shoulders and ushered Harry forward for introductions.

His Highness greeted them both warmly and accepted Harry's presence without question. Then he eased Derek's nerves by personally introducing him to the other gentlemen present. Granted the Prince's patent approval, Derek was assured acceptance by all, regardless of what stories they may remember of his family's past.

Nearly three hours later, Derek stepped onto the balcony to escape the heat of the dancing, the crush of laughing bodies and the candles' glow reflected in the many mirrors. Here a soft breeze refreshed him and offered a few moments of solitude. He'd lost track of Harry. His cousin had captured the interest of more than one female tonight, and Derek could only hope he wouldn't be asked to act as second in a duel at dawn.

"We meet again, Vaughan." The familiar voice from behind mocked him.

Turning, he discovered his nemesis, Lord Worthing.

They watched each other, eyes level, while the muted strains of the orchestra played within.

Worthing's eyes flickered. "Forgive me. I mean Lord Ambersley." He inclined his head.

"I wasn't sure you'd acknowledge my claim," Derek said softly.

"Prinny has already done so. I'll appear churlish if I don't follow suit." Worthing's teeth glinted in the moonlight as he smiled. "Though I'm rather aggrieved to find you, a half-brother born on the wrong side of the sheets, claiming a family title older than mine."

Wary at this seeming admission, Derek asked, "Do you have proof?"

"That my father sired you? No." Worthing's eyes narrowed in the darkness. "Do you?"

"No."

"Perhaps we don't share blood, only an uncanny resemblance."

Derek wished this were so, but Worthing's frown meant he agreed it wasn't likely.

After a moment, Worthing said, "I will share this—my father visited her in her jail cell once. He said she kept a diary, and she swore she would leave her sad story for all to read."

Derek's whole body tensed at this unwelcome news. "I knew naught of any diary."

Worthing rearranged the cuffs of his shirt and coat as if he had no other care in the world. "Perhaps your father burned it."

Derek could only hope, but then he remembered Rosalie telling him of his bastard birth. She'd said she and his father were going through papers—had she seen Alicia Vaughan's diary?

Worthing stepped closer. "I'll not have the Trevarthan name dragged into scandal again. Should you ever find her diary, destroy it."

"Did you fear I would demand your family acknowledge me?"

"I rather thought you'd blackmail us."

Derek's fingers closed into fists before remembering he could hardly throw blows at another guest in Carlton House.

"Of course, now Father's dead, and since you've inherited Ambersley, you need nothing from my family." Worthing leaned close. "I suggest we grant each other distance. Regardless of our titles, Trevarthans don't mix with Vaughans." He looked past Derek's shoulder and straightened. "Nor Coatsworths."

With a nod, Worthing shouldered past Derek to return to the ballroom. He didn't acknowledge Harry at all as he passed.

Harry approached Derek with a glance back over his shoulder. "Same old Trevarthan."

Derek silently disagreed. The St. John Trevarthan who'd warned him tonight was subtly different than the tormentor from his youth. The mystery was whether this new St. John was an improvement.

ço∽

The following day, Derek stopped at Vaughan House in Harley Street, where he searched for any sign of his mother's diary. On this he agreed with St. John—such a volatile document should be destroyed at once. No good could come from publishing Alicia Vaughan's memoirs. The *ton* would sooner castrate him than see their families' good names dragged back through such notorious scandal.

But the document was nowhere to be found, and Derek was forced to return to Ambersley empty-handed. Though it was the last thing he wanted to do, he broached the topic of the diary with Rosalie.

Her eyes narrowed shrewdly at his question. "How did you learn of it?"

"Worthing mentioned that his father once saw it. Do you

know what has become of it?"

She pursed her lips. "Reggie mentioned her diary, but I never saw it."

"Has it been destroyed?"

"I don't know. Awkward for you if it hasn't. Perhaps awkward for Worthing as well?"

Derek regretted bringing St. John's name into it. Still, if Rosalie had the diary, she would have put it to use long before now. He let the matter drop, though it plagued the edges of his mind like a tender bruise that refused to heal.

Despite the uncomfortable situation with his family, Derek drew solace from working on the estate. He marveled at each new experience the changing seasons of his first year introduced—frost gilding the ground to crunch beneath the coach wheels before the first dusting of snow, a new crop of bleating calves and lambs, the burst of flowers and birdsong as spring warmed the land and summer took hold. Through it all, he continued to lead repairs on the Hall as he could afford them, just as he continued to give silent thanks that Minton had yet to find any sign of Miss Amber.

Following a successful race meeting at Ascot in June, Derek opened the house in Grosvenor Square for two months and invited Rosalie and the children to London.

Rosalie arrived with alacrity and wasn't the least distressed when Derek announced his intention of returning to Ambersley. Having sole reign in Grosvenor Square suited her purpose. She'd bided long enough, and she lost no time renewing acquaintances.

One of the first notes she sent was to the Marquess of Worthing. His punctual arrival the next day brought a smile to her lips as they seated themselves in the elegant drawing room.

"I believe we may be able to assist each other," she said without preamble.

He raised a brow at her. "How so?"

"Derek tells me Alicia Vaughan's diaries may be of interest to you."

"He said he doesn't have them," the marquess said in a bored tone.

"He doesn't. But what if I did? The information therein might be valuable to many."

"Not the least of all would be your son."

"This isn't about my family. It's about yours." She watched wariness overtake his devilish eyes. Oh yes, Derek had been so good to feed her this little tidbit of gossip about Worthing's father.

"I see. And what sort of price did you have in mind for such valuable information?"

Triumph nearly in her grasp, she maintained her demur tone. "We both know my son Curtis is the real duke. There's a sizeable fortune that will settle on the dukedom in a few years, and then all my needs will be met. But in the meantime, I could use a little something to tide me over." She need not be greedy. Worthing came from one of the wealthiest families—a family that avoided scandal at all costs.

The marquess rose stiffly. "You'll excuse me, but I have no taste for your enterprise." He looked down his aquiline nose at her to add, "Perhaps you may find someone hungrier than I."

"But you don't understand—"

"Believe me, I grasp all the particulars. My sole interest in the diary is to protect my family from the stigma of my father siring a bastard. By offering to sell it to me, you've told me the diary contains no clear evidence of Derek's paternity." His eyes narrowed. "That, or you do not even have the diary in your possession."

"How—?"

"Because if you did, you would hardly be blackmailing me to keep it hidden." He retrieved his hat from the table by the door. "Go ahead. Publish it."

Disliking the challenge in his tone, she rose. "I may do so."

He gave an irritating chuckle, as if he found her bravado quite droll. "A word of caution. Don't do so unless it contains irrefutable evidence. Derek has gained Prinny's notice, and slandering him will do your children no good unless you can prove he must surrender his title." He opened the door. "Good day, Lady Vaughan."

Rosalie twined her fingers, unwilling to smash any of the porcelain decorations at hand. They were hers. All of this was hers, and one day, all of London would know it. She went to the window to watch Worthing ascend into his chaise. She hated him almost as much as she hated Derek.

Worthing had called her bluff, and now she would have to search for some new form of action. There had to be a way to get around Derek. Until she found it, she would have to wait. Fortunately, she had patience.

Yes, like a spider, she had patience.

༄

While Rosalie and her children enjoyed the entertainments of London, Derek and Harry returned to Ambersley where they disrupted the staff with their unbridled laughter.

"It looks better than it did," Harry remarked during Derek's tour.

"I could have burned it to the ground and made it look better than it did," Derek replied. "You're supposed to be admiring the craftsmanship of the plastering and woodwork."

"Craftsmanship—is that what you call it?" A smile danced on Harry's lips. "Were there, in fact, any craftsmen involved, or merely rank amateurs?"

"Rank amateurs? I'll have you know I'm a duke, young man. Step into the library, and we'll discuss this matter at length."

Harry laughed. "No, thank you. I stepped into your library once before, and fell at length."

Derek looked over his shoulder as the butler passed. "Paget, are you *humming*?"

The butler's stride faltered. "Certainly not, my lord," he said gruffly.

Beckoned by summer sunshine, the cousins spent their days by the stream, pretending to fish and sleeping under the shade of the willows. Once Johnny discovered their retreat, the boy made it a habit to join them as soon as he'd finished his chores.

One idle afternoon, Harry watched Johnny wade into the water intent on a fat frog. Something about the boy tickled his memory, and when the sun cast a glint of silver in Johnny's blue-green eyes, Harry swore beneath his breath.

Tossing his hat at his half-asleep cousin, he whispered loudly, "Have you ever noticed that Johnny looks exactly like the portrait of the late duke hanging in the library?"

Derek rolled on his side to blink at Johnny. His eyes narrowed. "You may be right."

"He must be the old boy's bastard. Didn't you tell me the late duke and his wife buried seven children in infancy? He must have found himself a sturdy yeoman's daughter to bear him a child and then placed the child secretly with Tom and Martha." Harry chewed on a blade of grass. "Do you suppose the rest of the servants know?"

With a yawn, Derek sat up. "The boy's underfoot everywhere. If you recognized the resemblance, I'm sure others must have."

Harry looked at his cousin shrewdly. "Will you acknowledge him?"

"He's a bit young to understand, I think." Derek watched as Johnny tried to mimic the frog's full-throated *ribbit.* "Still, it wouldn't hurt to encourage him. The boy is filled with admirable qualities."

"And what would those be, pray?"

Derek thought them through. "Good sense, a positive nature, resourcefulness, a generous spirit, but most of all honesty."

"Sounds like a recipe for a good mistress, even a wife."

Derek laughed darkly. "As if you could find half those traits in any woman."

"Oh, come now. They're not all bad."

"Maybe it's just my luck then, eh? Remember Helena?"

Harry let forth a crack of laughter. "Ha! Won't she be sorry she turned you down when she learns of your inheritance. She'll be eating her heart out over it, you may be sure. You were well out of that one."

"Indeed. 'Twas a hard lesson, but one well learned.

Women are mercenaries who will lie to achieve their ends."

"In her case, decidedly," Harry agreed. "But what of my mother? She has all those qualities you named." Harry tossed aside his blade of grass. "In fact, I have most of those qualities, Derek. Why not marry me?"

His dark mood broken, Derek laughed. "Because you subvert all your good points by being vain and far too gregarious."

"Whatever do you mean?" Harry batted his eyes and pouted his lips in jest.

"And you're a fool," Derek finished. "If I met a woman like you, I'd be forced to strangle her."

Harry lay back in the warm grass with a sigh. "If I found a woman just like me, I'd have to marry her."

From where she stood knee-deep in the stream, Johnny caught the second part of the men's conversation. *Admirable qualities. Good sense, a positive nature, resourcefulness, a generous spirit, but most of all honesty.*

But most of all honesty. But most of all honesty.

She blushed with shame, suddenly conscious of the lie she lived. She glanced at the duke. Should she tell him the truth? But then, he would send her away, for a girl couldn't apprentice in the gardens, and a girl couldn't play by the stream with him and Mr. Harry. Besides, he seemed to think all women were liars, and she hated to lose his regard. Swallowing the lump in her throat, she swore he would never learn the truth about her.

Autumn heralded the return of Lady Vaughan and Olivia from London, but Curtis remained away to attend Eton. Johnny was thankful he hadn't returned to torment her. Curtis's absence made it easier for Johnny and Olivia to see each other, especially since the duke found nothing wrong with their friendship. He encouraged Johnny's efforts to befriend Miss Olivia, even going so far as to ask Miss Trent to include the boy in Olivia's lessons. Johnny proved an apt pupil and even made Olivia pay more attention to her studies.

Tom marveled at her good fortune. "Reading is a gift, Johnny. You be sure to thank his lordship for this opportunity." But Johnny had to wonder whether the duke would encourage her to take part in Olivia's lessons if he knew she weren't a boy.

Ambersley, July 1808

As the months tallied to a year and then another, the duke traveled far more, assuming his seat in Parliament, visiting Mr. Harry and his mother in Bath, or staying as the exalted guest of other members of the aristocracy. Johnny sniffed the roses blooming in the garden and wished the duke could be home to enjoy them. She bore his absences with patience but missed him tremendously. Her favorite person on the whole estate was the man who owned everything around her.

"The duke's returned," Tom announced as he entered the cottage by the stream on a warm evening in July.

Johnny sat erect at the table, eager but frozen as a setter sighting game. "Please, may I go see him?"

Martha's hands gravitated to her wide hips. "What about your supper?"

Johnny threw a pleading look to Tom.

"Supper can wait an hour. Just this once." Tom said. "But don't be a nuisance to his lordship."

Martha tossed up her hands in defeat. "Go child, if it's so important."

Johnny raced around the table to hug the aging woman's fat waist. "It is. If all went well in London, he'll declare a special holiday."

Martha returned the tight hug with a chuckle. "What nonsense, declaring a special holiday. Whatever for?"

Halfway out the door, Johnny spun around. "Didn't you know? His Grace went to London with Mr. Minton to declare Miss Amber dead. If they succeeded, he promised he'd hold a big memorial for Miss Amber and declare it a special holiday so everyone could attend. I can't wait to find out!"

She dashed out, leaving behind a stark silence.

Settling her bulk into a chair, Martha worried her fingers in the folds of her apron. Tom rubbed his hand back and forth across his mouth. The silence stretched taut.

"Tom?"

"I don't know."

"They're going to hold a funeral for her. They're going to all but bury the child while she stands and watches. It's too horrible."

"Shh." Tom reached for his pipe. "Maybe we should tell His Grace and Mr. Minton the truth."

Martha wiped at her eyes. "But she'd have to live with Lady Vaughan."

"She's eleven now, and I think she'd be safe enough with her ladyship. I'd face jail to see her restored to her family, but for one thing—she don't remember." His voice broke on the last word. "I don't know if she could take learning the truth."

Martha tried to imagine Tom swearing Johnny's true identity to the duke's disbelieving household. They'd be put in Bedlam! And would Johnny herself ever believe them? Would it bring back the horrible nightmares she had suffered the first year she spent with them? And if they succeeded, Johnny would be taken away from them, and they might never see her again.

She pushed aside the guilt. "You're right, Tom. She don't remember anything about her past, and she's safe and happy with us. We should keep our silence. For her sake."

Tom nodded sadly. "And may God have mercy on our souls."

৩৵৶

Johnny ran all the way to the Hall and arrived out of breath at the front drive. The coach had left, and the Hall's doors stood closed. She knew knocking on the heavy walnut panel would only draw a severe scolding from Paget. Faster than a puppy on a fresh scent, she bounded to the rear of the Hall by the rose garden and was rewarded with a glimpse of the duke inside the library. She stole up to the French doors and tapped lightly on the glass.

He looked up from the paper he was studying, and Johnny grinned as she waved at him. His lips twitched in response, and he came to the doors.

"Shouldn't you be at supper?" he asked with a severe frown.

Johnny wasn't fooled. She threw her thin arms around his waist in a quick awkward hug. Recalling herself, she stepped back. "I missed you. You were gone forever."

He ruffled her hair. "I was gone less than a fortnight."

Unable to contain her curiosity, Johnny launched her many questions. "Did you see the magistrate? Did he give you the money? Did you—"

"Whoa, Johnny. One question at a time." The duke led her toward the rose bower where he seated himself. "Yes, my inquisitive little jay, I did speak to a magistrate, and so did Mr. Minton and a Bow Street Runner. The magistrate agreed with all of us that Miss Amber must surely be dead. So he signed a certificate and Mr. Minton is now transferring Amber Vaughan's money into my accounts."

Johnny leaned forward. "Was she awfully rich?" she whispered.

"Yes. Between you and me. Awfully," he responded with a wink.

Johnny whooped and spun around in her joy. When she came to a stop, the whole garden spun, but that was part of the fun. "Now you can finish repairing the Hall, and buy a new coach and four, and put the footmen in new livery."

"I can do all that and more," he agreed with a laugh.

"Will you open your London house and expand the stables here and re-thatch the cottages and bring a dentist to visit the tenants?"

He tilted his head at this last item. "A dentist? Do your teeth hurt?"

"Not mine, but Rory lost a tooth only last week." Her head bobbed with earnestness. "He was in awful pain. Tom told me the late duke brought a dentist to Ambersley every year to see all the tenants."

He sat quietly while she continued her list in a rush—the Vaughan crest over the front door needed repainting and what color coach horses did he plan to buy and how it must be so exciting to visit London.

When she paused for breath, he interrupted her. "What other things do the tenants need?"

She scrunched her face with concentration. "The Tate family just had a new baby, and Martha said they don't have enough room in the cottage for everyone. And this last winter, when it got so cold, Widow Sanders borrowed one of our quilts, and Tom won't let Martha ask for it back. And—" She grasped for other things she'd heard. "And Mrs. Chalmers wishes there was a new stove in the kitchen—she said so the other day."

"I see."

His deflated tone made her shoulders slump in response. She joined him on the stone bench beneath the arbor. "Should I not have told you about the stove?" she asked with concern.

Derek sighed as his responsibilities once again took precedence. "No, I needed to know it." With Miss Amber's coffers now open to him, he'd arranged with Minton to set up funds for Curtis and Olivia—funds their mother couldn't touch. He thought he'd taken care of things, but apparently there were more people depending on him.

He looked at the boy, so eager to please. "It's vital I know what's happening at Ambersley. Promise me you'll always tell me the truth, Johnny."

The lad blushed. "Why me, my lord?"

"Because I trust you." He watched Johnny's cheeks grow even pinker and noticed a discoloration of the skin surrounding the boy's left eye. "Here, what's this?" He touched the puffy skin, and Johnny flinched under his hand. "Who hit you?"

Johnny became engrossed in the toe of his boot. "I'd rather not say, my lord."

Anger simmered within him. "Was it Tom?"

Wide eyes flew up to his in reproach. "Never, my lord. Tom and Martha, they'd never strike me. Tom was right angry when I came home with this shiner. I got into an argument with someone, and this just happened."

Derek's lips tightened. Numerous times he'd warned Johnny to stay away from the stable lads. The child seemed determined to fit in among boys older and bigger. He studied Johnny's slight frame and doubted the eleven-year-old would ever grow large.

"My lord, what exactly is a bastard?"

The question caught Derek by surprise. He frowned, displeased anyone would sully the bright child with this word. "Does this have something to do with your shiner?"

The boy grimaced, and his gaze fled to his boots again. After a long pause, he nodded.

"Very well, lad. A bastard is a rather unfriendly way of saying that someone is illegitimate. By that, I mean a person's parents weren't married to each other when he was born."

Johnny mulled this over. "Does that make a person bad?"

"No, I don't believe that makes a person bad." Derek watched and waited while the child wrestled with this information.

Johnny met his gaze with solemn eyes. "Curtis told me he'd learned I was a bastard, and I wasn't fit to talk with him, or Olivia, or even you. I didn't know what it meant, but I've always known my parents weren't married. That's why I live with Tom and Martha. I got angry when he said I couldn't talk to you. I don't care about talking with Curtis, but Olivia's my friend. I didn't like him calling me names and telling me what I could and couldn't do. That's when we started to fight."

"Curtis blacked your eye?"

"Aye, but I bloodied his nose." The brief spark of fire in Johnny's eyes dimmed. "I've kept clear of him ever since. My lord, are there lots of bastards?"

"Lots of them. Some from the finest families—even the Royal family. Johnny, do you know who your parents are?"

"My mother was Martha's cousin. I've heard Martha say her cousin wasn't wed, and that's how I came to be apprenticed to Tom."

"You don't know who your father is?"

"No, my lord."

"I think—and I bet Curtis thinks it, too—that you are the image of the late duke. I believe he's your father, and you are his illegitimate son."

Johnny seemed to ponder this long and hard. "Is that why Martha wants me to talk right, and Tom won't let me help him with the heavy work in the garden even though I'm his apprentice?" The boy thought some more and then smiled. "My father owned Ambersley," he stated with a simplicity that tugged at Derek's heart.

He couldn't help but ask, "Would you like to own it one day?"

"That wouldn't be right," Johnny answered with immediate sincerity. "Ambersley is yours."

They sat in companionable silence as a few lazy bees hummed in the midsummer twilight, until the boy hopped off the bench and sketched a tiny bow. "I have to go eat supper."

Derek watched the small figure disappear into the chestnut grove. Alone in the rose garden, he grinned at the prospect of little Johnny swinging at Curtis. How like the boy to so casually accept the circumstances of his birth and defend his good name. He sobered as he recalled his own stormy confrontation with his father all those years ago. Goaded by his stepmother, he'd barged into Reginald Vaughan's study like a mannerless urchin.

"Stepmother just told me the truth about Mothe—That I'm a bastard. Father, tell me she's wrong." Derek prayed his father would sweep away the grimy soot of these lies. Instead, Derek read shame on the older man's face.

"I'm sorry. I hope one day you'll understand and be able to forgive your mother and me. Sit here, and I'll try to explain—"

"There's no need to explain, sir," Derek spat out with dignity. Inside he was shaking with humiliation as he recalled his mother's cold, selfish behavior. He'd always thought the blood in his veins was tempered by Reginald Vaughan's warmth and kindness. Now he didn't know who his father might be. "The story is plain. You were snapped up by a common trollop. She got what she deserved, and you've been stuck with me."

Reginald Vaughan came around the desk, and Derek never guessed his intention until the older man backhanded him sharply across the face. His eyes swam with unshed tears as he felt the stinging heat rise on his cheek. This man he had called father had never struck him before.

"You'll show proper respect for your mother around me, my boy. I loved her." Reginald's voice cracked on the last words, and he turned away.

"Then I am sorry for you, sir. I think, under the circumstances, it will be better if I leave this house. I cannot believe we will ever see eye to eye on this." Derek waited, but the older man said nothing. His heart urged him to run, to lock himself in his room, to cry the frustrated tears of a child. But he was no longer a child. He wished fervently he had never learned of this. He could have lived his whole life in contentment never knowing the truth. He marched toward the door.

Reginald's voice stopped him. "One day, my boy, you will love one woman with all your heart. Then, you'll understand."

"Indeed, sir, I sincerely hope not," Derek replied bitterly.

He went directly to his room where he packed a single bag to take with him. Shirts, hair ribbons, brush, razor, breeches and stockings all went into the bag without thought.

His stepmother opened the door a crack. "Derek?"

He proudly held his ground as she entered.

"Your father tells me you plan to leave us," she said quietly.

"Immediately." Derek lifted his bag from the bed.

She held out a small pouch heavy with coin. "You cannot go without means."

Derek battled with himself, but finally took the bag. He'd left for foreign lands and toiled in many kinds of work. The Army had been an enlightenment, though it unnerved him how fast he took to leading men into death and destruction. He had his mother's quick temper—did he have her killing instincts as well?

For three years now he'd planned to hand the title to Curtis once finances were secure and return to the simple, deadly life of the Army. But judging by taunts and fisticuffs, it was clear Curtis was yet unprepared for the responsibilities demanded by the estate. Derek glanced back toward the chestnut grove where Johnny had disappeared. The lad worried about all the tenants as if they were family.

Noblesse oblige. Derek no longer doubted Johnny's father had been the late duke. Unfortunately, Johnny had no means to look after the tenants, only his unwavering faith that Derek was the best duke ever. If only the boy knew the truth—Derek was another bastard son who shouldn't be admitted to the *ton*. With a resigned sigh, Derek rose and walked toward the library. He was already thinking of the letters he'd have Pritchard send to Minton and Broadmoor. One of them could arrange for blankets, new thatches and, God help him, a dentist.

8

The staff and tenants commemorated the tenth anniversary of the Hall fire with a candlelight vigil on Midsummer's Eve. They gathered in the wide drive as dusk surrendered to the stars, and Johnny listened to her elders reminisce while candles glowed upon faces of young and old alike.

Rory recalled the bucket brigade they had started. "We couldn't get the water fast enough. It was windy and smoke billowed everywhere. That's when I saw the ghost of Miss Amber."

A hush fell over his listeners, and Mrs. North murmured a brief prayer.

Rory continued his story while Johnny listened, enthralled. She'd heard the tale dozens of times over the years, but it always made shivers race across her skin. She noticed Martha's fingers nervously tapping the base of her candle and reached her arm around the older woman's fat waist to comfort her. Martha always grew weepy over the thought of Miss Amber's death.

Tom glanced over the lanky fourteen-year-old Johnny. Her short-cropped chestnut curls were swept forward into what he'd been told was a Brutus cut, and she'd mastered the neat folds of many neck cloth arrangements to hide her slim throat.

He knew—because Martha had shared with him—that Johnny had started getting her monthly flux, and he'd helped Martha shred their second best sheets to bind Johnny's budding breasts. It would never do for everyone to discover at this late date that he and Martha had been harboring Miss Amber for all of ten years.

From the Hall's large drawing room, Rosalie looked out over the flickering candles in the front driveway and barely suppressed a bored sigh. The high point of the Season, and she was still at Ambersley. She glanced sidelong at Derek, who stood at the next window watching the scene in the drive. She'd like to blame him for keeping her here, but this time it was Curtis's fault. One lark too many during his first year at Oxford, and the dons had rusticated him until the Michaelmas term.

She couldn't monitor Curtis in London. No, he'd give her the slip and be off with any number of his young friends, none of whom she trusted. Better to keep him here in the country. And perhaps it was time Curtis came to know his stepbrother better. After all, Curtis was now eighteen. Soon he'd be taking over Ambersley.

True to her expectations, she hadn't been able to budge Derek from his role as duke once he had his fingers in the Vaughan family fortune. Trapped with him in this hellish masquerade, she watched his expenditures as closely as he watched hers. His settlement of a generous allowance mollified her somewhat, and when he granted her leave to come and go at will to any of the family properties, she decided she could bide her time longer.

Stepping back from the window, she addressed her stepson. "Shall I ring for some port?"

Derek raised a brow at her. "The servants are all outside."

Her shoulders sagged at this reminder.

"It was kind of you to allow Curtis and Olivia to attend." Derek motioned her to the divan.

"They have so little to enliven their days." She seated herself with a sigh and watched as he moved about the room restlessly. "Did you wish to join them, or didn't Paget invite you?"

"Oh, he asked, but I never knew Cyril or Dianna Vaughan. I felt the staff should have a private memorial."

"Of course." She pursed her lips. Apparently, she was the only person on the property who hadn't been invited. "You're so considerate of all of them."

He stopped to look at her, but she felt confident that she'd veiled the sarcasm well enough.

"I've been thinking about Johnny," he said.

Rosalie tilted her head, immediately alert. "Indeed?"

"I'm setting aside some money for him. It's clear to look at him that he's Cyril's...son. I believe his father would have done something for the lad."

Throughout Derek's speech, she had to forcibly maintain her calm demeanor. Twice she had to uncurl her fingers from the pillow near at hand. That urchin was constantly underfoot, and Derek openly doted on him. Clearly, he preferred Johnny's company to that of his own brother, but how *dare* he throw money away on that worthless by-blow?

Pushing aside her frustration, she sniffed. "You spoil that lad, Your Grace." She drew Derek's attention by introducing a better topic. "I wonder if I might ask your help with Curtis."

"What trouble is he in now?"

"No trouble, nor does he need money." She withdrew a handkerchief from her sleeve. The white linen against her lavender silk gown looked quite nice as she laced it artfully between her fingers.

"Then what does he need?" Derek asked more kindly.

She looked at him over the back of the divan. "He's become a man, overnight it appears. I hardly know him anymore, and he won't confide in me the way he once did. He needs guidance, but I...well, this is something I cannot do for him."

He contemplated her words while she held her breath. Finally, he said, "I could show him the breeding operation and some of the colts we're training."

"Yes, anything to occupy his mind so he won't look for trouble while he's here. All he wants is a little of your time."

"I'll do what I can."

"Thank you, Derek." She smiled at the success of her ploy. She'd waited years for this day. Reggie's debts were paid, as were hers. That Vaughan chit's money was secured and the Hall repairs completed. Curtis was old enough to assume the role of duke, but young enough to be led by her. Yes, it was more than time. Curtis would be the next Duke of Ambersley.

Only one hurdle barred his path.

༼ঽৡ

The following morning, Curtis strolled down the stairs for a late breakfast. Even with the hour approaching noon, he doubted his mother had roused yet. The last time he'd sought out Olivia this early in the day, Miss Trent had been teaching her rudimentary dance steps. He'd be damned if he'd suffer through another morning as dance partner to his childish sister.

He entered the dining room and stopped short at the sight of his half-brother seated at the head of the table. "What are you doing here?"

Derek set down his teacup with a frown. "I was hoping you'd join me for a ride, but perhaps today isn't convenient." He started to rise.

Curtis felt his face heat. He hadn't meant to be rude. He'd always hoped his brother would notice him one day, and here he'd ruined it. "Wait. I'd like that. That's—if you still have time." He waited for the inevitable excuse.

"I set aside the day." Derek's lips twitched. "Though I had no notion you'd sleep half of it."

Curtis relaxed under the gentle ribbing. "I'm awake now. Shall we?"

Morning rides became their habit, first in silence, but as they became more familiar with each other, their conversation took on a natural flavor.

"Mother wants to go to London before the Season ends," Curtis shared one bright morning.

"And what do you want?"

"Me?" Expressing his own preferences was foreign to Curtis. "I never thought about it. Mother will just attend all the parties. I don't much care for them, and Livvie's too young."

"Would she leave you and Livvie here with me, do you think?"

Curtis rolled his eyes. "I doubt it. She always wants us with her, even when we drive each other mad." They waded into a shallow stream and paused while the horses drank. "Do you ever miss Father?"

Derek's back stiffened. "Why do you ask?"

Curtis shrugged. "He once told me the best I could aspire to would be to emulate you. He was always good and kind to me. I miss him."

His brother stared off into the trees. "As do I."

Curtis enjoyed the hours they spent, but all too soon, Derek left for Goodwood. Whether his brother didn't want him to come or his mother had negated any invitation, Curtis didn't know. He only knew he was left behind with little to do. All too often he was sent to retrieve Olivia. The tiresome chit was forever slipping away from her needlework to play in the sunshine. She had a particular penchant for that Bendicks urchin, which always put Curtis in a foul mood. In an attempt to curb her attentions to the servant, Curtis offered to teach her to ride.

Her eyes brimming with gratitude, she threw her arms around him. "Oh, yes!"

Curtis felt rather like a hero, which pleased him. He was still pleased the next morning as he waited for his sister to join him for their first lesson, until he discovered she'd disappeared again.

Biting back an oath, he strode to her favorite haunt, the rose garden. As he suspected, she was following Johnny while he weeded.

"Curtis says he will teach me to ride. I'm thirteen now, you know."

If the boy replied, Curtis couldn't hear it as he approached.

"Will you teach me about the greenhouses? Miss Trent said it would be unexceptional for me to learn to arrange flowers."

"If that's what you wish, Lady Olivia."

Fury engulfed Curtis. First this Bendicks brat had stolen Derek's regard, and now Olivia had grown fascinated with him. The skinny youth had managed to usurp Curtis's role with everyone here at Ambersley.

"Livvie! Come here at once."

Olivia giggled, in no way contrite. But she came to him immediately. "Johnny's going to teach me about the greenhouses."

"We'll discuss that later. Get along with you. I'll be right after."

Olivia glanced over her shoulder and waved farewell. Johnny didn't dare return her regard, but he did make eye contact with Curtis.

Curtis stared him down. "Stay away from her."

"Yes, my lord." Johnny cast his eyes back to the ground.

For a moment, Curtis wished he could bury the bastard.

❧

After that, Johnny did her best to avoid Curtis. When the duke returned, she had to forego his company as Curtis was prone to shadow his elder brother. She tried to remember her place. *The likes of them and the likes of us don't mix,* Rory had said all those years ago. The duke didn't seem to have time for her anymore, which only made her feel worse.

Once finished with her chores, the September afternoon's refreshing breeze beckoned her to the meadow by the stream. She stretched out to capture the sun's warmth, the smell of tall grass filling her senses. Dark clouds building along the tree line warned of an impending storm.

The clanging of the stable bell alerted Johnny of trouble. She clambered to her feet and ran to see how she could help. Before she rounded the final bend in the drive, she realized the dark clouds were caused by smoke, its acrid stench filling the air. When the stable came into view, it was ablaze.

Rory and Cushing, each leading two horses by their halters, yelled for the stable lads to look lively. A water brigade was already forming, and Tom was pumping the well. When someone shouted that the coach house wasn't safe,

Paget grabbed Mr. Pritchard by the arm, and the two set off to save the coaches.

In the midst of the mayhem, Johnny stood alone. Watching. Shaking. Unable to move. She didn't know why.

Then she thought of the barn cat, forever raising her kittens in the harness room. In all this activity, no one would spare her a thought. Johnny judged the harness room was safe from the flames licking the sky above the hayloft. With a deep breath, she dashed into the stable and found her way to the harness room. The mother cat, carrying a mewling kitten by its scruff, squeezed herself between two loose boards into the next stall and scurried from sight. Johnny found two more crying kittens behind the barrel and bent to scoop them up.

The harness door slammed. She whirled around only to hear the bolt shoot home.

"Hey!" she shouted. "Let me out! You've locked me in here!" Her breath hitched in panic as she threw her shoulder against the door, but only crackling answered her. Why would anyone close the door? She could *die* in here. Terrified by the prospect, she continued to shout until her lungs burned with smoke that grew thicker by the second.

Such a fire killed the duke and duchess.

Deep within her memory, images sparked to life. Johnny saw the upper west wing of Ambersley Hall, the many bedroom doors, until she opened the door to the duke's bedchamber. Through the heavy smoke, she saw the duke and duchess in their bed. She tried to rouse them, but to no avail. Only, she wasn't herself, she was their little girl.

Dizziness and nausea washed over her. She staggered and only managed to stay on her feet because of the mewling kittens in her hands. They needed her to save them.

She searched for the hole the mother cat had passed through. Setting the kittens aside, she tested the boards and, discovering some give in the top one, she kicked at it until it broke. With effort, she dragged herself through the hole, and reached back through for the two kittens. She ran from the stable to gulp fresh air into her aching lungs. Setting the kittens near a fence post, she trusted the cat would find them.

Johnny looked back to find one side of the stable engulfed in flames. Heedless of the wind-whipped sparks that burned her face, she stood riveted and shook uncontrollably. The billowing black smoke finally gagged her, and Johnny doubled over coughing. She longed to flee, but a stronger force kept her hunched over, her hands on her knees, trying to breathe... waiting...

A horse's terrified shriek pierced the air. Johnny immediately recognized Sabu's voice. The few seconds seemed like an eternity, but suddenly the bay stallion appeared in the doorway, his eyes white with fear. He parted the crowd with a rearing leap then dashed toward the east garden in a headlong gallop. A few people followed after him, but most continued to work. Johnny saw Cushing and Rory with water buckets, and she knew only one other person would have braved the flames to free the stallion.

As if entering a dream, Johnny straightened and walked toward the stable to duck through the smoke-filled portal. The interior had become a fiery apparition, and Johnny hesitated, wide-eyed at the resurrection of her childhood nightmares. She'd always awakened in a terrified sweat, but could never remember the images. Yet she knew with certainty she had done this before. Despite the heat, a shiver coursed up her back. It urged her to escape this inferno, but she refused to leave without the duke.

With a cough, Johnny realized she had precious little time. She dropped to her hands and knees—the dirt floor was cooler and less smoky—and crawled towards Sabu's stall. If that's why the duke had come into the barn, that's where she'd find him. The passageway stretched endlessly while she snatched shallow breaths that burned her lungs. Sweat trickled down her back, and her eyes watered painfully while she strained to focus through the smoke. Johnny shimmied along on her elbows and knees ignoring the intense heat surrounding her and the butterflies tying themselves in knots within.

She barely recognized Sabu's stall because part of the charred ceiling had collapsed, dumping hay and boards in a glowing mountain. Crackling sparks wafted toward her, but if any landed, Johnny didn't notice.

The duke lay in a heap near the far wall, which only frightened her more. She crossed the stall and turned his body over. Hair lay matted across his face and, as she smoothed it from his eyes, she discovered it was damp and sticky. Looking closer, Johnny discovered the duke's blood smeared across her fingers.

Eager to get him to safety, she grasped his jacket by the shoulders and dragged his inert body into the passageway. A loud crack warned her as more of the ceiling broke apart, dropping burning wood and fiery missiles. Johnny threw herself and her charge away from the worst danger, but the downpour barred her retreat with a pile of charred debris.

Wiping sweat from her eyes, she spied a pitchfork. Hope renewed her as she cleared an escape route. Oblivious to everything but the need to save the duke, she grabbed burning boards and flung them aside. When she'd cleared enough, she grasped him firmly under the arms. Despite her aching lungs and straining back, Johnny pulled him through the burning mass, down the passageway and outside where she collapsed.

Cushing appeared before she could call for help. He lifted his master with care and shouted a brusque order for someone to fetch the barber while he carried the unconscious man away from the fire. Johnny dragged herself to her feet to follow but a spasm of violent coughing doubled her over. When she again could draw breath, Cushing kneeled beside the duke's prone form. The big man sadly shook his head.

"No!" The cry wrenched from her heart as she stumbled to them.

Cushing's eyes were moist. "He's not breathing, boy. I don't know any way to make him breathe."

Johnny flung herself down beside the duke. He couldn't die! Hadn't his heart beat beneath her hands while she dragged him from the barn? But she saw no rhythmic rise and fall of his chest and could feel no breath when she laid her cheek to his face. Panicked at the thought of losing him, she pushed on his chest.

"No, you cannot die! Breathe, damn it, *breathe!*" she

sobbed as she pushed again and again.

Others had gathered. From behind her, strong arms tried to lift her away.

"Hold," commanded Cushing. "Leave the boy be."

With a faint rattling sound, the duke's chest rose and fell, then trembled violently as he began to cough and take in air on his own.

Johnny collapsed in a heap, tears spilling down her face.

"He lives," someone said.

Other murmurings were drowned out by Cushing's imperious tones. "Stand back and let His Grace breathe!" He dabbed at his master's brow with a wet cloth, wiping away soot and blood while the duke battled to control his lungs.

When the racking coughs subsided, the duke took hold of the bigger man's arm. "Cushing, you saved my life," he said in a hoarse whisper.

Cushing slowly shook his head and would not meet his eyes. "No, Master, not I. The boy pulled you from the barn." Cushing nodded toward her.

The duke turned his soot-stained face. "Johnny?" He looked again to Cushing and back at her. She sensed his confusion. "How? Why?"

She wiped away her tears and conjured up a brave smile. "Mr. Harry once said he couldn't always be here to look out for you. He told me to watch your back."

The duke's furrowed brow relaxed. "You did well, lad. I'm grateful." He offered his right hand.

Johnny stared in astonishment. The duke was offering to shake hands with her—like an equal. She tentatively reached out, in case he should change his mind. When his hand clasped hers, she yelped with pain.

"What's wrong? Good God, look at your arm. When did you burn it?"

Johnny discovered her hand and forearm were red and covered with white blisters. "I don't know," she answered stupidly for she hadn't noticed it before.

Cushing sloshed a bucket of water across to her with orders that she soak her arm until the barber came. With grim concern, the big man inspected the cut across his master's scalp.

Ignored for the moment, Johnny shut her eyes and tried to block out the memories that pounded in her head. They brought pain that surpassed her burns and plunged to the depths of her soul. Her intense need to save the duke had held the terror at bay, but now images careened about her mind until she could no longer deny the truth.

She'd unburied Amber Johanna Vaughan.

❧

The following day dawned gray and wet and progressed with a steady rain pattering a symphony on the leaves. Johnny didn't mind the rain. It suited her mood and her plans. It was a blissful reprieve to sit alone in the east meadow and contemplate the large monument erected to the memory of—her.

In Loving Memory of Amber Johanna Vaughan, 1797— .

She was glad the duke had decided against inscribing a final date on the plaque. Mr. Minton had been the one to point out that they had no conclusive proof when—or even if—Miss Amber had died. The duke had shrugged and said he cared not whether the chit lived, so long as he could have access to her fortune and finish repairing Ambersley Hall.

Johnny sat on the wet ground, her hands around her knees and wrapped in a large wool cape for some semblance of dryness. Bandages covered her right arm from fingers to elbow, yet the skin burned as if flames still licked her wrist. She tried to put the discomfort from her mind as she wrestled with yesterday's memories.

Who locked me in the harness room? Was it Curtis? I know he's hated me for years, but why would he do that to me? And what of the duke's injury? Was the fire merely an accident?

Johnny pursed her lips as she considered who would gain from the duke's death. Curtis was his heir. Was it possible Curtis had set the fire and then tried to kill his brother and do away with her while he had the chance? She hated to consider it—had no proof to take the story to anyone. But she couldn't forget Curtis's face in the rose garden when he told her to keep away from Olivia.

With a tired sigh, she stared at the monument. *What am I to do?* In the duke's eyes, masquerading as a boy was bad enough, but now she knew she was the girl everyone had sought for years. The duke had always told her he admired honesty more than any other virtue, and she'd lied to him. *Should I tell him?* She shivered at the thought of confronting him, of having everyone look at her differently, of leaving her beloved home. *And what of the money?* She still remembered how patiently the duke had waited for Miss Amber's fortune. Would he be forced to give it to her? *I don't want it! I've done naught to deserve it. The duke brought life back to Ambersley. He's repaired the Hall and the gardens and the farms; he's made the tenants happy. I just want him to be happy.*

Uncertainty crowded her, making her lay her face to her knees. *What about Tom and Martha?* Surely they knew. She'd never pressed Martha or Tom about her parentage, content not to dwell too deeply on a question that always made her heart race and her head ache. She recalled the Bow Street Runner who'd swept her up in the chestnut grove when she was a child. Martha had been frightened. Tom and Martha had hidden her true identity for ten years—the Vaughans would blame them. They might lock away the people she thought of as her parents.

But no one knows I know. I could keep the secret until there's some way to tell the duke without him hating me. She lifted her chin heavenward. In his fury, no doubt he would send her away forever. She wouldn't be able to wade in the stream or help Tom in the garden. She'd be forced to do all the things Olivia talked about—wear fancy dresses, learn to dance, to stitch, to talk French and laugh at compliments. It was all too depressing.

No, she wouldn't tell. She was content as she was. She wouldn't risk Tom and Martha's freedom and her happiness. For the past three years everyone had accepted Miss Amber was dead, and it was best that way. She didn't want the money or any fancy title. After all, the duke had both title and money, and neither made him truly happy.

The object of her thoughts leaned over her, accidentally draining the water that had gathered atop his hat onto her head. "What's on your conscience that you came to seek the counsel of Miss Amber?"

Acutely aware of her newfound secret, Johnny shaded her eyes with one hand to guard against the pelting raindrops as she looked up at the duke. Finally, she shrugged and lowered her eyes to the ground. "I don't know, exactly. Being in that fire yesterday made me think of her." She wondered if she'd be damned for all the half-truths she'd be telling from now until the end of time.

He hunkered beside her, his dark cape falling elegantly into the mire. "I understand. When I hit my head, all I could think was how damned unlucky we Vaughans are when it comes to fires. Luckily, you don't seem to suffer the Vaughan family curse."

With pounding heart, Johnny asked, "What do you mean?"

"I mean, thank you for pulling me out. I didn't think it possible for a boy of your size to rescue me, but you did." The duke slung an arm around her shoulders. "I'm proud of you, Johnny."

She turned to find his face very close, with its lean jaw, the clean-shaven chin with the tiny cleft in it, the waves of dark hair, and those penetrating blue eyes. Dear God, how had she never noticed how *handsome* he was? Even the bandage on his temple accentuated the *maleness* of him. She tore her gaze away. "Thank you, Your Grace," she mumbled, oblivious to the rain.

The duke rose and went to the monument. Johnny watched him caress the face of the marble lamb. Then he withdrew a nosegay of bright blooms from the folds of his cape and laid them at the lion's feet. "I always come here myself when I need guidance. Today I came here seeking answers about you, and here you are." He beckoned her over.

With trepidation, Johnny perched with the duke on the edge of the monument. Before them stretched the broad meadow, soggy beneath a laden sky.

"Johnny, no one's ever risked his neck for me before. Oh, once or twice in India, but the Army's different. The next man helps you because he's hoping to God you'll do the same for him. In the heat of battle most men don't think, they react. What you did yesterday was heroic, and I want to reward you for it."

Johnny's face warmed beneath his praise. "Your Grace, it's not necessary"

"I know it's not necessary. I've thought long and hard, and I want to make you my ward. You would live with me, get an education, and become a gentleman. What say you?"

Johnny pretended to give the proposal grave consideration, though her insides clenched with panic. She couldn't tell the duke, *no, I don't like the idea, thank you for the honor just the same.* He'd ask her to explain, and how could she without telling him the truth?

"You do me a great honor, but it's too much. I'm a boy of questionable parentage raised by a gardener. It's not my destiny to be a gentleman."

"Sometimes we must challenge our destiny." The duke looked away. "I did."

"Becoming a duke was within the realm of your imagination. I could no more imagine myself a gentleman than you could imagine yourself King of England."

"I see. Would you not be happy to be a gentleman?"

"I'm happy simply to be *me*. I hope you will be satisfied with what I am and not with what you would try to make me." With that, Johnny pushed away from the monument and walked slowly into the misty rain.

Derek watched him go. It wasn't proper for a servant to leave the presence of a duke without permission, but the boy had never stood on ceremony with Derek, and he preferred it that way. For a long time he stood in the rain and pondered the enigma that was Johnny.

9

Four days later, Martha died, and Johnny realized her own troubles were insignificant.

She came home to the cottage to find Tom kneeling beside Martha's prone form. His shoulders shook, though he made no sound. Johnny froze in the doorway, afraid to intrude upon his grief, yet unable to leave. She felt sick inside that she'd been so preoccupied with her own thoughts since the stable fire, as if she should have foreseen this possibility.

Tom sensed her presence and glanced over his shoulder. "Come here, Johnny. No need to fear. Martha's just passed on is all."

Is all. With the fresh memory of discovering her parents during the Hall fire, death held a finality that was deafening. But she braved it, for Tom's sake, and went to him. She wrapped his head in her arms, and he held her around her waist and wept unashamedly while her tears fell unheeded. Guilt stung, for as much as she wanted to comfort Tom, she longed to run to the duke and share this horrible news, convinced he'd find a way to erase the bitterness from this moment. If Death had come to Ambersley, had she somehow outwitted Him by rescuing the duke only to have Him collect Martha's soul instead? Her reserve broke in a sob.

Tom reached up to frame her face as she cried out grief and fear and loss. "There now, Johnny. Don't make yourself sick, child. You know Martha would never want that. In fact, she wouldn't put up with this nonsense of us grieving like this while she's lying on the floor."

At his gruff tone, Johnny smiled tremulously. Indeed, she could hear Martha ordering them to remember their duties. "I'll ask Mrs. North to gather the women to prepare her for burial."

Tom nodded. "I'll find Rory and Cushing to help me dig a grave. We can have the burial tomorrow. Help me lay her out on the table. Watch your arm."

She gripped Martha's stiff ankles, and they hefted her atop the long trestle table until it creaked beneath her weight. Tom and Johnny looked at each other across Martha's lifeless body.

"She was so proud to be your wife. You made her so happy," Johnny told the stocky man.

"She loved you, child. You know that, don't you? She'd lost her only child when he was but a little boy. You were a gift to us, and you meant the world to Martha."

Johnny swallowed the lump in her throat. "She was my mother." She looked at the relaxed planes of Martha's face. She'd never seen the woman with no trace of worry. "I'll fetch Mrs. North now," she whispered and escaped the cottage while she could still see.

She ran towards the Hall, until her aching lungs made her slow. The blood pumping through her injured arm made it throb viciously, but she saw it only as an inconvenience. Perhaps this was what the duke had meant when he'd told her that in the Army death made all pain seem minor in comparison. Silently, she gave thanks again that she'd been able to save him.

After the fire, he'd gone to London to see Mr. Minton, and Lady Vaughan, Olivia and Curtis had accompanied him. While having Curtis gone made Johnny feel safer, she didn't trust him with the duke. She'd been present when the barber had put three stitches in the duke's scalp. Everyone believed he'd been injured by the fear-crazed stallion.

Everyone but Cushing. "You did well to pull him out of there," he'd said darkly.

She'd been tempted to voice her suspicions, but as she had no proof, she remained silent. Instead, she watched as His Grace and Lord Curtis mounted a pair of hacks while Lady Vaughan and Lady Olivia rolled down the drive in the crest-emblazoned coach. The two men were laughing in perfect accord, but Johnny wouldn't be content until Curtis returned to Oxford. She'd certainly be on her guard whenever he visited Ambersley.

Whether or not he knew it, the duke needed her. Now, more than ever, she needed to hold fast to her secret.

Derek returned from London alone. "Curtis was invited cubbing, and Mother thought she should keep her eye on him," he told Paget, who reallocated the staff so some could help rebuild what was left of the stable.

Once more Derek doffed his waistcoat to work with servants and tenants in clearing away debris and salvaging what he could of a building. At least this time he could pay for the repairs.

"Curtis started teaching Olivia to ride this summer," he said to Rory one day as they took a break. "Did she take to it?"

Rory nodded. "Aye, we placed her on a gentle mare. She'll need some guidance, but I'd say she's got a sound seat."

"We'll need to set someone to ride with her when she returns to Ambersley in the fall. Is there a lad we can entrust?"

The groom bit back a laugh. "It would need to be someone immune to her fetching ways who could keep a tight rein on her. She'd give most lads the slip." He considered the question for a few more moments. "What about Johnny?"

"Johnny? Does he even know how to ride?" Derek's mind flew back to the first day he'd arrived at Ambersley when the boy had been nearly trampled.

"No, but he can learn. He's always around the stables when his chores are done. He understands the horses. It wouldn't take much to teach him to ride. I could do it."

"No, you're too busy with things around here. He can ride with me in the mornings. We'll start him off on Livvie's mare."

When told she was being promoted from gardener's apprentice to stable lad, Johnny trembled at the thought of taking responsibility for the headstrong Olivia. She could only hope the girl would take pity on her for all their years of friendship. In the meantime, the duke taught her how to brush down a horse, how to saddle it and feed the bit tenderly between its teeth.

Once she mounted Olivia's mare, he placed the reins in both her hands and positioned them low over the horse's withers. As he ran his hands down her leg to set her heel low in the stirrup, she tried not to flinch at the warmth radiating from his touch.

"You'll want to keep your seat in the saddle. And you might find you need to readjust yourself a bit, for comfort and safety." Derek patted the front of his own breeches and grinned.

Heat raced up her neck and face. Once they set forth, she regained her composure as she concentrated on staying astride.

As their rides progressed, Johnny lost her nervousness and treasured their time together. They discussed many topics until, one October morning, Johnny—aware Curtis's imminent return for the Christmas holidays spelled possible danger—gathered her courage to ask of him a favor. "Could you teach me swordsmanship?"

He shifted in his saddle to study her. "Why would you want to learn?"

Johnny tried to sound unconcerned. "You never know when I might need to defend Lady Olivia." She couldn't very well suggest she wanted to be better prepared should Curtis set upon her. Besides, were the duke ever attacked, she might be able to help defend him.

"Then, by all means, let us begin your training tomorrow. We certainly cannot leave my fair sister defenseless. Think of all the dangers lurking here at Ambersley."

He was laughing at her, she knew, but she chose to ignore

it since he seemed willing to teach her. Instead, she changed the subject to one that had been troubling her unaccountably. "My lord, do you ever think about marrying?"

The duke reined his horse into a crab stepping walk. "Why would you ask that?"

In truth, she'd lain awake nights thinking of the duke and the confusing emotions he'd inspired. She'd always wanted to be his loyal servant, but now that she knew she was his equal in birth, she found herself wishing for a different sort of relationship. The problem, of course, was she couldn't tell him of her birth without admitting that she'd *lied* to him for years.

Johnny met his eyes with what candor she could spare. "You seem content to live alone, but since Martha's death, Tom looks lost. I wonder if a man lives his whole life seeking his mate."

"Tom and Martha loved each other. Among the nobility, marriages are business arrangements made for power and prestige, money and land, or to beget an heir. Since I have all those things, I've no need to marry."

Johnny pondered this as their horses picked their way through the home wood. The marriage he outlined didn't sound happy. "So you don't ever plan to marry?"

"I won't say never. Perhaps if I find the right woman."

"What would she be like?" Johnny held her breath, awaiting his answer with anticipation.

Absentmindedly, he scratched his horse's shoulder. "She'd be beautiful but sensible, have good breeding, she'd understand that my word is law, and she'd be a good mother to our children."

Johnny exhaled a deflated sigh then took herself to task, for it mattered not what he sought in a wife. It wasn't as if he were ever going to marry *her*. Still, he hadn't mentioned any of the qualities she'd overheard him tell Mr. Harry all those years ago by the stream. Perhaps he'd changed his mind. "And you would love her for all that?"

The duke snorted. "What does love have to do with this?"

Warmth flooded her face, but she pushed on, above all wanting to understand his views. "But, if you have children together—" She stumbled, unable to finish the question.

Derek drew rein again to study the boy shrewdly. "Johnny, have you ever *been* with a woman?" He could tell the boy understood him by the way his face glowed bright red above his collar. Even flushed, there was no mistaking the delicate bones of the face, the skinny body and the smooth facial skin. No, the maids at Ambersley weren't fighting over the gardener's son. The lad's discomfiture finally drew a laugh from him.

"Johnny, don't be embarrassed. It's perfectly natural. Let me give you some advice. For your first time, find a woman older and more experienced than yourself. She'll be flattered, and she'll give you guidance that will serve you well with your future partners. Second, don't confuse love with lust. Women often do. Despite what the vicar will tell you, two people do not need to be married to bed together. You're living proof of that."

If possible, the boy flushed deeper crimson.

"Don't be ashamed. Some people risk everything to be together, they believe for love. But in my experience, love doesn't last. Men and most women enjoy the physical act of bedding together, lovemaking some call it. But love is not necessary for two people to share and enjoy that act. In truth, some men find the need to bed a woman so strong, they hire a woman to suit their purpose. They're called strumpets, and it's quite a trade in London."

"Have you ever hired a strumpet?" Johnny asked.

Derek's face warmed under the boy's intent gaze. "No, I have never hired a strumpet. But I do keep a mistress in London." To Johnny's knitted brows, he explained. "A mistress is a tasteful woman who commits to a man to be available for bedding at his leisure for so long as he pays her keep."

Johnny tried to assimilate this information. "What is your mistress like?"

"A gentleman never discusses his amores. I will say that she is beautiful and sensible, and she suits me quite well."

"If she suits you so well, why not marry her?"

"Marriage again." Derek shook his head at the boy's obstinacy. "Johnny, no man loves his wife half so well as he loves his mistress. And much of that is because his mistress never swears she loves him, but his wife swears it constantly. A woman is never as attractive after she tells a man she loves him. That's because you can never trust a woman to mean it."

This left the boy mulling in silence.

Fearing he'd become too didactic, Derek added more lightly, "Besides, a man's mistress is not of the same breeding he would choose for a wife. I cannot take my mistress out into polite society."

"If you cannot go out anywhere, what do you—Ohhh!" Johnny blushed again at the Duke's wolfish grin.

"Perhaps we should continue this conversation after you have acquired more experience with women."

She fervently hoped they would never touch upon the subject again.

છ✦ન

November arrived in a symphony of color. Johnny spent her mornings riding with Lady Olivia and her afternoons learning the art of fencing from the duke. Their foils tipped, they would feint and lunge on the lawn by the stream. Johnny proved more apt at fencing than at riding, and the duke commended her progress.

But before long, the duke left for Bath to join Harry and his mother for Christmas. With his departure, December's cold weather descended in earnest, and Olivia discontinued her rides until spring. Johnny took this dismissal in stride and returned to the conservatory to tend the winter chores. There were dozens of things she could do around Ambersley to occupy herself. She need not sit idle and wish for the duke's return.

She worried for Tom who took heart in nothing since Martha's death. He seemed to wither overnight. His movements slowed, his attention failed. The grizzled fur around his ears was all white now. By March, he developed a hacking cough and had to sleep with pillows propping his head. Johnny abandoned all her gardening tasks to care for him. At first he argued with her, determined this was nothing. When he no longer had the strength to leave his bed, Johnny asked Cushing to fetch the barber.

Burning with fever, Tom mumbled to his wife in a delirium while Johnny fought desperately to hold onto him. She tried every remedy Martha had ever taught her. Mostly she was there at Tom's side, willing him to live.

Cushing shook his head over the boy. "Tom's lived a full life. Let him go now. 'Tis time." The giant perched on the chair at Tom's bedside. "I'll keep watch a bit. Go get some air."

Johnny drew water from the well, impervious to the chilly fog settling with dusk. The scent of freshly turned earth reminded her that spring was a time of renewal, yet she knew it wouldn't be so for Tom. She needed to ease his final hours.

Returning inside, she found Cushing bent over the bed while Tom's voice rasped in the quiet cottage. She hurried to the bedside to find his sunken eyes were a trifle glazed but lucid.

"I hate to leave you, child." Tom's whisper rattled.

Tears blurred her vision, but she was determined to give comfort. "I'll get by, Tom. I wasn't ready before, but I am now."

Tom's hand moved on the quilt, and Johnny grasped the dry frail fingers. "I've told Cushing about your family."

Fear gripped Johnny as she noted that Cushing's normally ruddy face had drained most of its color. Clearly, Tom had revealed everything.

"It's time for you to know the truth—" Another cough racked Tom.

"I know. Tom, I know I'm Amber Vaughan." She smiled through her tears to see a sharp gleam reappear in his eye. "I've known since the stable fire."

Fidgeting, Tom started to speak, but she silenced him with two fingers on his parched lips.

"You'll ask why I said naught. What was there to say? You rescued me and raised me. You and Martha fed me, clothed me, taught me and loved me. You gave me everything I could have gotten from my real parents. You're my family—I didn't want to leave."

Tom turned to Cushing. "Look after her," he whispered.

"Aye, Tom."

Shifting on the pillow, Tom pierced her with his feverish gaze. "You must tell the duke."

Johnny glanced sidelong at Cushing. "Someday," she lied.

Tom's eyes closed, but his brow relaxed into smooth creases.

She kissed his ashen cheek. "I love you both. Tell Martha that for me," she whispered. Minutes later, she knew Tom had left her. She was on her own now, except...

He'd spilled her secret to the duke's faithful manservant. Even now, Cushing moved through the cottage as if to leave. When she turned to face him, he eyed her with caution.

"'Tis a miracle I can hardly conceive, lad. Er, Johnny. The Master will be...surprised."

"You mustn't tell the duke," she said without preamble. Her thoughts raced as she sought to connect them in a convincing argument.

"What's this? You cannot think to continue this way."

She went to him. She would have gone on bended knee if she thought it would help her cause. "It's the only life I know, Cushing. I've lost Tom and Martha. Do not take this from me, too."

"But you're an heiress—"

"What do I care for money? My world is here at Ambersley."

Cushing folded his arms, his lips hardening in a bullish line. "I promised Tom I'd tell the duke."

"No, you promised to look after me. How will you do that after you put me in Lady Vaughan's hands? For if you reveal me, that will be my lot."

This made the giant scratch his temple. "Nay. I've always served the Master's interests. I cannot lie to him."

Quickly, Johnny argued further. "During the stable fire, someone locked me in the harness room. Do you think that and the duke's injury were a coincidence? If someone meant him harm, Miss Amber could be in equal danger. Under Lady Vaughan's thumb I can do nothing to help the duke, but as Johnny, I can continue to help watch out for him. You know it's true."

Her gaze held his. Sensing his hesitation, she pressed her point home. "Truly, have you never worried that his own family might be a danger to him?"

Finally, Cushing released a long sigh. "How long do you think you can go on like this?"

"As long as I need."

"But you'll tell the Master one day?"

"I promise," she said. "Now, you must promise to tell no one. Let me do it in my own good time."

"I don't like it," he said, heavily. "Aye, lad, but only because there's trouble afoot."

❧

When Derek returned from his extended trip in early April, Cushing told him Tom Bendicks had died and that Johnny now lived alone in the gardener's cottage. Based on his valet's obvious concern, Derek expected to find a scared child. Instead, Johnny was unusually reserved.

"I'm sorry for your loss, Johnny. Tom was a good man." Confused by the lad's silence, Derek stepped into the cottage. "If there's anything I can do…"

The boy's face appeared leaner, his expression more guarded, as his gaze traveled past Derek to the valet. "If I take on all the gardening duties, will you pay me Tom's wages?"

The question stung. Derek had thought he was more than an employer to the lad after all these years. "Don't worry about that now, Johnny. I'll take care of you."

The boy shook his head emphatically. "I don't need anyone to take care of me. I want to earn my keep."

He smiled with understanding. "It's a painful lesson, but you're becoming a man."

"I wish I thought that were possible," the lad replied with feeling.

From the doorway, Cushing coughed.

"It will come in time," Derek said. "I'll ask Broadmoor to transfer Tom's wages to you. Let me know what assistance you need in the gardens, for Olivia's rides must not be neglected and there's no other lad I trust with her. Have you been practicing your fencing?"

Remaining mute, Johnny shook his head.

"Meet me tomorrow morning by the stream. Now that you are your own man, you'll need to defend yourself properly." He motioned to Cushing to follow as he left. The giant hesitated before matching strides with him.

"Is it wise to be teaching the lad swordplay, Master?" Cushing asked gruffly. "He's so small and delicate."

"Aye, he'll never be big-boned, but he must be, what, fifteen now?" Derek paused to look back at the cottage.

Johnny stood in the doorway, hands on his hips. His eyes narrowed with a haunting intensity as he watched their departure.

Derek turned once more for home. "The lad needs to learn to make his way in the world. His swordsmanship is sound, and it's a gentlemanly pursuit that may one day help him."

Cushing cleared his throat. "Very good, Master. I hope no trouble comes from it."

☜∙☞

The next morning, Johnny arrived at the stream worrying that Cushing had spilled her secret. Instead, she found the duke awaiting her, two foils in hand.

"Come. Let's see what you've retained," was his only greeting.

Johnny accepted the proffered weapon and weighed it in her right hand. Doubt filled her. With Tom and Martha gone, she knew she should confess her identity and beg for the duke's mercy.

He interrupted her reflection, and motioned her into position. He saluted her with his foil and then attacked. Unprepared, Johnny retreated from his advance, flailing her foil in the most elementary defense.

The duke stepped back. "You fight like a maid, Johnny. Come, let's mark it together." He patiently called out the moves, and she copied his actions. Satisfied with her performance, he stood opposite her once more and motioned for her to take the offensive.

She advanced in small steps, but he parried her attacks with ease. She countered him while her brain reeled. She shouldn't continue this charade, and yet if she told him the truth now, he'd see her only as a troublesome girl, and she'd be sent off to live with Lady Vaughan. Preoccupied with such thoughts, she barely noticed as the duke deftly turned the attack back on her. Suddenly, she found herself parrying his thrusts, trying to keep the foil from touching her body. In moments, the balled tip of his foil bounced off her arm and then hit home against her chest. She fell backwards with the force, tears of inadequacy filling her eyes.

"I'm sorry, my lord, I'm not concentrating very well today."

The duke looked down on her. "Don't apologize to *me*. If this were a real fight, you'd be the one dead now."

She stared up at him, surprised by his harsh tone.

"When someone attacks you, you have no time for any thought other than how to avoid being killed. If you *can* think of anything else, then you'd better be planning how to defeat your enemy. There's no room for emotions or excuses of any kind. In a real fight, it's kill or be killed. Understand?"

His words reinforced her very reasons for continuing her masquerade. She would risk anything to protect him.

"Yes, my lord."

"Good." The duke offered his hand. "Let's start again."

She rose without assistance and dusted off her breeches and waistcoat. With renewed determination to prove worthy, Johnny saluted the duke then met his attack. She predicted his moves and parried with a lightning quick wrist. Sweat dampened her shirt, but despite her aching arm, she refused to forfeit.

When the duke eased his attack, she took the offensive greedily, lunging forward as if she fought the devil. She feinted left to lower his guard, then lunged deep to pink him in the right shoulder.

The duke swore in pain and motioned for her to hold. Where she'd ripped his linen shirt, a red stain bloomed.

"My lord!" She checked her foil to find its tip gone. She dropped the weapon as if it burned her. "You're hurt."

He laughed as he inspected the wound. "'Tis merely a scratch." He sat on the ground and applied pressure to the nearby artery. "Help me remove my neck cloth. We'll staunch the wound with that."

Johnny's fingertips shook as she undid the intricate knot at his throat. Only when the neck cloth was wadded in place against his shoulder, did she believe he might actually live. She kneeled on the ground before him, but his color looked normal, and he didn't appear in any pain. "I'm sorry," she whispered.

"My own damn fault for lowering my guard. Don't blame yourself—you did exactly what I asked. You're a fighter, and that will serve you well. Remember, even if you're hurt or believe you've lost everything, you must keep fighting. If you give up, you'll never know what you might gain."

She drew strength from his approving smile as she fought down the panic. She might have *killed* him. Here she'd wanted to help him, and she'd wounded him instead. Of all the people in her world, she loved the duke best. The thought of being separated from him terrified her.

To stay with him at Ambersley, she would gladly portray Johnny to the end of her days, but one slip, and she feared Cushing would reveal her identity to all.

৩৹৵

Johnny didn't count the passing moons, but focused on the changing seasons as she toiled in the gardens surrounding the Hall. Wisteria and lupine heralded late spring. Summer conjured the red and pink sentinels of the rose garden. On long hot days, she trimmed the box hedges along the walkways of the formal gardens until her arms ached.

The hard work built strength for her ongoing fencing

lessons. After the duke left for London, she continued to practice with Cushing who remained behind to train the colts. The big bear of a man was not as young or nimble as his master, but he had a powerful arm. Still, she had to urge him to challenge her. He balked until she discovered his one weakness—Cushing had a yeoman's heart. He couldn't disobey an order.

This knowledge served her well, for whenever Cushing would look askance or suggest she renew her efforts to confess to the duke, she would silence him with the lift of a single eyebrow. They both knew she was a lady born, and now she understood that since Cushing had sworn to Tom to look after her, he would never betray her.

As one year passed, and then another, Johnny's frame filled out. But while her jaw was firm, it showed no trace of a beard. She lathered the shaving soap and rinsed the unused razor daily in case anyone should ever suspect she didn't shave. Each morning, she bound her breasts with torn sheets, wrapping herself until she looked barrel-chested. *Well*, she admitted looking in the mirror, *sort of barrel-chested*. She shook her head, her short-cropped hair curling around her forehead and ears. She rarely gave thought to her brown hair with its coppery streaks or her blue-green eyes, except—she tilted her head and raised her brows—she feared her eyebrows were too delicate in shape.

With a sigh, she turned away from the mirror to slip into her clothes. She'd never truly look like an adult male—she still looked like a lad of fifteen. But once dressed in her breeches and boots, with the long-sleeved linen shirt, brocade waistcoat and a starched neck cloth tied in a simple knot, she knew everyone would accept her as Johnny. It's all they'd ever seen. It's all they'd ever consider.

But there were times when she longed for the duke to see her in a different light.

⚬⚭

August always heralded the return of Lady Vaughan and Olivia, even if only for a short time. Aged sixteen, Olivia sought out Johnny to renew their friendship but wisely kept their continued association secret. With Curtis away at Oxford, this proved easy. Miss Trent took no notice of her lengthy rides, provided she selected suitable garments and didn't get too much sun. Mama had as little interest in riding as any other of her daughter's pursuits.

Johnny was the only person to whom she could confide, and the rides became an outlet for her frustrations. "Mama's buried me down here for the fall and says I cannot take part in the Little Season this winter. But next spring, I shall be presented at court, and then I shall attend all the fashionable London parties. We'll dine at midnight and dance until dawn."

"Why would you want to do that?" Johnny wrinkled his nose.

"To find a husband, silly!" She brushed a fly away from her horse's neck. "Do you ever dream of going to London, Johnny?"

"Me? Not a whit. I'm content right here."

Olivia gave him an appraising look. "Why do you not show me the same deference as the household servants?"

Johnny flinched at the question. "Lady Olivia, forgive me if I have displeased you." He bowed his head.

She waved her crop at him. "That's what I mean. You never say those kinds of things to me, and when you do, I feel as if you're laughing at me. Is it because your father was the late duke?"

"How do you know that?" Johnny sounded surprised.

"Oh, that." She curled her lip in disdain. "Curtis told me about it years ago. It doesn't bother you, does it?"

"Does it bother *you*?"

"Heavens, no. But it's why I don't tell Mama about our rides." Olivia's hand flew to her mouth as she gasped, "Oh Johnny, how awful! With Tom and Martha both dead, we must be the only family you have, and Mama absolutely forbids us to acknowledge you."

Johnny stared intently between her mount's ears, steeling herself from showing any emotion. "I don't need to be acknowledged. But thank you for the thought."

"There must be something I can do." Olivia's brow furrowed as she thought hard before squealing in triumph. "I have it. I shall celebrate your birthday with you!" Her exuberance drove her horse into a frisky trot. By no means an intrepid rider, she squeaked as she started to bounce.

Johnny quickly laid hold of the mare's bridle and brought both horses back to a sedate walk. She chuckled at Olivia's red cheeks. "That's a generous thought, Lady Olivia, but there is one difficulty to carrying it out."

"And that is?"

"I don't know my real birthday," Johnny lied. She couldn't confess the date, not when some of the tenants still delivered flowers to Amber Vaughan's memorial each March to commemorate the anniversary of her birth.

Olivia contemplated this with a nod. "Very well. We'll set a birthday. We'll do it next week, and I shall buy you a gift. That is, I don't have very much money, so maybe I could *make* you a gift."

"You mustn't give me anything, Lady Olivia. It wouldn't be proper."

"I shall come up with something," she promised.

Johnny assumed that would be the end of the conversation. Olivia had a habit of throwing herself into an idea one moment, only to forget it completely the next.

To her surprise, Olivia hunted her down in the rose garden one afternoon the following week. "Psst, I've got your birthday gift." Olivia giggled with delight. "You must come to the house tonight, and fetch it from my room."

"That would be highly improper, Lady Olivia." Johnny stuck her spade in the dirt and rose to face the girl. While Lady Vaughan was statuesque, Olivia was shorter and finer boned. The top of her head only reached Johnny's eyes, and Johnny looked down at her with a frown. "I cannot come to your room. Can you not bring the present to me at the stables tomorrow?"

Olivia stamped her slippered foot on the grass. "No! It must be tonight, and you must come to my room. I will complain of a headache, and I'll have Miss Trent bring me tea so that we may have a tea party. I have it all planned, Johnny! Don't spoil it."

"Lady Olivia, I cannot do this. Think of the trouble you would be in were we caught. And I might very well get sacked." For the first time, Johnny appreciated the duke's concerns about his high-strung younger sister.

Olivia's eyes took on a mulish gleam. "If you don't come to my room at nine tonight, I'll make sure Derek *does* give you the sack. You'll be turned out with no money, no references, nothing. Now what do you say?"

Johnny tensed at the quicksilver change in the girl's emotions. "How would I ever sneak through the Dower House to your room?"

"You'll have to climb the tree by my window to get in. If we're quiet, there's no reason anyone would ever suspect." She waited.

Silently, Johnny weighed the risks. She stood a fair chance of sneaking into Olivia's room and escaping again unnoticed, but if Olivia demanded that Derek sack the stable boy—a sense of foreboding permeated her. "Very well, my lady. I shall be there."

This restored Olivia's good humor immediately. "Good, then. See you tonight." She waggled her fingers as she backed away, then she lifted her skirts and dashed from the garden. Johnny watched her go then pulled the spade from the ground. Troubling thoughts made further work impossible.

That evening, the Dower House stood dark and quiet against the lingering velvet blue twilight. Wearing her best breeches and coat, a clean shirt and now gleaming boots, Johnny stood beneath a sturdy oak as she searched for her party.

"Pssssst!" Olivia waved from one of the second floor balconies.

With a last look around, Johnny pulled herself into the tree.

"I'm so glad you came!" Olivia's excitement was contained in a whisper. "Happy Birthday!" Her delight was palpable.

"Thank you, Lady Olivia."

"Come in, but do keep quiet, for Mama's room is just down the hall. She never leaves her room once she comes up, but then…" Olivia's words trailed off with a shrug.

Silently, Johnny agreed keeping quiet would be imperative.

Olivia's room was decorated in ivory and pink. The four-poster bed with its canopy above had a quilt of the sheerest fabric Johnny had ever seen, while the room itself was nearly as big as the whole first floor of her cottage. Next to the unlit fireplace, candles burned on a small table holding a teapot, two cups and some cheese and bread.

Olivia poured tea for them with the elegance of long practice. "Do sit down, Johnny. We'll have our tea first. Do you feel older?"

Johnny sat on a cane chair. Unaccustomed to this feminine finery, she didn't trust it. "Older? No. Does one ever feel older?"

"I felt ever so much older when Miss Trent let my skirts down, but I suppose it's different for boys. Your clothes never seem to change."

Johnny belatedly removed her hat and laid it on the floor. She fingered her coat as if it might feel as awkward as she. "I put on a clean shirt for this, and I even shined my boots."

Olivia beamed at her. "That was so good of you, for it would be impossible for me to explain how my bedroom began smelling like a stable. Do you care for anything in your tea?"

Johnny shook her head and received her cup then watched Olivia lace her own with cream and dunk two sugar cubes in it. She tried to mimic Olivia's way of sipping from the delicate china cup, but felt as graceful as an ox sitting across from a swan.

With a little squeak, Olivia set her cup down. "Let me get your present, and you may open it at the table." Her pink dress swished around her ankles as she glided to her bed and pulled something small from beneath her pillow. She presented it to Johnny then resumed her seat.

Johnny looked at the oval-shaped gilt box. It was hinged

on one side and had a clasp closure on the other.

"Open it, silly." Olivia giggled with her excitement.

Johnny gingerly worked the clasp and opened the box. It spread open to reveal two miniature portraits and the box became their frames. The man she recognized immediately as the late duke, her father, and the woman in the other portrait could only be—

"It's the late duke and duchess. I thought you'd like to have a picture of your father. This has been in my room ever since we moved here. I doubt anyone else even knows or cares it exists. They certainly won't miss it. You can get rid of the one side if you like. The duchess probably doesn't mean anything to you."

Johnny stopped breathing. She had never seen a picture of her mother, and she recognized the same shape of her face, the same eyebrows, even the same lips. "No, I'll keep both portraits, for they died together." Swallowing the lump in her throat, she whispered, "Thank you." She closed the box, secured the clasp, and stood to tuck it into her coat pocket.

"I'm glad you like it." Olivia glowed with satisfaction. Hopping to her feet, she came forward with hands outstretched. "Now for your birthday kiss."

Like a deer held at bay, Johnny froze. All her worries about coming here had not prepared her for this.

Olivia giggled. "Don't be shy, for we are kissing cousins in a way. Mama always gives me a birthday kiss, and since you're a Vaughan, you should have one, too."

Olivia took both Johnny's hands in her own small ones, and stood up on tip-toe to press a quick kiss to each of Johnny's flushed cheeks. She leaned in to place a third kiss on Johnny's lips when the bedroom door swung open.

"What the hell is going on here?"

Johnny recognized the voice immediately, but had no chance to react before white pain blazed through her skull. As she dropped to the floor, everything turned black.

Olivia's limbs shook as she grabbed the pewter candlestick from her older brother. "Curtis, what are you doing here?"

"Saving you from ruin, it appears. What the hell is *he*

doing here?"

Olivia kneeled to check on Johnny, but Curtis grabbed her arm and tugged her to her feet again. She jerked away from him with such force that the sleeve of her gown separated at the shoulder with a rending sound.

"Don't touch me! I invited him here," Olivia explained defiantly. "We were celebrating his birthday, and I was giving him a birthday kiss."

Curtis laughed. "Olivia, what have you ever seen in this bastard? He is so far beneath you." Curtis nudged the unconscious boy in the ribs with his toe. "I think he broke in here and tried to rape you."

Olivia's eyes grew large. She was not quite clear what rape was, but knew it was very bad. "No, listen Curtis, I invited—"

"Is that what you're going to tell Mother? That you invited a bastard stable boy to your room? She'll cancel your presentation. She'll lock you away."

Tears streamed down Olivia's face. "No," she whispered. Her presentation in London was all she'd dreamed of for years. It spelled freedom from Miss Trent and the beginning of a whole adult life. She heard a door open down the hall.

Curtis heard it, too. "Mother will be here any second. You decide."

"What in heaven's—Curtis what are you doing here?" Mama swept into the room, but stopped short at the sight of Johnny's lifeless form on the floor. "What is the meaning of this?"

Curtis looked to Olivia. "I came home for a visit, Mother. When I came to see Olivia, I found *this*," he kicked Johnny again, "kissing her. I struck him."

Lady Vaughan's eyes flew to Olivia. "Is this true, Olivia?"

Tears coursing down her face, Olivia looked at Johnny and wished there was some way out of this. Curtis watched her, daring her to speak the truth. But seeing her mother's judgmental frown, there was only one thing to say.

"He broke in here, Mama. He tried to rape me!" She burst into an angry sob, hating her brother for ruining everything.

Rosalie embraced her daughter and said nothing about the

table with its two teacups. Whether Olivia was at fault was not now in question. "There, there, baby. You're safe now. Curtis, remove him. Lock him in the stables and leave him for Derek to punish." Her eyes narrowed with satisfaction. Finally, she would prove to Derek what a treacherous viper he'd been harboring all these years.

10

Harry arrived in Bath midday, travel weary and exhausted from over two years of constant work with the Foreign Office. Castlereagh had come to rely on him. *Coatsworth will talk them 'round. Clever as a fox, he is.* Even after that devil Bonaparte was beaten and sent to Elba, restoring the Bourbons to the throne had required a great deal of diplomacy.

His mother clucked over him, ordered his bed aired and a bath carried up, and promptly canceled her plans for the evening, as he preferred to stay in. She ordered a hearty meal boasting quail and ham, and they lingered over supper while he bestowed upon her some of the better stories of the court as well as an excellent bottle of wine he'd carried home from France.

Though fatigue and the evening's simple activities should have relaxed him, sleep eluded Harry. Late into the night, he sat at his desk writing letters. While many thought he did nothing but talk in the Foreign Office, diplomacy required a shocking amount of correspondence as well.

A rapping at the front door disturbed his work and Harry squinted at the clock. Past midnight. Not even Taft, his mother's butler, would be awake at this hour. Carrying a taper, Harry hurried down the stairs to answer the summons.

Opening the door, he took a step back at the sight of Cushing. The man's normally swarthy jowls looked drawn and haggard. Behind him, a big-boned hunter stood beneath the streetlamp, steam rising from its heaving sides.

"Good God, man!" Harry pulled the servant inside, his imagination already rampant with what could only be bad news. "What brings you here at this hour?"

"You must come and help, Mr. Harry. Johnny needs you."

❧

Johnny spent the dark hours holding her splitting head. Between the large knot and the disjointed thoughts whirling through her brain, she was too distraught to sleep. As the first cock crew, she faced the truth—she had to confess her identity. Cushing may have already done so. With a sigh, she acknowledged there would be hell to pay with the duke.

Rory arrived to open the stall door and peer at her in the thin light of dawn, and his first words confirmed her suspicions. "His Grace wants you, Johnny. He's in a black mood, so I'd watch what I say." The groom stood back and let her pass.

"Where's Cushing?" she managed.

Rory frowned. "Rode out of here last night without a word."

Rode out of here... Had the duke sacked Cushing for lying to him? Fear mounting, she followed Rory outside to find two horses saddled and ready. Johnny pulled herself atop one, though the effort cost her head dearly. Her vision still swam with dizziness as she resolutely gathered the reins. She would face the duke now, tell him the truth and accept her punishment.

Rory led her down the long drive away from the buildings. She was glad he remained silent, for it took all her concentration to direct her horse. She continued to seek words to broach the subject of her identity as they splashed across a shallow stream and left the drive to cut across a vast meadow. In the center, a lone rider dismounted from his steed and awaited them.

The words of her confession scattered on the breeze as the duke roughly grabbed her by the collar and pulled her from her snorting horse.

"You wanted so much to be a man, let's see if you're ready to fight like one,"

"What?" She fought to squelch her dizziness and retrieve her wits.

"Don't play stupid with me. I warn you, you'll be lucky to survive the morning." Derek dragged her to where two rapiers speared the ground and flung her toward them. "Choose!"

Johnny darted a quick glance at his granite face and then gingerly plucked one of the rapiers from the ground. She stared at it dumbly for a few moments. "There's no tip."

"They're redundant in a duel."

A duel? "I don't understand," Johnny stated, panic blossoming.

"Then allow me to outline the rules for you." His eyes narrowed in fury. "You betrayed me. You're a threat to my family. I thought about whipping you, as I might have any other servant, but you're a Vaughan. That should account for something. Rory is here to offer witness that you had the chance to defend yourself."

Johnny blanched at the unemotional menace of his words. He was planning to kill her. They'd caught the stable boy in Olivia's room, and the duke blamed the boy Johnny.

"My lord, there's been a mistake—"

The duke raised his arm, and Johnny dodged reflexively when it looked as if he would backhand her across the face. He stayed his hand—why, she didn't know. His eyes narrowed until only thin shards of blue showed. "You're the one who made the mistake, and you're about to pay for it."

He tugged at his neck cloth before tossing it aside and removing his coat and waistcoat. Johnny tried desperately to control her trembling fingers as she unbuttoned her coat. The duke still didn't know her secret, and though these weren't the ideal circumstances for revealing herself, of one thing she was certain—unless she told him the truth now, in his fury, he would kill her.

The duke yanked the other rapier from the ground. "Are you ready yet, boy?"

She winced at the way he spat 'boy' out as if it were truly a foul word. "If you'd let me explain. I meant no harm—"

The duke lunged at her with his rapier, making her leap back. Rage transformed him to something evil and dangerous. Johnny defended herself, diverting the thrusts as she'd been taught over the years.

He accused her across their swords. "You lie! You broke into her room. You exacted your price from Olivia!"

"I took nothing from Olivia," Johnny fit her words between thrusts. "She begged me to come to her room last night. I only did as she asked. Curtis caught her kissing me, but if you hold, I can explain it all."

Immersed in her argument, she misread his parry and left herself open. He nicked her right arm, but she spared it only a glance. She recalled the duke's own words after Tom died.

When someone attacks you, you have no time for any thought other than how to avoid being killed. If you can think of anything else, then you'd better be planning how to defeat your enemy. There's no room for emotions or excuses of any kind. In a real fight, it's kill or be killed.

Johnny steeled her resolve with these words. Loving him as she did, she would have sworn she would do anything for the duke, but she found she couldn't bring herself to die without a fight. Countering his assault, she advanced on him.

Derek was caught unprepared as the boy's first thrust tore his shirt. He retreated, parrying Johnny's vicious lunges as he went, biding until ready to renew his attack. But the boy had planted seeds of doubt in Derek's brain. Had Olivia encouraged Johnny? Even welcomed his advances? With his upbringing, would Johnny even know the magnitude of the crime he committed with a girl of noble blood? Derek swore under his breath. Here he was preparing to kill a boy half his age. A boy who had been like a brother to him. A boy who had once saved his life. All for the honor of a young girl—a vain, overindulged girl who had played with fire, ignorant of its consequences.

As the rapiers locked with a clang and slide of metal, Johnny stepped on a stone and tilted off balance. In that moment, she felt the stinging slice of the duke's blade below her left breast.

Derek was certain his thrust had touched the boy, but saw no blood. The boy renewed his advances, and Derek continued the fight until he noticed the growing red stain on Johnny's side. "Johnny, hold. You're hurt."

Johnny tried to focus on him, and saw he'd lowered his weapon. Her legs gave way, and she dropped to the ground. The duke waved for Rory, then kneeled beside her. When he tried to turn her to view the wound, she clutched her side, and pushed him away.

"Johnny, let me see it. It looks worse than I thought. I never meant to hurt you—"

"No, you only meant to kill me. Me! You called me your friend. I saved your life, and you want to kill me. Why don't you do it now?" Johnny drew a ragged breath to control her bitterness.

Derek stilled at the betrayal reflected in Johnny's blue-green eyes. But the boy was right—an hour ago Derek had planned on dispatching him in a duel. It seemed fantastic now. They'd known each other so long. The boy couldn't be guilty of such a deed, but if he weren't—

"You're right. I wanted to kill you for what you did to Olivia. Tell me the truth for I couldn't draw a coherent answer from her. Did you take her virginity?"

Johnny raised solemn eyes to Derek's face while her skin grew clammy. No wonder he was furious. What could have prompted Olivia to say such a thing?

Derek read the boy's answer in those amazed, disbelieving eyes, but he needed to be sure. "Did you?" he prodded.

"No. Did she say that?"

"Yes, after Mother and Curtis—"

Johnny's eyes rolled upwards even as his lids closed. The look was not lost on Derek. And then the truth burst on him. While Olivia adored Johnny, she idolized Curtis as only a sixteen-year-old girl could love her devoted older brother.

Torn between the two young men, Olivia had obviously chosen sides last night. And of course, his stepmother had always hated Johnny. Realizing he might have killed an innocent, Derek raised an anguished hand to cover his face.

With an effort, Johnny focused on the duke. He'd hidden his face, unwilling to look at her. The smell of her own blood made her stomach roll, but she fought down the nausea. He still didn't know her secret, and it was now vital that she explain. "There's something I must tell you." She was interrupted as Rory joined them.

"Shhh, lie quietly for a moment, Johnny." Derek gave ground to the servant. Rising, he wiped his damp face on his sleeve.

Rory ripped open the shirt along the tear in the left side. At the sight of torn bandages beneath the shirt, he ran a hand through his silver hair. "What the…" Withdrawing a knife from his coat, he deftly cut through the bandages.

Johnny tried desperately to remain conscious long enough to tell the duke…to explain…if Rory would only give her a minute…

At the servant's loud gasp, Derek wheeled around to find Rory shaking his head in bemusement. "He's a she," the groom stated.

Derek looked down at the shapely white breast surrounded by blood-soaked bandages then raised his gaze to Johnny's face. It was the same face, and yet, it was a girl's face. It was so obviously a girl's face. Tears glistened in her aqua eyes.

His mind whirled. Were Johnny a girl, then everything he knew was wrong. Were Johnny a girl, she was clearly innocent of his family's lies. Yet Olivia had stood in his office and wept and accused, no doubt goaded by Curtis and Rosalie. His darling unspoiled sister, Olivia. And he'd been so sure she would never be false like other women in his life.

Derek gave vent to his anger with a single curse. "Damn all women for the liars they are!"

It was the last thing Johnny heard before she lost consciousness.

∞∽

Harry dozed fitfully in the coach, until a rut in the road brought an end to his dreams. It took but a moment for him to gain his bearings and recall why he wasn't drowning in the comfort of his own bed with the curtains drawn against the sunrise.

"Where are we?" he asked his mother.

"We just passed through Ambersham." Prim and pressed, no one would ever guess he'd roused her from her sleep hours before and dragged her on this rescue mission. She shook her head, her lips in an uncharacteristic frown. "That poor child, masquerading as a boy all this time."

"If Cushing's account of the situation is accurate, Johnny's revealed her identity by now."

The coach swept over the dew-covered countryside, slowing only to rattle across the old wooden bridge that marked the beginning of the Ambersley property. Not long after, the coachman pulled up the horses.

Harry leaned his head out the window as the coach swayed to a stop. Already, Cushing was clambering down from the perch seat.

"It's the Master," Cushing said as he yanked open the coach door. "I fear his temper's led him to something awful."

Harry jumped down. "Stay here with Mother."

With long strides, he approached the scene. A trio of saddled horses stood tied to a thicket of small trees. On a grassy knoll two men knelt over a third person. As Harry drew close enough to recognize his cousin and the silver-haired groom, Derek rose and cursed.

Johnny lay limp on the ground surrounded by blood-stained bandages. Fearing the worst, Harry ran the last few paces. "Did you kill her?"

Derek spun around, surprise widening his furious eyes. "You knew about her?" He barked a bitter laugh. "Fear not. She'll live."

"Thank God for that."

His face a scowling mask, Derek strode past him toward

the horses.

"Derek, wait. We need to talk."

"Not now, Harry," Derek bit out as he mounted his horse. "First, I need to talk with *my family*!" His frayed temper split on the last two words.

With ease of practice, Harry withstood his cousin's storm. "And what shall I do with her?" He pointed to the prone figure, but his gaze never wavered from Derek's flinty eyes.

"Do as you damn well please!" Derek wheeled his horse and galloped across the field.

11

Derek stormed the front door of the Dower House, which brought Stokes running into the main hall.

"Your Grace!" Shock painted the footman's features.

"I want to see Lady Vaughan. Now."

Indecision flickered in Stokes's eyes. "She's still abed."

"Wake her!"

With barely a nod, the footman ran up the stairs to find the maid to wake the mistress.

Derek cooled his heels in the ivory drawing room, though his temper burned unchecked. It flared again when his stepmother arrived.

Her fingers still fumbled with the sash of her wrapper, her dark hair with its hints of gray was pulled into a soft braid that fell over one shoulder. She hadn't even drawn slippers on her feet. "Why, Derek, whatever is amiss?"

Her outward guile might have fooled him, but for the gleam of anticipation in her eyes.

"Pack your things. You and your children leave Ambersley today, and I never want you to return."

Her jaw tilted open. Gathering her wits, she regarded him with more caution. "You cannot mean that. What has happened? What have you *done*?"

"Did you think I wouldn't uncover the truth?" he said. "The three of you conspiring to destroy a poor servant boy?"

From the doorway, he heard a soft gasp. Olivia, her reddened eyes beseeching from her pale face, stepped forward. "No, tell me you didn't hurt him. It was all a lie, Derek. I'm so sorry!" She covered her face with her hands and burst into fresh tears.

Behind her, Curtis appeared, his face likewise pale, his dark hair rumpled. He placed comforting hands on Olivia's shoulders, and she turned her face into his chest and wept. He watched Derek over her black curls, his eyes unblinking.

Derek matched his unwavering gaze, man to man. "Remember this as the day you betrayed not only me but your conscience as well."

Curtis said nothing, but the early morning sun revealed a glistening of moisture in his eyes.

"Lud, Derek, all this drama." Rosalie drew his attention back to her as she sank into a chair. "They weren't all lies. Curtis did find the boy in Olivia's room. Who knows what nefarious purpose he planned? But I suppose he's convinced you of his innocence," she said with a bored sigh, "and you've found some way to reward him."

"The boy has been dispatched," he said coldly. "All that remains is to deal with you."

"Dispatched?" She looked up, her eyes narrowing. "Do you mean—?"

Olivia issued another sobbing wail.

"I'll not discuss it more. Pack your things and go. I'll arrange an allowance—"

With growing agitation, Rosalie stood. "You cannot do this."

"This morning of all mornings, do *not* attempt to tell me what I may or may not do."

"But you're not yourself. Look at you, disheveled and bloody." Her eyes widened as she catalogued that detail. "These fits of tempers will lead you to madness and murder, if they haven't already. Admit it, Derek, 'tis time you give over the title to Curtis."

Derek released his pent up fury on a bitter laugh. "Like hell."

The demonic vow drove Olivia to hide her face in her brother's shoulder again, but Rosalie never cowed. "You cannot refuse this. You've denied him his due long enough. He's of age now, and the Vaughan title deserves Vaughan blood."

He turned on her as a hungry lion would stalk prey. "Did you think of that when you asked me to spill Johnny's Vaughan blood? How can you ask me to believe any of you give a damn about what it means to be a Vaughan?"

"And what of your noble promises to fulfill your duty? To do what's right for the peerage? I've been patient. I've waited *years*. For what, to have you forswear us now?"

"I forswear nothing," Derek growled. "You've brought this upon yourselves, with your lies and deceit. Curtis has proven he's not mature enough for the responsibilities Ambersley demands, nor will he ever be so long as you have his ear. He must first learn to be a man before he will ever be a duke."

Rosalie vented a frustrated whine. "I could destroy you—"

"Try it," Derek said. "But I warn you, publicly discredit me, and I'll cut you off without a farthing."

This silenced her.

His fury spent, Derek's words calmed. "You've crossed me and forced me to choose. Someone must protect the people of Ambersley from your—and your children's—machinations. To play with people's lives—" He shook his head, ruing his own actions.

"Now pack your things and go. I have much to do to reconcile the events of last night and this morning." No one stopped him as he left the house.

He returned to the meadow, but found it empty. The only sign of the dawn's furious struggle was a torn piece of muslin stained with blood.

Derek brought the fabric to his lips and closed his eyes. He'd nearly committed a heinous crime, but he vowed to redeem himself by championing Ambersley from all threats. His family had nearly destroyed him. Opening his eyes, he focused on the muslin in his hand. Anger kindled anew at the memory of Johnny's betrayal. A girl! The magnitude of her lie still astounded him. That Harry had also known only injured him more.

He released the scrap of fabric and stood alone, desolate, as it fluttered away on the breeze.

ᔊᐧᔊ

Enveloped in the downy security of a soft bed, Johnny came to slowly. A fire burned low in the grate, and a crisp morning breeze stirred the curtains with scents that were foreign to her. Wary, she would have sat up but for the sharp pain knitting her side. Images assailed her—the duke's accusations, a duel, blood, Rory bending over her, traveling in a coach and—

"Harry." Had it been a horrible dream? The last she knew, Mr. Harry was in France.

From the foot of her bed came a shuffling sound, and Harry bent over her. "You're awake," he noted with relief. "I feared the barber gave you too much laudanum."

Johnny searched his weary blue eyes for disdain or reproach, but he was the same Harry she'd always remembered. Except, she'd never seen his blonde hair so disheveled nor his shirt and neck cloth so rumpled.

As her memory slowly assembled the chain of events, one moment sparked with the clarity and fire of a prism. When the duke had discovered her secret, he'd been shocked and then enraged. *Damn all women for the liars they are!* He hated her—and with good reason. Every day she'd spent with him, she'd lied. He valued honesty. She'd betrayed him, and he would never forgive her.

"How did I come to be here?" she asked softly.

"I was hoping you would tell me," Harry said. "When I arrived, you were out cold and Derek was in the very devil of a fury. Rory was shocked nearly speechless by your secret."

She turned her head away. "The duke thought—"

"I know what he thought. Cushing told me the Vaughans had accused you."

"Is that why you came?"

"Cushing said you needed my help. If I'd known you were determined to continue your masquerade as Johnny, I would have come even quicker. Derek might have killed you." Harry leaned back. "Good God, he still doesn't know the whole truth."

Her pulse skipped at this words. "You know about...?"

"Cushing revealed everything to me."

"He'll have told the duke by now," she said listlessly.

"Cushing's here." Harry rose. "We brought you to my mother's home in Bath. Cushing swore he wouldn't fail you again. Damn. Derek must still think you're the old duke's bast—, er, I mean..."

She raised beseeching eyes to him. "You and Cushing are the only ones who know. Please don't tell anyone. I'll go away. I don't want any inheritance; let the duke keep the money. I've already hurt him once with my lies. If he learns the truth, he'll only hate me more than he already does."

Harry watched her argue his cousin's defense. Her delicate cheeks were wan against the pillow and the overstuffed bed made her appear small and helpless. He recalled so distinctly the child Johnny had been—small but boisterous, a charming gamin with a ready smile and quick wit. Instead, here lay a young lady with pale cheeks and large aqua eyes.

"Nonsense," Harry assured her. "Derek will want to know the truth. Now get some rest, and after awhile, I'll bring you up some breakfast." He patted her hand, but she turned away. Ill at ease, he left her to her sleep.

For two days, Harry and his mother hovered solicitously over Johnny. Harry tempted her with rich food and offered to play backgammon or read to her. Mrs. Coatsworth talked of taking measurements for the dressmaker as soon as Johnny was well enough. Johnny remained feverish, picking at her food and begging to be left to her rest. Instead of showing vast improvement as the barber had promised when he helped Harry load her in the coach for the trip to Bath, her health seemed to be declining.

On the third day, Mrs. Coatsworth asked her physician to have a look at the girl. His diagnosis was mixed. "There seem to be few physical complications caused by the large cut along her right side."

Harry leveled the man with a gaze meant to quell any curiosity.

The physician cleared his throat. "She appears to be out of humor. There's a deep gloom hanging over her, and if she won't eat, there's very little we can do."

While his mother showed the physician to the door, Harry leaned against the mantle, rubbing fatigue from his eyes. There had to be a simple way to help Johnny.

"You're worried about her, aren't you, dear?"

"I've been trying to see this situation through her eyes." He began to pace. "There she was, living a happy life with Tom and Martha. Even after she remembered who she was, she didn't tell anyone. Cushing claims she swore him to secrecy. Now, we've taken her away from everything she's ever known and she cannot return to that life. At seventeen years old she must become a new person. But worst of all, she's convinced Derek—a man she's idolized since she was a small child—hates her and will never forgive her."

His mother sank into a chair. "I'd have thought she'd be glad to have this masquerade behind her, but she must be frightened to death of her future."

Harry stopped in his tracks. "She's frightened to death of Derek. And Derek—he needs to know we've found the Vaughan heiress."

৩০৫

Alone in his study, his mood black, Derek poured another brandy. The Hall was silent. Tired of confronting his tyrannical behavior over the past four days, the servants now avoided him as if were diseased. No doubt conjecture thrived below-stairs, but he no longer cared.

After two days without a sign of Johnny, Paget had braved Derek's temper to ask what fate had befallen the boy.

Derek's answer had been succinct. "The boy is no more."

Paget had cleared his throat. "If I could clarify, my lord—"

Derek's wrath had exploded afresh. "That's all you're

going to get, Paget. I don't want the boy's name mentioned around here ever again. Now, get out!"

Staring into the flames, he jabbed at the fire with the long-handled poker. He'd tried to curb his emotions, but his anger festered. Anger at his selfish stepmother, vindictive brother, weak-willed sister, and at himself. This incident had proven his own shortcomings and now he couldn't lay hands on the real instigator.

"My dear, little friend, Johnny," he whispered to the crackling sparks. "Damn your lying soul." The curse did nothing to vent his frustration. He slumped in his chair. If only he could get his hands around the girl's throat and choke... some sort of explanation from her.

The whole scandalous episode had destroyed his illusions of the successful life he'd built. He'd worked hard these past years to provide Olivia and Curtis with everything they could need, and they had repaid him with lies. They'd pushed him to the point of murder, and Derek was disgusted with himself. And Harry—that betrayal didn't bear scrutiny.

But for the girl, he had every right to be infuriated with her lies. He should be glad to be rid of her—she was bound to cause trouble. He leaned back and rubbed his gritty eyes, wishing he could forget the happy sound of Johnny's footsteps skipping through the Hall, Johnny's voice ringing out with delighted laughter. Realizing where his thoughts strayed, his fury turned inward, because he shouldn't be missing the boy—the girl—whatever.

Why? Why had she carried out this charade for years? He thought he'd befriended a buoyant lad, a bastard like himself. Instead, that bastard girl had masqueraded as a boy, much the same way he'd been masquerading as a duke. Derek reviewed the primary lesson about women—never trust them. Given the opportunity, they'd cut out your heart.

"May she never return," he muttered. He drained his glass and wished he could drown his memories of the past nine years.

In the kitchen, Stokes interrupted Paget's momentary peace over a cup of tea. "Mr. Coatsworth's coach is pulling up the drive."

Paget responded with alacrity and was able to meet their guest as he reached the front door. "Good day, Mr. Coatsworth, sir."

"Good day, Paget." Harry shrugged out of his greatcoat and handed it with his hat to the retainer. "Awfully quiet here. Where's the family?"

"Lady Vaughan and her children have gone to London, sir."

"Indeed?" Harry caught the butler's eye, and by mutual consent, they let the topic go. "And where might I find my cousin?"

"His Grace is in his study, sir. Shall I announce you?"

"No, for I don't want him to have the chance to avoid me." Delaying the inevitable, he checked his neck cloth in the mirror and straightened his cuffs. "Is he in a rare temper?"

"If I might say so, sir, I have seen His Grace in better spirits than he's been the last few days. Perhaps your visit will improve his mood."

Harry choked out a laugh. "I wish I thought so." With that, he braved his cousin's sanctuary.

"Go away," Derek said bitterly without turning in his chair.

Harry responded in a light tone. "Come now, Derek, you might acknowledge my presence before you throw me out."

Derek looked around the chair back, a grimace his only welcome. He rose but did not so much as offer his hand. "I wondered when I would see you again. Come, join me for a drink." He crossed to the sideboard and looked at its contents. "I seem to be out of brandy, but there's some cognac here."

"Thank you, maybe a glass of wine to take the chill from the road." Accepting the glass Derek brought him, he studied his cousin. *Not good.* Derek's eyes were bloodshot, his face haggard. His hair, usually neatly combed, looked rumpled and unwashed. Derek looked as if he'd lost his best friend and, Harry supposed, one could say he had.

Derek sank back into his chair, Harry into its partner. They sat in brooding silence, each unwilling to open the subject that occupied both their minds. Harry noted ashes piled deep beneath the grate. So, Derek had been here all night. Seeking further details, he spied the glint of broken glass on the floor, a telltale spot on the wall where an object had impacted and shattered. He stole another glance at his cousin.

"If you clench that wineglass any harder, you'll break it, too."

Derek started, but his grip on the glass eased. "And to what do I owe the honor of this unexpected visit, cousin?" He relaxed in his chair and crossed his ankles before the fire. Harry knew the casual demeanor meant nothing. Derek was still simmering from having his life upended. He mimicked his cousin's pose, stretching his boots toward the flames.

Setting his wine aside, Harry steepled his fingers. "I came to hear your account of what happened here the other morning."

Derek's eyes narrowed. "What did you do with her?"

Harry baited him by feigning surprise at the question. "Why, I took your advice and did as I damn well pleased."

In a flash Derek shot out of his chair and dragged Harry out of his by the collar. His fist drawn back, he visibly struggled to control his reaction. Slowly, he released his cousin.

Harry straightened his neck cloth. "She's in Bath with Mother, recovering from her wound." He retrieved the two broken pieces of Derek's wine glass from the rug and threw them into the fire. He weighed his cousin's temperament, then crossed to the sideboard to replace his drink. From a safe distance, he said, "Rather a shock to learn Johnny's a girl, wasn't it."

"I don't want to discuss it," Derek growled.

Harry handed him his drink and resumed his chair. "That's going to be most awkward, because she's precisely what I've come to discuss. You can't avoid it, Derek. Hasn't it occurred to you who she is?"

"What the hell is that supposed to mean?"

"Think about it. When she was a boy, we all noticed her resemblance to Cyril Vaughan. We thought Johnny was his bastard son come to live with the Bendickses around the time of the hall fire. But if Johnny is a little *girl* who resembles Cyril Vaughan and appears at the Bendickses after the fire, doesn't that suggest something to you?"

Derek's expression grew thunderous. "Is that little bitch claiming to be Amber Vaughan? Is that her game? What did she tell you?"

"Very little. Cushing came to me the other night to tell me Johnny's secret." Harry recounted what he'd learned of Johnny's past, her amnesia, how Cushing had learned her identity and his deathbed promise to Tom to look after her.

Listening through it all, Derek stared into the fire, transfixed by this stunning turn of events. For years, he'd accepted that Amber Vaughan was dead. Even in his fury these past days, he'd been convinced Johnny was no more than the late duke's love child. Instead of toiling her childhood away, she should have had an army of servants waiting upon her. He could return her money—even if it crippled him financially, he would do that immediately—but there was no way to make amends for the years she'd lost nor the indignities she'd suffered.

Finally, he sat up and met Harry's eyes. "How long has she known?"

"Her memory came back to her the day she pulled you from the stable fire."

Derek tensed, recalling that day with vivid clarity. She'd lived in his care for three years knowing he'd had her declared dead so he could refurbish Ambersley Hall with her fortune. Why would an heiress never have given him any sign she was anything more than a gardener's apprentice? What had she hoped to achieve?

Despite his doubts, the next step was clear. "We must lay this information before Minton and see what is to be done."

"Agreed." Harry replied. "But first, I need your help. I'm worried about Johnny. The wound is healing, but she remains feverish. Mother's physician thinks she may continue to decline."

"And of what help can I be?"

Harry rose. Turning his back to the fire, he faced Derek. "The last time she saw you, you tried to kill her in a duel. Guilt preys upon her—she's convinced you want her dead."

Derek snorted into his glass. "On that day, I did."

"But knowing what you know now, I thought if you could tell her you forgive her—"

"No!" Slamming his glass down, Derek stood. Outrage drove him to pace the room. "I will do right by her. Ha! I tried to do right by that boy, and he—hell, *she* betrayed me. Now you tell me she knew the truth but willfully lied about everything."

"Not everything. She's always admired and trusted you—"

A dark laugh erupted from Derek. "*Trust me?* If she'd done so, she would have admitted her secret long ago. Now she's experiencing a little guilt over her masquerade, and you rush here to convince me she's dying. Tell her she need never see me again and that I'll restore her fortune to her forthwith. You'll see how quickly she recovers." His fury spent, he stopped at the window to look out over the garden.

Silence hung in the room until Harry stalked up behind him. "You have little reason to fault her for her honesty. You, who prize honesty so highly—what happened when Curtis and your precious Olivia accused Johnny? Did you give her a chance to defend herself against their allegations? No, you made her defend herself against your wrath."

Derek winced. His cousin rarely unleashed his temper.

Harry barely paused to draw breath. "The truth isn't always plain to see, especially when you wallow in self-pity. After today, I don't think you're fit to black Johnny's boots, but you're my cousin, and I feel it incumbent to point out that if anything happens to her, you're going to have a hell of a time explaining it to Minton." Though calmer, his tone still held a vicious bite. "I've asked Rory for a change of horses. Will you come with me or no?"

Derek continued to stare out the window.

His cousin's tone softened. "Johnny only lied about being a boy. Other than that, she's the same person she's always been. When she realized I knew her true identity, she begged me not to tell you. Ever. She doesn't care about money—she cares about *you*. She said she was afraid she'd hurt you when you discovered she was a girl. Pity to see her waste her heart." Harry's boots clicked toward the door but paused on the threshold. "You have such a capacity to give, Derek, it baffles me that you don't *care*." He left with a slam.

Dampness had collected on the window, and Derek traced the moisture with his forefinger while the barbs of Harry's words continued to prick him. They served as a painful reminder of his last words with Reginald Vaughan. Words that had left much more unsaid than said. Words that had pushed him from his home and denied him the chance to ever understand the man's reasons for continuing to treat Derek as his firstborn son. He'd nearly committed a similar mistake with Johnny.

Amber Johanna Vaughan. His orphaned seventh cousin. He and Minton were co-executors of her fortune. Like it or not, he'd never be rid of her. There was nothing for it but to face her.

"Damn," muttered Derek as he leaned his head against the pane. But somewhere deep within his chest, that knot—which a more emotional man might have termed heartache—slowly began to uncoil.

With a soft knock, Paget entered the study. "May I get you anything, my lord?" he asked tentatively.

Derek drew himself upright and scrubbed his stubbled chin as he turned to the butler. "Yes, Paget. I want a bath taken up to my room. Send someone to air this place out." He strode to the door with purpose. "And tell Rory I'll need a coach and pair."

Paget's shoulders relaxed, and he bustled from the room to do the duke's bidding.

Part Two:

Johanna

12

Derek arrived in Bath after nightfall.

His widowed aunt, Elizabeth Coatsworth, her once blonde hair turning silver at the temples, hugged him warmly and welcomed him without reproach. Seeing her silent smile, Derek recalled the gauche youth he'd been. He searched for words to explain away this transgression.

"I'm sorry to arrive so late, Aunt Bess."

She clucked her tongue. "You should have come with Harry, but no matter. We're glad you're here." She directed her footman to carry his trunk up the stairs.

Derek removed his gloves. "Where is Harry?"

"He's gone to play cards with some friends. He was in a foul mood when he returned this evening, and I suggested he take himself out."

"I'm sorry," Derek repeated. He knew only too well why Harry's temper had been frayed.

Roughly half his size, Aunt Bess eyed him up and down. "I know you are. You'll have to sleep in the back bedroom. I gave your room to Johanna." She waited while Derek removed his cloak. "Would you like to see her?"

Surprised, Derek stalled. "It's late. Surely she's asleep by now."

Aunt Bess shook her head.

"I hear she hasn't been well. I can wait until morning."

She handed him a candle. "Once she learned Harry went to Ambersley today, she refused to eat supper. You may be able to wait until morning, but she cannot. Go to her." She steered him toward the staircase.

Derek climbed the steps still unsure what to say. Outside the door of her chamber, he stopped and listened. No sound issued forth, but light spilled from under the door. If she were asleep, he should at least snuff her candle. He opened the door quietly and peered inside.

The four-poster bed was awash with candle glow. Propped against a mountain of pillows, she watched him as if he were a ghost. "Johnny." He entered the room and closed the door behind him.

She eyed him warily while he leaned against the portal and searched for some hint of the boy he'd known. He was struck again by her delicacy, this frail looking creature with the huge eyes. Seeing her now, he couldn't believe he'd been deceived for so long. Embarrassment swamped him as he recalled the many intimate discussions he'd shared with Johnny during the past few years. Certainly their discussions were not the sort a young girl should have heard. With her pale face, large eyes, and the brave blue ribbon tied in her short brown curls, she should barely be out of the schoolroom. Instead, he'd almost killed her.

She met his eyes for only a moment before her gaze skittered away to a far corner.

He maintained his distance and tried to think of something to say. "Aunt Bess called you Johanna."

"I cannot answer to the name Amber. It's not *me*," Johanna replied. Even her voice sounded different. Johnny's voice had always seemed high-pitched for a boy, but as a girl, her words resonated in a vibrant alto.

"She said you didn't eat supper." Derek stepped closer.

Johanna shrank against her pillows. "I wasn't hungry." She looked like a cornered rabbit hiding in the snowy white bedcovers. What, did she think he still meant to murder her?

"I see." Derek dragged a Chippendale chair next to the bed. He didn't want to tower over her—she looked scared to death already—and he shouldn't sit on the bed with her. Hell, he shouldn't even be in her room alone. What was Aunt Bess thinking, condoning such conduct? If Harry came home, he'd call Derek out.

Derek eased onto the chair, and looked over Johanna again. Her eyes were as wide as the Indian Ocean, and almost the same shade of aqua. Her lower lip appeared fuller, or maybe her chin's quivering made it appear so. Her cheekbones were thin and high, and dark circles wallowed beneath her eyes. No wonder Harry had been worried about her. She looked like hell. "John— I mean Ambe—, Johan— oh, damn..." he finally muttered.

The corners of Johanna's mouth twitched but failed to smile.

Derek resorted to calling her what he'd always called her. "Johnny, I came here because you and I have unfinished business."

Johanna swallowed hard and nodded. Even though the fury had left his eyes, she was scared to trust him. When he'd first appeared, his face wrenchingly handsome, her heart had leapt with hope, but now she had to make amends.

Again she heard those last words he'd spoken—*Damn all women for the liars they are.* How he must hate her. Here was the man she'd wanted only to please since they'd first met nearly ten years ago. Now they were strangers. If only he knew she'd maintained the deception because she'd loved him so.

As he seemed to be waiting, she tried to muster her apology. "My lord, if you knew how sorry I am about...everything," she finished lamely. "I wouldn't blame you if you never forgave me." She couldn't meet his eyes.

His back stiffened in the chair. "Forgive *you*? Is that what you thought—that I came all this way at this hour of night to *forgive you*?"

Johanna bit her lip. She'd promised herself she wouldn't cry no matter how he hated her.

He stood and ran one hand along the back of his neck. "Johnny, I came here tonight to beg you to forgive *me*."

She lifted her eyes to study him. "There's nothing to

forgive."

"I tried to kill you." Bitterness, not anger, tinged his voice.

"You had your reasons."

"Certainly, I had reason—because I refused to give you a chance to explain. You'd been my friend for years, and I refused to consider you might be innocent."

"But I wasn't. I'd lied to you from the first day we met. You always told me how horrible women were. I wanted to be a better person—to be like you—but every day I knew I was lying to you. I prayed every night you would never discover the truth about me."

A pang of guilt struck Derek as she tried to accept the blame for his actions. He knew he'd been free with his opinion about women around Johnny, but he'd never guessed how much the boy had taken to heart.

"Harry tells me you had no memory of who you were until a few years ago. I'm not saying what you did was right, but I understand why you did it."

Johanna sat upright against the plump pillows. "And I understand why you forced the duel upon me. You were defending Olivia's honor."

Separated by scant feet, their eyes met. In unison, they both said, "I'm sorry."

Johanna smiled first, and it brought an answering grin from Derek.

"That's my girl."

Johanna's heart bloomed with hope. He wouldn't cast her off completely.

"Let us start anew." He offered his hand, palm up. "Lady Johanna, I am your cousin, Derek." He faltered at the end, remembering he wasn't a Vaughan.

But Johanna never hesitated. She laid her hand, small and trusting into his. "Your Grace—"

"Tut-tut," Derek corrected lightly. "You must call me Derek now."

She drew a breath. "Thank you, Derek." To her amazement, he raised her fingers and bent his head to kiss her hand. Her heart pounded as she watched the play of candlelight against his dark hair. Lifting his head, his blue eyes captured her and stole her breath.

"Get some sleep now, little one." He smiled kindly before he turned to leave.

"Will you still be here in the morning?"

"Yes, if only to make sure you eat something." The door clicked quietly after he exited.

Johanna blew out the candle. Settling her head on the pillow, she watched a moonbeam slipping in through the window. She recalled how Derek had taken her hand, the warmth of his fingers closing around hers, the ticklish brushing of his lips across her skin. She could never have imagined such a thing. Did she dare risk loving him in truth?

She nestled her head into the fluffy cloud of her pillows and fell asleep with a smile.

ڡﻮﻤ

The transformation from gardener's son to heiress began the next morning and proceeded non-stop until Johanna's head spun. Two days after Derek's arrival, she descended the stairs for breakfast in the first dress she remembered donning. The store-bought creation of pale green muslin fit well and the matching slippers were more comfortable than her boots. Still, Johanna felt naked revealing so much of her unbound bosom and with the skirt billowing around her legs, bare but for sheer stockings. Aunt Bess nodded approval, and Harry drew out her chair for her.

Derek stood across the table, shock so clearly painted on his face, Johanna didn't know whether to laugh or retreat to her room. He finally acknowledged her after everyone was seated. "You must excuse my surprise, Johanna. It never occurred to me that you would be beautiful." The hint of his smile made her pulse trip.

Aunt Bess covered her eyes at his words.

Harry laughed. "Now there's a left-handed compliment."

But Johanna didn't mind.

The Coatsworths were generous and affectionate, but the highlight of her days was any moment when she came across

Derek. Constantly chaperoned, she missed the freedom she'd enjoyed at Ambersley and the times she'd spent alone in deep conversation with him. Now they were considered social equals, yet she had less access to him, which made no sense to her. But then, her whole life had changed.

For all her petite size and frail appearance, Aunt Bess—Harry's mother insisted Johanna call her this, as everyone needed family, she said—had a will as strong as Martha's had ever been. Other than Lady Vaughan, Aunt Bess was the first lady of quality with whom Johanna had ever had contact. She was impressed by the effortless good breeding and knew Paget would approve. Johanna determined to emulate her, for she saw this as a way of earning Derek's favor. Thus, she willingly partook of Aunt Bess's lessons on deportment and listened in rapt silence whenever the older woman told her stories of the *ton*.

When Bath's top dressmaker arrived at the house to measure her and pore over sketches for a proposed wardrobe, Johanna grew nervous at the sheer number of things Aunt Bess ordered.

Aunt Bess silenced her. "Nonsense, child. Derek insists that you be outfitted as your station demands."

"But surely I don't need all of this." Johanna pointed to the pile of sketches they'd selected. I couldn't wear this many clothes in a year."

"My dear, during a Season in London, you could wear everything we've ordered in a week."

Johanna tried not to gape, and from then on, she kept her doubts to herself.

October was on the horizon when Derek announced he'd be traveling to London and then returning to Ambersley. They were enjoying the end of a quiet supper, and Harry expounded for the ladies' benefit.

"Derek's already written Minton about Johnny's true identity. Now they must take the evidence before a magistrate and have you declared alive again." He winked at Johanna.

Aunt Bess paused with a spoonful of trifle in midair. "Derek, you're welcome to return here and stay as long as you like."

"Thank you, but I've missed much of the harvest as it is. Besides, my business with Minton will result in a significant change in my finances. I must speak with Broadmoor about the impact it will have on the running of Ambersley." Derek didn't mention that telling the staff to economize would be easier than explaining how he'd suddenly found the young woman who should have been their mistress these past dozen years. "When I arrive home, I'll ask Mrs. North to select a suitable girl to act as Johanna's personal maid and send her here."

From her seat, Johanna stared at him. "Will I not be returning to Ambersley with you?" Her voice sounded small and shaky.

The others shared a look before Aunt Bess said, "That's not possible, child."

"Mother and I would like very much to have you live with us for now," Harry added.

Derek contemplated Johanna's pale face. "Aunt Bess and Harry, could you excuse us? I think it's best if Johanna and I discuss this alone."

Aunt Bess opened her mouth as if she might object, but Harry shook his head at her. Rising, he offered her his arm. With a backward glance, she accompanied him from the room.

Derek moved restlessly around the dining table. "My dear girl, it is impossible for you to live at Ambersley with me unchaperoned."

"Why?"

He gave a sardonic laugh. "That very question proves to me you must stay here under Aunt Bess's tutelage."

Johanna's eyebrow lifted at the commanding tone he used with her. He'd never ordered her about so when she was the gardener's apprentice. "But I don't want to stay here. I want to go home."

Derek turned at her entreaty to find she watched him with huge eyes. The boy Johnny had always trusted him, and he hated to fail her. "I'm sorry, Johanna, but I cannot allow it. If you were to appear at Ambersley now, everyone would recognize you as Johnny, and they'd all realize the truth."

"Pray, what's wrong with the truth?"

Knowing Society's ways were still new to her, Derek tried to explain. "It's imperative no one know about your upbringing. Minton and I both agree on that. We're working on a more suitable story to tell the public once we announce you're alive."

"And you expect people like Paget and Mrs. North not to notice any resemblance?" Johanna quirked her brow at him—a clear, if unspoken, challenge to his authority.

"I expect them not to say anything, just as Cushing and Rory have said nothing."

"I'm not your tenant any longer," she reminded him.

"No, you're my ward, and you'll do as I bid. For now, you'll remain in Bath with Aunt Bess." Derek wanted to be firm, but hated himself when he saw unexpected moisture swim in Johanna's eyes.

Johanna could barely breathe as she realized he didn't want her at Ambersley. The knowledge hurt more than when he had stabbed her. "Yes, Your Grace." Crying was a weakness she abhorred, and she fought valiantly to check her tears. Only a telltale sniffle escaped.

Derek recognized it immediately. "Why are you crying?" She remained silent. "There's no need to be unhappy, you're an heiress."

"I don't want to be an heiress," she choked. "I want to go home."

"What—you wanted to spend the rest of your life playing a boy?" Derek shook his head. "Don't talk nonsense, Johanna."

She looked up at him as if he'd slapped her. "Is that what you think it was? Playing? I *am* Johnny. That's all I remember, being a boy to everyone, and no one gave it a thought. Only now it turns out I'm the daughter of a duke, and suddenly I should forget everything that's happened to me for the past thirteen years. Now I have wealth and position, and I should be grateful to claim my identity. But has it occurred to you what you're asking me to relinquish? Everything!" She ended on a sob.

Derek stood numbly during her tirade, but as her shoulders shook, he went and pulled her into his arms. She was so young, so fragile, so *feminine,* the desire to protect her struck him a sharp blow.

Johanna hung on his chest and shoulder, her fingers curling into his coat. When the worst of the storm had passed, she whispered, "I was *happy.* I would have been Johnny for the rest of my life. Now it's as though he's dead, and I don't know who I am. I miss him."

Derek rested his head atop hers and smoothed her chestnut curls with his hand. "I know," he whispered in soothing tones. "I miss him, too."

୨∞৫

Following Derek's departure, Johanna resolved not to think about him or Ambersley.

The first week, she received a visit from Mr. Minton. Aunt Bess received him in the drawing room, and when Johanna entered, he bowed to her. She smiled, a little afraid of the dapper solicitor.

Minton adjusted his spectacles as he looked over her face. "I cannot believe how blind we all were," he said with a rueful smile. "Thank God we can make this right." He then spoke privately with her regarding the state of her fortune and her father's will.

Johanna entreated him to let Derek keep the money, but he firmly refused, saying the duke had been adamant about wanting to return her full fortune to her. She understood he and Derek would act as executors of her fortune, and they had arranged for a quarterly allowance to be given to her. She had no idea how she could begin to spend the exorbitant sum he called "pin money" every three months.

Over supper, Mr. Minton reiterated the importance of keeping Johanna's upbringing a secret. Harry nodded and agreed no one must know Lady Johanna Vaughan had been raised on the Ambersley estate by the gardener and his wife. Johanna felt insulted on behalf of the Ambersley staff and tenants, but knew by now her arguments would meet deaf ears.

She listened to the details of the story Mr. Minton and Derek had devised with detached curiosity. It began with her mysterious arrival at a priory with no memory of who she was. The priory was more than one hundred miles from Ambersley, and it was considered a miracle she'd arrived there unharmed.

Johanna considered it would be a miracle if anyone believed this story, but wisely held her tongue.

Only last year had she started recalling snippets of her childhood, and this had prompted the prioresses to widen the search for her family. Learning of the Ambersley Hall fire, the prioresses sent a letter to Derek, and he and Minton had traveled to the priory and positively identified Johanna. When presented with facts and names, she'd miraculously recovered her memory. She'd then returned with them to Bath.

"Which is why you've been kept so closely here in the house," Harry explained.

Aunt Bess smiled at Mr. Minton. "It's a very plausible story, and will capture the *ton's* imagination. Did you pick a specific priory?"

"Oh yes, and Lord Ambersley and I have already been there to make a sizable donation. They assure me they will answer any inquiries with a sincere, 'We've been asked by the family not to discuss the matter,'" Minton replied.

Harry laughed. Johanna tried to appreciate the humor, but something else troubled her. "What about Johnny?"

Mr. Minton pushed his spectacles higher on his nose. "His lordship is telling all at Ambersley that Johnny has been shipped off to America. He felt it would be inappropriate for Johnny to ever return to Ambersley when Lady Johanna was unaware of his existence."

Johanna had to be satisfied, but she didn't like it.

A month brought no word from Derek other than the arrival of Nancy, Johanna's new maid. She realized the girl had been the perfect choice. As a second maid for Olivia when Olivia visited, Nancy had never come face to face with Johnny. Johanna tried to appreciate having someone to do every task she bid, but it seemed unnatural. She was more apt to send Nancy away and undress alone in the huge bedroom once occupied by Derek.

Being restricted to the house began to wear on her nerves, and she sought diversion in the most mundane things. When Harry caught her reading a book on animal husbandry she'd found, he suggested his mother take Johanna to the lending library or the Pump Room. Aunt Bess agreed, and so Johanna ventured out onto the Royal Crescent for the first time. The hills surrounding Bath were ablaze with autumn color when she and Aunt Bess strolled down High Street toward their destination.

Aunt Bess told her how she'd tried drinking the waters, believing it would improve her spirits following her husband's death, but nothing had helped. She patted Johanna's hand. "But you've brought me great joy these last few weeks. I hope you're as happy with Harry and me as we are to have you as part of our family."

Johanna blushed and agreed she was most happy.

It being the season for grouse shooting, the Pump Room wasn't crowded. Aunt Bess introduced Johanna simply as Johanna Vaughan, a cousin. Matrons nodded approvingly at her, and she tried to appear self-assured. She wished Harry had come with them. After tasting the nasty waters, which gave her a fit of sneezing, Johanna followed Aunt Bess to the lending library where they whiled away an hour looking at *The Times* and choosing a novel for Aunt Bess and a book of poetry for Johanna. They admired the many display windows as they strolled along Milsom Street and so back home. Johanna's feet hurt from so much walking in the thin slippers, but her cheeks glowed with color at having finally gotten some welcome exercise.

After that, Johanna began to taste Bath society. One night, they attended a musical entertainment at the Lower Assembly Rooms. Another night, a group of young people played charades while the chaperones occupied themselves at cards. Johanna laughed until tears trickled down her face at Harry's outrageous playacting of a turkey.

But the day Harry turned up at the front door with two riding horses, one wearing a side-saddle, all Johanna's decorum fled as she threw herself into his arms. After that, she and Harry spent mornings riding. She laughed at herself and was grateful Harry understood how awkward she felt. She longed to straddle a horse again, but when she said so before Aunt Bess, she feared the older woman would faint.

Fall turned to winter, and Johanna missed her home fiercely. *Who will prune the roses? Has someone turned the plants in the conservatory to face the southern sunlight like Tom taught me to do every December? What is Derek doing today?* The questions teased her so she couldn't concentrate on her chess game with Harry.

Aunt Bess entered the drawing room, a letter in hand, a smile beaming. "Well, children, it's done. An announcement has appeared in *The Times* that Lady Amber Johanna Vaughan has been found and is now residing with relatives in Bath. We can expect to receive invitations everywhere."

Her prediction proved accurate as their home was besieged with morning callers. Matrons approached Aunt Bess in the Pump Room to invite her and her charming guest for supper or a card party or a small gathering with perhaps some dancing for the young people. Women admired anything Johanna perused in the Bath shops and praised her taste. She was dumbfounded by this behavior until Harry pointed out the one thing these women all shared in common—all were related to a man who desired to make Johanna's acquaintance.

"You jest," Johanna responded from atop her mount as they walked the horses back to the Royal Crescent.

"I wish I did," he said darkly. He helped her dismount.

Aunt Bess leaned out an upstairs window. "Johanna, thank goodness you're home. Come in and change. We must go to Milsom Street and arrange for a new dress."

Johanna cast a despairing glance at Harry who only laughed and led both horses away. She stared up at the window, hands on hips. "Why would I need another dress?" she called up.

Aunt Bess's capped head popped back out. "We've been invited to a Christmas Ball at Lord and Lady Sedgefield's, and Derek has given permission for you to make your debut there.

His letter even said he might make time to attend himself."

Johanna didn't know whether to be flattered or scream in frustration at his casual disregard of her for the past three months.

Lord and Lady Sedgefield's estate was little more than an hour from Bath, but owing to the unpredictability of the December weather, Aunt Bess accepted the invitation for her party to stay overnight. Johanna simply stared at the small trunk while Nancy packed five dresses, shoes and stockings, curling irons, hair ribbons and miles of underclothes and silently prayed she wouldn't disgrace herself. Unnerved by the activity in her room, she escaped to the library for some quiet. She'd had three hours of dancing lessons each day this week, and she longed to rest her sore feet before the fire and fall asleep over a book.

Every moment had become a flurry of activity in preparation for her debut. Aunt Bess's sole concern lately was whether a fabric's color enlivened Johanna's skin or clashed with her eyes. Johanna opened a book to a picture of a fish. Immediately she pictured the fish fork she must use and knew precisely how many inches to the left of her plate it would rest on the dining table. She shook her head in disgust. No wonder men thought ladies were such trivial creatures—they had nothing but trivialities to entertain them. Fashion and etiquette weren't details important enough to worry her, yet Aunt Bess believed the entire trip to Sedgefield hinged upon them.

Snapping the book shut, she drew a steadying breath. This would be her first Christmas away from Ambersley. Candles lit throughout the Hall, hot punch in the kitchen, a fat goose for every tenant family, carols sung in the stable yard—the memories of past winters made Johanna smile. But the aura faded as homesickness chafed her like a raw wind across chapped skin. Here, alone in the library, she could admit she longed to return to Ambersley.

But she wouldn't have traded her evening at the Sedgefield estate for anything. As their coach pulled up before the monstrous manor house, Harry told her in a whisper there were at least thirty bedrooms, and he'd heard tell of someone who had taken a wrong turn and been lost more than an hour.

"Have you been here before, then?" Johanna asked.

"Good heavens, no," he answered in good-natured horror. "The Coatsworths aren't in the same league as the Duke and Duchess of Sedgefield. Aunt Bess was only invited because she's your chaperone."

Bemused, Johanna asked, "What of you?"

Harry shrugged. "Every hostess is always seeking an extra unmarried man to even out her numbers. But it's you they wanted here. You are our *entréz* into the first circles of Society."

When she started to object, Aunt Bess interrupted her. "Don't make her nervous, dear. It's true, Johanna, that you've raised our status. While Harry's father was a wealthy man, he earned that money through trade. There was no reason to single us out for an invitation—until now. Don't be embarrassed. These are precisely the sort of people you would have grown up knowing had your parents lived. They're so looking forward to meeting you."

A footman opened the coach door and handed Aunt Bess down. Harry started to follow, but stopped long enough to look back at Johanna. "Of course, they're looking forward to meeting you. Their son is busy gambling away the family fortune and needs a rich wife."

Johanna's anxiety doubled.

Her room adjoined Aunt Bess's with Nancy acting as maid to them both for the night. Aunt Bess immediately called for a hot bath, and Nancy began unpacking their things. Within the hour, Johanna found herself scrubbed and preened. Her dress of pale pink silk dipped low exposing the creamy smoothness of her throat and small bosom. Johanna eyed herself critically in the cheval glass. No, she wouldn't allow Aunt Bess to persuade her to purchase another pink dress. It simply wasn't her color.

Aunt Bess came up behind her. "My dear, I knew pink would be perfect on you." She presented a strand of matched pearls. "You must wear these. They were your mother's."

Johanna had never received anything from her parents. She reached but didn't quite touch them. "How?" she whispered.

"Derek sent them earlier this week. He promised to come tonight but feared he might be delayed. He wanted you to wear them, and I agree they're most appropriate for a girl your age."

Johanna bent her head while Aunt Bess fastened the cool orbs around her neck. She touched them. Delicate yet invincible. Derek had sent them to her, and she would see him tonight. Happiness spread through her with a warm glow.

They sat down nineteen for supper. Johanna wished she were ignorant of the great honor bestowed upon her by being seated at Lord Sedgefield's right hand. On her other side sat a handsome man with blonde curls who was introduced as Reed Barlow, a cousin of Lady Sedgefield. Smiling politely at him, she stole a glance down the table. Harry and Aunt Bess were seated across from each other halfway down. Harry sat between two pretty young ladies and seemed entirely at ease. Further down, a handsome dark-haired gentleman seated at Lady Sedgefield's right made Johanna's heart skip. But then she realized it wasn't Derek, only another gentleman who looked rather like him.

When Lord Sedgefield escorted her into the ballroom, she forcibly reminded herself not to gawk. Large and drafty as a barn, the room's floor was waxed to a golden sheen and four crystal chandeliers bathed everything with light from over a hundred candles. More candles burned in candelabra, their tiny flames magnified by the mirrored walls. She saw her first palm trees, and the marble statues in the alcoves were all nude.

Before she knew it, Harry swept her into the first of a set of country dances. She swallowed her nervousness when she saw how many guests improvised their own steps. Harry always danced with carefree abandon, and she soon caught his contagious grin. For the next two hours she bobbed amidst the dancers throughout two reels and a cotillion. She smiled at each partner introduced to her but couldn't help wondering whether Derek would ever show.

The moment he entered the ballroom, electricity sparked

the air, and a murmur rippled through the guests. Even Johanna was impressed by his appearance, and she realized she'd never seen him dressed so formally. Derek had chosen unadorned black, relieved only by the snowy folds of his neck cloth and shirt. The striking simplicity put the more colorful combinations of the dandies to shame. His commanding height, broad shoulders and well-muscled leg added to his imposing entrance.

Beside Johanna, a young lady said on a sigh, "Lord Ambersley has arrived."

Johanna blinked at the worshipful tone. He was, after all, the same Derek she'd always known. They were old friends.

But when he caught her eye from across the room, her composure deserted her. The ballroom suddenly felt as confining as her stays, and she longed to be outdoors wearing her familiar breeches. Then she might have been able to breathe. Derek nodded politely to her, then returned to his conversation with Lady Sedgefield.

Johanna's face heated. Apparently she wasn't as important as her hostess. She tried to bury her disappointment.

"Please, don't develop that same bored look everyone else wears at these events."

The male voice made Johanna turn to see the handsome man from dinner. This close, his resemblance to Derek was more pronounced, except his nearly black hair curled more, his blue eyes were flecked with silver, and his jaw formed a sharper angle. His lips twisted into a wry smile as she studied him.

She dipped a curtsey, unsure how to proceed when they hadn't been properly introduced.

He bowed, revealing broad shoulders beneath his dark green coat trimmed in black. With his black satin breeches and buckled dancing shoes, he cut a very dashing figure.

"St. John Trevarthan, Marquess of Worthing, since we've no one to make the introductions," he said. Even his voice reminded her of Derek's rich timbre. "My eldest sister is the lady of the house."

"Johanna—"

"Vaughan, yes. I heard tell Derek uncovered the heiress."

She didn't know what to say to that. "Do you know Lord Ambersley?"

"Went to school together—as close as brothers, you might say. Come, let us dance."

Across the room, Lady Sedgefield handed Derek a glass of champagne. "Your ward does Elizabeth Coatsworth justice. She has very pretty manners."

He sipped his drink. "Yes, I'm told she's always been an obedient little thing," he lied smoothly.

"I see Worthing's taken an interest. High time my brother was married." She smiled blandly at him.

Recognizing the man leading his ward onto the floor, Derek checked his temper and smiled back. Fortunately, the music ended as Johanna and Worthing joined the group of dancers on the floor. Swift action was imperative.

"I wonder, Imogene, if you had planned to include any waltzing this evening?"

Lady Sedgefield eyed him shrewdly. "You know many still consider it a wicked dance. Whatever would Sally Jersey think if I allowed waltzing at my party?"

"You shock me," he said with well-feigned surprise. "I never dreamed you would worry yourself over Sally Jersey's approval, especially when she's not here. It's Christmas, and we're all among friends. Let the young misses skip the waltz to protect their reputations, but don't deny us." He raised her hand and kissed it.

An accomplished flirt herself, Lady Sedgefield wasn't immune to his persuasiveness. She motioned to the orchestra leader, and as the strains of a waltz sang out on violins, Derek led her to the floor.

"And will we find you waltzing at Almack's this season, my lord?" she asked as he swung her into the three-quarter rhythm.

"Perhaps, if I can be sure my ward won't disgrace me."

As the music started, Johanna watched many young ladies desert the floor. She stepped to the side, clearing the way for couples to whirl past, young bucks and matrons whose reputation couldn't be spoiled by so scandalous a dance. Johanna looked on in envy.

Beside her, Lord Worthing's eyes narrowed. "Lady Johanna, I regret we made so brief an acquaintance."

"Must you leave so soon?" she asked.

"No, but unless I mistake, you're about to be claimed for this dance."

"No," she said with disappointment. "For Aunt Bess expressly forbade me to waltz tonight."

"I somehow think he'll override her very proper directive." He bowed again to her. "It was a pleasure."

She'd barely curtseyed to him when Derek and Lady Sedgefield drew to a halt before them.

"Come dance with me, St. John," the lady said.

Lord Worthing raised a brow at Johanna. "Your servant, my lady." He took his sister by the hand and whisked her away among the other couples.

To Johanna's surprise, Derek held out his hand to her.

"I'm not supposed to—" she began.

"I'll bear Aunt Bess's ire," Derek said as he beckoned. "Come, it's best we talk."

Doubts fled when his fingers clasped hers, and elation consumed her as she soared through the dance in his arms. His hand warmed her waist, and his face hovered inches above hers. Her eyes roved over the features she had long since memorized and missed so much.

He tilted his head to study her. "I don't believe pink is your color."

"Is that all you have to say?"

"No. Stay away from Lord Worthing."

Her radiance fizzled. "Damn you," she breathed.

"Don't swear at me, young lady." Derek pinched the small of her back. He glanced around, but the other couples appeared oblivious to their conversation. His lips twisted into a fake smile. "Pretend you're enjoying yourself," he ordered.

With her newfound knowledge in etiquette, Johanna pinned a tight smile in place.

"Where did you learn such language?" He would have

used the same polite, disinterested tone to ask about the weather.

"From you, of course." She was equally polite. "You taught me to swear, you taught me to ride, you taught me to fence and fight. You taught me everything so one day I could be a gentleman and make you proud." She batted her eyes at him.

Derek's forced smile turned to a genuine grin. "Instead, most of what I taught you was useless."

"Oh, not at all. You taught me ladies are senseless creatures with no thought in their heads beyond making an advantageous marriage. And you were absolutely right." There was no hiding the disillusionment in her voice.

Derek frowned. "Men of fashion are little better, wanting only to win the prize of a beauteous or rich wife."

"How very true."

"Have you been misused tonight?" Though his tone was light, his eyes narrowed with concern that somewhere in the place was a person who had injured her feelings. The desire to protect her settled upon him warm as a familiar cloak.

"Not at all. I'm the toast of the ball. I'm sure when everyone sees us together, they see your title and property dancing with a sack of money." She laid aside her façade of gaiety. "Is this truly my lot in life? For if my childhood was intended to be a training ground for fish forks, dancing and idle chatter, I was much happier living with Tom and Martha."

"You mean the prioresses," Derek corrected.

Johanna quirked an eyebrow at him.

Seeing that familiar mannerism, Derek added softly, "We've all gone to great lengths to make that story stick because we care about you." He would go to any length to protect her from the mockery of the *ton* should they ever learn the truth of her highly improper upbringing. Indeed, he was still reeling from his first vision of Johanna as he'd entered tonight. He could barely assimilate the transformation Aunt Bess had wrought in turning the stable lad into this fairy princess. Johanna had looked at him from across the ballroom, and he'd had to quell the urge to rush to her side.

Johanna stared at him as they continued to twirl around the floor with perfectly matched steps. Finally, she managed to push words past the lump in her throat. "Do you? You haven't written. I haven't seen you in ages, nor heard one word. You arrived tonight and seemed more intent on making an impression with Lady Sedgefield than speaking with me. Do you know what I've been through these past few months? Have you any idea how much I've missed you?"

Derek's gut clenched as he recognized the hurt in her aqua eyes. The quivering of her chin parted her lips, making his arm tighten with the involuntary desire to pull her closer and taste her. With an effort, he recalled his duty as her guardian and went about the painful but necessary task of reminding her of her place.

"Has it occurred to you that, supposedly, we've barely met? We're practically strangers as far as Lady Sedgefield knows, and it's important people never know how much time we've spent together." He brought her to a stop as the music ended and added, as much for his benefit as hers, "A duke would never take an interest in his naïve ward. Now come, let us find Aunt Bess."

Johanna followed him mechanically from the floor, still smarting from his words. How foolish she'd been, thinking he could ever love *her*. He had little faith in women in general, and he clearly had no patience with her in her new guise.

Derek escorted her toward a settee occupied by his aunt. As Johanna sank down next to the older woman, he wondered when she'd acquired that fluid grace of motion. He bowed and offered to fetch them some lemonade. Aunt Bess thanked him, but Johanna remained silent. Derek berated himself for destroying her pleasure as he crossed the room. *But it was necessary. She shouldn't be looking at me in that way.* He recalled her smile, the way her eyes had lit as he'd held her during the dance. The way they'd lifted to him in unspoken offer—damn, she shouldn't be looking at *any* man in such a way.

When he returned with two glasses of lemonade, he found Aunt Bess sitting alone.

"Johanna's dancing with Harry." She patted the seat beside her. "Don't they look well together?"

Derek felt a rush of emotion he didn't care to name. He sat and sipped the noxious lemonade and never took his eyes from the beauty laughing with Harry while she danced.

13

"My dear, don't fidget so. With all your pent up energy, perhaps we should harness you to the coach."

Aunt Bess's gentle admonishment checked Johanna's drumming fingers. She pulled the lap rug higher and tried once more to retrieve the warmed brick with the toe of her kid boot.

"Never mind, child. It's grown cold by now. We're nearly there."

Johanna's gaze returned outside the window. Seeing the familiar roofs of Ambersham, she grew giddy with anticipation.

She was finally coming home.

Rory pulled the horses to a halt before the Hall, and he and Cushing climbed down from their perch. Derek and Paget greeted them from the flagway. "Did you meet any trouble?"

Rory shook his head. "No, my lord. The weather held for us the whole way." He cast his gaze to the fat clouds that promised snow yet to fall.

Derek opened the coach door, and smiled inside. "Welcome to Ambersley, ladies."

Johanna forced herself to sit still as Derek handed his aunt down first. When he offered his hand again, Johanna took it deftly and hopped lightly to the ground, all the while drinking in the familiar sights of Ambersley. She longed to rush to Cushing and Rory and Paget, give them each a big hug in their turn and tell them what it meant to be home. But neither by word nor gesture did they betray an inkling of her true identity, and so she followed Derek and Aunt Bess in docile silence.

"Ladies, I hope the journey didn't prove too cold. I believe Mrs. North will have some hot tea ready. If you're not too tired, Lady Johanna, Mrs. North can show you around the Hall."

Johanna quirked a brow. It had only been a four-hour coach ride from Bath—did he think she would swoon from her exertion? She held her tongue, for she knew Derek would be angry if she didn't behave exactly as Lady Johanna who had never visited Ambersley before.

Paget followed them in and took the ladies' pelisses. Tea awaited them in the drawing room, along with a tray of Mrs. Chalmers' scones with clotted cream and jam. Johanna felt a pang at the thought of baking day at Ambersley, and how as the gardener's son, she'd been permitted to help. She longed to visit the kitchens. She leaned toward the fire to warm her chilly hands while Aunt Bess poured tea.

"Did Harry travel to London as he planned?" Derek asked his aunt.

"Yes. He was disappointed not to join us here, but he'll see us in Town when we arrive for the Season. When duty calls, one must respond as he says. For myself, I still cannot imagine him working in the Foreign Office." She handed Derek his cup.

"Harry was made for the diplomatic corps. They do nothing but talk forever."

Johanna smiled from her position by the fireplace. She would miss Harry dreadfully, but knew he couldn't forever hold her hand.

She toured the Hall with Mrs. North and did her best to pretend she'd never seen it before. The housekeeper showed her the main floor, all the bedrooms and even the nursery and servants' quarters. Viewing the nursery sent a shiver flashing up her spine. She recalled the night of the fire as a shadowy blur, but here stood a room with a tiny bed and walls of robin's egg blue. Peering out the window, she recognized the view of the home wood her dreams had etched in her memory.

Johanna requested to see the duke's chamber, and to Mrs. North's slack jaw, explained she wanted to see where her parents had died. Mrs. North agreed, and after assuring herself the duke wasn't there, she let them in. Johanna breathed with relief when she saw no sign in here of the fiery night when she couldn't wake her parents and had nearly suffocated herself. There were no ghosts here. Perhaps now the nightmares, which still visited her from time to time, would disappear completely.

Her own room was a golden yellow, as if sunshine radiated from within. A rich Aubusson carpet and cherry furniture added elegance and comfort. Nancy had arrived and was busily hanging Johanna's dresses in the armoire. She selected one of dark green wool with long fitted sleeves that gathered at the shoulder. The neckline scooped low across Johanna's breasts, leaving her throat and breastbone bare to chilly drafts. Nancy supplied a crocheted shawl in a paler green for style and warmth.

She arrived at the dining room to find Derek and Aunt Bess already there. The three sat at one end of the long table while Paget and Stokes served supper *a la russe*. Derek and Aunt Bess discussed Johanna's presentation in April, whether she should keep a horse in Town for the Season and compared notes on all their friends and acquaintances. Johanna might have thought Derek was planning a military campaign, he looked so serious over his wine as he outlined for Aunt Bess the most advantageous people to know in London. They didn't cut her out of the conversation, but Johanna had so little to add, she remained silent through most of the meal.

Across the room, Paget waited by the sideboard for someone to need his service. She smiled at him, but he didn't respond. When he cleared her plate from the first course, she thanked him, but he didn't seem to hear. It became a contest to see if she could get the straight-faced butler to acknowledge her. She tried dropping her fork, but he replaced it wordlessly. She requested a second helping of the chicken fricassee, but he only nodded to Stokes who brought it to her. In a final gambit, she waited until Derek became engrossed in what Aunt Bess was saying to him, and she winked at Paget across the way. *Surely* he would recognize that little wink as something Johnny used to do.

Aunt Bess rose from the table and suggested they go to the drawing room so the servants could clear the table. Johanna followed in frustration.

Derek offered her a game of chess, but Johanna couldn't concentrate on the moves and lost the first and subsequent game rather quickly. She'd returned home to Ambersley, just as she'd wished, only now she wanted a reunion with the familiar faces from her childhood: Cushing, Mrs. Chalmers, Rory, Paget and the others. After losing the second game, she admitted she might be more tired than she had thought. Aunt Bess agreed it was time they were both abed and followed her upstairs.

Nancy had already turned down the covers and lit the small lamp on the table. With a touch of envy, Johanna had granted the maid the next two days off to visit her family. She drew back the heavy drapes to watch snowflakes swirl in the darkness to the now-white ground. Johanna warmed the frosty window with her breath, and an idea formed while she traced designs with her fingertip. She wanted to see the staff, and there was no better time and place to find a group of them than in the kitchens after supper.

With care, she tiptoed down the back stair to the kitchens at the bottom of the house. As she drew closer, she heard Mrs. Chalmers' familiar voice. "Tell me more, Cushing. Does she look just the same as Johnny?"

"Aye, just the same, yet completely different. You'd recognize her with a flick of your eye, but she's so cool and reserved. She's a lady now." Cushing drained his pint of ale.

Rory chimed in. "And it fair breaks your heart, knowing what an imp Johnny was, to meet the most delicate and proper Lady Johanna." He stared into his tankard.

"But I'm still me." She stepped into the kitchen firelight.

Cushing turned around and nearly toppled his chair. "Lady

Johanna!"

Rory scrambled to his feet while Mrs. Chalmers bobbed in a fair copy of a curtsey.

Johanna smiled warmly and came forward with outstretched hands. "No, friends, ignore the gowns. I'll always be Johnny with you."

Mrs. Chalmers dabbed at her eyes with her apron. "Bless you, child, for coming down here so I could see you meself. I worried so about you."

Johanna drank in the kitchen's aromas of gravy, yeast and herbs. Gleaming copper kettles she'd once polished hung above the long trestle table where Mrs. Chalmers carved the meat and rolled out the pastries. Mrs. Chalmers in her white smock, with her wrinkled sinewy hands and sagging bosom, remained just as Johanna remembered. She glanced at Cushing and Rory, but they stood transfixed as if she were the ghost Rory had always claimed he'd seen.

Her gown somehow managed to tangle up her tongue. Dressed as Lady Johanna, she couldn't think of what to say to them.

Footsteps descended the stairs, and Johanna nervously stepped around the corner, afraid Derek would find her here.

Instead, she heard Paget talking to Mr. Pritchard and Mrs. North. "We shall need to take the best china, for there will never be enough at Grosvenor Square to accommodate so large a gathering." Paget entered the kitchen, very much the general in command. He stopped to contemplate the others standing about like scarecrows in the field. "Is something amiss?"

"Only me," Johanna admitted meekly from her corner.

Paget stared hard at her for a moment, as if she couldn't possibly be there. Mr. Pritchard and Mrs. North were likewise struck dumb.

Mrs. North found her voice. "Is there aught we can get for you, Lady Johanna?"

Johanna took an angry stride forward. "It's *me*, Johnny. Don't you recognize me?"

"Of course we recognize you." Paget's authoritative voice checked her temper at once. She looked to him with hope, but his face was, as always, stern. "But there is no more Johnny."

"You're angry with me because I lied. I couldn't tell you. I couldn't tell anyone—" She broke off, afraid she'd never make them understand.

Rory shook his head. "Nay, Johnny. Cushing explained all that."

"Lady Johanna, may I speak my mind?" Paget commanded her attention.

"Of course."

"What was that business in the dining room tonight?" He drew himself even taller, as if the topic were distasteful to him. "You behaved no better than a child still in the nursery. I've never been so embarrassed in my life."

"I—I was just trying to get your attention."

"Don't. I know my place in this house even if you do not. I am the butler, and the only courtesy I expect is for you *not* to call attention to my presence. If your mother were alive, I shudder to think what she would have said of your behavior."

Johanna held her stance, her chin up despite the chill settling upon her shoulders. "Very well. If you're determined not to acknowledge me." She moved toward the stairs, but stopped to look at the sea of familiar faces. "You're the only family I've ever known. I missed you. Is that so hard for you to understand?"

Mrs. Chalmers stepped forward to wrap the girl in a motherly embrace. It smelled of flour and meat drippings and heaven. Johanna thought her wonderful. "We missed you too, Johnny. Don't ever doubt that, child."

"But you live in a different world now," Mrs. North pointed out.

"It's only upstairs."

"It may as well be on another continent," Cushing muttered.

Johanna tilted her head to look at him. What he said made sense. She had left this world—whether by choice or no—and had landed on a far distant shore. She stepped out of Mrs. Chalmers' arms and gave the woman's hands a squeeze before nodding to the other servants. "Then I have no choice but to move forward with my life."

She turned to leave again, but stopped before the hawk-nosed butler. "Paget, one of the few things I've ever wanted was to win your approval."

"Johnny had my approval, for he knew his place and duty. Lady Johanna may earn it as easily."

Johanna stared at him intently as she absorbed his advice. Without a word, she exited up the stairs.

In the kitchen, silence prevailed over the company. Rory retrieved his tankard, intent on fetching more ale. "That wasn't very pleasant."

"It was, however, necessary," Paget responded stiffly.

Cushing shook his head. "The Master had her pegged. He said she'd come looking for us. I didn't believe she'd come this fast."

"Poor lamb." Mrs. Chalmers chafed her empty arms. "She looked as if she had to face the world alone."

"She's headed for London soon. 'Tis better she grow accustomed to that feeling now," Mrs. North replied.

"Ladies and gentlemen, may I remind you of our commission to the late duke and duchess—to raise their daughter as befits her station. Lady Johanna may still face hard lessons, but she'll not embarrass herself—or this staff—in public."

"The duke will be happy to hear of tonight's work," Mr. Pritchard noted.

They regarded each other wordlessly. Each knew no one would speak of tonight's encounter to His Grace.

ৎ৽৵

Johanna acted the model of decorum during the next few weeks. Around the staff, she remained coolly reserved, ever polite but distant. She took her cue from Paget himself, whether or not the butler wished to know it.

With Derek she built the foundation for a new relationship. Though not as easy-natured as Harry, Derek was one of her oldest friends. Yet, while she viewed Harry as her same friend, she couldn't see Derek as anything but a man—a handsome man who scattered her pulse every time he looked her way. With effort, Johanna learned to treat him with the deference appropriate for a ward to her guardian. It was far more difficult than any of the deportment lessons Aunt Bess had tried to teach her, for she constantly had to guard her tongue.

For Derek, Johanna's return to Ambersley spelled sweet torture. Her mere presence lightened the mood of those around her even while she remained the proper young lady they'd taught her to be. He found he missed those days when he could have demanded she share her thoughts, but that easy camaraderie they'd shared seemed to have disappeared along with her breeches. It would be improper to press a young lady to speak the feelings he read in her eyes as she watched him. In fact, the proprieties were a damn nuisance.

At her request, Derek took Johanna to the conservatory where she lost herself among flowers and greenery and joy. Even Aunt Bess agreed it would be unexceptional for her to repot the plants. She was never happier than covered with dirt, pruned leaves gathering at her feet.

Seeing the work she accomplished, Derek allowed that perhaps he needed to hire a new gardener. As they left one March evening, he watched Johanna kneel and brush the last of a snowdrift away from a handful of green shoots sprouting from the ground.

She smiled at his bemused expression. "Daffodils." She feathered her fingers through the tenacious stems. "It's practically spring, you know."

Derek offered his hand to help her up. The sweetness of her fingers curling through his unnerved him. "You got your dress muddy," he said.

As they walked home, her hand in his, he thought how happy a child Johnny had been and compared it with the young lady beside him. Today, playing in the conservatory and tugging on daffodils, he'd caught a glimpse of her happiness. He hadn't realized how vital that was to him. In truth, he had the uncomfortable sense that his own happiness was somehow twined with hers.

Images of her plagued him well past the time Aunt Bess

and Johanna bid him goodnight. Derek stared into the fireplace and saw Johanna kneeling beside snow-covered daffodil shoots. An unexpected heat flared up as readily as the flames before him. *He wanted her.* He couldn't explain why or how or when it had happened, but desire was there, so obvious he couldn't ignore it.

He pushed away from the fire to stalk the drawing room. Useless to fantasize about her ivory skin, or her vibrant aqua eyes, or the eyebrow that lifted in its maddening way. He would never dream of breaking the proprieties with Johanna. She was the daughter of a duke and entrusted to his care. Never would he taste the sweet response of her first kiss, or the delicate skin behind her ear, or watch her eyes dilate with desire. He'd seen her slender but strong legs in breeches, but he'd never see them as his imagination did, wrapped around his waist as she experienced the most intimate ecstasy. He would never share any of these moments with Johanna.

Not unless he married her.

Derek laughed bitterly to himself. As her guardian, he had no business contemplating such a union. As the bastard son of a murderess, even less so.

Marriage was something he'd avoided for obvious reasons. Since his commitment had always been to hand over the reins to Curtis and return to India, a wife and child would have been a shackle. But uncovering Johanna's true identity had muddled all his plans. He wouldn't relinquish Ambersley to his half brother until Curtis proved his worthiness, and yet he refused to foist an heir upon Ambersley that wasn't of Vaughan blood.

But Johanna was a Vaughan, and her son would be a fitting heir to Ambersley. It had been clear in Bath she was infatuated with him, like a schoolgirl experiencing her first stirrings of love. He stared into the fire and tortured himself with another vision of her as she'd been in the conservatory, dirt on her hem and joy in her eyes. Even the smell of moist earth and greenery came back to tease his memory. The rush of desire struck him again. Would a lifetime of marriage be too high a price for bedding Johanna?

His thoughts turned to the alternative and sparked

jealousy. If she wed another, he would be forced to bury this attraction he felt forever. He doubted it would release him; it had taken hold upon him like a sturdy vine, and the thought of her with another man only strengthened the vine's grasp. With a frown, he acknowledged there lay a place in his heart reserved for Johanna alone.

Was this love then, this explosive mix of desire and jealousy? He admitted to little familiarity with the emotion. But this he could recognize—she seemed to favor him.

And he wanted her with an intensity that would brook any cost.

The ides of March heralded spring, and bright shafts of light pierced the thick mists blanketing the east meadow as the pair of riders broke through the tree line. Derek watched Johanna slow her gelding and inhale the morning air fragrant with pine and hyacinth.

As she crested a grassy knoll near the meadow's center, Johanna stopped her horse and pointed toward the monument on her left. "My memorial's still here."

Derek followed as she urged her horse toward the marble edifice. He jumped down and crossed to Johanna's mount.

She gazed fondly at the familiar lion and lamb. "Someone still tends it. Do I have you to thank for that?"

Derek helped her alight. "I didn't think it should be neglected, but some of the local women have started treating it like a shrine. When a child grows sick, the mothers leave flowers here."

Johanna's face lit with delight. "How sweet!"

"The vicar doesn't think so," Derek replied. "He's told the women that sick children should be treated with medicine, and if prayers are needed, mothers should look no further than God. Mrs. Cleary told the vicar that she would never look *further* than God, but that Lady Johanna was much closer, and since Providence had been so good to you, you might be able to spread your good fortune to other helpless children."

Johanna quirked an eyebrow at him as her lips curled into

a saucy smile. "So now I'm a saint."

"I never said so." Derek smiled back. "But then I know you too well."

She reached for his hand and squeezed his fingers. "And you have no idea what a comfort that is to me. These past few months have brought so many changes, I feel like a...butterfly."

"A butterfly?" asked Derek, not sure he'd heard right.

Johanna's musical laugh pealed through the quiet meadow. "Yes, a butterfly. When I lived here, I was as invisible as a caterpillar. Then Aunt Bess taught me to be a proper lady, and that was like being in a cocoon. Now everyone treats me like a fragile butterfly, as if the slightest breeze would send me tumbling. They dance around me, concerned for my health, my welfare, my entertainment." She stopped her pacing and folded her hands, her back to him. "But they never take time to learn about me, my hopes, my dreams, my ambitions."

"You're a young lady. They believe you have no ambition beyond marriage."

"Is that what you think?"

He turned her to peer into her worried eyes. "You were raised as a boy, and your ambitions were always encouraged. Merely because you've changed your clothes doesn't mean you've changed your heart. You're still a rascally little caterpillar inside a very charming butterfly."

Johanna's smile warmed him more than the sun. "You *do* understand. It's not that I don't like being a butterfly. Sometimes it's rather fun, but I miss being the caterpillar."

She had given him the perfect opportunity, and Derek lost no time. "I miss the caterpillar, too, Johanna. It's been good to have you home this past month. Your absence has—what I mean is...Ambersley has been lonely without you."

His compliment drew a warm blush to her cheeks.

Encouraged, Derek took her hands. "Ambersley has always been home to you, and I think it fitting that it should always be. You and I know each other rather well, and I think we could live together quite happily. Johanna, I'm asking you to marry me."

He had surprised her, he could tell by her luminous blue-green eyes. Not wishing to frighten her, he tamped down the urge to pull her to him and kiss her. "You don't have to answer me now, but consider it. I've rather avoided the notion of marriage, but I cannot imagine another woman who better deserves to be mistress of Ambersley. You belong here."

Johanna swallowed and reminded herself to breathe while her heart raced. To call Ambersley home forever was the answer to her prayers. But marriage... Unsure, she withdrew her hands from his. "I'm flattered by your offer, my lord, but I'm not sure I should accept. You see, I've always believed I'd marry for love." She turned away, unwilling to show how much she hoped he would declare his feelings for her.

Derek watched her turn away, hurt brimming within him. When he'd contemplated proposing, he'd believed her response would be joyous and emotional. Instead, her practical negotiation stung with the sharpness of a disturbed wasp nest. He retreated to stiff formality. "Then perhaps 'tis better you refuse my offer. I wouldn't have made it except I've obviously misinterpreted your feelings—I thought you did love me."

Disappointment settled coldly upon her, but pride demanded she face him with a tremulous smile. "At one time I did. As a child I idolized you, but that's not the kind of love on which I could pin a marriage. Thank you for your offer, but I'm afraid our marrying would be a grave mistake."

Derek made her a small bow. "Very well. I hope you find the happiness you seek."

"Thank you, Derek. I hope we shall always remain friends."

Though neither moved, the distance between them widened.

"Of course," he finally said. "Shall we return for breakfast?"

Johanna rode beside him through the home wood in silence. Derek had taken her refusal well—too well. He didn't love her. He'd suggested a marriage of convenience. What else was she to think when he proposed marriage but had never tried to kiss her? While she remained mistress at Ambersley, he would keep other mistresses in London. She couldn't bear the thought of being married to him only to share him with other women he cared about more than he cared for her. Refusing his offer was for the best. So why did she feel so miserable?

Derek glanced at Johanna occasionally as they rode. Gone was the confiding imp who had ridden out with him at dawn. Here was a coolly reserved lady. He'd ridden out with the caterpillar, he mused, and was returning with the butterfly.

And yet, he still wanted her with a passion more consuming than carnal, a new and unwelcome experience for him. He had proposed to two women in his life. The first, admittedly, had been a great mistake, and when he considered the unholy mess his life would be if Helena had said yes, he was grateful for her selfishly stormy refusal. At the time, the pain had been intense but quick to come and go, as if he'd been struck by lightning but left with no permanent damage.

Johanna's refusal today, so calm and quiet, had been resolute nonetheless. He felt rather a fool for assuming she'd developed a *tendre* for him. He had a title and Ambersley to offer her, and while the title might not be important to her, he knew Ambersley was. Yet she had turned him down for the simple reason that she didn't love him.

Thinking back, Derek recalled he'd never won a woman's affection, not his mother's—certainly not his stepmother's. Helena had proven her only interest was in the status a husband could bring her. Olivia claimed to love him, but she barely understood the emotion. He'd grown accustomed to Johnny's childlike worship—a love akin to a dog for his master—so the loss of Johanna's regard now left him oddly bereft.

He wanted to be worthy of her love, Derek realized. He wanted it desperately. That desire filled him with disquiet for he knew not how to begin such a quest.

At breakfast Aunt Bess remarked on Johanna's heightened color. "I hope you haven't given yourself a chill or a headache from too much riding."

Johanna cast him a look, clearly begging him not to

mention their earlier words.

Derek paused, his teacup midair. "Nonsense. Fresh air did her good. To listen to you one would think she was as fragile as a butterfly."

Johanna choked on her tea. She tried—none too discreetly—to kick him under the table, but when she couldn't reach, she satisfied herself by glaring at him.

Derek's lips twitched at this reminder of how well they knew each other.

Aunt Bess looked from one to the other in bewilderment. "*I* never compared her to a butterfly. I just don't want her to wear herself out before we go to London."

"A morning ride doesn't require nearly as much stamina as a night of *ton* parties," Derek replied lightly. "Don't worry, Aunt Bess. She won't come to any harm with me. Now, how soon do you leave for Town?"

"Friday." Aunt Bess dabbed at her lips with her napkin. "There will be fittings for her Court dress next week, and then her presentation is the following Wednesday."

"Are you planning a suitable ball for her?"

"Well, I've been planning, but I haven't scheduled one. I wanted to wait until we'd arrived in London to work out the details."

"Allow me, Aunt Bess." His decision made, he buttered a slice of toast. "I'll be spending a good deal of time in Town this Season, what with my sister and my ward being presented. I should probably look over the field of suitors."

Aunt Bess beamed at him. "Of course, and perhaps you should look over the young ladies as well."

"Yes, I'll do that," he responded.

Johanna concentrated on her plate while she digested that Derek was coming to London. He didn't care for Town very much, he cared for his stepmother even less, and Johanna had refused his offer of marriage only that morning. Derek was going to London to visit his mistress and possibly to seek a wife.

Sometimes, she wished she didn't know Derek quite so well.

14

London, April 1815

Johanna arrived at the Coatsworth's house in Portman Square, reeling from her first impressions of city life. London seemed to be nothing but narrow streets and tall buildings, with chimneys smoking and people shouting all day. She was relieved to discover the square offered some trees and greenery, but she hoped it would be quiet enough at night to sleep.

Harry awaited them in the drawing room, and she was so happy to see him, she threw herself into his arms without a thought.

"I missed you so," she said to his shocked look.

Harry held her at arm's length with a pained smile. "That's for certain, but do remember Johanna, that in public, we must not be so familiar." With a laugh, he gave her a smacking kiss on the forehead as he lifted her off her feet and spun her around the room. "I missed you, too."

Aunt Bess entered the drawing room followed by Taft bearing a tray of wine and cheese. "Harry, put her down and let Taft take her pelisse."

"How was Ambersley?" Harry asked after Taft left them.

Johanna glowed with her memories of the month-long visit. "It was so good to be home. So little has changed there."

Then she remembered Derek's proposal, and her smile faded.

Harry didn't notice. "Did the staff recognize you?"

"Of course they recognized me," she said with a touch of asperity. "They're not idiots. You cannot fool them simply by putting me in a dress and asking them to look the other way."

Harry nodded at her outburst. "Foolish of us, I'm sure. But will they hold their tongues?"

"Oh yes, for Paget gave me quite a dressing down when I was too familiar with them. It seems now that I've become a lady, no one wishes to take responsibility for my childhood—no one except the prioresses whom Derek and Mr. Minton bribed. I'm no longer fit company for the servants, and I feel so awkward at times with the *ton*. I'm afraid even after all the effort you and Aunt Bess have taken to prepare me, I'm going to say or do something frightful."

"The beauty of it is that it won't matter." Harry gave her shoulders a gentle shake before crossing to the sideboard to fetch her some wine. "Johanna, the *ton* will lie at your feet and worship you. You're a mystery—a gloriously rich and beautiful mystery. Should your behavior be considered unladylike, you'll be labeled eccentric, but it won't detract from your charms."

"My charms," Johanna sighed. She looked up at Harry as he presented her wine to her. "The *ton* may worship me, but will any of them *like* me?"

Harry sobered immediately. "I like you," he said with simple candor. "Mother likes you. The people at Ambersley like you. Do you truly care for the opinion of anyone else?"

Slowly, she smiled. They clinked glasses and toasted the *ton* to perdition.

ॐ

Derek's coach pulled to a stop before Vaughan House. Paget and the rest had gone directly to Grosvenor Square, but Derek thought it time to confront his family. He'd not seen them since that fateful day he'd discovered the truth about Johnny.

He was greeted by a sterile butler and shown to the

drawing room where he waited to discover whether her ladyship was at home. Apparently she was, for a minute later, she entered with Olivia at her heels.

Derek barely recognized his young sister, so great was her transformation. She'd left Ambersley seven months before an adolescent girl, but here stood a young lady in the latest fashion with her high-waisted ivory gown and ivory ribbons in her coifed and curled raven locks. Derek tried to overlook that she resembled a very young version of her mother complete to the feline smile gracing her lips. At some point he would need to discover how much his stepmother had paid for Livvie's new wardrobe. Undoubtedly, Rosalie had included a number of new dresses, like today's coral silk, for herself.

"Derek, what a lovely surprise. We weren't expecting you in London so soon." Rosalie beckoned him to take a seat. Her actions paid no heed to the difficult terms on which they'd parted.

"Hello, Derek," Olivia stopped on the threshold. Despite her polished appearance, she looked too frightened to enter the room.

Derek reached out to her. "Come here, Livvie. Let me look at you. You've changed."

She rushed to grasp his hand with tears glistening in her eyes. "If you only knew, Derek. I know how angry and disappointed you were with me when—" She faltered and looked at the ground.

Derek squeezed her fingers gently.

She lifted her eyes to his and found the courage to continue. "When I was at Ambersley. I know what I did was wrong. I hate knowing I ruined Johnny's future, that I spoiled the friendship between you. I didn't want to disappoint you, and yet, that's exactly what I did." Her dimpled chin quivered slightly, and Derek was reminded of the first time he'd seen it, of the child she'd been, seeking approval and love. She still sought them, he realized, because she didn't get them from her mother. Derek knew too well what that was like.

Rosalie interrupted his thoughts. "I'm sure Derek has forgiven you, my dear."

"Of course," Derek agreed at once. "My temper was at its worst that day, but you needn't fear me in future. I was very angry, not so much with you as with the circumstances. As for Johnny, his destiny was not ruined, merely changed. He'll make a new start in America." Derek smiled at the way his words masked the real situation. "I would have you tell me the truth from now. I don't appreciate lies of any sort. Do you understand?"

Olivia nodded shyly, but when he smiled at her, she cast herself into his arms with a single gulping sob. "I'll never do it again, Derek. I swear!"

While Derek soothed her agitation, Rosalie stood by, smothering a yawn. Emotional displays still bored her, he noted.

Derek pulled back to look upon Olivia's wet face. "Are you ready for your presentation?"

Her eyes sparkled between tears and excitement. "I think so. Mama and Miss Trent have had me practicing for weeks. Exactly how to curtsey, exactly where to look, exactly what the Queen or the Prince will say. My dress arrived a few days ago. It's so beautiful. Mama says you paid for it, thank you!"

Rosalie dared him with her smile. "It was quite generous of you to buy it for her."

Of course, she wouldn't tell Livvie he paid for all her clothing. "Don't thank me, just pray the colts keep winning. Now, have you considered a presentation ball?"

Rosalie's eyes lit with hope immediately, just as he'd expected. "I've considered it, but I wasn't sure how we were to pay for such an extravagant affair."

And she would still expect it to be an extravagant affair.

"I've discussed this with Minton, and here's what we propose. Since Olivia and my ward, Lady Johanna, are to be presented this spring, I shall host one presentation ball for both ladies at Grosvenor Square. Lady Johanna's funds shall pay a large portion of the bill. This will allow us to make the ball the most lavish event of the Season, and with two such debutantes present, it should be well-attended."

Rosalie curled her hands into fists, her fingernails biting

into her palms. *That Vaughan chit.* It still irked her that the girl had turned up after all these years. Once again, her children had been forced to make way for another of more means and precedence. "Lud, Derek, I cannot fathom why you didn't put Lady Johanna into my care from the outset."

Because she's safer away from you. Derek looked to his sister. "And divide your attention? You already have charge of one of the true beauties of the Season." He smiled at Olivia. "No, she needed a great deal of preparation, and Aunt Bess had time on her hands over the winter in Bath."

Rosalie considered her daughter carefully. She wanted the largest ball of the Season to be her daughter's success alone, but there was no denying that Johanna Vaughan's money would allow them to stage an event everyone would remember.

Olivia truly was a beauty with her black hair and bright blue eyes, and she was gaining the polish of a rare gem. Her lips curling into a smile, Rosalie decided she would stake Olivia against any other young woman in London. Lady Johanna might be rich, but she was bound to be a plain little drab having been raised in a priory. "Very well, Derek. I agree to your plan. When shall the ball be held?"

"A fortnight after the presentation. Everyone will have returned to Town by then. Provide me a list of guests, and I'll have Pritchard send the invitations."

This met with her approval. Thank heavens Derek was through flying into the boughs over that whole stable boy incident. "Olivia will need another dress. I'm afraid she doesn't have anything suitable for a ball."

Olivia opened her mouth but closed it again when Rosalie caught her eye.

Derek's lips thinned then bent into a tight smile. "By all means, allow me to buy her a gown. Choose something that will bring out her eyes. Oh, shall I invite Lady Jersey? Perhaps you can procure Olivia's vouchers to Almack's."

"Certainly, my lord." Pleased, she dipped a small curtsey.

"And be sure Curtis attends." In truth, Derek wasn't sure his brother was even now in London.

"He fears you'll not acknowledge him anymore."

"Good God, tell him he's becoming more dramatic than Olivia." Derek retrieved his hat. "All men make mistakes. Good men also make amends."

Their interview over, he let himself out the front door and strolled to his coach. He knew Rosalie would take immediate advantage of his softening toward her. She might be pliant and agreeable now, but once Olivia was launched on Society, he had no doubt his stepmother would revert to her insatiable demands. Were she to discover her attempt to destroy Johnny had been the catalyst to Lady Johanna's discovery, he hated to think what she would do.

He studiously avoided visiting Portman Square, reasoning he might fare better with Johanna if she didn't see him for a few days. He'd missed her after she'd left Ambersley. The Hall had never felt emptier.

Through Harry, he learned all the details of her presentation. Dining alone at Grosvenor Square, the two gentlemen nursed their port at the table while Paget cleared supper. All three pretended Paget wasn't glued to every word.

"The Prince Regent was on the throne yesterday, and Johanna said he smiled most graciously at her. Being a duke's daughter, she was permitted to kiss his hand, and he told her she was quite lovely." Unable to suppress a grin, Harry stared into his glass. "Johanna asked me last night if that's all a man thought was important in a woman—her beauty. I told her that, of course, the Prince—like all men—wasn't immune to a woman's charms, but that he also had a healthy regard for her fortune as well."

Derek coughed up his last sip of port and dabbed at his lips. "Was she angry?"

"Furious," Harry said on a laugh.

"Paget, remind me to ask Pritchard if he included His Highness on the invitation list."

"Yes, Your Grace." Paget withdrew, a smile on his lips.

Derek poured more port while Harry watched him through narrowed eyes. "Derek, you know I hate to pry—"

Derek snorted. "Of all the outrageous lies, Harry. Why

would you say that when you're constantly doing it? Isn't that what they teach you at the Foreign Office?"

This last made Harry rise, stiff-backed. "Well, if that's what you believe, I won't bother you anymore tonight."

"Don't you dare leave. I'd rather have you prying information from me than bribing my staff."

"I *never*—"

"Then I'm sorry I suggested it," Derek shot back. "Pour yourself another drink and tell me what's on your mind."

Harry pursed his lips for a moment. "Do you plan to marry Johanna?"

Caught completely off guard, Derek blinked at him once then threw his head back and laughed.

"I'm serious." Harry relaxed back into his chair. "You're about to set all of London on her. With her beauty and her fortune, she's going to attract the bucks faster than a doe in heat. How can you stand for that? Don't you love her?"

Derek sobered at the final question. Not even to his cousin would he reveal the depth of his feelings for Johanna. In truth, she held his thoughts with an unsettling tenacity. Leaning forward, his elbows braced on the table, he met Harry's eye and said quietly, "I proposed last month."

"Capital! So, the two of you are secretly engaged?"

"No. She refused my offer."

Harry's euphoria was quickly doused by this surprise. "What? You jest."

"I wish I did." Derek sipped his port. "I proposed in March. It was spring, it was dawn, it was the east meadow. Oh, what the hell—it was foolish. I had this notion she loved me."

"But she does," interjected Harry. "I mean, she *must*."

Derek eyed his cousin's idealism ruefully. "That morning she told me she had loved me as a child idolizes a hero, but she didn't love me in a way to want to marry me. I was disappointed, I won't deny, but—" He smiled into his glass. "Even the Prince Regent has failed to make any impression upon her. I believe she won't care for Society. I intend to renew my suit following the Season, when I can do so without the *ton's* prying eyes."

"Then you don't believe your situation is hopeless."

"Hopeless? Never." Derek drained his glass. "Make no mistake, I'll marry Johanna before the end of the year." Love or no, the restlessness in his heart couldn't bear the thought of living without her any longer.

Over three hundred guests replied favorably to the duke's gracious invitation to a ball honoring his sister and his ward. Nigel Minton found himself among the select guests included for an early supper at the house on Grosvenor Square. "My lord, I'm here, but I fear there may have been a mistake, for surely you didn't mean to include me at table. I'll certainly understand and wait elsewhere if—"

Derek drew the solicitor forward. "Pritchard and I made no mistake. You're one of Lady Johanna's guardians. Of course you're to be included at the supper table. Fear not, Minton, it's not as if I've seated you next to His Highness."

Minton's eyes widened behind his spectacles.

Knowing the situation could turn explosive as a powder keg if Rosalie recognized Johanna as the former gardener's son, Derek had laid his strategies with as much care as any precarious battle. The invitation to Minton and the Coatworths asked them to arrive a full half hour before anyone else, allowing Johanna to prepare to meet his stepmother. Dressed in a simple cream-colored gown with aqua colored ribbons drawn under her high breasts, her chestnut hair piled atop her head with a single ringlet of curls allowed to escape over one shoulder, and the prized choker of pearls adorning her throat, Derek could hardly believe the heiress had once been a grubby boy.

The Vaughans arrived punctually. Derek had expected no less since his stepmother was acting as hostess for the evening. He would have preferred bestowing that honor upon Aunt Bess, but saw no sense in baiting Rosalie's ire needlessly. Derek greeted his family as they entered the drawing room and knew the moment Rosalie's gaze lighted on Johanna. Her lips closed together in a thin line of displeasure. Derek wisely avoided all eye contact with Harry.

Barely concealing her contempt, Rosalie's eyes narrowed on the heiress. After all her years of toil and patience, it was galling to meet this girl whose reappearance had robbed her family of their fortune. The girl possessed an uncanny resemblance to the gardener's son—the same coloring, the same eyes. But then, Curtis and Olivia shared many of the same features. No, Lady Johanna, nervousness reflected in her huge aqua eyes, was a princess who'd never known a day of toil. If she ever learned her dear father had sired a bastard, she'd probably faint.

Rosalie contemplated that lovely possibility as the heiress stepped forward at Derek's invitation to be presented. "Lady Vaughan, 'tis a pleasure to finally meet the rest of my distant cousins. Thank you for inviting the Coatsworths and I tonight. It was most gracious of you." She smiled demurely and dipped a curtsey.

Rosalie perused her from head to foot. "You're wearing the Vaughan pearls. How lovely." Forcing a smile, she motioned to her children. "This is your cousin, Olivia, and your cousin, Curtis."

Johanna expected a friendly welcome from Olivia, but seven months of her mother's constant tutelage showed its effects as Olivia lifted a brow and spoke with icy courtesy. "How do you do, Cousin Johanna?"

Curtis stepped forward to bow over her hand. "Your servant, Cousin. I hope you'll save me a dance this evening."

Johanna had to acknowledge that if she'd never met Curtis before, he would have made the most favorable impression of the three. As it was, she saw past the present—his raven hair, smiling blue eyes, and handsomely curling lip—to the tormentor of her past.

Despite her reservations, she drummed up a smile. "Of course, for you, Cousin, anything."

Olivia frowned, but Lady Vaughan's satisfaction broadened at this exchange.

Derek had no trouble foreseeing where Rosalie's mercenary mind would lead her. She was already busy arranging a marriage between Curtis and Johanna, granting her direct access to the Vaughan fortune.

Supper was a formal affair with sixteen at table. His Highness the Prince Regent sat at Lady Vaughan's right while Lady Jersey earned the distinction of being seated to Derek's right. Johanna found herself seated mid-table with Mr. Minton on one hand and Curtis on the other. She suppressed the urge to shift her chair away from her cousin and tried to engage in normal conversation. She was pleasantly surprised his manners were that of a gentleman throughout the meal. The Prince Regent smiled and waved at her from his position at the foot of the table, and Lady Vaughan looked as if she'd snapped up a canary. It was the most exhausting supper in Johanna's memory.

Following supper, both Johanna and Olivia and their families participated in the receiving line. Johanna silently hoped she would never hostess another ball in her life. If not for Harry's sense of humor, she might not have survived. At the head of the line, Derek had trouble focusing his attention on Lord and Lady Sumner when Johanna's laughter pealed through the hall.

Not one to go unnoticed, Lady Sumner raised her voice to introduce her youngest daughter, Charis.

Derek took the lady's hand and bowed over it. When he raised his eyes, he was astonished to see a true beauty before him. Charis Sumner, blonde and green-eyed, had a glorious complexion of ivory and dusty rose. Her dress was a pale yellow color, and clung to her well-formed frame. Derek, foreseeing a long night with few pleasurable moments, requested Miss Sumner to save him a dance. She blushed prettily, and her mother smiled broadly.

"There now, Your Grace, I knew you'd enjoy meeting my Charis. She's the best of the lot, just been presented this week. This is her first ball, and I hope she'll take."

Derek murmured a polite reply as he sighted the Sedgefields and Lord Worthing approach. Damn, he should have reviewed Rosalie's guest list. He steeled himself to parry pleasantries with St. John.

Paget and Mr. Pritchard looked on as the ballroom filled with gentlemen in knee breeches and young ladies in sheer dresses every color of a pastel rainbow. "You are to be commended, Mr. Pritchard," Paget acknowledged. "We are well-attended tonight."

Pritchard gave a deprecating shake of his head. "My task was simple. With the duke's and Lady Johanna's names on the invitation, practically everyone accepted. You and Mrs. North had the difficult chore of preparing the house. Not an enviable undertaking, I'm certain."

"Yes, Mrs. North and her staff made a heroic effort. The house is fit for royalty." The two men allowed themselves to smile. After a quick meeting of eyes, they returned to their duties.

Derek entered the ballroom with Sally Jersey on his arm.

"Emily Cowper has told me she's approved your sister for admission to Almack's," Lady Jersey said. "I shall want to meet your ward. She looked a fetching thing at dinner. Does she know her right foot from her left?"

"Well enough to lead the dandies on a merry chase. But she has a good heart, and a wit which may one day rival your own."

"Flatterer." Lady Jersey laughed. "Her fortune's intact?"

"More so than mine these days," Derek said with a rueful smile. "She comes with the largest dowry London has seen this generation. There's no property or title, but her money is invested in the Exchange and will grow annually. Invite her to Almack's and you'll have the highest male attendance you've seen in years."

"As if that's all we care about," she replied indignantly. But they both knew it was the truth.

Aunt Bess watched couples forming for the quadrille and experienced a pang of longing. How many years had it been since she'd stepped onto the floor?

Nigel Minton sketched her a bow. "Might I beg this dance, Mrs. Coatsworth?"

She pictured herself as one of the light-hearted women before her, and her pulse quickened. Despite his thinning gray hair and wrinkled brow, Mr. Minton had a wiry athletic figure, and she suspected he might prove a most able partner. "Thank you, Mr. Minton, I would enjoy that. Perhaps this one dance, and then, do you by chance play cards?" She spotted a gleam in his eyes even behind his spectacles.

"I have a penchant for whist, madam."

"Then let us retire to the card room after, for I'm sure Johanna is in very capable hands." Aunt Bess allowed Minton to squire her onto the floor.

Having promised to deliver the coveted Almack's vouchers to the house on Portman Square, Lady Jersey continued her rounds, leaving Derek, Harry and Johanna to sip their champagne.

Johanna touched Harry's sleeve. "Tell me about Lord Worthing. Don't you think he resembles Derek?" She tilted her glass toward the nobleman, looking equally elegant to the first time she'd seen him.

Derek coughed up his drink.

Harry looked from one to the other. "You'd best steer clear of Worthing, Johanna. He's a bit of a rake."

"Him?" She'd heard the term, but this was the first time she'd seen such a man. "He was most courteous to me at the Sedgefield ball."

"Lady Sedgefield is his eldest sister. Stickler for propriety. The Trevarthans have never known scandal, publicly at least."

"Johanna, I'll not countenance you associating with him," Derek said.

"But he said he was your friend."

"Did he?" Derek replied cordially. "He lied." He set his empty glass on a table and quit their presence.

Johanna turned wide eyes to Harry. "How am I ever to understand him?"

"Worthing and Derek were in the same class at Eton, but Worthing's connections were far superior then. He ostracized Derek, made his life at school pure hell."

"Why?"

Harry shrugged. "Prove his power, prove his worth. Derek was only eleven when his mother was tried for murder, and his family lost many friends and supporters. No one wished to be associated with such a notorious scandal."

She thought upon this while she watched Derek wend his way through the crowded room. She'd known the story of his mother's dark history since her childhood, but she'd never stopped to consider how it affected him. Derek was simply…Derek. "Why did he leave home?"

"He and his father argued over something. Derek won't discuss it."

For the first time, Johanna saw Derek as more than the handsome duke or even a friend. He was a man with a troubled past, a youth whose mother committed a heinous crime and blackened his whole family's reputation.

"But, Johanna," Harry cautioned, "I wouldn't trust Worthing. Though he and Derek have had a truce, I think he'd like to see Derek embroiled in another scandal."

She had no opportunity to reply before Curtis arrived with a flourishing bow. "Cousin Johanna, they're forming up for the *Roger de Coverley*. Won't you join me?"

Johanna smiled, and handed her glass to Harry. "Most assuredly, Cousin Curtis."

Derek traversed the ballroom, greeting the masses with a tight smile, until he ran his quarry to ground. "Worthing."

"Ambersley." St. John nodded. "So kind of you to invite me."

"I believe my stepmother invited you."

"Ah, did she? No doubt she fancies a title for your sister. Thank you for the warning."

"I'll give you another," Derek said. "Johanna is not for you."

St. John blinked then his mouth widened into an uncharacteristic grin. "I've barely met the young lady, much less declared my intentions."

"I've never had reason to trust you intentions, St. John, and I won't see her hurt." Derek stared into eyes as blue as his own. "Take whatever revenge you seek on me, but leave her alone."

His rival sobered. "Revenge is overrated." He stepped

away then turned back. "I regret I destroyed our friendship, Derek. Your duty to your ward is to be commended."

Derek watched St. John move among the throng, a man assured of his place in Society. He, too, was sorry their early friendship had suffered, but protecting Johanna far outweighed trusting St. John now.

Johanna tripped by on Curtis's arm as they danced. The way she smiled at his brother hit him like a bayonet lunge to the gut. Derek released a slow breath to control his reaction. He would have to bear watching her with numerous potential suitors for the next few months. At this rate, it was going to be an interminable Season.

"I say, Ambersley, been wanting to ask you all night, who cuts your coats?" The Prince Regent creaked up to stand beside Derek who cooled his thoughts as he lost himself in idle prattle with royalty for the next half hour.

Seeing Derek delayed by His Highness, Lady Vaughan left the ballroom to supervise the laying out of the midnight buffet. The evening was *not* going as planned. First, Derek was looking and acting every inch the duke. One day, he would sorely regret his betrayal, for she was even more determined to see Curtis take over Ambersley.

Second, Lord Worthing had proven as elusive as a fox. Though she disliked him, she recognized that he rivaled Derek in being the marriage catch of the past five seasons, and she wanted to introduce him to Olivia. Instead, she'd watched her daughter dance off with Worthing's young, handsome, and *poor* cousin, Mr. Barlow.

Olivia was faring well tonight, despite her nerves, but she was being eclipsed by Lady Johanna and that Sumner chit. Who would credit it? The elder two Sumner girls had been drab little birds. Why did the youngest have to be a diamond of the first water? It was not to be borne. Rosalie would have her revenge—on all of them.

Approaching the table, she checked her reflection in the silver punch bowl and touched the feathers in her hair. Her façade was unshaken—poised, polished, unflappable. She may seethe within but knew how to bide until the right moment.

Tonight she must portray the successful chatelaine.

Further down the table, Paget was deeply engaged in supervising the arrangement of chafing dishes. Finally, someone she could command without question.

"Paget, it's been too long. How is everything at home?"

He gave a brief nod of acknowledgment. "Very good, my lady."

She eyed the table's length. "It's quite a spread you're preparing. But the staff has been serving champagne since the dancing began. You must put a stop to it."

Paget bowed. "My apologies, my lady, but as the champagne was purchased by Lady Johanna, only she or his lordship may stop the serving of it. Believe me, we'll not run out." He watched her without blinking.

Her hands clenched, fingernails biting into her palms despite her gloves. Again, that Vaughan chit denied Rosalie her due. She'd find a way to dominate the heiress. The obvious solution was for Curtis to wed her. The more she contemplated the idea, the more she approved the potential results. Curtis would become wealthier than Derek, and that little heiress could be buried at Ambersley raising a passel of babies. Indeed, the only hindrance to her plan was securing Derek's approval to let the girl wed his brother.

Heavens—he wouldn't have designs of his own on the heiress, would he? Gathering her skirts, Rosalie hurried back to the ballroom to watch the heiress's every move.

As they sashayed through the country dance, Harry regaled Johanna with the story of his meeting Lady Charis. "A true beauty, and very elegant on her feet, but absolutely lacking in conversation. I asked if she were enjoying the evening, and she said 'yes.' I asked if she wanted to partake of the buffet, and she said 'no.' I was tempted to ask if she wanted to sneak away with me onto the balcony for a kiss just to see if it would shock her into more than a single word answer."

Johanna laughed at his foolery in a most unladylike manner. "A kiss on the balcony? How wicked of you— imagine your horror if she'd answered 'please!'"

Harry shouted with laughter.

"You're disrupting the floor," Derek whispered loudly as he danced by with none other than Charis Sumner.

Harry and Johanna shared a look and retired to the refreshments table where they could laugh their fill.

"Are you enjoying your evening, Lady Charis?" Derek asked the beauty.

"Yes, Your Grace," she managed to reply, a pretty color rising in her cheeks.

Derek tried again. "Will you be remaining in London for the Season?"

She nodded mutely.

Derek sighed inwardly. It was so often the case with the nonpareils—they shone like diamonds, but there was nothing beyond the first flash. He wondered how long the dance would last, and then sighted Johanna and Harry from the corner of his eye. Harry handed her a glass of champagne with a smile. Johanna accepted it and took a long slow sip, her eyes never leaving Charis. There her smile faded.

Derek considered the beauty in his arms in a new light. They'd told Johanna how sought after she would be, but did she understand what a prize Derek was considered on the marriage mart? Perhaps an illustration might make her look upon him more favorably.

He spun his partner and spied Rosalie on the opposite side of the room. Her tight-lipped smile and narrow eyes revealed her displeasure. Derek's lips twitched, but he held back from gloating. His stepmother's resentment toward Johanna was palpable. If she ever guessed he planned to wed his distant cousin, she'd do everything in her power to destroy his plans.

15

The Ambersley ball was accounted a masterful success, and Olivia recognized as one of the belles of the season. But Harry's prediction proved most accurate: the *ton* laid themselves at Johanna's feet. Calling cards arrived at Portman Square in such volume that Taft had to replace the small salver with a delicate silver basket. Johanna and the Coatsworths were included on every hostess's list for suppers, breakfasts, balls, musical evenings and more.

A month after her London debut, Johanna ransacked her wardrobe for something to wear to that night's round of parties.

Aunt Bess smiled at her vexation as she discarded dress after dress as having been worn too recently. "Now do you understand why we purchased so many things?"

Johanna shook her head. "It's a ridiculous waste, but I agree it will never do to wear the same dress twice in one week." Johanna finally settled on a peach gown that complimented the chestnut streaks in her brown hair. After visiting three parties, she calculated over seven hundred people would see this dress. With a sigh, she admitted she would need to suffer another trip to the dressmaker.

As little interest as she had in the endless merrymaking,

Johanna was determined to impress Society for Aunt Bess's sake. And so she suffered the tedium of dances, courteous introductions, endless glasses of lemonade and determined to have a good time. Were Harry present, this was easy. If he had other plans for the evening, Johanna donned a mask of vivacity and set forth with Aunt Bess. She wore the mask well, though it slipped a bit each time she caught Derek with Charis Sumner.

They met at many of the same functions, but in their guise of guardian and ward, he rarely sought her out for more than a perfunctory greeting. Whether he was complimenting the host on a successful party, chatting with the patronesses of Almack's or dancing with a wallflower, Johanna was aware of him. He was the most popular man in London—so popular, he didn't have time for his ward. While she danced and laughed at whatever her partner said, she tried to ignore Derek.

But he proved impossible to ignore. His rare laugh carried to her ears, or she spied his broad shoulders from the corner of her vision. Once she caught his blue eyes glowing by candlelight as he seemed to follow her movements, and she grew so lightheaded she feared she would faint.

She'd met countless men of varying ages and degrees, but none lingered in her thoughts to rival Derek. Except for Lord Worthing. Which was odd, because she'd only ever spoken to him at the Sedgefield ball. She saw him often at parties she attended or while riding in the park. He never approached her, and on such scarce acquaintance, she didn't dare approach him. She'd heard one young man say Worthing was famous for his set downs.

Not that his opinion scared her. After all, why should it? She'd learned he was a leader of the Corinthian set, a member of the Four Horse Club and he had four sisters—Lady Sedgefield being the eldest, and the youngest, a Miss Marianne, who had yet to be presented. Whenever he deigned to visit Almack's, the patronesses preened as if the rooster had entered the henhouse. But even Lady Jersey admitted he didn't seem to have an eye for any particular young lady.

Except, Johanna had the uncanny sense he watched her.

When asked, Aunt Bess had sighed over him. "Don't set your cap at him, Johanna. I've heard tell he's broken a fair number of hearts. Although," she said, tapping her forefinger against her chin, "you two would make a fitting match. I'll mention it to Derek." But Aunt Bess didn't speak of Worthing again after that.

Johanna didn't view him as a potential match. Nor did she agree with Harry that Lord Worthing still meant Derek any ill will. He roused her curiosity, nothing more.

By late May, Johanna had grown comfortable enough in London to walk with Nancy to Clark & Debenham in Cavendish Square whenever she needed to purchase ribbons, trims or other trifles. She'd just handed her purchase to Nancy and started down the haberdasher's steps when she spied Lord Worthing.

He saw her, too, and stopped to tip his hat. "Good day, Lady Johanna." Dressed for riding, he showed a good leg in his fawn-colored breeches and gleaming Hessians. Brightened by the early afternoon sunshine, his coat of pale blue emphasized the silver flecks in his eyes.

She dipped a curtsey. "Lord Worthing."

He looked about. "What, no warden today?"

"None but Nancy. It's only a short walk home."

"Then allow me to escort you."

Pleased to have an opportunity to speak with him again, Johanna agreed.

"Miss?" Nancy drew her attention. "Remember, you'll want to change before you go driving."

Worthing raised a brow. "Do you handle the reins?" He fell into step beside her.

"Not with any skill. Mr. Ardmore is taking me to test his new pair of matched bays around Hyde Park."

"Ardmore? I think not. He left for Sussex this morning. I was told he'd applied to Derek for your hand and was refused."

So great was her surprise, Johanna tripped on the hem of her skirt.

Lord Worthing steadied her elbow and peered down into

her face. "Did you not know?"

"That he planned to propose? No." She tried to fathom young Mr. Ardmore taking her in a passionate embrace, but the vision only made her skin turn clammy.

"Has Derek discussed any of your suitors with you?"

"There's been more than one?"

He tucked her hand into the crook of his arm and moved forward again. "It's hard to trust the rumor mill, but I can vouch for four men who've claimed they addressed Derek on the subject." He looked down on her, the intensity of his eyes unnerving. "May I be frank with you?"

With trepidation, she nodded. "I wish someone would be."

"Guard your heart, for there are a number of men at White's who've entered a pool of wagers concerning you."

"I don't understand."

His brow furrowed as he frowned. "There's no polite way to say this. A number of men are betting on who will become your husband. You have your own page in their betting book."

Embers of incredulity kindled deep within her and sparked to outrage. "I've never heard of such a thing!"

"No, and I shouldn't have told you, except—" His features softened as he smiled. "Except you strike me as rather an uncommon female. I felt you deserved to know."

Beneath his appraising gaze, Johanna's face warmed, and she tried to blame it on the sun. She touched her bonnet, but then a thought struck her. "Are *you* considering offering for me?"

Lord Worthing's lips curled into a wide grin, and the silver flecks in his eyes sparkled with repressed laughter. "My dear outrageous girl, how am I to answer?"

"Honestly, if you please."

He laughed at that. "I doubt Derek would look favorably on my suit. Besides, he'd be a damn fool not to marry you himself." He drew them to a stop.

She looked away from him and discovered they stood outside the Coatsworth house.

His finger touched her chin, and he tilted her face back to meet his gaze before releasing her. "You deserve a better husband than I would be, but I hope you shall count me as a friend."

"Derek has warned me away from you."

"Has he?" Worthing looked away, the sun lighting a tic in his cheek. "He's first and foremost your protector. He's probably right to keep you from my lecherous clutches."

Though his tone was dark, Johanna smiled. She liked his unexpected candor. Bravely, she laid a hand on his sleeve. His muscle tensed beneath the fabric at her touch. "I choose my own friends, and I shan't allow you to disparage yourself so."

His features softened again. "Brave girl. Now run along inside before Mr. Coatsworth sees fit to chase me off."

She doubted anyone could chase Lord Worthing away. "Thank you," she said.

He tipped his hat, turned on his heel, and strode away without a backward glance.

Nancy sidled up beside her. "Miss—?"

"I'd appreciate it if you'd forget everything you just heard, Nancy."

"Aye, Miss."

Johanna let them into the house and, leaving her bonnet on, went in search of Harry. She found him in the front drawing room dozing over a book. Normally, she would have allowed him to sleep, for he'd been keeping all sorts of odd hours, but her conversation with Lord Worthing pressed her to wake him. "Harry!"

"Huh?" The book slid from his fingers as his head shot up, and he shook it slightly. "Oh, Johanna. Say, got a note from Ardmore. He's been called out of town."

"Hmm. So, the rumors are at least partially true."

"Rumors? What rumors?" He retrieved the book and laid it on a table.

"I heard he asked Derek for my hand. Tell me," Johanna pinned him with an angry glare, "Is this the first man Derek has turned away, or have there been others?"

"Well, um…no. Not the first."

"How many?"

"Seven, maybe eight."

Johanna threw her arms upward. "Seven!" She wheeled back to face Harry. "You *knew*. You knew yet never said a word to me. Do you know of the bets at White's, too?"

His brows knit. "What bets?"

"On who will win my hand. Lord Worthing told me I've earned a page in the betting book."

"You in the betting book?" Harry pushed a hand through his hair. "The blackguard. He should never have shared such indecent information with you."

"Oh, so it's fine for men to be placing bets upon me so long as I know naught about it." She snorted with contempt.

"It wasn't Worthing's place to repeat such stories to you."

"No, it was yours."

"Mine? I'm not even a member of White's, how was I to know?"

"Then it was Derek's place." She stalked about the room, her anger continuing to build. To have men treating her as if she were no more than a pawn—it was too demeaning to be borne. "Derek should have put a stop to it."

"Aye, if you can trust Worthing's word. He might be trying to brew trouble."

"I doubt that. I'll take it up with Derek." So saying, Johanna swept out the door, leaving Harry behind in her disturbed wake.

Fueled by outrage, she defied convention and walked to Grosvenor Square unescorted.

Paget's smile dimmed when he saw she was alone, but Johanna speared him with her gaze and demanded to see the duke. With a bow, Paget led her to Derek's private study where he informed her His Grace was out this afternoon. No, His Grace hadn't said with whom. He'd taken his pair of matched grays and the landau. He was expected for supper, Paget assured her, and had expressed the intention afterward of attending a fireworks display with Miss Sumner and a party of friends.

Upon hearing this news, Johanna announced her intention to wait. Paget took her pelisse and bonnet away and returned with a glass of lemonade and some teacakes.

Johanna waited half an hour with ever-dwindling patience. She ignored the lemonade and teacakes, as she desired no hospitality from Derek. Another quarter hour frayed her temper to the breaking point, and she strode to the sideboard and poured herself a brandy. She downed a dainty portion with a gulp just as Derek, Charis and Lady Sumner entered the room laughing.

Spying Johanna with the open brandy decanter, his laughter stopped abruptly.

Her gaze swept from Derek to the two ladies, and she slammed down her glass.

Derek steered mother and daughter out the door. "Excuse me, Lady Sumner, Miss Sumner. My ward apparently needs to have a private word with me. Paget will show you to the drawing room, and I'll join you in a few minutes. Paget!"

With Charis and her mother safely out of earshot, Derek turned to scowl at her. "Will you never learn propriety, Johanna? Whatever must Charis Sumner think of you?"

His attitude stung. Charis must have the proprieties protected, but Johanna's name could be bandied about at his club. "I don't give a damn what she thinks of me."

"Very pretty, my dear." He opened the door. "Perhaps we should continue this discussion tomorrow."

"We'll discuss this now. I want to know what you said to Geoffrey Ardmore that made him leave town today."

A crack of laughter escaped him, but he shut the door again. "Left town, did he? I didn't think I gave him such a scare."

"Why should you scare him at all? What threat could he possibly be to you—unless, oh, don't tell me he had the audacity to ask you for my hand. Could that have been it?"

"And if it were? He's a boy. He's no business proposing to anyone at his age."

"Harry tells me there have been seven other men who have offered for me, Derek—*seven of them.* Who were they?"

"Would you like me to list them alphabetically?" he asked with maddening calm.

"Damn you—this isn't a joke!"

"No, it isn't. Very well, your suitors were Braithwaite, Terrelson, Campion, Halloran, Penbury, Burton and Goodwyn. Oh, and Ardmore of course. Now, *will* you go home?"

Johanna ignored this blatant attempt to be rid of her. "And did all of them have bets on me at White's?"

He pinned her with an intense stare. "Did Harry tell you of that, too?"

"No, Lord Worthing told me."

Derek's jaw hardened, and his eyes grew dark and glittery beneath hooded lids. "When did you speak with him?"

"I came upon him in Cavendish Square today." She lifted her chin. "He walked me home."

"Beware of him, Johanna." His tone, though quiet, was menacing.

She refused to back down before his anger. "Why do you fear him? So far, he's been nothing but honest with me."

An unpleasant laugh broke from him. "Honest? This paragon who sets upon you when I've warned him away?" With an effort he uncurled his fingers from the fists they'd formed.

Johanna blinked. Derek hadn't only warned Lord Worthing away, but Ardmore and all those other suitors, too. Suddenly, she understood. "I refused your offer, and now you're withholding your consent. And all because I hurt your pride—*your pride.* What about my pride? Oh, I keep forgetting, I'm but a woman, worthy of nothing more than a wager!" Intent on escape, she shouldered past him.

He grabbed her arm, alarmed at how she'd interpreted his actions. "Johanna, wait—"

"Don't touch me!" She fought to break free, but Derek's viselike grip only tightened until she stilled. "I hate you," she whispered.

"Maybe so, but we'll finish this now," Derek responded grimly. He'd waited patiently, but now he wanted answers. "So think carefully of all the men you've met this Season. Is there one among them you favor? Tell me his name, and I'll send out the banns."

She chose the name guaranteed to wipe the smirk from his

face. "Lord Worthing."

Derek released her as if she'd bitten him. "Has he addressed you?" he demanded.

Sensing she'd wounded him, Johanna looked away, afraid he'd read her guilty expression. "Not in so many words."

"Forget him."

"No." She braved meeting his gaze, unaccustomed to being at odds with him. "All I ask is the freedom to choose my own husband. Do you think me incapable of that?"

Sunlight from the window cast a gleam in his blue eyes. "No. You're wise enough to know your money makes you very attractive. And that bothers you, doesn't it?"

With a frown, she looked away, but he tilted her chin to study her face.

"You want a man to fall in love with you, not for your wealth or even your beauty, but for whom you are inside." Derek studied her flushed face, the parted lips, the brightness of her eyes, and tried to still the emotions roiling within him. "Perhaps one day a man will come along who steals your heart, and it'll never beat the same again."

She became conscious of the pounding of her heart as his arms enfolded her.

"Perhaps one day, he'll take you into his arms, and with one kiss he'll change your destiny."

Before Johanna could utter a protest, Derek's mouth swooped down and hungrily claimed hers. She stiffened, shocked by the sudden display of such intense emotion. Almost immediately, his lips became less insistent but more tempting. The soft coaxing caress of his mouth across hers was impossible to withstand. Her arms crept up to his shoulders, and she returned the kiss with an awakening hunger of her own, unwilling to allow this moment to escape. Though she'd secretly imagined this day, the kiss eclipsed her dreams.

As his lips moved to her ear and nape, Johanna found herself shivering against him. *Now,* she thought, *now he will tell me he loves me.*

His whisper penetrated her fogged brain. "We were made for each other, Johanna. End this mad quest, for your suitors may profess deep, undying affection, but they desire only your fortune. I, at least, won't play you false."

The proud moment shattered, Johanna's chin tilted up. Without a thought, her balled fist connected with his chin, and snapped his head back. She withdrew a step and nursed her knuckles while Derek rubbed his bruised jaw in disbelief.

"I wish you were dead," she said with conviction. She willed her shaking limbs to move and stalked from the room with dignity. She didn't wait for her bonnet and pelisse, but let herself out the front door.

Derek stood alone in his library for a long time after Johanna left, berating his own stupidity. She'd rejected his proposal, she'd sworn she hated him and she'd admitted to favoring Worthing. Yet, even after all that, Derek had been fool enough to kiss her. His sole excuse was that when she'd said she wanted the freedom to choose her own husband, he'd had an irrational desire to have her choose him. He knew he shouldn't have pressed her, but he'd needed to prove she still felt something for him.

He smiled ruefully and rubbed his chin again. She felt something—that was certain—though at the moment it was closer to hatred than any form of affection. Derek sank into the chair at his desk and tried to picture his life without Johanna. The bleak canvas filled him with disquiet.

Johanna and Worthing. The very thought repulsed him. Damn the man for involving himself in Johanna's affairs. As for the wagering at White's, Derek had torn the pages from the betting book that listed her name, and made his displeasure clear with the younger members—and some older ones who should have known better. But Worthing hadn't been present to witness Derek's gallant defense of his ward. Still, the man had no business repeating such tawdry details to Johanna.

Cushing entered the study and cleared his throat.

Derek glanced up with a sigh. "Cushing, I'm a fool."

"Yes, sir. Paget asked me to remind you that Lady and Miss Sumner are still waiting in the drawing room."

"Oh, yes." Derek stood. Damn, he was in no mood to play the besotted suitor to Charis. Unfortunately he had no plausible reason for excusing himself from his duties as host, and so he followed Cushing to the drawing room where Lady Sumner beamed at him, and Miss Sumner never guessed that most of Derek's thoughts were on another woman.

Lying on her bed in the house on Portman Square, Johanna's pulse finally slowed to its normal rate. Then, without warning, tears spilled forth a flood of anger, frustration, disappointment and yearning. She muffled her racking sobs with her pillow and tried her best to stifle these unwelcome emotions. She hated him, she reminded herself. He'd had no business kissing her, and *certainly* not when Charis Sumner was waiting for him in the next room.

She needed to forget ever loving him, to wipe from her memory the security of being held in his arms, the thrill of his kiss. He didn't love her, nor did he respect her. What he'd shown her today was the lust he'd explained to her in her youth. Let some other woman throw caution to the winds and share his bed. Johanna had her pride. *Yes*, responded her pride, *but I'm not fooled. You'd cast me aside in a trice if you thought you could make him love you.*

Johanna meekly acknowledged the truth of this, and set about seeking some bright side to the situation. Miserably, she decided, there was none.

16

If Johanna had thought attending the *ton* parties difficult before, following her fight with Derek the chore became unbearable. Pride forced her to continue the round of gaiety for she was determined Derek should never know she'd spent her tears on him.

Harry noticed the change and commented that her happiness seemed to have a vengeance about it. This drew him a withering look but no reply, and so he let the subject drop. He hoped Derek would tell him what had transpired between them, but his cousin only grunted the one time Harry noted how happy Johanna looked these days. When they met, Johanna and Derek spoke in icy monosyllables and parted company as quickly as decorum allowed, leaving Harry to mutter under his breath that the French court had less intrigue.

Their cold war lasted a fortnight before Rosalie caught wind of it and moved to take advantage of Derek's lamentable failure to control the heiress. Losing that chit's fortune was not acceptable. Eagerly, she cornered him at Almack's. "My dear, we haven't seen you in Harley Street all Season."

"I've been busy." He sipped his lemonade and wrinkled his nose.

She didn't care for his look of distaste. "Is it true, these rumors I hear about you and the Sumner chit? She's a fetching little thing, but somehow not just your style."

"And what do you consider my style?"

"I thought you would prefer a milder looking girl— someone with less flash and more fortune. She seems an unwise choice when there's an heiress available." She covered her mouth with her hand. "Oh, forgive me, she's your ward. Most awkward for you, I'm sure. Especially when the two of you can't seem to be civil with each other."

Derek set his glass down and folded his arms, his jaw tense.

"Did you think no one had noticed? How like you. It's the talk of the *ton*. Everyone is wondering what you did to put her in such a rebellious mood. She's walking the edge, and I believe she'll do something outrageous any day. Why, there she is with Reed Barlow. Isn't he Worthing's cousin? They say Barlow's the most handsome and charming man of the Season. Of course, he's a younger son, but still, Johanna seems to consider him most eligible."

Gritting his teeth, Derek did his best to ignore the pricks of her needling.

Rosalie fanned herself lazily. "Curtis is quite taken with her, too. He won't confess it, but I know him. I've tried to steer him away from her, feeling you might have some interest in that direction yourself. Of course, if you don't..." She allowed the statement to hang.

"Don't hold him off on my account. Lady Johanna has demanded the right to choose for herself."

She weighed his answer in silence. Finally, she nodded and left him in peace.

Derek rubbed the back of his neck to ease the tension there. His head had been pounding all evening. He shouldn't have come, for in his present mood, he was bound to say or do something regrettable. Watching Johanna's carefree behavior only darkened his mood. She'd all but dismissed him from her life. His only consolation was that Worthing seemed in no hurry to pursue her. Still, whether it was Worthing or another, Derek feared he may have lost Johanna's regard forever.

Worse, he had no idea how to redeem himself in her eyes.

With little interest, he danced his obligatory dance with Charis. After his attentions to her these past weeks, he couldn't cut her directly, but he was weaning her of his notice. He'd discovered that after getting past her nervousness, Charis could talk at length, just as her mother did. Unfortunately, neither Charis nor her mother ever had anything of interest to say.

He began the tedious process of departing, weaving through the crowd and chatting with his many acquaintances. It was nearly midnight, and Almack's was teeming, so he might make it out the door in half an hour. He'd hoped to avoid another *tête-a-tête* with Charis or Lady Sumner, but both stood in his path. They alone delayed him twenty minutes and tested his patience ten-fold. He finally excused himself by saying he would be leaving for Ambersley early the next morning.

Johanna watched Derek leave from the corner of her eye as she whirled through a waltz in Curtis's arms. The dance felt a little flatter after his departure. He hadn't even bothered to speak with her tonight. *I wish you were dead.* Five syllables she wished she could take back, but she didn't know where to begin.

The music ended with a flourish of strings, and Curtis conveyed her to the edge of the dance floor. "Would you like some punch?" he asked solicitously.

She nodded assent. His manners were impeccable, and he continued to surprise her with his humor and consideration. Had she misjudged him all this time? Had the barn fire been only an accident? Except someone *had* locked her in the harness room that day. Johanna strolled to an open window to catch the summer breeze. From the alcove, she overheard two familiar voices.

"Mama, why must he go to Ambersley now? There's a balloon ascension next week, and I wanted to go with him in his phaeton so everyone could see us together."

"Shhhh, my pet. There will be many other opportunities for that. Depend upon it, if he's gone to Ambersley, it's to ensure all is in order for his new bride. You must be patient and not breathe a word to anyone."

Johanna's darker emotions warred. There was jealousy, which she did her best to ignore. Then came a sickening frustration that Derek would marry that girl when Johanna couldn't comprehend what he saw beyond her beauty. Then anger and outrage bubbled to the surface, for how dare he leave for Ambersley without so much as a farewell to the Coatsworths and herself?

I don't know what I expected. We've barely spoken since that day. He's entitled to do as he pleases, but why her*?* Derek married to Charis Sumner. It dimmed her mood as if someone had trimmed the wick of her candle—gone was the excessive flickering she'd been casting for the past fortnight.

ঙ৵৻৶

The end of the week brought Aunt Bess a letter bearing the sad tidings of her cousin's death. She and Harry were discussing travel plans when Taft announced a visit from Lady and Miss Emily Brindle.

"Show them up, Taft. I promised Lady Brindle she and I could have a quiet coze while you escorted the girls on a walk around the park," she admitted to Harry. "We shall have to make our apologies, for we need to pack and be on the road as quickly as possible."

As soon as Taft ushered in their guests and quit the room, Aunt Bess apologized to Lady Brindle. "I'm afraid the girls will have to forego their walk today. I've just received word my cousin passed away in Tunbridge Wells."

Lady Brindle expressed her sympathy at once.

Aunt Bess nodded her thanks. "I haven't seen him for years, you understand, but he had no family except Harry and me. His wife died years ago. Harry, Johanna and I will need to leave in the morning."

"Then Emily and I will take our leave. Such a pity. Emily was hoping to get to know Lady Johanna better, but that can certainly wait." Lady Brindle rose with a rustle of silk.

Aunt Bess stood with her. "Yes, and it's such a shame to leave Town now, when I know Johanna was looking forward to attending the ball and fireworks display on Friday."

"It's not vital that she go with us to Tunbridge Wells, is it?" asked Harry.

"No, of course not. She won't know anyone there. But I can hardly leave her here unchaperoned."

"May I make a suggestion, Mrs. Coatsworth?" interrupted Lady Brindle. "I would be very happy to have Lady Johanna as our guest during your absence from Town. I'm sure Emily would be happy for the company, and Johanna could join our party for the fireworks on Friday."

Emily clapped her hands at the notion. "Famous! Johanna, please say yes!"

Johanna looked at Aunt Bess, not sure whether to accept or refuse. She liked what she knew of Emily, a pretty and outgoing girl with a bright wit and friendly manners. At one time she would have been terrified of staying as a houseguest without Aunt Bess's tutelage, but now she was curious to stay and keep watch on Charis. Still, her duty to the Coatsworths meant she should go with them, and she therefore deferred any decision. As if reading her thoughts, Aunt Bess accepted Lady Brindle's invitation.

Later that afternoon, Lord Brindle's coachman drove Johanna with Nancy and their trunks to Emily's house. Johanna, who had never before had a female friend her own age, marveled at the speed with which she and Emily formed a close-knit tie. It was extraordinary to talk to someone who understood and agreed wholeheartedly with all her own thoughts and feelings. The two girls talked without pause.

"Johanna? Have you ever been kissed?" Emily asked one night. It was late, and they were curled up in their wrappers on Emily's bed recounting their evening.

"Me?" Johanna squeaked. She'd been considering whether she could send a note of apology to Derek, and wondered how Emily had lighted on such a subject.

"You have, I can tell. You're blushing!" said Emily. "Famous! I never even guessed. Are you in love with him?"

Johanna felt the flaming heat rise through her cheeks straight to the roots of her hair as she recalled Derek's kiss.

Even as she willed herself to shake her head, she answered, "I think I am." *Heaven help me.*

"What's he like?"

Johanna considered not answering, but it seemed harmless enough to share secrets with Emily in the security of the darkened bedroom in the dead of the night.

She recalled Derek as he'd been around the boy, Johnny. "He doesn't have many true friends, but he's devoted to the ones he has. He says he doesn't like children, and yet he befriended a little boy and will risk anything to defend his sister. He's patient and kind and gentle. He's honest and righteous. He's brave and sweet. And all he wants is a peaceful life."

Emily smiled. "For a moment I thought maybe you were talking about your guardian, the duke, but those last few things don't describe him at all."

"No," Johanna replied, for the Derek she was describing was not the duke that everyone else knew. "He's someone I knew growing up."

"Are you going to marry him?"

Johanna shook her head. "I haven't seen him for years," she said, closing the subject.

ৡৼ

Two days later, Lady Brindle interrupted Johanna and Emily, their heads bent in discussion. "I've received a note from Mrs. Coatsworth that she and her son will be delayed in Tunbridge Wells a few more days. I hope you won't mind bearing us company a little longer, Lady Johanna."

"Not at all," Johanna replied with all honesty. She missed Harry and Aunt Bess, but Emily and her family had made her feel welcome.

"You'll still be with us to view the balloon ascension," Emily said. The idea of a man sailing up into the sky had captured her imagination.

Johanna forced a smile but wished Derek would return to Town, even if it meant watching Charis sit in his phaeton with him.

The rest of the day crawled along, until she looked forward to the evening at Almack's with anticipation—a first for her—as a way to escape her thoughts. She wore a dove gray silk, nearly silver in color, with a new pair of slippers that pinched her toes a bit. The late June evening had turned muggy following an afternoon of rain, but as they set out, the twilight skies appeared to be clearing, and she felt the soft warm breeze ruffle the single feather in her hair.

Almack's glowed with light and laughter, and happy music poured forth from the small orchestra. Mrs. Burrell greeted them as hostess, and Johanna looked upon the sea of familiar mothers and daughters sprinkled with dandies parading like peacocks—many dressed as brightly as the raucous birds.

"Come girls," Lady Brindle said, ushering them forward. "Let us find some chairs and a glass of punch for me, and then you may run along and dance your fill."

Pinning the familiar mask in place, Johanna pretended to enjoy the next hour. She remained politely suspicious of the men who requested a dance. Had this one placed a bet upon her at White's? Was the next hoping to apply to Derek for permission to propose to her? She was heartily sick of the topic of marriage, yet all around she witnessed the ritualistic mating dance.

Curtis claimed her for a reel, to her relief—another first. For the moment she could forget her woes and enjoy easy conversation. When the set ended, he escorted her to the punch bowl, where they met his mother, Olivia and—to Johanna's surprise—Lord Worthing.

Lady Vaughan wore a smirk as bold as her garnet-colored dress braided with pink. Her raven hair was dressed high with an ostrich plume. Johanna had always thought herself tall, but Lady Vaughan appeared to tower over all of them except his lordship.

"It was so condescending of you to dance with little Olivia, my lord," Lady Vaughan said. "She's still learning her way through the steps. I hope she didn't tread on your toes."

Olivia's lips tightened into a thin line.

"Not a bit," Worthing said with a smile for the girl. "She

was a charming partner."

"Ah, Curtis, you found your cousin, I see." Lady Vaughan's smile faded as she recited introductions. "I thought you had gone from town, dear," she said to Johanna.

"Harry and Aunt Bess went to Tunbridge Wells, but I'm the guest of Lord and Lady Brindle."

"How lovely. If only I'd known, you could have stayed with family."

Johanna's skin prickled as if a spider walked across it. "Perhaps some other time, my lady."

"Yes," Lady Vaughan agreed. Her eyes narrowed. "I've had word from Ambersley that Derek is suffering from an odd fever."

Johanna stiffened. "How—?"

"Cushing sent a groom to seek out Mr. Coatsworth." She waved a gloved hand at the triviality of the situation as she spoke. "But when the man found the house on Portman Square empty, he sought us out. Don't worry yourself, I've sent my own physician to see to him."

Instead of soothing Johanna, this only made her more anxious. "Has someone sent word to Harry?" she asked.

"No need for that," Curtis said. "Mother sent her physician. I instructed him myself to give Derek special care."

Concerned by his words, her teeth tugged on her bottom lip, but she held her silence as the orchestra launched into a familiar waltz.

"Lady Johanna, might I beg this dance?" Lord Worthing asked with a bow.

She gratefully accepted and allowed him to whisk her away from Lady Vaughan's palpable displeasure. But Johanna was too concerned by other things to give much thought to displeasing her distant aunt as she followed her partner's lead.

Lord Worthing chuckled softly. "It's quite humbling. I finally get you to myself with no fear of Derek tearing us apart, yet he still monopolizes your thoughts."

Her gaze swept up to meet his.

"It's written plainly on your face." He spun her in a tight, fast turn. "Why do you worry so? He's young and hale. The fever shan't trouble him long."

"He took a fever in India, and sometimes it recurs." Memories plagued her. "One time, a few years ago, Derek returned from London all pale and thin and drawn. Cushing told me his Master had suffered for over a week and nearly died."

"Cushing?"

"His valet."

He watched her, his brow knit, and one corner of his mouth pulled back. "You've known Derek a long time."

Belatedly, she cursed her slip. She waited, but he didn't press her with questions. Finally, she gave her thoughts words. "You asked me to count you as a friend. I'm in a need of a friend now."

"I'm at your service, my lady." He tilted his head to better hear her request.

"I must go to Ambersley at once," she whispered.

He drew back, though his steps never faltered. "Is that all?"

She waited for him to laugh at her—Derek would have. But he only studied her in that disconcerting way of his. "The fever might endanger him, and I don't—" She drew a breath and plunged into a confession. "I don't trust his stepmother."

This sharpened his attention. "Have you cause to distrust her?"

She allowed a tiny nod. "Please, Lord Worthing, if I try to explain, Lady Brindle will apply to Lady Vaughan for permission, and she won't want me to go. But I know about nursing, and I can be of help to Derek. He has no one else."

The silver flecks in his eyes glittered, and the hand resting at her waist tightened. "Then he's lucky to have you. What do you propose?"

She thought for a few moments. "We could step out to the balcony, then slip away and you could drive me to Ambersley in your coach."

"Without a word to anyone?" This time, his lips definitely twitched.

"You won't help me," she said, feeling foolish.

"My dear, I'd like to, but while Derek may be too sick to shoot me, Harry is not."

Johanna nodded with a blink, and they continued the waltz in silence.

Worthing sighed. "A woman's unshed tears will most definitely prove the death of me. Don't despair, my sweet Johanna. I shall call upon you tomorrow morning, and if you're still determined to leave for Ambersley, I shall find a way to convey you there."

"Thank you," she whispered. But even as she said it, she was considering a more immediate—and daring—plan.

ço≪

Within an hour, Johanna pleaded a headache, and the Brindle party returned home.

"What you need is a good night's sleep," Lady Brindle said as she climbed the creaking staircase with a candelabra flickering light onto the walls. "You girls have been staying up too late talking every night."

"I am rather tired," Johanna said quietly. She placed a hand to her head.

"I'll bring you a cool compress," Emily offered.

"No. I'm sure once I lay my head on the pillow, I'll fall right to sleep."

"Leave your friend be, Emily." Lady Brindle opened Johanna's door and handed her a candle. "We'll see you at breakfast, my dear."

"Thank you." Johanna stepped inside and closed the door. Quietly, she lit the candles by her bed and started to undress. Her stays gave her some trouble, but she'd rarely used Nancy's assistance at night. Stripped to her chemise, she opened the trunk at the foot of her bed and dug beneath the folded fabrics to withdraw a bundle wrapped in white paper and tied with cord.

As she unfolded the paper and withdrew the worn pair of breeches, voluminous white shirt, and embroidered waistcoat, doubts hammered her. But Derek's words from long ago soothed her. *Once you decide on a course of action, you must see it through. You can make a wrong decision and still come out of it in one piece. But when you begin to have doubts, when you don't take any action because you can't decide what to do, that's when you get your men killed.*

Quickly she donned the garments she had worn in another life. She rummaged in the bottom of the trunk until her hands fell upon her riding boots. The leather felt snug and stiff with inaction as she tugged them on. Thank heavens she'd decided to wear her hair up—all she needed was a hat. There, the battered tricorne was a little old-fashioned, but no one would question it on a servant.

Johanna checked her shadowy image in the tall looking glass and smiled at the reflected countenance of a tall boy who would never be mistaken for Lady Johanna Vaughan. Whether or not she could carry off this masquerade in the bright light of day she wasn't sure, but by dawn she'd be safe at Ambersley. She grabbed a sprigged muslin gown and a wool blanket. Looking at the myriad underclothes, she knew she'd never fit them in a saddle roll. With a philosophic shrug, she rolled up the dress, a chemise, a pair of stockings and shoes. She'd just make do until Harry and Aunt Bess came.

Like a mouse she descended the stairs and tiptoed into Lady Brindle's drawing room. By the light of her single candle, she found paper and ink and dashed off a quick note. *I've gone to Ambersley. Please, don't worry.* It dismayed her to think how she would anger Bess and Harry and frighten Emily and her mother. But she dared not risk time to write more.

She left the note on a table and snuffed the candle before sneaking through the empty kitchen and out to the Brindle's tiny mews. Saddling her horse in the dark was a chore, and she had to remind herself to move about slowly and quietly. As she led her mount from the stable, its clopping hoof beats thundered loud as cannon in the silent night. But her luck held, and no one stirred in the house.

She heard the watch cry out half past eleven o'clock as she reached the dark street. Only now did the enormity of her plan strike her. She wanted to ride to Ambersley by dawn. She needed to take the Bath road but had no idea how to find her way. At the street corner, she stopped to consider her next move.

A rustling in the moonlight provoked a nicker from her horse. She stepped closer to the animal's shoulder as another horse and rider materialized from the nearly black shadows. When the man dismounted, his lithe movements were unmistakable.

"Lord Worthing?"

"Damn," he muttered as he led his horse over. "What is that getup you're in?"

She pressed her lips together, though it was a little late to try to hide her plan. Finally, she stepped forward into the moonlight. "Why are you here?"

"Because, like you, I must be fit for Bedlam." He motioned for her to turn around, which she did. "You've masqueraded like this before. Can you ride astride?"

"Yes." The beginning of a smile dawned. "You'll help me?"

"How else am I to sleep, knowing you're traipsing about like a lamb in the dark?"

"I thought you'd send me back to the Brindles'."

"As if you'd stay." He shook his head. "I knew from the moment I first saw you, you'd be trouble. Do you need a leg up?"

She wanted to hug him, but settled for a happy leap onto her horse's back.

"You *have* done this before." He mounted his horse. "Someone should put you over his knee and beat you soundly."

"Try it," she challenged in a jaunty tone. When he looked at her, she cocked an eyebrow at him.

Lord Worthing barely checked his laughter. "I'll leave that for Derek. He may not be at all happy to see you, you know."

Her throat tightened as she recalled their fight. "I know."

"And you have no concern about riding off in the middle of the night with no protection but mine and, I might add, no protection *from* me?"

Her horse sidled up next to his. "Do I need protection from you?"

He raised his forefinger as if to lecture her, then his shoulders slumped. "No, I suppose not. Come, and while we ride, please apply your mind to how you'll explain away this fit of madness once we arrive at Ambersley."

"Is that all, my lord?"

"One thing more—remove your ear bobs."

Chagrined, she quickly pocketed the jewels, and with a nod of thanks to him, they set forward at a smart trot. The full moon bathed the two dark riders in its silvery light as they cleared the city gates and whipped their mounts into a ground-eating gallop.

17

Cushing gritted his teeth as Dr. Wardlaw placed the leeches, one by one, on the duke's prone form. Cushing wasn't sure which he hated more, the leeches or the physician himself, but as the barber—who'd cupped the duke thrice in as many days—had already shaken his head in defeat over the duke's illness, Cushing didn't dare turn this man away.

Derek hovered between a feverish state of consciousness and oblivion. The fever had run its course for four days now, and its toll was pronounced. He lay inert, an unhealthy pallor to his normally rugged skin. The dozens of leeches left tiny trickles of blood as Dr. Wardlaw moved them. It gave Cushing the chills, but he felt powerless to defend his master.

The physician stopped his ministrations long enough to pour himself a glass of brandy from the crystal decanter. Cushing stoically didn't react to this open thievery even when the man turned and saluted him before downing the liquid in a gulp.

"Ahhh, if one has to sit up all night with a patient only to lose him, the least one should get is a good brandy."

With a start, Cushing approached the bedside and saw his master's labored breathing.

The physician nodded. "His lungs are getting worse, and I can't remove blood from him fast enough. You may be seeking a new job before the day's over."

Cushing soothed his outrage with the promise that if the duke died, he would seek out and pay a visit to the good physician.

Outside, Johanna jumped from her lathered horse and ran up the wide steps to the front door before Worthing could dismount. She slid into the front hall and called up the stairs. "Paget?"

Paget peered over the railing. "Johnny!" His eyes widened as Worthing entered behind her.

She spared no breath on explanations. "How is the duke?"

"Very ill. Cushing is upstairs with him and Lady Vaughan's physician."

Johanna didn't like the dark emphasis the butler placed on the last word. Taking the stairs two at a time, she ran unerringly to the master bedchamber door and burst through it like a whirlwind. She quickly surveyed the candlelit scene then raised her eyes to a surprised Cushing. "How is he?" she entreated.

The burly valet shook his head grimly. "It's not good."

"Cushing, who is this?" Dr. Wardlaw demanded. "How dare he barge in here and interrupt? You—what are you doing? Stop that! Stay away from him."

Johanna leaned over the duke and tried to swallow the lump in her throat. Derek was far more ill than she'd imagined. She turned to Cushing. "How long has he been like this?"

Dr. Wardlaw spun her by the shoulder. "The duke has been ill for nearly a week. Now you must leave at once," he said forcefully.

Nonplused, Johanna cast her eyes over the physician's pudgy face, badly tailored coat and worn shoes. "Pack your things, and I'll have the coach deliver you to Ambersham. Your services are no longer required here."

The physician gave a blustery laugh. "Young man, I'm here at Lady Vaughan's own direction. Who do you think you are to order me around?"

"I'm the duke's ward."

"You look no better than a servant. You've no authority here."

"Then you may leave on my authority," came a voice from the door. "Tell her ladyship the Marquess of Worthing discharged you."

Dr. Wardlaw sputtered and turned crimson. "This is an outrage!"

"I agree," Worthing said, his bored tone barely concealing contempt. "The whole night's been outrageous, so don't try my patience further. Now *leave*."

Cushing blew out a breath and turned on the good doctor with a predatory smile.

The physician grabbed his bag and fled the chamber.

"Thank you," Johanna said.

Worthing stepped closer to look over her shoulder and shuddered at the sight of the many leeches. "You were right to come. I'm not sure the bloodletting is helping."

"He continues to grow worse," Cushing murmured. Fatigue etched the giant's face.

Johanna touched his arm. "I wager you haven't left his side since he fell ill."

He grunted a non-committal reply.

"You're not alone anymore, Cushing. I'm here, and I won't let anything happen to him."

"Admirable, my dear," Worthing said behind her. "But don't you think we should remove those…those…" He didn't seem to be able to name them.

Johanna peered over her shoulder to find their long ride had left him rumpled and wind-blown. "Would you fetch Cushing a brandy, my lord, and perhaps one for yourself?"

That slow smile of his appeared. "An excellent notion." He went unerringly to the table holding the decanter and glasses.

Cushing stayed with her. "I don't need spirits, my lady. What may I do to help?"

"For now, I want you to sit. You look dead on your feet." Before she could ask, Worthing corralled the servant and drew him to a chair where Cushing's knees all but collapsed as he dropped into it.

Johanna drew a ragged breath, but with firm resolve began to pluck the leeches from Derek's body. "I need something for these."

Cushing tried to rise. "There's a bowl—"

"I'll get it," Worthing said as he pushed the bigger man back into the chair. "Your mistress said sit—I expect you to comply."

Cushing blinked, but didn't question the voice of authority.

Worthing brought the bowl and held it for her to dispose of the slimy creatures. "Those *things* don't make you squeamish?" He winced as one of the creatures fell onto his hand.

"They're not so different from slugs or snails," she said. She lifted a wet sponge from the bucket near the bed and wiped Derek's chest as she cleared away the leeches, erasing the tiny trails of blood they left behind.

Derek twitched under her ministrations, but his sounds and actions were unintelligible.

As she dropped more leeches in the bowl, she glanced up to find Worthing contemplating her.

"Is there anything you cannot do?" he asked. His normal sarcasm was conspicuously absent.

So many things. "Needlework," Johanna replied, holding her fears at bay. She paused to smooth Derek's brow, hot and dry beneath her hand. "I dislike it so, I have no heart to apply myself to it."

Worthing touched her shoulder. "Apply your heart to the important things."

She closed her eyes at his words. "I would have come sooner had I known."

"I hope Derek appreciates his good fortune at having you."

Reopening her eyes, a sad smile pulled at her lips. "He doesn't even know I'm here."

"He will." Worthing squeezed her shoulder before dropping his hand. "Don't leave him."

She turned to look at him, but found he studied Derek's haggard face. "What lies between the two of you?" she asked.

"The same thing that separates us."

There was no mistaking the regret in his voice, which

perplexed Johanna.

Derek muttered something in a dry rasp, drawing her immediate attention. She bent over to take his hand in hers while she considered potential remedies to fight his fever.

A soft rap heralded the arrival of Paget with a fresh bucket of cool water. Behind him Mrs. North carried Johanna's saddle roll, and Mrs. Chalmers brought a welcome tray of food.

"Rory is taking the physician to town in the pony trap," Paget announced.

"And good riddance," murmured Mrs. Chalmers. "I never liked the way that man always cleared his plate but never made His Grace eat."

"How is he, Johnny?" Mrs. North asked.

Johanna straightened and studied their solemn faces. They all awaited her leadership, and she knew she couldn't depend on better people to help her.

"He has a high fever, and his breathing is labored and shallow, but we *will* save him. Do you understand me?"

They nodded, one by one.

"Good. Mrs. Chalmers, I'll need some broth and milk. Also, find some mustard seed, flour, yeast and vinegar to mix a mustard plaster. Mrs. North, please leave my roll in my bedroom, then this room needs to be aired out. Paget, thank you for the fresh water—the duke will need more bathing. Cushing, I want you out of here until after dawn, and I expect you to sleep. You'll be of no help to us if you go down sick. Take these things with you, and dispose of them." She handed him the bowl of leeches.

Mrs. Chalmers set down the tray and left for the kitchens, Mrs. North in her wake. Cushing looked like he might argue, but Johanna quirked a brow at him, and he gave a silent nod and left.

Worthing stepped forward. "What, no commission for me?"

"I hesitate to ask."

"You have only to name it." The silver in his eyes glittered in the flickering candlelight.

"Harry and Aunt Bess should be told—"

"I should have foreseen a ride to Tunbridge Wells," he said with a curl of his lip that somehow wasn't a grin. "Allow me a brief meal and a fresh horse, and I'll leave at once."

"You've had no sleep," she said.

"Neither have you, and I doubt you'll see a bed any time soon. Leave it to me. I'll have them here as quickly as possible."

"What will you say to Harry?" she asked, remembering that Harry didn't trust Lord Worthing.

"I shall simply tell him *Johnny* needs him at Ambersley because the duke is ill. I suspect that will fetch him and his good mother."

Johanna's shoulders slumped. *Yes, they'd definitely respond to that message.*

"Fear not." Worthing chucked her under the chin until she met his gaze. "Your secret is safe with me."

"How shall I ever repay you?"

"Help Derek. He needs you." Worthing released her. "And perhaps, one day, you'll entrust me with the story of your past." With that, he quit the room, leaving her with only Paget and the duke.

Johanna dipped a fresh handkerchief into the bucket and dribbled water into Derek's mouth. The scar he'd received the day of the barn fire flared angry red from the fever.

Paget cleared his throat. "I'm glad you've come, Lady Johanna, I won't deny, but if you'll pardon me for—"

Johanna stopped him. "I won't pardon you, Paget. Don't bother to judge my actions, for I care not for your or anyone's opinion. This is where I belong, and so I am here. Now, will you help me or not?"

Paget nodded. "I'll do my best, Lady Johanna, but none of us know anything about nursing."

"I do. Martha taught me. And for the time being, Paget, think of me as Johnny. It'll be easier on all of us."

❧

Johanna watched the full moon ascend in the sky. Over the past three nights, she'd formed quite a bond with the luminous disc. She'd ridden at a full gallop beneath its light, and this was the second night it had borne her company while she watched over her patient. Most people misunderstood the moon. It wasn't cool and distant, shrouded in mystery. The moon waited in the sky and offered its friendship to the people below, but was often overlooked in favor of its brilliant rival. The moon encouraged silence. It kept your secrets. It presented your worst fears, yet it offered hope when the bright reality of day denied there was any hope left.

Throughout the day, Derek had thrashed about, muttering incoherently. By dusk he grew quiet, but his breathing was labored and uneven, his pulse raced, and his haggard face had turned ashen. Alone with her patient, Johanna felt her own panic rise. She feared she was losing him.

Throughout the evening she and Cushing continued to bathe Derek with sea sponges dipped in cool water. Whenever he was conscious, they lifted his head and spooned ale or broth into his mouth. Finally, Cushing convinced Johanna to get a breath of air and eat some supper. She took a crust of bread and a glass of wine to the window and marveled at the huge fiery orange full moon rising in the east. Never before had she seen the moon so large or brilliant, and she recalled Derek had once told her of the moon's beauty in the wilds of India. She wanted so much to share this with him—

Cushing's voice broke into her reverie. "Johnny, he's shaking—come see!" Johanna rushed to the bedside to find Derek covered in perspiration and shivering.

"He's sweating, Cushing. The fever's *broken*." Tears stung her eyes.

Cushing laughed in response as he grabbed a quilt to toss over his master. Johanna fetched two more blankets while Cushing went to bank the fire. Their tasks complete, he led her to the fire and lowered her into a chair. "One thing is certain— we wouldn't have saved him if you hadn't come. I was never so surprised to see anyone as I was to see you the other night."

"Why should you be surprised?" she asked as he handed wine to her. "You knew if you sent word Derek needed me, I would come immediately."

"No, I didn't. You and the Master must have had one hell of a row. I wasn't sure I'd ever see you at Ambersley again."

Johanna bowed her head. "'Twas but a foolish argument, Cushing. I said things I shouldn't."

He nodded. "That explains it. The Master has been mighty grim ever since he returned. Now, you should get some sleep."

"No, Cushing. I slept some last night, and you made me nap this afternoon. You should sleep now because in the morning Derek will need you. Come, help me make him comfortable before you go."

After the servant left, Johanna snuffed all but one candle. She glanced Derek's way, but his steady breathing was less labored than the previous night. She left him to his rest and quietly tidied the room. Wiping her hand down her waistcoat, she glanced over her clothes. She still wore the same breeches and shirt in which she'd arrived, and until now hadn't spared them a thought. While she longed for a relaxing soak in a tub full of hot water, she pragmatically opted for a sponge bath. For years she'd taken sponge baths at the little cottage, and since she'd revived her role as Johnny, it seemed fitting.

She doffed her clothes, and sponged her lithe body by firelight. She twisted her hair up and out of the way—washing it would have to wait until the morrow. Soon she was scrubbed and glowing, and only a little chilled as she dried herself by the hearth. Too late, she recalled asking Mrs. North to take her saddle roll to the bedroom down the hall.

Pushing her hair back, Johanna convinced herself Derek wouldn't mind her borrowing one of his shirts. She quietly rifled his wardrobe and donned a white shirt with full sleeves that covered her thighs halfway. The fine linen felt soft against her skin, and she was grateful for anything after the three-day-old clothes.

She checked once more on Derek, who slept with only the faintest of wheezing as he breathed. His cheeks were still flushed with fever and overgrown with black stubble. Johanna had never imagined him with a beard, and it was all she could do not to trace the outline of its growth across his normally smooth skin. She reached a hand toward him, then pulled it back to stroke her own neck instead as she recalled how intimate she'd become with Derek's body while nursing him. She'd seen every inch of him, and every inch was magnificent. He'd be angry about the impropriety of her behavior, but she'd been a good nurse and never thought of anything beyond making him well. Only now could she afford to let her mind wander back to that fateful kiss he'd given her in Grosvenor Square. The memory left her yearning to feel his touch again.

Johanna turned a wing chair so she could watch over Derek as he slept. Dragging a blanket around her hips and legs, she curled up in the chair and tucked her bare toes under her. She watched over his prone form and considered her impetuous action of coming here. Harry would have rushed to Derek's side as quickly as she had, she knew. But Harry was a man, and Derek's devoted cousin. Johanna found it demeaning that Harry could travel about unquestioned while she would have to recite a litany of answers. She preferred not to consider those answers too closely just yet. With a last glance at Derek, she resolutely closed her eyes and courted sleep.

Derek awoke with a crushing headache and parched throat. It took him a moment to gain his bearings and realize he wasn't feeling the ill effects of a night of drinking but was simply *ill*. Slowly, he raised his head. A single candle glowed, and the fire burned low in the grate, but neither shed enough light for him to focus on anything. Overheated, he couldn't summon the strength to throw off the heavy bedcovers.

A soft rustle stirred the darkness, and suddenly Johanna was setting the candle beside the bed. In the soft light, Derek noted dark shadows beneath her eyes. Her competent hand smoothed his forehead and he almost groaned with pleasure when she bathed his cheeks with soothing cool water. It was a compelling fantasy he'd entered with Johanna, clad simply in one of his shirts, ministering to him. Only when she tilted a glass to his lips and he tasted barley water, did he doubt his fertile imagination. With effort, he raised his hand to touch the cool glass and her warm fingertips.

"Johanna?"

"Shh," she replied with a little smile. "Johanna's not allowed to be here. I'm Johnny." She tried to withdraw her hand.

"Don't go."

"I must heat up the broth. You've eaten very little these past few days." She eased her hand from his.

"I'm not hungry."

"You need to eat anyway." When he started to disagree, her tone became firm. "Don't argue with me. I'm much stronger than you for the moment. Let me put another pillow behind you."

Derek had a dozen questions, but he didn't raise a single one as Johanna leaned over to adjust the pillows. He recognized a faint familiar scent of lavender when she put a capable arm behind his back. The curve of her breast pressed against his shoulder and he smiled at the unexpected pleasure. She padded barefoot to the fireplace, candlelight playing across the backs of her calves. Derek didn't care what good fortune had brought her to Ambersley, he only knew that already she'd dispelled the bleak loneliness he'd felt since returning home. In moments, the smell of simmering beef and sage filled the room and Johanna returned with a small bowl.

"I can feed myself," Derek croaked as she raised a spoonful of dark broth.

Her brow quirked but she passed him the bowl. "Fine, but you'll wear yourself out."

She pulled the blankets back and Derek was grateful to lose their heavy weight. He spooned the watery stew carefully into his mouth and heard his stomach growl its thanks. Johanna moved about the room, adding another log to the fire, lighting a candelabra on the table, folding a blanket and laying it on the chair.

She returned to his side. "Tired now?" She took the bowl from him and, seeing it still half full, shook her head. "Weak as a kitten, but at least you won't waste away overnight."

Derek met her gaze squarely. "I would have rather thought you'd prefer me out of the way."

"Oh, don't say that," she protested.

To his surprise, a single tear traced its way down her soft cheek. "Here, now. What's amiss?" Derek pulled her down to sit beside him on the bed.

"I feared you might die before I could apologize for the awful things I said in London. You were very provoking, but I was wrong to behave so."

"I fear you provoked me as well."

"I should never have wished you dead."

"That was the most provoking of all," he admitted.

"You know I didn't mean it."

Derek gently wiped her damp cheek with his thumb. "Ahh, but at the time, you see, I thought you might."

"Oh, Derek, don't say that. You must know that I've…come to count on you—your counsel—ever since I was a child." She lifted aqua eyes to gaze directly at him. "I'd be lost without you."

She locked her fingers with his and gave his hand a squeeze to add evidence to her statement. It was a gesture she'd often used as Johnny, but Derek saw no traces of the gardener's son. She was the daughter of a duke, beautiful and unobtainable. Yet she was here in his bedroom sharing confidences with him.

Johanna smoothed a stray lock of dark hair from his forehead, her cool hand soothing his brow and even more his soul. When she finally withdrew, he snatched her wrist midair and pressed a kiss against her palm.

Instead of pulling away, she leaned forward.

Encouraged, Derek traced his fingers up the collar of her shirt to stroke her nape in a slow caress. Her hand dropped softly to his bare chest, and with a moan, he pulled her to him and hungrily captured her lips in a lingering kiss. Her tentative response, the splaying of her fingers on his ribs, the opening of her mouth beneath his gentle onslaught undid him. He plunged his hands into her loose hair as if afraid she would withdraw from his lips even as he branded her with their sensual warmth.

He wasn't sure whether a moment or an eternity had passed when a noise at the door made her pull away from his viselike grip. He released her with reluctance and even more reluctantly she lifted her head.

Derek looked up into her dilated eyes. Her lips, red and moist from his kisses, parted as she tried to catch her breath. His gaze roamed over her features, down to her white throat, pausing to wonder how it would taste, and further to where the linen gaped open. He caught his breath—until now he hadn't realized she wore not a stitch of clothing but for his shirt.

"Well, well. Isn't this a cozy picture?" Rosalie Vaughan stood in the open doorway and removed her gloves. "I'm so glad I told Curtis and Olivia to await me at the Dower House, for this scene would scarcely be fit for their eyes."

Johanna deftly slipped off the bed and would have retreated, but Derek still held her by one hand. She clutched her shirt collar close to her throat and stared back with wide eyes. "What are you doing here?"

"Saving you from utter ruin, apparently—or is that what you want?" Rosalie stepped into the room and tossed her gloves onto a stool by the wardrobe. "Here I thought I was rushing to protect Derek from the misguided notions of that stable boy, Johnny. Now I see the truth. I've been very stupid, haven't I? To think you've been enjoying each other under our very noses all this time." She smiled darkly.

Cold fury brewed within Rosalie, but at last, she held the power. To think that bastard stable boy Johnny had metamorphosed into Lady Johanna—they'd played her for a fool. But now she had them cornered, and she would exact her revenge. "Congratulations, my dear. You've been very discreet—until now."

Derek squeezed Johanna's hand then released her before trying to sit up.

Immediately, Johanna pressed his shoulders back to the pillow. "No, you'll bring on the fever again. Lie still."

Rosalie watched their tender interaction but noted the fatigue etched in Derek's features. "In truth, you don't look well at all." She reached toward his forehead. "Perhaps we should fetch a physician."

"Stay away from him!"

Rosalie recoiled, biding her time to strike. "Watch your tone with me, *young lady*." Sarcasm laced her final words.

The distraught little chit stepped between Rosalie and the bed. "You won't touch him while I'm here. I'll throw you out myself if I must."

Rosalie allowed herself a small laugh as she stepped to the foot of the bed. "The kitten has discovered her claws but I warn you, my dear, do not sharpen them on me. If indeed you nursed Derek back from death's door all by yourself, I'd be the first to commend you. Were your methods not so *painfully* obvious," she added with a sniff.

Derek's jaw tightened. "She didn't come alone. Aunt Bess and Harry are here."

Johanna froze as Rosalie raised her brows. "Is that so, Johanna? I was told you arrived three nights ago on horseback. And we both know the Coatsworths are in Tunbridge Wells."

"What's this?" Derek succeeded in pushing himself to a sitting position with, it appeared, much effort.

The chit shook with suppressed emotion as she explained herself to him. "Aunt Bess's cousin died and they went to the funeral, but I stayed in London. When Lady Vaughan told me you were ill, I came immediately, as was my duty."

"Your duty," Derek said slowly.

Rosalie's eyes narrowed on them. "I suppose you felt it was *your duty* to crawl into bed with him, too."

"I didn't—" Johanna began.

"Enough!" Derek commanded.

Rosalie pursed her lips at the way he always protected his precious heiress. A pity she hadn't been able to convince him to murder that boy Johnny on the dueling field.

"Decidedly enough," she said. "But for one thing, Johanna. Whatever have you done with poor Lord Worthing?" Pleasure surged through Rosalie as she watched the chit blush crimson before her head fell forward and hid her face.

"Worthing? What's this?" Derek looked back and forth between her and the chit. Oh, yes, she'd agitated him.

"Did you not know?" Rosalie made no effort to hide her condescension. "Dr. Wardlaw returned to London and told me the *oddest* story that he'd been ejected from Ambersley by the Marquess of Worthing and an impudent servant boy who claimed to be the duke's ward. They arrived unannounced in the wee hours of the morning. Tell me, Johanna, did you leave Worthing in sated slumber then come here to awaken Derek?"

Johanna raised her head but, instead of the frightened child she anticipated, the eyes of an angry tigress blazed back at her. "Do not insult him so. Lord Worthing has been nothing but good and kind to me. Even now he's gone to fetch Harry and Aunt Bess. The staff will tell you he left nearly as soon as he delivered me here."

"Oh, of course, Paget and the rest will tell any story you ask of them." She spoke to Johanna but watched Derek from the corner of his eye. His jaw tightened as the chit argued Worthing's defense. That long rivalry might prove as tragic as the bare heel of Achilles. If nothing else, she could count on Derek to ensure the girl never married the marquess.

Derek contemplated Johanna with stony eyes. "Worthing brought you here in the dead of night alone?"

The chit took a step toward him but something, perhaps his icy demeanor, made her hesitate.

Mistake.

"I was already disguised as Johnny. Worthing caught me sneaking away from the Brindles' house. I would have come on my own, but he provided me safe escort. I'm indebted to him."

"How indebted?" Derek's voice had taken on a decided edge.

"Now, Derek, don't blame the child," Rosalie said. "Mayhap she had no scheme in mind when she involved him in her little escapade. But if Worthing knows her secret, he may try to force your hand. He may have an eye to her fortune."

"Worthing's never courted me," Johanna protested.

"Now, he need not." Rosalie couldn't be happier with the way the girl had played into her hands. "Worthing could create a scandal the Vaughans haven't known since Derek's mother—" She covered her lips, but let the thought hang without apology.

He flinched at her barb.

Now was the moment to strike.

She looked at his implacable face and dredged up that beseeching tone she'd used all too often with him over the years. "We must rally around Johanna now. I don't think she's any idea how disastrously she's endangered the whole family. What can one expect after the upbringing she's had? And I hate to see Worthing take advantage of her so." *Especially when he has no need of her fortune.*

Derek's eyes narrowed and slid sideways to meet her gaze briefly. "And what do you propose?"

"Curtis will marry her."

"What?" Johanna cast beseeching eyes at Derek. Did she expect him to defend her? How quaint.

Rosalie held her breath while Derek contemplated the suggestion. "Curtis and Johanna."

"Her fortune will secure the entire Vaughan family, yet the scandal will be kept one step removed from the Ambersley title," she explained. "I'll let it be known she left the Brindles to visit us in Harley Street. All we need do is silence Worthing."

Derek's lips flattened in a grim line. "I'll handle Worthing. And I'll secure a special license. But Johanna will wed me and no other."

Victory slipped from Rosalie's grasp and she clawed to regain it. "You? No, you're to offer for the Sumner chit. Think of the scandal—"

"'Tis my scandal, so I shall marry her." Perspiration beaded Derek's now-flushed face. "No need for Curtis to clean up my mess."

Johanna trembled. She'd gone so white, it looked as if she might faint. "Derek, you don't need to do this."

He eyed her coldly. "Did Worthing compromise you?"

"No." She responded as if he'd bitten her.

"Then I will marry you." Fury welled up within him, for this wasn't how he'd planned to win Johanna's hand. Yet, cornered as he was, he wouldn't allow the opportunity to slip through his fingers.

"But—"

Derek cut her off, afraid she would convince him to release her. "You said it was your duty to come to me when I was ill. You gave no regard to the cost. Now it's my duty to marry you. I'll brook no argument."

Bravado abandoned Johanna, and she crossed her arms before her. "I never meant for this to happen," she stammered.

"Nor did I," Derek conceded with a tired sigh.

"I'm sorry," Johanna whispered before fleeing the room.

Rosalie watched her go and barely tempered a tight smile. "Poor child. She seemed upset. Shall I go after her?"

"Leave her be," Derek said bitterly. "You've done enough for one night."

"You cannot mean to marry her."

"I do."

"You've denied Curtis his title, and now you'll deny him a wealthy bride?" With the chit was gone, Rosalie unleashed her frustrations.

"Curtis denied himself the title by exercising dangerously poor judgment."

"Don't you *dare* marry her and try to keep Curtis from his title—"

"I warn you, Rosalie, do not dictate to me." Derek slumped back against his pillows. "I shall marry Johanna, and nothing you say shall dissuade me from it."

He'd always been a stubborn, proud man. But then it occurred to Rosalie that perhaps she could persuade Johanna against such a marriage.

"Very well, I'll leave you to your sleep, my lord." She gathered her gloves and left his room, closing the door behind her. She whispered a brief prayer that Derek Vaughan would simply die.

Alone, Derek closed his eyes. Guilt preyed upon him for he felt like a thief stealing Johanna from under Worthing's nose, but if the man had wanted to press his advantage, he'd still be here, laying his claim. Whether she believed she loved the marquess Derek couldn't say, but he did know that she'd said she favored Worthing, and she'd turned to him when she needed help. Meanwhile, she felt a *duty* to Derek, as if she'd never overcome being one of his servants.

Clearly, given a choice of husbands, Johanna would choose Worthing. That, and his stepmother's machinations, had prompted Derek to claim Johanna at once. He'd long since admitted he wanted her at any cost, but this…

Visions of her haunted him. Johanna, padding to the fireplace in the white shirt. Johanna, her brow quirked, daring him to feed himself. Johanna, lying across his chest with passion lighting her eyes. Johanna, standing defiantly nose to nose with his stepmother. Johanna, beaten and retreating from him, her life in ruins.

Some day, Derek swore, he would make it up to her.

18

In the relative safety of her chamber, Johanna paced in agitation. The bed offered no respite, for she knew she wouldn't be able to sleep now that the pre-dawn sky had turned pale blue. How she missed the moon.

Opening the armoire, she discovered her things had been unpacked, and Mrs. North had considerately found a moment during the past few days to press her gown. She slid the linen shirt off only to clutch it to her face when another wave of tears threatened. Stoically, she laid the shirt aside and pulled on her stockings and chemise. When her bedroom door opened, she shielded herself with the sprigged muslin.

"I'm so glad you brought something ladylike with you." Lady Vaughan prowled into the room. "Pity, I would have thought everything you owned was pure silk. Well, there's no accounting for taste, I suppose." She closed the door silently behind her.

Johanna backed against the bed and kept a wary eye on the older woman.

"I thought we should have a little chat, just you and I."

Johanna had never trusted the woman's feline smile. "I don't think we've anything further to discuss, my lady. It appears everything is settled."

"Tut, tut, child. Don't be bitter." Lady Vaughan stepped forward and motioned to Johanna's dress.

As little as she appreciated the older woman's help, Johanna desperately wanted to be clothed. She presented Lady Vaughan with her back.

Lady Vaughan spoke her mind while she laced Johanna's stays. "You and I are both women of the world. We see what we want, and we take it. I can see it all through your eyes. Derek was on the verge of offering for Charis Sumner, and you didn't want to lose Ambersley. And we both know Charis would *not* have welcomed you here, ward or no. She's neither a clever girl nor a fool. Am I right, thus?"

Johanna fought for composure. As a child, she'd always feared Lady Vaughan. Though she was no longer the helpless son of the gardener, she shivered at her memories. "I came to help Derek because he's my guardian and my friend, nothing more. Do you understand?"

"Yes, dear. I understand completely. Stick to that story. Most people would believe it—I'm sure Elizabeth and Harry Coatsworth will. Of course, I caught you atop Derek, and I needed no imagination to see where both of you were headed. Tell me, Johanna, are you still a virgin?"

"I—I, how... yes, *yes.*" Johanna finally sputtered.

"Why, how pretty you are when you blush. And I don't believe you could feign that outraged look, so you must be telling the truth." Finished with the laces, Lady Vaughan helped drop the dress over her head. "My dear, I'm interested in your welfare. You think you are gaining a title, land and security. Did you know Derek is not truly a Vaughan?"

Johanna turned to regard the older woman's pursed lips. "What do you mean?"

Her services no longer needed, Lady Vaughan stepped back and ran a hand along the footboard of the four-poster bed. "You're aware of his mother's notorious history—liaisons made public, murder, hanging."

"Yes, Derek has no secrets from me." Even as a child, she'd been privy to the gossip at Ambersley about the new duke and his tragic family history.

"Indeed." There was that smile again, but Lady Vaughan's eyes glittered like a serpent's. "Did he tell you his mother foisted him upon Reginald Vaughan, that he's not Reginald's son at all, but the issue of that whore and one of her paramours?"

Johanna inhaled sharply and only when dizziness assaulted her did she remember to breathe.

"Derek learned the truth as a young man about your age. He was so disgusted by it, he quite rightfully left home—we thought never to return. But Reggie didn't have the heart to disown the bastard, and now Derek's usurped the dukedom that should belong to Reggie's real son."

"No. I don't believe you," Johanna said. "Derek wouldn't do such a thing."

"Oh, he had me fooled, too. Told me when he first arrived here that he merely meant to hold the title until Curtis came of age. Now he blatantly denies us."

Johanna tasted doubt, bitter as bile. "Harry would have told me."

Lady Vaughan chuckled. "Noble young Harry—he doesn't know. Otherwise, he wouldn't have traveled all the way to India to drag Derek back here after Reggie's death. Derek never told him this black secret, just as he never revealed it to his young pet, Johnny. Tell me, did you not wonder why a duke would befriend a small boy of doubtful breeding?"

In truth, she'd accepted Derek's friendship as easily as his presence at Ambersley, so greatly had she idolized him as a child.

"Guilt," Lady Vaughan enunciated the word like a judgment. "Reggie did everything he could for that boy, and when Derek learned the horrid truth about his mother, he spurned Reggie's generosity. How natural, then, to bestow fatherly attention on the next bastard he encountered."

Johanna put her fingers to her throbbing temples and sat upon the bed. "Why do you tell me all this?"

"I'm sorry if it pains you, my dear, but I would hate to see your heart broken. I'm afraid Derek isn't capable of loving anyone."

"I am well able to protect my heart, my lady." Johanna met the woman's gaze.

Lady Vaughan nodded. "I'm pleased to hear it. Believe me when I say I want only the best for you. Derek needs your money because he knows he must one day hand Ambersley over to Curtis. When that happens, you'll have neither this home nor the title. Society will shun Derek when they learn the truth of his parentage, of his charade as the duke, and as his wife, you'll lose all your connections."

The picture she painted was as dark and muddy as charcoal on wet paper. Realizing she'd crumpled her fists into her skirt, Johanna tried to smooth the muslin.

"That's why I urge you to reconsider and wed Curtis." Lady Vaughan stepped forward to pull Johanna's nervous hands into her own. "Curtis will secure a special license, and I will help the two of you escape. Once you're married, Derek cannot harm you."

Johanna looked up into the woman's face, the blue eyes bright with hope but not a drop of sympathy. She slipped her fingers free. "I need to think on it." Evasion was simpler and safer than refusal.

Lady Vaughan straightened and folded her hands before her. "But, of course, my dear. This is all so sudden—you shouldn't be pressed for an answer right away. You may send me word at the Dower House should you need me." She sauntered toward the door but looked back over her shoulder. "There is one additional factor you might consider as you tally your options."

"Indeed?" More than anything, Johanna wished the woman would leave.

"It's obvious an attachment of sorts exists between you and Worthing. Should you marry Curtis, I can guarantee he could be persuaded to...ignore any discreet liaisons you may wish to enjoy."

Johanna rose to her feet, certain she couldn't have heard right. "Are you suggesting—?'

"For your safety, Johanna, I warn you not to make a cuckold of Derek. If you think to marry him and still enjoy Worthing's attentions, you're misguided. He'll murder you before he allows you the liberties his mother exercised. Once wedded, he'll control your fortune, and you'll have no escape. Take that to heart."

"So, no matter whom I wed, I'm still a pawn," she said.

Lady Vaughan chuckled. "What, were you expecting love and happiness? Heavens, what sort of notions were they teaching you in that cottage across the way? You're a lady now, and you'll be judged by your fortune, your manners, even your clothing. No one will give a thought to your happiness, least of all your husband. Don't despair—marriage will afford you much more freedom than you've had. The standards for a young matron are far more lenient than for a debutante."

Johanna's brain whirled with all this information. While she'd given some thought to the possibility of marriage, she hadn't contemplated these miserable details. She'd heard of husbands and wives who made children together but lived practically as strangers within their house. Was that to be her lot?

"You have much to think upon, my dear. I'll leave you alone to get what rest you can." Opening the door, Lady Vaughan threw back one last appraising look. "And Johanna, welcome to the family."

Johanna stood tall and proud until the older woman left. Only then did she bow her shoulders and retreat to the window. Perhaps the sight of the sunrise and the promise of a fresh day would restore her hope. She leaned her head on the glass and looked out over the manicured lawns and clipped hedges with their hundred hues of green. The sky was painted blue, and the rising sun washed it with rays of gold and pink. How could the world be so colorful, yet her future appear so bleak?

Marry Curtis. There was a daunting proposition. While she'd once thought she couldn't live without being at Ambersley, she knew better now. Home was not defined by a place, but by people. Marrying Curtis wouldn't bring her happiness any more than the title of duchess.

Her head still reeled with all the information Lady Vaughan had imparted about Derek. But now that she'd had time to consider everything she'd heard, Johanna discovered she felt no revulsion. He was still the same Derek he'd been before she'd learned these secrets about his past. The man who'd rebuilt Ambersley, the man who'd defended his sister's honor and provided for his family. Was she to believe his stepmother's stories or the deeds she'd witnessed over the years?

She turned away from the window to look about the familiar bedroom. She had strength enough now to leave Ambersley and never return. Harry could help her escape, and Mr. Minton could supervise her fortune until she reached her majority. She need not marry—ever.

But she couldn't bear the thought of living without Derek. His illness fresh in her mind, she tried to imagine what she'd feel now if he'd died. An abyss opened where her soul dwelled. Now that she was assured he would live, would she be any happier if he married someone else and she never saw him again?

Degrading to admit, but she didn't want to live her life without him, no matter how he felt about her. She accepted he didn't love her. Now that she'd trapped him into marriage, she'd simply have to do her best to make sure he didn't grow to hate her.

೪๑

Johanna thought nothing could be more painful than her interview with Lady Vaughan. Nothing, that is, until later that day when she faced Aunt Bess and Harry.

She'd witnessed Harry's arrival on horseback. Hatless, he'd flung himself off the lathered steed and run up the front steps. She'd heard him in the lower hall shouting her name but hadn't the nerve to face him. She'd left that to Derek, even though he could barely leave his bed. Aunt Bess arrived later by coach, serene as always and with Johanna's trunks and maid. One of the housemaids came to Johanna's room to tell her she was wanted in the duke's library.

With trepidation, Johanna answered the summons to discover Derek and the Coatsworths awaiting her.

Aunt Bess came forward to place a feathery kiss on her

cheek. "Child, we were so worried."

"I'm sorry," Johanna whispered as tears pooled in her eyes. She had never wanted to disappoint Aunt Bess.

Harry came forward to wrap her in a tight brotherly hug. "Worthing said you'd save Derek. And now Derek tells us the two of you are to be wed."

Derek stood by the empty fireplace, a hand on his hip, the other arm leaning on the mantle. "I told them everything," he said in a tired voice.

Harry loosened his grip on her, and she searched his face. But Harry never judged, she'd learned. He looked at her with boyish earnestness. "Is this what you want?"

With a helpless shrug, Johanna shook her head. "I don't want to fight anymore. I'm resigned to the fact Derek and I belong together. There doesn't seem to be any way to escape it." She swallowed the lump in her throat.

Derek stepped away from the fireplace, his face a blank reaction to her words. He faltered once as he came toward her, and Johanna surmised it took every ounce of energy he possessed to stand and entertain his guests.

"We'll forego the reading of the banns," Derek explained to Harry and Aunt Bess. "I'll procure a special license, and we'll hold the ceremony in the chapel here. The Season's drawing to a close, and it makes no sense to plan a large Town wedding when everyone will be eager to escape to the country."

Aunt Bess cleared her throat. "Derek, the *ton* will reschedule their shooting parties for something as momentous as the Duke of Ambersley's wedding."

"Perhaps, but it seems hypocritical to stand before an audience and profess our love."

Johanna stiffened at this reminder that he didn't love her. Derek may as well have said he saw her only as a rich purse or a fertile field on which to sow future generations.

"When do you plan to hold the wedding?" Harry asked.

Derek rubbed his tired eyes. "As soon as I procure the license, but I should wait to hear from Minton. I sent him a note formally requesting his approval of the marriage."

"Johanna, are you feeling well, child? You've gone all pale," Aunt Bess noted.

Johanna touched her forehead and noted that even her hand looked translucent. "I have a headache is all. Perhaps I'll lie down before supper." With encouraging words from Harry and Aunt Bess, and silence from Derek, Johanna quit the room. She padded up the stairs, her mind tumultuous, until she recalled Aunt Bess hadn't mentioned Emily and Lady Brindle. Had anyone told the Brindles she was safe? Her note was so brief, whatever did they think of her disappearance? Embarrassment washed over her, but she retraced her steps toward the library until she heard Derek's voice, vibrating with frustration.

"Of course we neither look happy." His words froze her in her tracks. "I could throttle my stepmother for forcing us to marry like this. It's the worst thing that could have happened."

Mortified, Johanna backed away from the door silently praying no one would hear her.

In the room, Harry asked, "Then why go through with it?"

Without waiting, she fled to her room, already knowing Derek's answer—he would say it was his duty, both to protect her and to secure her fortune for his family. Either way made her less of a person than she'd been when she was a gardener's apprentice.

In the sanctuary of her room, Johanna tried to control her shaking limbs. Derek didn't want to marry her. Not at all. Undoubtedly, she'd spoiled his chance to wed Charis Sumner. She'd so hoped she could find a way to make him love her, yet she should have known better. He thought all women were selfish and manipulative, and now she'd proven to be the same, despite her noble intentions. How could she blame him for not loving her? Oh, he desired her. They liked each other. Marriages were often built on far less. She drew a breath, determined never to let him know she'd dreamed of more. If a marriage of convenience was what he wanted, so be it.

In the library, Harry repeated his question. "Why marry her if it's not what you want?"

Derek rubbed his aching eyes in an effort to blot out the

vision of Johanna's pale face. He was so damned tired of this emptiness that threatened to swallow him. "If I don't marry her at once, I fear Worthing will." He stalked from the room leaving silence in his wake.

Bess watched him go. "Derek looks so unhappy. And Johanna—I feel as if I've failed her, somehow." She pursed her lips in thought for a moment. "Have you ever considered offering for her?"

"Mother," Harry looked her in the eye. "There has only ever been one man for Johanna, and that is Derek."

Aunt Bess frowned at the conviction in his voice. "You've always followed behind him and offered him first choice of everything. Yet, you've asked nothing in return."

"That's not true. Derek and I are different people. He wants great things from life, but he won't admit it even to himself. Marrying Johanna will be the making of him." Harry thought for a moment, then his brow cleared as his lips twisted into a smile. "I wonder if that's what Worthing meant when he said she'd save Derek?"

"And what about you?" she asked with exasperation.

"Me? I'm a much simpler and infinitely happier man," Harry said with a laugh. "When I wed, I assure you, there will be none of this drama."

৵৹৵৹

He pulled a laughing Johanna into his arms. She came willingly and needed no coaxing to meet his kiss. His lips took hers hungrily, tasting and teasing a response from her. But when she responded by darting her tongue across his lips, the conqueror became the vanquished, and he surrendered completely to his passion. His arms locked around her, he pulled her against his full length. He whispered words against her hair that stopped her sensual exploration of his throat.

Leaning her forehead against his chin, she asked in a husky whisper, "Did you say something?"

His arousal grew more pronounced than when her fiery kisses had branded him.

She lifted her head, and he gazed into those magnificent

blue-green eyes. "I thought I heard you say something," she repeated and her left eyebrow lifted. God, he loved that eyebrow, those eyes, everything about her...

On the precipice of repeating the three words he'd whispered into her hair, his world toppled into a gray mist.

Derek awoke from his dream with a start. The images were vivid in his mind and he smiled at the desire it provoked. He hadn't desired another woman in months—ever since learning Johanna's true identity. There had been times when he'd needed a woman, thought he wanted one, but when faced with the actuality of visiting his mistress, he'd done so only to end their relationship.

His smile faded at the memory of those three words he'd been prepared to say to her in his dream. *I love you.* Three tiny syllables that wielded so much power. He'd never said them to any woman, nor had he believed the few women who'd said them to him. Love was as rare and fleeting as a shooting star. When dawn came, not only did the star's luminous trail fade, so did the passion inspired by it.

This uneasiness in his heart would dim along with his mad desire to gather Johanna in his arms and beg her to love him, for the lady of his dream wasn't the lady he was to wed. Granted, there had been similarities that night he found her in his bedroom. Just the memory of those few torturous minutes could arouse him.

But since she'd agreed to marry him, she'd become withdrawn. Her words of the previous day still stung. *I don't want to fight anymore. I'm resigned to the fact Derek and I belong together. There doesn't seem to be any way to escape it.* She wouldn't be marrying him but for his stepmother's meddling. Derek wished he understood her feelings, but unlike most women, Johanna didn't advertise her emotions. He only knew that when she looked at him, he felt like her captor.

If he truly loved her, he'd stop this wedding and deliver her into Worthing's hands. Johanna hadn't spoken a word of how or why St. John had brought her to Ambersley, but Harry had shared the brief, straightforward story St. John had presented him when he arrived in Tunbridge Wells. Clearly,

Johanna had asked for the marquess's aid, and he'd assisted her with gallantry and honor. He was the better man, and could provide Johanna a home, a title, even love, without fear of reprisal.

Derek's hold on Ambersley and the title was tenuous at best, his fortune minimal, his relationship with his closest family members precarious. If he loved Johanna with the selfless devotion she deserved, he'd release her and grant her the one thing she'd asked of him—the freedom to choose her own husband.

He climbed from his bed to prowl restlessly about the chamber. He should put everything right. He should grant Curtis the Ambersley patent, he should confess the sins of his birth to Society and leave once more for India as he'd planned long ago. He should release Johanna to find a love more deserving than his. He stopped at the window to look down upon the rose garden, its once meticulous care abandoned until the bushes now grew wild in riotous clumps. Johnny could reclaim that garden in less than a week.

With a sigh, Derek acknowledged he'd do none of the things he *should* do. He needed Johanna as desperately as those roses needed sunlight—for sustenance. He'd been granted an opportunity to bind her to him forever, and by God, he'd take it.

For the hundredth time, he considered whether this marriage was ill-advised and came to the same conclusion—it most decidedly was. He was a selfish bastard to force her into it.

So be it.

19

The marriage of Derek Preston Vaughan, twelfth Duke of Ambersley, to Amber Johanna Vaughan, heiress to the Vaughan fortune, took place on July 22, 1815. It was a small affair, with only family members and Nigel Minton present.

Rosalie Vaughan stood outside Ambersham's tiny chapel with her children, reluctant to witness more of her hopes dashed. She seethed with frustration that both Derek and that chit had spoiled her plans. Her only consolation was that both bride and groom looked miserable.

"Mark me, Curtis, Derek will pay for this indignity to us today, and you shall get your due."

"Mother, leave it be. Today of all days, please. Derek owes me nothing."

Rosalie raised her hand and barely repressed the urge to slap him. He stood half a head taller than she now, and he no longer regarded her with any fear, only a wariness that frustrated her. He'd become a man—worse, he'd become his *own* man, one who didn't seek her guidance.

"I've set my hopes in you, Curtis. Do not disappoint me." She gathered her skirts to climb the steps into the church, but paused to look over her shoulder at the children. "After the ceremony, we leave for London."

Curtis raised his brows. "But the party—"

She shot him a look that silenced him. *Party. There was nothing here for any of* her *family to celebrate.*

"We've missed enough of the Season as it is." Rosalie looked beyond her troublesome son to her daughter. The fresh air and rest had added a glow to the girl's eyes and skin. "Now that the heiress is wed, we need to see to proper matches for both of you."

"Yes, Mama." Olivia dropped her a curtsey, ever dutiful and obedient. She might yet be the salvation of the family.

Rosalie turned and climbed the steps, leaving Curtis and Olivia to follow.

Mr. Minton, assigned the task of giving Johanna away, stood with her at the back of the church. He watched her with solemn bespectacled eyes. "I came to Ambersley to write your father's will after you were born. Your parents loved you dearly, I remember. They would be very proud of you today."

Johanna's hand covered her mouth in surprise. "Thank you," she managed to whisper, but there was no time to say more before he led her down the aisle. Throughout the ceremony, her vision remained misty with memories of what had been and dreams of what might be. Derek's jaw tightened when he pulled back her veil and spotted the telltale moisture. Johanna braced herself for his kiss, but his lips lightly touched hers in a brief caress. She swallowed hard and smiled tremulously in response. He didn't smile as he led her from the church.

Johanna was grateful to climb into the barouche for the ride back to Ambersley Hall and avoid Lady Vaughan's bitter scowl and Aunt Bess's frown of concern. She sat beside Derek, who remained silent, while she tried very hard not to think about what this day could have been if only he loved her. Derek's own words returned from her childhood to haunt her—words he'd spoken when he was convinced she was a boy. *No man loves his wife half so well as he loves his mistress. And much of that is because his mistress never swears she loves him, but his wife swears it constantly. A woman is never as attractive after she tells a man she loves him. That's because you can never trust a woman to mean it.* She worried her lip with her teeth. How long would it take her to conquer these unwanted emotions?

Derek's gaze slid over her dispassionately. Well, he'd done it. He'd married the one woman he wanted above all others. She was his—and she'd never looked more unobtainable than she did at this moment. She studied the landscape as if it were the only important thing in her life. Derek silently cursed his luck.

As the barouche pulled up before the Hall, Johanna heard a cheer rise on the wind. Derek hopped down from the carriage and offered his hand to assist her. Johanna gaped at the sight— the entire staff of Ambersley, and all the tenants as well, had gathered before the front doors to greet them. There were smiles and laughter, a few tears and much applause until Derek held up his hand for silence. He motioned Paget forward.

In his most commanding tones, Paget announced, "Presenting the Duke and Duchess of Ambersley. Welcome home, Lady Ambersley!"

Another cheer burst from the crowd, and a lump formed in Johanna's throat as her family—for that's how she'd always think of these people—applauded her. They were so obviously pleased to welcome her as their new mistress, she couldn't help but smile. Looking over the sea of faces, Johanna saw Mrs. North dabbing her eyes, Stokes blowing his nose, Mrs. Chalmers nodding sagely, and Paget grinning like the village idiot. Johanna would have loved to celebrate this day with all of them, but knew it was inappropriate to her new station in life.

Derek interrupted the applause with a shout. "Luncheon will be served on the back lawn in half an hour!" Cheers erupted anew, but this time the crowd started to disperse. He looked down upon Johanna. "I thought you would like to include them in the celebration."

"Thank you." She couldn't find words to say more.

Derek cleared his throat. "I'm sorry Tom and Martha couldn't be here today. I would have asked them to give you away."

"They would have liked that," Johanna said softly.

Derek wondered if he'd upset her, but her smile appeared genuine as she took his hand and led him through the Hall to the back lawn. At least he could make her smile.

Johanna radiated sincere delight as the afternoon progressed. Her happiness today was all that mattered to him. Still, as the shadows lengthened, and people began to depart for their homes, he found himself unnerved at the prospect of being alone with her.

Harry and Aunt Bess took their leave during the afternoon. Johanna clung to Aunt Bess, as if she were only a small child and someone were taking away her favorite doll. "Must you go so soon?"

Aunt Bess tucked one of Johanna's stray locks behind her ear. "You have no further need of a chaperone. Derek tells me you're planning to return to London by the end of the week, so we will await you in Portman Square."

Johanna nodded silently. This was the first she'd heard of her impending return to London. Apparently, Derek wanted to finish out the Season, or worse, he couldn't wait to return to his mistress. At least she wouldn't have to watch him squiring Charis Sumner about Town. Small consolation.

Supper was an affair of sumptuous delicacies. There was a turtle soup, and turbot with lobster and oysters followed by lamb cutlets with early peas from the little garden Paget still tended. Johanna picked at her plate as dishes came and went, for even the tiny meringues with chocolate cream tasted like dust. Her mouth felt so dry... She couldn't remember ever being this nervous.

Following the meal, Derek asked if she'd care to join him in the library for a brandy. Surprised by his outrageous suggestion, she accepted, and he offered her his arm.

They sat in companionable silence while candles flickered in the breeze from the open French doors. Johanna nursed her dainty portion of the strong spirits, while Derek downed his in fiery gulps. Finally, his glass empty, he stood and offered her his hand. "Come Johanna, 'tis time we were abed."

She let him lead her up the stairs to his room, his words

echoing through her. She hoped she would get through this night without humiliating herself. She desperately wished she were experienced in the ways of lovemaking. Certainly, Derek would find no appeal in the gauche fumbling of an untried girl. Getting an heir was an integral part of any marriage, but Johanna remembered Derek telling her men and women derived intense pleasure from the act as well. She hoped she'd feel such pleasure—even more, she hoped Derek would.

Derek's bedroom was awash with candlelight, and pale pink rose petals were strewn across the snowy sheets of the turned-down bed. Johanna's stomach fluttered with nerves. She drew strength from the waxing moon, luminous outside the open window. The same glowing orb that had offered her friendship when she fought for Derek's life had now returned from its monthly trek to shine away the worst of her fears.

Derek watched her step to the window where moonbeams bathed her in haloes and cast golden glints to her chestnut curls. Her skin shone ivory with a pale flush to her cheekbones as her eyes swept the room and landed on the bed. Her aqua eyes flickered with a silvery light under upswept lashes, and Derek longed to say something to drive her left eyebrow up in that maddening habit it had. He didn't deserve her, this ethereal being who held the power in her eyebrow to fulfill or destroy him. He would need to tread delicately.

She tugged at her bottom lip with smooth white teeth. "I have a peignoir Aunt Bess helped me pick out—" She hesitated, and he glimpsed the thousand questions in her eyes.

"Perhaps later. I see no need for you to change clothes when what I want is to see you without them entirely."

His voice was a caress, and Johanna had to moisten her lips before they'd form words. "Is that what you want?"

Derek groaned at the sight of her tongue darting briefly across her lips. It only took a heartbeat for him to pull her into his arms. "That and so much more, Johanna." Only then did his lips descend to hers.

Johanna quickly forgot the chaste kiss at the wedding altar. As their lips melted together, the simmering heat traveled through her body and pooled in the pit of her stomach where it glowed among embers of desire. Tentatively, she closed her fingers over the taut muscles of his shoulders and was rewarded with a viselike embrace as he pulled her to his full length. One of Derek's hands pressed along the curve of her buttocks, and she experienced the heat of him as he held her.

He raised his head slowly to gaze into her eyes. Johanna smiled weakly. "I should ring for Nancy to help me undress."

Derek laughed softly. "I think not. That door is locked, and I will murder with my own hands the first person who dares so much as knock upon it." His tone was vehement and he took a steadying breath. "I've waited for this night for so long, Johanna. You have no idea how much I've wanted you."

Her left eyebrow flew up in surprise and—maybe—hope. "Truly?"

He turned her around, unwilling to reveal how her unconscious gesture touched his heart.

"What are you doing?" Johanna asked.

"I'm undressing you. Do you mind?" Derek responded. His fingers began the arduous task of unbuttoning the length of her back. By the time he'd reached the tenth satin covered barrier, Derek experienced fully the exquisite torture of anticipation. Inhaling the soft fragrance from her nape, he plied gentle kisses along her shoulders as his fingers continued their downward advance.

Johanna breathed a slow sigh of pleasure at odds with her racing pulse. Already, she could feel a drawing sensation below her stomach where her legs came together. It was a totally new experience that emboldened her to speak. "Derek, I want to be a good wife, but—" She paused in indecision.

Derek turned her to face him. The white dress slipped down Johanna's shoulders and she unconsciously shook it free until it slipped to her feet. She stood before him in nothing but the thin silk chemise and stockings, all smooth and ivory except for the pink tips of her breasts.

As close as he stood, he couldn't touch her until she finished her thought. "But what?"

"Will you teach me to please you? I know it's not what wives usually want, but I—will you teach me?"

Derek's heart hammered in response to her words. "Darling, if you pleased me anymore, I'd embarrass myself."

Johanna frowned. "What do you mean?"

In response, Derek pulled her hand toward the buttons of his breeches.

She drew back in hesitation, but curiosity, not repugnance, lit her face.

Tenderly, he offered, "Let this be a gauge of my desire for you. Touch me." Her gaze flew from their hands to his face, and he grinned with delight. "You asked me to teach you. It would please me greatly if you unfastened and touched me."

Johanna nodded at his encouraging smile, and began the disconcerting task of undressing her husband. She feared he would be disappointed with her fumbling fingers working at his buttons, until she heard a groan of pleasure escape him. With the buttons undone, it took only the nerve to touch the power of his manhood through the fabric of his small-clothes.

If he had thought undressing her was sweet torture, than surely her hesitation would kill him. Derek's laugh sounded strained. "You would truly test the patience of a saint."

"I would never mistake you for a saint, my lord," Johanna responded with a smile. She gave a squeal of surprise as Derek swept her up in his arms.

He carried her to the bed where he dropped her unceremoniously atop the rose petal strewn sheets. "Then you'll forgive me if I tell you I cannot bear this waiting anymore." He undid his neck cloth while he kicked off his shoes. The buttons of his shirt took only a twinkling, and suddenly he stood bare-chested before her. When he'd removed his breeches and stockings, Johanna tried not to stare. She'd seen him naked before, had sponged his body when he was delirious with fever, but she'd never imagined his manhood erect. She shivered in anticipation.

Derek saw her tremors and paused in the act of removing her stockings and garters. "You're not frightened, are you?"

Johanna shook her head until she could find her voice. "Should I be?"

"Never of me, sweetheart. I would never hurt you," he

promised.

"I know," she answered softly. Trust shown in her eyes.

Nothing had ever touched him more.

He loosened her garters and drew them with her stockings down her legs before kneeling on the bed and capturing her lips in a tantalizing kiss. His hand caressed her throat and shoulder, playing with the strap of her chemise. She lifted her hands to his face and traced the stubble along his jaw as she opened her mouth for him to delve inside. He did so with a moan of pleasure, and she ran her hands up into his hair. He had dreamed of the ecstasy of feeling her fingers in his hair.

His kisses moved down her chin and throat to the lace at the top of her chemise. With one hand, he gently cupped a firm breast. She reacted to the heat of his hand with a throaty sigh. He rubbed his thumb back and forth across her silken-covered nipple and watched her back arch in response. Buttons decorated the front of the chemise, and in a moment of passionate savagery, he gripped the fabric with both hands and tore it open, sending the fasteners flying. *A plague on buttons.*

Johanna's eyelids fluttered open in question.

"Forgive me, sweet, I couldn't help myself. You're so much more beautiful than I imagined." He bent to kiss her breast.

Sensations rippled through her. No wonder men and women did this. Derek's hot tongue tickled her nipple, and every muscle in her body grew taut as a bowstring, yet she had never felt so at peace, so complete. He spread his large hand over her other breast, warming her with his palm. Then cool air swept her as he withdrew his hand until only the tips of his fingers traced her nipple. He closed his thumb and forefinger over her aroused pink bud and squeezed gently, sending sparks shooting through her body. Many of them seemed to fly and land between her legs. Johanna squirmed with the embarrassed realization that she wanted Derek to touch her there.

Derek lifted his head from her breast at her wanton movements. Seeing the doubt and embarrassment in her eyes, he smiled slowly. "What you're feeling is perfectly natural, Johanna. Your body is responding to my touch. It's beautiful, and it's flattering. This is how men and women arouse each other."

She pondered this for a moment, her brow furrowed, her lips slightly parted. "But I don't know how to arouse you."

Derek chuckled softly at her disarming innocence. "My dear, I assure you, I am aroused simply by being near you. Seeing your beauty, feeling you move beneath my touch, knowing you are willingly sharing yourself with me, teaching you this pleasure—all these things arouse me." He rolled on his side and pointed to his erect phallus. "See? Did I not say it would be a gauge of my desire?"

Johanna shyly gazed down Derek's full length. From the broad chest with its light furring of crisp black hair to the trim hips and muscular thighs and the— Johanna blushed hotly to see that indeed, Derek's arousal was quite obvious. She looked back at his shamelessly rakish grin and was swept by emotions she barely understood and didn't dare name. Tentatively, she touched her lips to his. He tasted of brandy and something eternally male. Gaining courage, she brazenly ran her tongue across his full lower lip.

Derek's reserve broke. He pulled her to him and deepened the kiss, forcing her own lips apart and invading her mouth again with his clever tongue. His hand stroked the center of her ribcage, past her belly to her thigh. He traced the curve of her hip, and cupped her bottom.

She felt the heat of his hand brand her wherever he touched. He caressed the length of her back and the side of her breast before his hand traveled lower a second time. His fingers brushed feather-light across her leg to her inner thigh. Johanna's legs tensed, but as he gently stroked them, she opened them slightly. With surprise, she realized he had somehow read her secret thoughts, and she awaited his touch with guilty anticipation. When it came, she responded like tinder as his torch-like fingers explored her, tendrils of fire spreading throughout her being. Johanna whimpered a need she didn't understand against Derek's mouth. He withdrew from their kiss, and she looked up at him with undisguised passion as he taught her to surrender to the sensations.

Derek quivered with restraint. She'd already been slick with desire when he first touched her. As much as he wanted to sink himself into her and relieve the agony of the past few months, he wanted more to teach her the full power of lovemaking. Her fingers bit into his back, but the pain only made him more aware of her scent, her taste, her sweet trusting response. He continued to stroke her and watched a flurry of reactions flit across her face until she gasped his name from the brink of some mysterious plateau.

He stopped her sighs with a kiss, his tongue roaming her mouth at will, and she responded with wanton abandon as he adjusted himself above her. They twined together, the full length of their bodies touching, and Johanna opened her eyes in wonder at the feel of his manhood radiating against her belly.

"Do you still want me to touch you?" she asked softly against his ear as he devoured her throat.

Derek paused a moment to collect his thoughts. He raised his head to look into those aqua eyes with their liquid silver flames. More than anything he wanted to enter her, to pump his desire into her. He'd die if he had to wait much longer. He swallowed.

"Yes." His voice was little more than a growl. He rolled onto his back, willingly committing himself to torture.

Johanna's gaze roamed over him, and she felt proud knowing this magnificent man was her husband. Even if he didn't love her, she would do her best to make him a good wife in every way. She closed long cool fingers around the pulsating heat of him, and he reacted with a resonant purr. She continued her tentative fondling, exploring his body at her will, until he muttered something like a curse.

"Did that hurt?" she asked with concern.

"No, sweet, but I cannot withstand much more of this." He took her hand in his, and rolled her onto her back. Her cheekbones were flushed with color and candlelight while rose petals adorned her hair. For the first time in his life, Derek felt foolish with a woman in his bed. "I've never taken a woman's virginity, Johanna. I'm told it can be painful, but the pain will be brief. I promise, after this, I will never hurt you again."

Johanna nodded, moved beyond reason to know she was the only woman to give this gift to Derek. He touched her with experienced fingertips until she sighed with pleasure once more, then he slid inside her. She felt the pressure of live heat as he slowly filled her. When he stopped all motion, Johanna opened her eyes to see his face taut with strain. He caught her liquid gaze, and leaned down to kiss her. Just as she lost herself in the velvety clutch of his lips, he pulled back, and drove in again with enough force to break through her barrier. She winced with the sudden pain, and Derek stopped moving again.

He raised his head to look at her. There were tears at the corners of her eyes. He wiped them gently with the pad of his thumb. "Does it hurt still, little one?"

Johanna shook her head slowly. Derek framed his hands about her face, as if he would hold her still and prolong this moment indefinitely. She was totally aware of him—this joining of their bodies seemed to fuse their very souls. Now she understood why men and women coupled. She never wanted this moment to end.

Until Derek began to move, and Johanna realized the fires he had stoked within her still raged unchecked. He thrust himself into her with long rhythmic strokes, and her body welcomed his movements. Unconsciously, her hips rose to meet him as he sank into her fervid softness. Derek ran his hand down her leg, and lifted her knee. She followed his lead, and wrapped both her legs around his waist. He groaned with pleasure as his shaft burrowed deeper into her. Beads of perspiration dotted his body as his tightly controlled passion strained to the breaking point. He increased the tempo of his movements, and Johanna felt the dizzying spiral of heat rise within her. She panted in rhythm with him until his name broke from her lips.

Derek watched her closely. "Soon, sweet. We're almost there."

Johanna didn't know what he meant until suddenly a cry burst from her lips in a choking convulsion of delight, and with one last stroke, he poured himself into her and collapsed, rolling her next to him on the bed.

She lay still, damp and dotted with petals while her breathing returned to normal. Never had she imagined anything as beautiful as what she and Derek had just shared. Surely, he couldn't be this intimate with someone he didn't love. But then she recalled all the conversations she'd overheard between Derek and Harry and other men around Ambersley—men who spoke of keeping mistresses for pleasure, of begetting heirs, of sharing a bed with their wives only when necessary. None of these men had ever mentioned loving the women they bedded. Derek had spoken no words of love to her, and he didn't want to hear them from her.

She looked over at him. He lay with a hand flung over his head, his eyes closed, his face blank of emotion.

Derek felt his pulse returning to normal. He'd never dreamed lovemaking could be so fulfilling yet leave him incomplete. But, even as he reached for Johanna, eager to gather her close, she rolled away from him. Before she could rise, he snared her arm. "Where are you going?"

"My room?" she said, unsure.

Cold water couldn't have doused his ardor any faster. Immediately his guard went up. Clearly, Johanna had enjoyed her initiation to lovemaking but now that her wifely duty was fulfilled, she was eager to escape his bed. This was the price he paid, free access to the charms of her body while she reserved her heart for another.

She cleared her throat. "I know husbands and wives keep separate bedrooms. I didn't know what you would want."

"It's our wedding night. Stay with me tonight." With care, he plucked petals from her hair while her luminous eyes reflected flickering candles. He bent to kiss her nose, her mouth, to trail kisses down her throat. He knew he could lose himself in her—perhaps, if he carried her over the horizon of passion, that haunted look would leave her face.

"Derek, what are you doing?" Johanna asked. Her body was already turning fluid and supple from his caresses.

"You said you wanted to please me. It would please me

very much to do this more than once tonight." He stopped any further questions with a searing kiss.

കൈ

Johanna found her first week as a wife filled with the unexpected. Despite what she'd heard about husbands and wives keeping separate beds, Derek made clear his preference to have her sleep with him in the large master chamber. This wasn't a hardship—except they rarely slept. During their passion, Johanna would lose herself entirely and hold him with all the love she felt in her heart. Afterward, she longed to broach with words what their lovemaking implied, but Derek never gave her reason to believe that he loved her. Afraid that she would drive him away by committing too much, she said naught.

Derek had never imagined marrying a woman could make him feel so complete. Yet the guilty knowledge that he didn't deserve her gnawed upon him. During their passion, he would see what looked like love shining in Johanna's eyes, but afterward, when they lay spent and sated, he couldn't escape the knowledge that she should have married a worthier man. To ward off the fruitless thoughts, he made love to her endlessly until she fell into exhausted slumber, and he could do the same.

The end of the week found Lord and Lady Ambersley and their household returned to Grosvenor Square for the final weeks of the Season. Harry had delivered the wedding announcement to *The Times* upon his earlier return, and it appeared the day before they arrived. This opened a floodgate, and a fleet of invitations awaited them. Wishing to stem any rumors resulting from their sudden marriage, Derek responded favorably to nearly all of them.

Johanna obediently directed Nancy to turn out the wardrobe Aunt Bess had sent from Portman Square. Apparently her prayers that she be finished with this round of gaiety were not to be answered. How she wished they might have stayed at Ambersley, where she might have continued to chip away at Derek's reserve. All she needed was time and patience to win his love.

Their first night out as man and wife, she encountered the gossip that Derek had feigned leaving London so he could steal her away from the Brindle residence. Throughout the supper party, Johanna held her counsel and left the truth unspoken. Despite the speculative looks and whispers, she smiled and assured all who asked she couldn't be happier.

But her heart grew heavy as she sipped her wine and watched Derek. Seated across from her chair, his gaze rested on Charis Sumner halfway down the table. Reminded of the other women he'd pursued, Johanna wondered how long it would be before he visited his mistress. Men loved their mistresses more than their wives, she recalled him telling her long ago.

When the dancing began, Derek escorted Johanna to the floor for the first waltz. Though their steps matched in perfect accord, she couldn't help but feel they were on display.

"I commend you on turning the rumor mill in our favor," she said.

He frowned slightly, his jaw tight. "That wasn't me. Worthing must have set the rumors in motion as soon as he returned to London."

"He kept his own name completely out of it?"

This made Derek's lip pull back into a half smile. "St. John has always avoided scandal."

"So the *ton* believes we're in love?" She lifted her eyes to his, and her breath caught to find him studying her with a smoldering intensity. Belatedly, she realized this was the first time the word 'love' had been spoken between them.

He turned his head to scan the crowded ballroom. "Only the naïve," he said. "Wealth seeks power. Power seeks wealth. As far as Society is concerned, it's the most natural thing for you and I to wed—especially so suddenly and secretly. After all, you're my ward."

Johanna tried to blend this cold rationale with the man who made love to her tirelessly, who brought her to the brink of heaven and back. She considered the other married couples around them. Did they commit their bodies with such abandon in private while maintaining such a public façade of detachment? With a sigh she silently acknowledged she still had much to learn about Society and its ways.

At the next rout they attended, Johanna renewed her acquaintance with the Honorable Reed Barlow. Mr. Barlow, the younger son of an earl, was tall and fair, a prince of a man. A bit of a dandy, he knew all the courtesies, and danced with a natural athleticism that made even the same old steps of the quadrille take on a new zeal. His conversation would never rival Harry's, but if Johanna did not stray far from the weather or the doings of members of the *ton*, Mr. Barlow seemed able to hold his own.

As they danced a waltz, Johanna was amazed to hear Mr. Barlow murmur in the vicinity of her ear. "Hair like a raven's wing, and a gleam of sapphire in her eye." He left it at that, and Johanna, perplexed, sought what had given his normally staid mind a poetical bent. Across the room she spied Olivia, and when she glanced back at Mr. Barlow, there was no mistaking the look of longing on his face.

"Do you know Lady Olivia, Mr. Barlow?" she asked.

Immediately his attention snapped back to her. "We've been introduced a few times," he said. He then went on to relate each of the meetings at great length. Johanna was only saved from his monologue by the end of the dance. Taking pity on the smitten young man, she led him to Olivia and suggested they stand up for the next dance together. Olivia blushed prettily, and agreed that since her sister—for so she referred to Johanna now—thought him a suitable partner, she would be happy to join him. He offered his hand to Olivia gallantly, and Johanna watched the two match steps perfectly while they maintained an animated conversation.

Olivia cornered her later in the ladies' retiring room. "Thank you, Johanna," she said with a kiss on the cheek before she whisked off again.

Mr. Barlow requested another dance, and Johanna agreed. At least he wouldn't step on her toes during a waltz as two of her other partners had that night. She breezed along in his arms, his steps always easy to follow. She gave herself over to the strains of cheery violins and tried to imagine she was dancing with Derek.

"I wanted to beg your assistance, Lady Ambersley," Mr. Barlow said. This was the first time he'd started a conversation while they danced. "Olivia tells me you're her friend, and I appreciate you giving us the opportunity to dance together tonight. You see, Olivia and I are in love!"

Johanna barely managed to suppress her mirth at his declaration. Two more ill-fitting people she could scarce imagine. Seeing his serious expression, she nodded gravely. "I see."

"Lady Vaughan has warned me off in no uncertain terms. She feels my prospects aren't adequate to ensure Olivia's happiness."

"And what does Livvie think?"

"She's an angel. She swears if I join the Army, she'll become a camp follower. I don't think camp life would be good for her, so I've given up the notion of the Army as a career. I thought of the Navy, but she cannot go to sea with me." He paused as if he needed to piece together his next thought. "I've no desire to see her risk her life, you know."

Johanna nodded agreement with his noble care for his beloved.

"I thought about becoming a vicar, but I would have had to have studied much harder at school, I'm afraid. Besides, Olivia told me she wants to live in London, and there's not much chance of finding an opening in the city. So, I informed Lady Vaughan I plan to support my wife through my poetry. I've written quite a lot of it, so as soon as it starts selling, there should be plenty of money."

"And Livvie approves of this plan?"

"Whole-heartedly," Mr. Barlow responded. "She says she fancies being the wife of a famous poet."

"No doubt she fancies it," replied Johanna. Any irony was lost on Mr. Barlow. "Lady Vaughan didn't approve of your plans, I take it."

He shook his fair head. "No. She forbids me to see Olivia any longer. I cannot take her for a stroll, or escort her in to supper, and I shouldn't dance with her, except that tonight you partnered us up. I was hoping you'd deliver our correspondence back and forth. I should much rather trust you than my servants, and Olivia says her maid tells her mother everything." He flushed like an embarrassed cherub. "I thought, since you flaunted convention to have *your* love, you might help. Would that be asking too much?"

Despite that *her* love hadn't turned out so well, Johanna contemplated his request. She was certain this flame of love would burn itself out, and all the more quickly if Olivia had constant contact with Mr. Barlow. Johanna had no compunction about meddling with Lady Vaughan's directives. Certainly, Lady Vaughan had meddled in Johanna's life enough to deserve a little recompense.

"Mr. Barlow, your story has touched my heart, and I'd like nothing better than to see Livvie happily situated. Tell me what I may do." Johanna smiled her first carefree smile in days.

Derek stepped from the card room into the candlelit ballroom and watched Johanna waltzing in the arms of the tall and handsome Reed Barlow. There was no mistaking the happy gleam in her eye or the soft smile on her lips. Mr. Barlow, his face flushed, talked passionately. The pair of them didn't seem to notice anyone else existed in the room. Jealousy bit into him sharply, but what could he expect? She deserved admiration—even adoration. If he couldn't bestow those upon her, should he deny her seeking them from others?

No. Not within reason.

20

Derek made love to her that night, and she welcomed the heat of him against her, inside her, as he ravaged her with sweet savage kisses and pillaging hands. His greedy lovemaking bore a desperation Johanna had never experienced before, and she responded to him with equal passion. Here was freedom from thought, mindless escape from words, nothing but sensations cascading through both their bodies.

As he stroked her to a quivering response with the tips of his fingers, she whispered his name on a shuddering sigh. Slowly, he bent down to kiss her in that most intimate of places.

Johanna's eyes flew open when she felt his lips move across her. "Derek, what are you—oh!" She gasped as his tongue invaded where his fingers had so recently driven her to spasms. The heat of his mouth unnerved her, and she spiraled in a dizzy ecstasy.

He kept her hovering at that peak while he held his own needs in check, watching the play of wonder and emotions upon her face. Her purrs and gasps punctuated his own enjoyment and gave him a feeling of limitless power. She stroked his shoulders and finally clutched his sinewed arms as her body rode the convulsive wave he brought her.

She opened slumberous, sated eyes, while her breasts rose and fell with her deep quickened breaths. She smiled upon him, and Derek tucked her satisfaction close. He'd come to treasure this intimacy between them. Here, there were no trappings of titles or money. Here, they were a man and a woman, and as such, he felt worthy of her. But would this always be enough for her?

On the verge of entering her, Derek was overcome by a vision of Johanna with another man, giving herself with this same passion. His fingers bit into her hips as he thrust into her, determined to destroy the image. He expected her to pull away from his punishing strokes, but her hips rose to meet his increasing tempo. "Look at me," he demanded hoarsely. Her eyes met his and held while he pushed them both over the brink of passion's oblivion.

Afterward, she welcomed his weight, the trusting surrender that allowed him to lie atop her, sweating and spent while she ran her hands lightly over his back. Surely, after what they'd just shared, she need not fear opening her heart.

"I love you," she whispered into the silence.

"Don't," he answered. He didn't move, but his eyes were now open. Her words struck him like arrows, piercing him with searing heat and bittersweet pain. He was a bastard and a cheat, a man who had taken her virginity by promising her Ambersley when he knew he couldn't guarantee it to her. She'd been forced to give up a worthy man and marry against her will. He didn't deserve her love, nor could he sully her by returning it.

Tears stung her eyes. "Do you doubt my heart?"

"I doubt your experience." He rolled on his side. "Johanna, I know you still believe love is the natural mate to marriage, but passion—not love—prompts you to say those words." He watched the glow fade from her eyes.

"Do you not believe in love at all then?"

Unable to resist, he traced his finger along her soft throat. "If I speak words of love, will that please you?"

Johanna sensed his reticence. "Not if you don't mean them with all your heart."

"And you love me unequivocally?" He smiled ruefully. "What if I were not a duke?"

She pursed her lips, knowing he referred to his bastard birth. While she longed to reassure him, he didn't know Lady Vaughan had spilled his secret. Johanna desperately wanted Derek to tell her himself—if he could admit his secret to her, it would mean he truly trusted her. She wanted his trust as much as his love. "I've always loved you, Derek. I will love you no matter what happens."

He frowned, for her actions before they wed belied these protestations. "I fear I don't deserve you." Lying back, he folded his arms beneath his head. "Get some sleep, Johanna."

She lay on her side and watched him surreptitiously. She longed to reach out and touch his face, but the moonlight silhouetted the harsh relief of his features. He'd withdrawn into troubled silence, and she feared by broaching it, she would lose what small ground she'd gained. She doubted he understood his own capacity to love, and she'd never be able to convince him—not until she'd won his trust.

Long after his wife slipped into slumber, Derek lay awake and contemplated her words. She'd kindled a hope within him that perhaps, were he worthy enough, he might one day win her undivided love. To make her happy, he'd face down his family and keep Ambersley forever. He'd made her a duchess and he would give her free rein with her fortune. Yet he couldn't help but fear how she'd react when she learned the truth behind his birth. For the first time, he became conscious that he guarded a secret identity that made Johanna's charade as the gardener's son pale in comparison. The irony weighed heavily upon him.

Johanna awoke late the next morning, still distracted by her thoughts, which turned more turbulent when she learned Derek had gone out. He'd been so silent and preoccupied the previous night. Had she pushed him away by talking of love? Had he gone to his mistress?

Uneasy, she set out with Nancy for the Coatsworths, hoping Harry might be able to alleviate her doubts.

The house in Portman Square was in disarray, but Aunt

Bess smiled upon seeing her. "Johanna, have you come to say farewell?"

"Are you leaving?" she asked.

"Yes, for the Season has worn me to the bone. Harry returns with me to Bath, though I've told him to stay. It's high time he started shopping for a bride of his own."

"No bride for me," Harry said as he entered the drawing room. "I've got quite enough trouble looking after you, Mother."

"And here I thought I looked after you, dear," she said sweetly.

"Not that I'll admit to it in public." He bussed his mother's cheek. "Taft has questions about covering the furniture and whether you want the chandelier stored for the winter."

"Heavens, is he that far along with packing? Excuse me, Johanna." Aunt Bess retreated, a tiny general in a mobcap.

Harry seated them both on the divan and took Johanna's hand. "Is something amiss?"

"Not exactly." She squeezed his fingers and released her hand to smooth her skirt while she summoned her courage. "May I speak with you on a private matter?"

He studied her. "Something you cannot broach with your husband?"

"No, I—oh, Harry, does he still keep a mistress in Town?" she blurted out.

"Johanna! How do you know about—?" Harry muttered an oath. "Derek should never have spoken to Johnny of such things. Put it from your mind."

"It's rather a difficult topic to forget now that I'm his wife," Johanna said.

"Do your best."

"Just tell me yea or nay, that's all I ask."

Harry hopped up and stepped away as if distance from her were vital. "I don't know. Derek doesn't discuss his amours with me." He turned horrified eyes on her. "And don't you dare ask him, nor hint that you asked me. He'd be livid to learn you gave any thought to it."

Johanna sank back into the cushions with a huff. Harry

was right, but her mind was even less easy than it had been. Indecision gnawed at her, for if he couldn't help her, she would need to seek further advice. And awkward as it may be, there was but one other source she could trust.

‿❧

The rest of the week sped by in a blur. During the days, Derek would leave the house for places Johanna sensed she was safer not contemplating. In the evenings, they dressed and made their committed appearances where Derek would often adjourn to the card room and leave Johanna to her own devices. At an impasse with her husband, Johanna centered her attention on Olivia and Mr. Barlow.

Johanna delivered the lovers' missives and tokens surreptitiously. She often accepted notes from Mr. Barlow at the parties and delivered them safely to Olivia while they strolled along New Bond Street together. She even agreed to a carriage ride with him one afternoon, which raised Paget's brows. Once in the carriage, Johanna regretted her impetuosity. Mr. Barlow had brought along sheaves of parchment on which he'd scratched his poetry, and he urged her to follow along while he recited his finest pieces praising Olivia's beauty. After an hour, Johanna wondered what she'd ever done to deserve such punishment.

Derek seemed to take no notice of the time she spent with Mr. Barlow, and Johanna found it a depressing sign that she couldn't inspire jealousy in her own husband. She might have thought he didn't care for her at all, except that each night in the privacy of his bedroom, he lavished her with the most intimate of attentions. When she whispered words of love to him, she swore a yearning ignited in his eyes, but he said naught in return. Humbly, she accepted his silence and awaited the day he would willingly share his secret with her.

‿❧

July gave way to August on the night of the Worthing Ball, and fanning herself amongst the crush of guests, Rosalie Vaughan was forced to admit that the Season, overall, had been dismal. Olivia had failed to snare the attention of a duke, a marquess, even an earl. Curtis still didn't have the dukedom he deserved. Derek and his bride continued to thwart her at every turn—she'd cornered them into a forced marriage, and they still managed to appear content. Happiness would be on the horizon next.

Unless she prevented it.

From her vantage point near the punch bowl, Rosalie scanned the ballroom. Her eyes narrowed as she caught Lord Worthing ushering Johanna onto the terrace. The night was warm, and torches would be lit along the paths in his gardens, Rosalie knew. The perfect spot to share a secluded *tête-à-tête*. She couldn't have asked for a more perfect opportunity.

Gathering her skirts, Rosalie pushed through the crowd until she found Derek near a potted fern opposite the orchestra. If her luck held, he hadn't witnessed his wife's escape with another man. She hurried to Derek's side and laid hold of his arm. "My dear, I swear you've been avoiding me."

Her accusation hit its mark, but Derek dredged up a polite reply. "Have you need of me, Mother?"

Aware she might have but this one chance, she launched her attack. "You married your heiress. I want to know when you plan to relinquish Ambersley to Curtis."

He stiffened. "Curtis must show some maturing before—"

"Nonsense," she hissed. "You've delayed this for years. You now have the money you promised to set aside for your brother and sister, Curtis has reached his majority, and Ambersley is in good repair. You can have no further arguments to prevent you from fulfilling your promise to me— and Reginald's son."

Derek watched the crowded floor, but could find no hint of Johanna in her rose-colored gown. "Have I not been clear? I'll not dance to your tune. Until Curtis is ready for such responsibility, I'll not hand him—or you—Ambersley."

She straightened with a huff. "After all I've done for you, you continue to cross me."

Derek snorted. "You've done nothing but drain my pockets. And that will stop, too."

"After I made sure you got your heiress? Let's be honest, Derek, she wouldn't have married you without the threat of scandal." Rosalie leaned back to watch her adversary while a smile hovered on her lips. *Oh yes, that very word 'scandal' put him on the defensive.* "You should thank me."

"Go to hell."

Venom rose to her tongue. "How *dare* you? I've waited ten years to see *my* son get his rightful inheritance while you strutted about and put him off with your tales of duty. You took his father's love, his title, his bride—you even supplanted him with that stable boy."

Derek didn't flinch at her litany of injustices. She pursed her lips and patted her turban. In a calmer tone, she said, "Cross me in this, and I swear you'll regret it."

This time, he laughed outright. "You cannot touch me with your threats."

"No, but I can tell some very damning stories about your stable boy wife that will destroy her reputation. Be warned." A smile lit her face as she backed away from him to toss her final verbal dagger. "Oh but then, she's well on her way to destroying her reputation already."

A tic in Derek's cheek was the only sign of movement in his rock-hard face. His eyes glittered with tightly leashed anger. "You speak of her attentions toward young Barlow. He's a pup—

"Barlow?" Rosalie allowed herself a throaty laugh, enjoying the delicacy of this moment. Finally, she would have her revenge on that interfering little chit. "My dear, Johanna's moved far beyond impotent dandies. She's out in the garden with our host as we speak."

Fury flashed across his features before he masked it. Without a word, he strode toward the open doorway leading to the terrace.

Derek's little wife was in for it now. Rosalie almost felt sorry for the girl.

Almost.

֍

Grateful for Worthing's silence as he escorted her outside, Johanna drank in the clear night air, hoping it would refresh her spirits. Without hesitation, she descended the steps from the terrace into the small formal garden. The hedges formed a maze of sorts, where many a reputation had been trapped, but even in the dark she felt no fear.

Worthing pulled her to a stop. "Is this wise, Johanna?" he asked with unflappable calm. "You said you wished to ask me a question, but I should think the terrace would be sufficient for that."

"Please, my lord. My need is of a most delicate nature." She looked up to find torchlight cast an amber glow that reflected the haughty aristocratic line of his nose and jaw. He looked cold and implacable, but she knew better. "If I may still claim you as a friend?"

His jaw softened with a reluctant smile. "You shall ruin my reputation." He tucked her hand into the crook of his arm and continued down the steps with her. "But I think it's high time you called me St. John. It seems hardly fair to stand on ceremony when you continue to entrust me with delicate secrets."

"Thank you, St. John." Johanna squeezed his arm. Releasing a heavy sigh she gazed at the heavens. "I'd rather no one overhear us."

He drew her to a bench and waited as she smoothed her skirts and sat. "You have my undivided attention, my dear. How may I be of service?"

Nervously, Johanna tried to find words to broach the painful topic.

"Come. Out with it. Have I not proven trustworthy?"

"Most trustworthy, which is why I must impose upon you, that is—oh…" She paused once more before blurting out her troubles. "Do you keep a mistress, my lord?"

To his bark of laughter—quickly muffled—she added, "I do not mean to pry, but I'm curious to know why a wedded man still has need of a mistress, and I thought you might provide…some insight."

She feared the question might offend him, but only

concern painted his features as he seated himself and drew her hands into his. Just this tiny consolation made her sigh with all the pent up misery of the past two weeks.

"What's this?" he asked. "You're unhappy. Has Derek misused you? He's not hurt you, has he?"

"No, not hurt me, except—he cannot love me." She bent her head with the shame of it.

"He cannot...has he not bedded you?"

Johanna's face warmed, and she looked away. "Oh, yes, we've..."

"Then, is it that you find no pleasure in his touch?"

She swallowed. She'd known this conversation would be awkward, so she could only be grateful that he treated the topic as commonplace. Bravely, she met his worried gaze. "He gives me much pleasure, more I suspect than many wives receive from their husbands."

Worthing leaned back to study her. "Then forgive me for not understanding—"

"He speaks no words of love, and I cannot help but worry that he reserves them for another."

"Ahhh." Worthing nodded. "Now I see. But Johanna, you must understand, a man can feel love without speaking the words."

"But that makes no sense to me."

"No, I'm sure it doesn't. Nevertheless, it's the truth. As for mistresses—they rarely inspire deep abiding emotions. I've had a string of them and never loved a one."

Johanna dared a glance at him, but not by a flicker of his eyes did he appear to be lying. "So, you think it's possible Derek loves me, but says naught."

"Have *you* told *him*?"

"I've tried, but he believes women are incapable of sustaining the emotion. He has so little reason to trust any woman."

"All the more reason for him to discover he is wrong. Take heart, Johanna, I believe his feelings run deeper than you imagine."

She stood, agitated by the hope he might be right. "Oh,

would that were so." Then an idea struck her. Before she could reason herself out of it, she sank back onto the bench and laid a hand against his firm jaw. "You're a man, St. John, can you not teach me ways to make a man love me?"

He said nothing, and fearing she'd offended him by stepping so far beyond propriety, she met his eye to gauge his mood. He stared off over her head, his lips set in a grim line, his eyes glittering in the torchlight.

Behind her, she heard footsteps.

"I'm sure Worthing could teach you many things." Derek's voice sounded from the shadows. "But he knows too well the dangers he risks by dallying with another's wife."

Johanna stumbled to her feet, berating her own foolishness. Already, Worthing had stepped forward to shield her from her husband's wrath. The two men squared off like roosters preparing for a fight to the death.

"I should think no one knows those dangers better than yourself, Derek," Worthing replied.

Derek's jaw locked in an uncompromising line. He looked her way, spearing her with angry eyes. "Johanna, go inside and wait for me in the ballroom."

"No, you don't understand—"

Worthing interrupted her. "Johanna, be a good girl and do as your husband bids. I promise, no harm will come from this."

Her teeth tugged on her bottom lip as she considered both men once more. Their attention was so riveted on one another, she wasn't sure either would heed her explanations. Knowing she'd driven the wedge between them even deeper, guilt enveloped her.

"Go!" Derek's command spurred her retreat, leaving the two men alone.

"She's misjudged you," St. John said after she left. "She thinks you do not love her."

Derek's hands fisted at his sides, but he managed to control the initial urge to bash St. John in the face. "I'll thank you to remember my wife and I need no help from you."

"Your wife seems to think otherwise," St. John replied evenly. "If you continue to hold her away as you have me, I fear she'll stray."

Derek tensed. "In your direction? Is that your excuse?"

"Don't be an ass. You bloodied my nose once. I'm not inclined to provide you cause to do so again. But then, neither did I put her in your keeping to see her hurt."

"I would never hurt her."

"No?" St. John stared at him in silence. "She's been married a fortnight and she's unhappy. Whose fault is that?"

"My wife's happiness isn't your concern."

"No, it's yours. See to it." With a nod, St. John shouldered past Derek.

Derek gripped his arm, bringing them nose to nose.

St. John's teeth glinted in a warning grin. "What, will you mill me down at my own party? Take a little brotherly advice—stop fighting the world at large. Your worst enemy is yourself."

"I hold what is mine," Derek warned, his words vibrating with anger. "If I catch you with her again, I'll run you through."

St. John didn't flinch at the threat. "Know this—I'll not betray my friendship to her. If she comes to me again as unhappy as she is now, I'll do anything in my power to help her. If that insults you, then I suggest you call upon me tomorrow to demand satisfaction." With that, he pulled free from Derek's grasp, straightened his coat, and returned to the house.

Derek exhaled slowly, expelling the murderous thoughts that had gripped him since he first saw Johanna touching St. John's face. He thought of Reginald Vaughan's silent acceptance of his wife's promiscuity. *One day you will love a woman with all your heart*, he'd said, *and then you'll understand.*

Derek did understand now, but he would never accept it.

And he'd make damn sure Johanna knew it.

Derek's fury was further strained when he returned to the ballroom to find Johanna had disappeared. He was only slightly mollified to learn from Worthing's porter that Lady Ambersley awaited her coach on the flagway.

With angry strides he stalked her, catching her as she ascended the coach. Without preamble, he pushed the footman aside and hopped in behind her, slamming the door upon them.

Across from him, she slid into the corner.

"The party is no longer to your liking, Madam?"

Her chin lifted a notch. "The present company even less so, at the moment," she countered.

Damn her, she was looking down her nose at him. "Forgive me, wife, I hadn't realized I hindered you so." Derek's words dripped sarcasm.

"You're angry now, and there's no point in discussing this until you will be reasonable." She pinched the bridge of her nose, whether from a headache or to hide her tears, he knew not.

"I warn you, Johanna, on this topic, I fear you will never find me *reasonable*. So let me be clear." He leaned forward, crowding her in her corner. "Whatever your plans with Worthing, forego them."

"My plans—my God, what did Worthing say to you?"

"He didn't compromise you with words, but it's obvious he's your devoted servant. Nevertheless, you're my wife, and I'll not share you."

The lantern outside the coach window cast pale shadows across her face. "So, my lord, that is what you think of me." Her words shook with repressed fury. With a half-hearted laugh she leaned forward and her eyes narrowed to dagger slits as they pierced him. "If you thought I had so little regard for my own reputation, I'm surprised you wed me to save it."

"It was a mistake, I own it now," Derek retaliated.

She jerked as if he'd struck her, but recovered quickly. "Be that as it may, I spoke those vows. And what's more, I meant them. I love you, Derek."

"And what am I to believe? Your words or what I witnessed tonight?"

"When have I ever lied to you?" she cried.

He watched her steadily until her gaze dropped and her

shoulders sagged in defeat. Softly, he said, "So, be warned. Give yourself to another man, and—at the least—I will spurn you forever. At the most, I'll kill the blackguard. Do you understand?"

She remained silent, her face averted.

"*Do* you?" Derek exploded.

"More than you know." Her voice sounded dead. "May I go home now?"

He said not another word but wrenched open the coach door and hopped out. With a wave, he directed the coachman to pull away at a smart trot.

Left alone on the flagway, Derek silently cursed Johanna, his own folly and his traitorous heart, now deflated and empty.

Unwilling to return to Worthing's hospitality and even less willing to follow his wife home, Derek walked through the cool night to his club. Here, he tried to blot out the evening's events by drinking and playing cards with three gentlemen he would barely have tolerated on a normal day. The gentlemen were pleased to count the Duke of Ambersley at their table and lost their money almost as happily as they won it. Derek left the table well after midnight, his pockets significantly lighter and his heart significantly heavier.

He returned to Grosvenor Square to find his room empty. He'd known it would be, but hadn't expected the emptiness to be so bleak. He knew Johanna was only through the adjoining room, but the threshold may as well have been an ocean for all he could cross it.

He sat on the bed, his head in his hands, still haunted by the vision of her cloistered with Worthing in a puddle of torchlight. Approaching from behind, he'd seen a golden cast to her hair and noted the upturned chin as she spoke to the marquess. But it had been the way she'd boldly placed her hand on the man's jaw that had cracked his calm. That and the deference Worthing showed her. Worthing truly cared for her. Worthing was the better man.

Damn.

A shiver descended his spine as Derek dragged himself to his feet. More than anything, he wanted to look upon his wife, to ensure she was safe. He stepped quietly to the door separating their rooms. No sign of light bled beneath the door, and the room was silent. By the light of a single taper, he pushed the door open.

Johanna lay curled on her side. Wearing a sheer white nightgown, her chestnut curls spilling about her shoulders, she resembled a sleeping angel. If not for the frown bending her lips, he might have faced her with a clearer conscience. As it was, he couldn't blot out the horrible accusations he'd flung at her.

He desperately wanted Johanna to love him. And therein lay his painful dilemma. He couldn't bring himself to believe her words of love now—not after he'd ignored her refusal to marry him and denied her the freedom to choose her husband as she'd begged him. The fault was not hers but his, for even if he believed she loved him, he couldn't accept her love. He was so far beneath her, and his parentage had little to do with it.

Your worst enemy is yourself. St. John had hit home with that remark, and now Derek understood why.

Despite the power and prestige he commanded, he knew himself to be a usurper. He wouldn't confess his love without also revealing to her the truth behind his ignoble birth. And how could he face telling Johanna of his birth without first doing right by the true Vaughan heir? In Derek's determination to deny Rosalie access to the Ambersley coffers, he'd unfairly denied Curtis his birthright.

He'd dishonored Reginald Vaughan. Generations of Vaughans. Would he continue to dishonor the woman he loved?

No. Derek now understood he would never be worthy of her love until he mended this situation. How Society viewed him no longer mattered. He needed to look in the mirror and see a man deserving of Johanna's love—a man with the courage and honor to restore Ambersley to the Vaughan family. A man who was St. John Trevarthan's equal, if not in rank, than in character. A man with the selflessness to place his wife's happiness first. Even if it left him with nothing.

He stole back toward his room but stopped in the doorway to gaze again upon his wife.

"I do love you, don't ever doubt that," he muttered with ferocity. Snuffing the candle, he exited her room and closed the door without a sound.

21

Johanna awoke with a blinding headache, the kind that only comes after a night of tears. She'd lain awake for hours trying to find the words that would somehow convince Derek she held nothing but an abiding friendship for Worthing. She still wasn't sure if her husband had ever come home last night.

She reached for the hand bell to ring for Nancy, but her arm brushed across something on her pillows. She leaned up on an elbow while her head swam, and focused on the notepaper sealed with a wafer. Lifting it, she recognized Derek had addressed it to her. Nervously, she broke the seal and read the brief note.

Forgive me. Last night has reminded me of a duty I cannot forswear. Believe that I want only your happiness, so while I denied you your right to choose a husband, I grant you leave to choose your love. Should you wish to leave, Paget will help you make preparations.

Johanna frowned over the words, trying to decipher their meaning. *Choose your love...should you wish to leave...* Was he such a dolt that he didn't believe her word when she said she loved *him?*

Johanna threw back the covers and paid with a reeling head. It was a small price, and she pulled on her wrapper as she ran to Derek's adjoining room. Sunlight poured in through the open curtains, but the room was empty. Retrieving her slippers, Johanna rang for Nancy. The girl appeared in less than a minute with her breakfast tray and apologies.

"I'm sorry, my lady. I know you don't usually like to sleep late, but his lordship made me promise not to disturb you until you awoke."

"Never mind, Nancy. Where is his lordship?"

"Why he's left. Called for Cushing to harness a coach and four this morning. He took a bag with him. I heard him tell Paget he'd be gone for a few days."

Disappointment descended like a cloud, but Johanna fought valiantly to hide it. She allowed Nancy to prepare her bath while she sipped tea and pretended to eat a piece of toast. An hour later, bathed and dressed, she descended the stairs in search of Paget. She found him in the pantry packing away silver.

"Good morning, Your Grace," he said at his most formal. That never boded well.

Johanna tried to sound nonchalant. "Paget, I understand Lord Ambersley left this morning. Did he say where he was going?"

"No, my lady."

"Did he say when he would be back?"

"No, my lady."

Johanna bit back her frustration with an effort. "Did he say anything?"

Paget bowed slightly. "He said you might be taking a journey yourself. Will you be leaving us today?"

Johanna wished for the days when she could have stuck her tongue out at the old hawk. Instead, she settled for her haughtiest tone. "No, Paget. I will *not* be going anywhere. My husband will have to come home and face me eventually."

Paget gave a silver spoon a final rubbing before placing it with its brothers. "His lordship did mumble something about making repairs. I do not think he was talking about any of his estates." He looked meaningfully at her.

"He and I both need to work at repairing things, Paget."

He nodded. "I suspected as much."

Johanna smiled ruefully, then stood on tiptoe and gave the

butler a quick peck on the cheek. "Thank you, Paget. You've made me feel better." She started out of the pantry, but turned for one last directive. "Oh, and Paget—I want to know the minute Lord Ambersley returns."

"Yes, my lady."

❧

Derek hadn't slept a wink the previous night, and if it weren't for his concern for the tenderness of his horses' mouths, he would have sawed the reins like any common carter. Mid-afternoon saw him pulling into the busy streets of Bath, where he looked longingly for the Royal Crescent and Harry.

He didn't expect to be greeted at the Coatsworths' door by Nigel Minton, and from the look on the older man's face, Minton hadn't expected this visit from the duke.

"Your Grace." Minton bowed slightly.

"Minton," Derek acknowledged as he entered. "Taft's day off?"

"As a matter of fact, it is." The older man's face reddened a bit.

Aunt Bess's voice wafted down the stairs. "Who was it, Nigel?"

Despite his preoccupation, Derek smiled. *Nigel?* Why had he never seen this coming? Aunt Bess's china doll face with its capped curls peered over the stair railing from above. She was surprised but not embarrassed to see him.

"Whatever brings you to Bath, Derek? Is anything amiss? Where's Johanna?"

"She's still in London." Derek turned his hat in circles by the brim.

"Come up, dear, come up. Nigel, don't keep him standing in the hall."

Derek smiled again at Minton's discomfiture. He was sorry circumstances didn't allow him to enjoy this situation to its fullest. Harry would be making rare sport of the solicitor by now.

As he topped the stairs, Aunt Bess gave him a warm hug.

Derek kissed her forehead and apologized. "I seem to arrive here at the most inopportune times."

"Nonsense, you know you're always welcome in this home. Come into the drawing room. Nigel will pour you a glass of wine."

"Is Harry home today?"

Before Aunt Bess could answer, they heard the door open again, and Harry called up the stairs. "Fair warning—I'm home now, and I'm coming up to the drawing room!"

Derek watched Aunt Bess color up crimson. "He went for a walk."

Harry strode into the drawing room with a smile on his face that only broadened when he saw Derek. "I thought that was your four-in-hand I saw drive through town. It's good to see you. Where's Johanna?"

"She stayed in London," Aunt Bess said.

Harry nodded at his mother with a wink to Derek. "Have they told you the news?"

Derek smiled. "No, but I can guess."

Minton cleared his throat. "Your Grace, Harry has already granted me permission to address myself to Mrs. Coatsworth, but as head of the family, it would mean a great deal—"

"Minton, my aunt has been leading her own life for years now. She's not a Vaughan nor is she dependent on me. If you've already secured Harry's permission, there's no more I can add, except perhaps to ask that you secure her permission and promise her happiness."

Minton smiled broadly. "Then I must inform you, she has already agreed to become my wife."

Harry laughed and clapped Minton on the back. "This calls for a toast." He went to the sideboard and splashed Madeira into four glasses. Derek looked from Minton to Aunt Bess. Even across the room from each other they both beamed like mooncalves. Glasses were raised, and Harry proposed, "May your lives together be long and filled with happiness."

Derek drank a healthy dose of the fortified wine and then stared dolefully into his glass. "May you be happier in marriage than I have been," he said to no one in particular.

Aunt Bess touched his elbow. "Did you and Johanna quarrel, dear?"

Derek laughed bitterly and drained his glass. Last night could hardly be summed up by so simple a word. "It's a bit deeper than that, Aunt Bess."

She sat upon the divan and patted the cushion beside her. "Tell us about it."

Derek shook his head. "This is no time to hear about my problems."

"Nonsense. You drove all the way to Bath for some reason. I can only assume you wanted to talk to us about something."

"Perhaps I should be going." Minton rose and tried to excuse himself gracefully.

Derek stopped him. "No, Minton, please stay. All of you need to know what I am going to do, and why I must do it."

Minton joined Aunt Bess on the divan while Harry stood by his chair, but Derek paced about as he formulated his thoughts.

"I'm going to grant the Ambersley title to Curtis. He has much to learn yet, but I'll remain at his side to teach him. Can I do that, Minton?"

Minton pushed his spectacles higher on his nose. "You may do so, Your Grace, but one must ask why you would wish it."

Derek bowed his head. "I cannot face my wife and expect to win her love until I confess to her that I've been masquerading as the Vaughan heir all these years. She deserves the truth."

"The truth? What truth?" Harry asked.

"I'm not Reginald Vaughan's son," Derek stated quietly.

Aunt Bess gasped. "What mean you?"

Minton grasped her fingers, and she clutched his hand, slack-jawed, as if recovering from a shock.

Harry, for once silent, seated himself.

Derek forged ahead. "I'm the bastard son of my promiscuous mother and one of her many lovers. How she convinced Reginald Vaughan to accept me, I'll never know.

We all know she was convicted of murdering one of her paramours."

"Derek, who told you this?" Aunt Bess asked quietly. Tears sparkled in her eyes.

"Rosalie. She discovered it when she and my father were going though his personal papers. He explained it all to her. She came at once to me, to gloat that Curtis was his true son."

Aunt Bess shook her head. "And did you never question Reginald about it?"

With a contemptuous laugh, Derek responded. "Oh yes, immediately. Like a small child, I wanted Father to make it right. I asked him if it were true that I was a bastard. He said yes. He apologized to me, as if that would make up for the fact that I had no last name. I left his home that night and never spoke to him again."

On the mantle, a clock ticked into the stillness. Minton removed his spectacles and rubbed the pinch marks on his nose. He held the spectacles up toward the light from the window and peered at them for a few moments, then settled them again on his nose.

Derek bowed his head. "Rosalie has threatened to expose Johanna's upbringing and the scandal behind our sudden marriage unless I grant Curtis the Ambersley patent. She's held the knowledge over my head for years, but it's not her threats that prompt me to do this. I love Johanna, and I cannot feel worthy of her while I live a lie and cheat Curtis out of his birthright."

"You never told me any of this, Derek." From his chair, Harry looked like a wounded cub. "You've held this secret for years."

"How could I sully you with this, Harry? You always stood by me. I couldn't bear what you might think of me if you knew the truth."

Harry rose to refill his glass. "I think you're a fool if you believe my friendship is so casual."

Minton cleared his throat. "I must say, Your Grace, that for all my research into the Vaughan family, I never found reason to doubt your parentage. I don't believe anyone can offer proof that you're illegitimate."

"I can," Aunt Bess set her glass on a table and rose. "Derek, I never addressed this subject with you because I'd no idea you were so misinformed. Reggie told me you left because you'd learned the truth and were disgusted by it. It's true you're illegitimate, but you're not Alicia's child. You're the son of Reginald Vaughan and his mistress, Deborah Preston."

Derek stared at her, unable to comprehend her words.

"When you left home, your father thought you couldn't forgive him for having an affair with a servant."

Harry set the Madeira bottle down. "Mother, how came you to know this? This is not a subject for gently reared young ladies."

"Nonsense." She retrieved her glass and had Harry fill it and the others. "In my day, women were not as missish as they are now. Alicia was my sister-in-law, and I learned the story first from her. It wasn't my secret to tell, and truth be known, Reggie and I both hoped neither of you boys would ever hear of the scandal, for the secret was well-guarded. Even Alicia never betrayed it." With every glass filled, Aunt Bess sat down again, and motioned Derek to an empty chair.

Mechanically, he folded his legs and sat while she started her tale.

"As a young man, your father fell in love with a maid who worked in his family's house. Her name was Deborah Preston. When Reggie set up an establishment of his own in London, he moved his beloved Deborah into it and made her his mistress. He begged her to marry him, but she refused, saying his family would never accept her. Eventually, he did as his family thought proper and offered for Alicia Coatsworth. Alicia was the toast of the Season with beauty, elegance, and what she lacked in breeding, she more than compensated for with her dowry. She could have had any man she wanted, but she'd set her heart on Reggie. They were wed, and soon thereafter Reggie discovered Deborah was with child. He immediately removed to the country with Alicia and found lodging for Deborah nearby."

Aunt Bess shook her head sadly, her lips forming an uncharacteristic frown. "Alicia told me she thought Reggie leased their romantic cottage because he wanted her to himself. In fact, Reggie was concerned because Deborah was losing her health. On the eve of delivering the child, she begged Reggie to promise her he wouldn't abandon their baby. He promised, and when Deborah died in childbirth, Reggie brought the newborn home and unfolded his tale to Alicia. To her credit, Alicia stood by the man she'd wed and said that if he were determined to keep his son, she would like it presumed that it was her son, too. And so she willingly signed your birth record, even when Reggie insisted you be given your mother's family name."

"My middle name," Derek muttered. His whole world tipped on its axis. Summer was winter and night was day. He wasn't his mother's son—he'd always been grateful he didn't look like Alicia Vaughan, and now he understood why. He rubbed his cheek with one hand as he recalled his final interview with his father.

"*I hope one day you'll understand and be able to forgive me and your mother. I'd like to explain—*"

"*There's no need, sir. The story is plain to see. You got caught up with a common trollop. She got what she deserved and you've been stuck with me.*"

"*You'll show proper respect for your mother, around me, my boy. I loved her.*"

"I called my mother a trollop, and Father struck me. He'd never hit me in his life, and I couldn't understand why a man would attempt to defend the honor of a woman who clearly had none."

Aunt Bess took hold of Minton's hand. "Alicia's story was tragic. She'd always been a flirt, was accustomed to men struck by her beauty and declaring their undying devotion to her. It galled her to discover the one man to whom she'd lost her heart didn't return her love. She took her revenge with that string of torrid affairs that had everyone's tongues wagging. Reggie didn't care a fig about it, as long as she held to her bargain never to divulge your true parentage." Derek recalled his childhood with parents who barely spoke. A mother who eyed him warily, a father who watched him with pride. Then another thought occurred to him. "If Alicia Vaughan wasn't my mother, than we're not truly related."

Harry rose. "Derek, so help me, if you try to deny us as family now, I'll personally mill you down. Hasn't it occurred to you family has little to do with the blood that runs through your veins? Do you think Johnny loved Martha and Tom any less, or they her, because she was not their true child?"

Aunt Bess rose and came to take Derek's hand. "Derek, I've known you since you were a baby, and Reggie believed the sun rose and set because of you. Brothers are often not as close as you and Harry are. You'll always be a part of my family."

Derek's brow furrowed as he contemplated his mother. Deborah Preston had been so young when she died. If he died tomorrow, his one regret would be that he hadn't told Johanna he loved her. A vision of her awaking and reading his note hit him. He'd not had the nerve to face her. He'd urged her to leave when he should have begged her stay.

Convinced he was the usurper at Ambersley, he'd been unworthy of her love. Once again, Rosalie had manipulated his emotions and done her best to destroy him. Derek closed his eyes, aware he may have destroyed Johanna's love last night.

He looked to Harry. "I need to return to London."

"Of course. I'll go with you. We can leave first thing in the morning."

"No, I must get back immediately." Seeing their shock at his urgent tone, Derek tried to explain. "Aunt Bess, I sacrificed my relationship with my father because I wasn't brave enough to stay and hear him out. I cannot risk the same thing happening with Johanna. She's far too important. We fought last night about her...preoccupation with Worthing. This morning I left her the choice to follow her heart, but I denied her the one piece of information that might sway her decision in my favor—I didn't tell her I love her. If there's any chance she loves me—"

"I'm sure she does," Aunt Bess replied with a nod.

"Harry, I'll need fresh horses for my coach—"

"You cannot drive back to London tonight, Derek," Minton interrupted. He turned to Harry. "My boy, saddle up your fastest mount. Derek will need to ride if he expects to reach London before midnight."

Aunt Bess beamed at her husband-to-be.

For Johanna, the day had progressed with as many highs and lows as a hungry hawk over an open field. She'd felt awful when she awoke, then been elated by Derek's note, only to be felled by discovering he'd left town. She tried to imagine Derek's joy when he returned to find her waiting, and she could finally tell him she'd chosen her love. Then doubts assailed her—would he be joyful, or was he hoping she would leave him? But surely his selflessness in letting her leave him to find her happiness spoke of love. *Didn't it?*

By mid-afternoon, she decided love was the most miserable emotion on earth.

In desperation, she sifted through their invitations to see if anything prompted her to go out for the evening. Finding a theater party invitation from Lord Worthing, she weighed the merits of speaking with him against the dangers. But Derek wasn't due back for days, and she wasn't making an assignation to see Worthing alone. Decided, she dashed off a quick note and had a footman carry it to Worthing's townhouse with directions to await his reply. Within the hour, she had Worthing's assurance that she'd be a welcome addition to his gathering.

Johanna waited as Nancy affixed the mother-of-pearl comb in her hair. When finished, she rose and allowed the girl to assist her into a dress of rich turquoise silk. A single glance at her reflection, and Johanna nearly surrendered the notion of going out. Aunt Bess had selected this fabric because it matched Johanna's eyes, but since she'd slept so little the previous night, she felt it might not be best to call attention to her eyes. With a shrug, she decided to brave it. She couldn't stay home all night and wait.

She sent word for Rory to bring the coach around in an hour and descended the stairs to face the lonely ordeal of supper. She was just finishing a veal cutlet under Mrs. Chalmer's watchful eye, when Paget entered. "Mr. Barlow is downstairs inquiring whether you are at home, my lady."

With a frown, Johanna dabbed her lips with a napkin. Whatever business could Reed Barlow have with her? Anything was a welcome diversion, she decided, and so asked Paget to send him up.

"Thank you for agreeing to see me at this hour, Lady Ambersley." Mr. Barlow bowed formally over her hand. "Is the duke not at home?"

"He's gone out of town for a few days. Is there some way I may help you?" Johanna motioned to a chair across from her, and he seated himself.

"If I could have some private conversation with you." None too discreetly, he nodded his head at Mrs. Chalmers and Paget.

Mrs. Chalmers cleared Johanna's plate and left, but Paget looked as if he were permanently molded to his spot by the door.

Mr. Barlow leaned forward and whispered, "It concerns Olivia. She sent me personally."

Johanna nodded. "Paget, if you would excuse us for a few minutes." It wasn't a question, and for a moment, she feared the retainer would refuse to do her bidding. Although he visibly warred with himself, Paget stiffly withdrew and closed the doors behind him. She had no doubt he stood as close to the keyhole as he dared.

"Whatever is amiss?"

Mr. Barlow rose and began to pace the room, his hands shoved in his pockets. "Lady Ambersley, you've been in Olivia's confidence. She told you she hoped to wed me, yes?" Gaining her nod, he continued. "We knew we would never be able to win her mother's consent, and a few days ago, Olivia suggested we elope. I agreed I thought we could make it to the border and be wed, and so, today we made the attempt. Only, the coach broke down, and we knew we would be stranded

314

overnight. Olivia started to cry and swore her mother would send her to a convent on the Continent, and, oh, Lady Ambersley, it was horrible."

Johanna, who had experienced Olivia's bouts of hysteria when things didn't go her way, nodded. "Where is she now?"

"She's at an inn outside the City. I've already heard Lady Vaughan and Curtis are scouring the town for her. She begged me to come here and find Lord Ambersley or you so she had an ally when they find her. I hate to ask it of you when your husband is away, but would you—"

"Of course I'll come to her. Let us fetch Olivia and bring her here. I haven't left the house, and the staff will readily agree she's been with me all day."

Mr. Barlow sighed as if the weight of the world had been lifted from his shoulders. "Thank you, Lady Ambersley. Olivia and I will be so grateful if you can find a way to patch this up."

"Does this mean you've given up the notion of eloping?" she asked hopefully.

"Absolutely," he replied with conviction. Relief eased the worried lines in his brow.

With a nod, Johanna rose. "Then let's set out. I was going to attend the theater tonight, and Rory is bringing my coach around—"

He interrupted her. "I have a hired coach parked out front. We can leave immediately."

Johanna agreed. In the event she had trouble with Olivia, it might be better not to have her own staff offering unwanted assistance. In fact, it was best if they suspected none of this until she brought Olivia back. She called for Paget.

His quick entrance bespoke that he'd waited with his hand on the knob.

"Paget, there's been a change of plan. Mr. Barlow is going to escort me to the theater tonight. We'll be taking his coach, so thank Rory for me and tell him I apologize for troubling him needlessly."

Paget emanated disapproval, but remained silent until he'd followed her down to the lower hall. "What shall I tell his lordship if he returns while you're out, my lady?"

"I don't think that's likely, do you?" She looked him in the eye until he shook his head. She tugged on her gloves. "If he does return, tell him I've gone to the theater with Mr. Barlow, and I'll be home when I get home."

"Anything else?" Paget asked as he opened the door for her.

Exasperated by his over-protectiveness, Johanna called back, "Don't wait up!"

Paget stood in the doorway, golden light spilling from behind him onto the flagstones until long after the jingle of harness and the clop of hooves had faded into the mist.

A heavy damp fog made for slow going as the coach picked its way through the London streets. As annoyed as she was with Olivia's prank, Johanna couldn't help but be grateful she had solid activity to occupy her time and thoughts. She would be able to resolve this, and with luck, no one in Derek's family need know what poor judgment Olivia had shown. Johanna looked across at Reed Barlow. He was strikingly handsome, had exquisite manners and about as much sense as a sheep. Johanna couldn't imagine what Olivia still saw in him.

The lights on the carriage helped not a whit with visibility, but bounced off the fog as if it were a solid wall. The moist cloud also deadened all sound, and with her preoccupied thoughts, it was a long time before Johanna realized they'd left the city streets of London and picked up speed to a brisk trot.

"How far out of the City was this inn?" she asked.

He ducked his head a bit in penitence. "It might take longer than you'd planned, Lady Ambersley. I'm afraid I've brought you here under false pretenses. I assure you, it's the only way for me to marry Olivia."

৵৵

Paget was grateful to hear an imperious rapping on the front door less than two hours later, and he responded with a smile that faded once he discovered it was Lord Curtis and Lady Olivia on the doorstep and not his mistress.

"Where's Johanna? I need to see her at once," Olivia

demanded in her high-strung tone. Her eyes were bright and cheeks flushed.

Paget winced slightly, but saw no polite way to bar them entrance. "I'm afraid Lady Ambersley has gone to the theater this evening."

Olivia gave a huffy sigh.

He recognized Lord Curtis had been saddled with his sister's woes for hours and took pity when the young man asked if they could wait. Paget showed them to the front drawing room and took Olivia's pelisse and Curtis's hat.

"When will she be back?" Olivia asked.

"I couldn't say, miss."

Olivia gave a melodramatic throaty groan, an exact, if unfortunate, copy of Lady Vaughan. "I cannot understand why she would go out when she knew I would want to speak with her tonight. Honestly, she can be the most self-centered, thoughtless creature that—"

"Olivia!" Curtis sharply interrupted her tirade. "Paget, that will be all."

Paget bowed and left the room with no expression on his face.

Curtis looked at his flushed sister. "Livvie, you cannot say things like that about Johanna in this house, especially before the staff. I suspect they repeat everything to her."

"I'm sorry, Curtis. I shall be more careful. I just wish she were here to tell me whether she knew Reed would be leaving town."

"I told you, he said he had to go to Dover to help a friend. I don't think he'd planned his trip at all."

Olivia looked out at the swirling fog. "I wish he hadn't gone in such rotten weather. Do you suppose he'll arrive safely? You don't suppose he'll get lost in this?"

Curtis gave a snide laugh. "Reed Barlow won't even notice the fog. The question is whether he could find his way to Dover on a clear day in broad daylight."

"Don't say nasty things about him." Olivia stamped her slippered foot. "I'm going to marry him."

"Heaven preserve us," swore Curtis.

ౡ∕ల

Derek pushed his steed as much as he dared, but the journey from Bath to London ran close enough to the river that fog made for dangerous traveling. He didn't dare lame the horse by galloping into mists with no visibility, and once or twice even feared he'd taken a wrong turn.

The ride gave him ample time to remember his childhood and his father. He replayed the events leading up to his departure from his father's home and saw clearly how his stepmother had manipulated him. She had to know Derek had misconstrued the truth. Natural enough, when you grew up as the son of the most notoriously promiscuous lady in London. How was he to know Alicia Vaughan had been a devoted bride until she learned her husband loved another?

Derek drew rein to get his bearings when the road forked, and chose the high road through Richmond. His thoughts returned to Rosalie. She'd tried to rule Ambersley during his absence, clearly hoping he would never return from India. For years, she'd made him feel like a thief within his own house, allowing him to rebuild Ambersley while plotting to strip him of his title. Then there was her role in unmasking Johnny— she'd driven her own children to tell lies about the boy because she felt Johnny had usurped Curtis's position as Derek's younger brother. And she'd forced Johanna's marriage to secure her fortune for the Vaughan family.

Clearly, he had to remove Rosalie, once and for all, from their lives.

He knew he would be successful in dealing with his stepmother. He prayed he would be as fortunate with his wife.

The clocks chimed eleven as Derek's horse crab-stepped along the cobbled streets of St. James. Derek had never been so happy to see the house on Grosvenor Square, lit up and welcoming. He strode into the hall, unfastening his cloak.

Paget bustled in to relieve him of the damp fabric. "Your Grace, we'd not expected you back tonight."

"Where's Johanna?" He glanced up the stairs in hopes of catching a glimpse of her.

"She's not here, my lord." Paget cleared his throat. "She went to the theater with Mr. Barlow."

Derek stilled, his anticipation dwindling to disappointment. "When do you expect her home?"

"She said she would be home when she came home," the butler said quizzically.

He didn't like the butler's downcast eyes. "And—?"

"She said we shouldn't wait up."

Uneasiness hummed through Derek's veins at those words. He'd seen Johanna dancing and laughing with Reed Barlow, but that was nothing but innocent flirtation. Surely she didn't love the handsome dolt. A glance at the hall clock told him the theater would only just have ended. With the crush of carriages, it could be another hour or more before she returned. There was no need to fret. Yet his uneasiness remained.

"Very well, Paget." Derek handed his gloves to the unhappy old hawk. "Anything else I should know?"

Paget cleared his throat. "Your brother and sister are awaiting Lady Ambersley in the drawing room."

Derek frowned, but the butler offered no further information. Their eyes met and held for an instant before Derek nodded dismissal. He climbed the stairs to the drawing room slowly.

Curtis and Olivia pounced on him as soon as he opened the drawing room door.

"Derek!" Curtis exclaimed with relief.

"Where's Johanna?" Olivia demanded.

Derek smiled ruefully at her unconscious selfishness and strode to the sideboard to pour a glass of brandy. The fog had left him chilled. "I'm told she went to the theater with Reed Barlow."

"What?" Olivia gave a horrified shriek. "That conniving little witch—she *stole* Reed. She must have planned it all along. What a fool I was to trust her." Her cheeks turned red with rage, and her eyes grew icy.

Derek looked to Curtis for a clarification of this tirade, but his brother had stepped to the sideboard to fill a glass for himself.

"Livvie, if you're going to call my wife names, I'd appreciate an explanation."

Instead of the guilty apology he expected, Olivia raised her chin. "We've been made fools, Derek. Your wife has run off with my fiancé. These past two weeks, she convinced me she was helping my cause. Mama didn't approve my choice, so it was difficult for Reed and I to see each other. Johanna delivered notes between us, but apparently she spent so much time with Reed, she decided she wanted him for herself."

Tension built within him, but he knew Olivia was prone to overreact. He took a hearty gulp of the strong amber liquid, hoping to warm his stiff fingers and cold toes. "It seems a bit far-fetched to assume they ran off together when Paget said they only went to the theater."

Curtis drained his glass. "I must agree with Olivia. I believe they've left town together. Reed told me he needed to help a friend, and he'd be leaving London for a few days. He hired a coach this afternoon to take him to Dover and asked me to make his apologies to Livvie for they'd planned on meeting at a party this evening."

"How do you know about the coach?" Derek asked.

Curtis laughed. "I lent him the damn money for it. He said it was imperative that he go today, said his future happiness depended on it. I didn't give it any thought. Reed is always over dramatizing things. But he didn't have the money for the coach, and I lent it to him." Curtis looked at his stepbrother's stony face. "There must be some logical explanation, Derek. I cannot believe Johanna would run off with Reed Barlow. It makes no sense."

The truth settled on him, denser and colder than the fog. She'd left him. He'd offered her a choice, and she'd chosen to go at once. "On the contrary. It all makes perfect sense," Derek responded quietly. "Johanna and I fought last night. I suspect she convinced Reed to help her escape me." He downed the remainder of his brandy.

His earlier euphoria fled before the engulfing pain of this loss. There would be no re-kindling of Johanna's love if she'd left him. Just as St. John had predicted, Derek had held her away—despite his noble reasons—only to lose her. Perhaps it was best this way.

"I want to kill both of them," Olivia announced to the room at large.

Curtis looked from one to the other. "Why don't we go after them? Derek, you cannot tell me you're willing to have it known Johanna left you for Reed Barlow. They must pay for this. There's no reason for them to go to Dover unless they're leaving the country. High tide isn't until afternoon, and we could reach Dover by midmorning."

Olivia tugged on his arm. "Yes, let's. Derek, you should call Reed out for trying to steal your wife."

Derek couldn't imagine calling out someone as inept as Reed Barlow. He'd derive much more satisfaction by calling out Johanna. No doubt she was the real culprit who'd somehow convinced Reed to carry her off at the opportunity Derek had allowed her. Besides, she'd be a far fairer match for him than Reed in a duel. Derek cursed himself. If he'd forced her to go to Bath with him, none of this would have happened. He could have saved his whole family another scandal.

Then another, more unnerving, possibility occurred to him. Reed Barlow was Worthing's cousin. What if the dandy were conveying Johanna to her true love in Dover? Derek tried to picture Johanna living happily with St. John. After all, he'd offered her the chance to choose her love. A vision of Johanna naked in St. John's arms obliterated any noble thoughts of letting her go. He was damned if he would allow any other man to steal what was his—not without fighting for her. St. John might be a better man, but he couldn't love Johanna more than Derek, and he would move heaven and earth to tell her so.

"Paget!" Derek turned to Curtis and Olivia. "I'm going to Dover. You may accompany me, but no complaining. The trip will be fast, and probably uncomfortable."

"I want to see them pay," Olivia responded.

Curtis's eyes flashed in agreement.

Derek nodded assent, but then seemed to catch himself. "Where's your mother?"

"Holed up with a headache," Curtis said. "She took to her

bed hours ago. I doubt she'll know we're gone."

"I'll have Stokes deliver a note, so she won't worry. Ah, Paget, tell Cushing to harness the grays to the chaise. We leave for Dover as soon as he's able."

Paget's brows flew up in surprise, but he responded immediately to the command.

Derek turned back to his brother and sister. "We shall find them, fear not. And then we will lay bare the truth of this matter."

❧

Less than an hour later, Derek stepped out to the mews lit by torches and lanterns. The horses were hitched, tossing restless heads and held in check by yawning grooms. Man and horse alike knew this was no hour to be traveling.

Paget handed a basket up to Cushing on the box. Wise man. No doubt the basket contained food to sustain them on their trek. Derek tucked the box he carried under his arm and went to join his siblings as Curtis handed Olivia into the chaise.

"A family outing, at this odd hour?"

Derek turned at the familiar sarcasm to find St. John handing the reins of his horse to a groom. *Damn.* Even in the midst of this remarkable activity, the man appeared nothing but bored. Derek handed the box to Curtis. "Wait inside while I have a private word with Worthing. Store the box on the floor beneath the seat, but make certain we can reach it if we meet trouble."

Curtis nodded before climbing into the chaise.

Derek strode to confront St. John. "Where is she?" he demanded.

St. John's eyes glinted in the torchlight. "She's not here?"

"You know damn well she isn't."

"I only know Johanna sent me a note earlier this afternoon saying she planned to join a theater party I was hosting. She never appeared." St. John's eyes narrowed. "What did you do to her?"

Derek's jaw tightened at the accusation. "I drove her away.

My wife has run off with your young cousin." After last night, he hated to admit the situation to his rival, but his earlier uneasiness had returned. He needed answers, and St. John might have them.

"Reed?" St. John snorted with contempt. "Unlikely, at best."

"Be that as it may, he laid his plans and stole away with my wife earlier tonight. We have reason to believe they've gone to Dover and may be sailing for the Continent. We hope to catch them. My brother and sister go with me." Eager to set forth, Derek turned back to the coach.

"May I come, too?"

The request, sincerely made, caught Derek off-guard. "To what purpose?"

"To help my brother reclaim what he's lost." St. John regarded him steadily.

Derek swallowed. "I may have lost Johanna for good."

"I doubt that." St. John put out his hand. "If you'll have me, I'd like to help."

Derek considered his former nemesis. So many of Derek's judgments had been driven by wrong beliefs. They had much to forgive, but this man had proven a true friend to Johanna when she'd needed someone. He clasped St. John's hand firmly. "Let us be off then."

22

"Do you think Olivia would mind if we only came to London for part of the Season? I'm not sure how I shall afford it, but if the duke lets us live at Ambersley part of the year—"

A burst of birdsong caught Johanna's attention and warned her of the coming dawn. She didn't bother to point out that Derek wasn't likely to allow the man who had disappeared with his wife to marry his sister *and* live at Ambersley.

Her experience during the night had taught her that reasoning with Reed was useless. He listened to her arguments, nodded politely and then launched another flight of fancy. In self-defense, Johanna had resorted to addressing him by his first name, as if speaking to a not very bright child. Eventually, she did her best to ignore him.

They arrived in Dover after sunup. The bumpy road and damp chill had left her stiff and irritable from lack of sleep when Reed nudged her awake. She'd quickly abandoned the notion of jumping from the moving carriage in the middle of a foggy night, but as they drew to a stop at an inn yard, Johanna planned to demand assistance from the innkeeper.

Her plan was thwarted when Reed pulled a small pistol from his cloak. Upon descending from the coach, he announced he was a Bow Street Runner. He proclaimed her his prisoner and demanded a private dining room. The innkeeper, a surly man with hair grizzled around his ears and an overbearing wife, apologized that his inn didn't boast private dining rooms, but he could close up the coffee room and tell everyone to go elsewhere. After much cogitation, Reed agreed this would do.

Though Johanna appreciated his talent for playacting—indeed, he was fit to rival Edmund Kean on the Drury Lane stage—she knew Reed could never have hatched this ploy on his own. Unable to judge his familiarity with firearms, she dared not cross him. The last thing she needed was to get someone killed. Instead, while the coffee room was being prepared for them, she bent her thinking toward who would convince Reed to abduct her. Who would be able to promise him a chance to win Olivia if this went well? Who would stand to gain from her own disappearance? The answer burst upon her with rays of enlightenment—Curtis. He was Reed's friend, he was Derek's heir, and he had always wanted to cause trouble for her.

His interference couldn't have come at a worse time. If Derek returned and found her missing, he would assume the worst. She should have left him a note before leaving the house. Gnawing the tip of her fingernail, Johanna tried to uncover some way out of this stupid mess.

The innkeeper returned to the coach to tell Reed the coffee room was prepared. "We shuttered the windows, and there's only the one door. She won't be able to give you the slip. But I'll need the coffee room to use when the Mail Coach arrives at two this afternoon. The customers are always mighty thirsty when they get down from the Mail."

"Where does the Mail go from here?" Johanna asked.

The innkeeper looked at her as if she'd bitten him, but he wasn't impervious to a pretty girl in a bright blue-green dress. "It goes back to London."

Johanna didn't dare speak another word until the innkeeper had shown them into the darkened coffee room. He called to his wife to bring their guests breakfast, and bowed himself out to Reed.

As soon as the door clicked shut, Johanna faced her abductor. "Reed, you must get me a ticket on the Mail. I haven't money enough with me, but I'll repay you when we return home."

Reed smiled with the success of his playacting. "Be patient, Lady Ambersley. Someone *is* bringing you a ticket."

"For the Mail?" Johanna asked suspiciously.

In answer, he smiled and pretended to lock his lips closed and throw away the key.

Johanna gave an exasperated groan. "I've had enough of this nonsense. I shall find some way back to London. Oh, shoot me if you must!" She saw him raise the pistol, and did her best to bluff him.

Reed didn't give ground as she thought he would, but leveled the pistol at her with what looked like remarkably accurate aim. "I cannot allow you to ruin this for me now, Lady Ambersley. You must wait with me here. Otherwise, I might never win Olivia."

The innkeeper chose that moment to enter with their breakfast, his eyes widening at the sight of the pistol. She crossed her arms and pursed her lips as he laid two steaming plates of eggs and sausages on the table. She watched him wipe his hands on his dirty apron and then lean toward Reed.

In an exaggerated whisper, he said, "I've some rope if you'd like to tie her up." He winked at Reed.

Johanna reminded herself that throwing something at them wouldn't improve her situation in the least.

After the innkeeper left, with the clink of Reed's coins in his pocket, Reed motioned her to sit. She watched him set his pistol beside his plate, and finally she sat across from him and played with her food.

She contemplated the gun, but quickly discarded the option. She never knew if a gun's aim would be true, and they seemed far more difficult to control. Reed appeared more confident than she about the pistol, therefore, she wouldn't chance wrestling it from him.

She picked at her plate. The sausage grease was coagulating, and the sight of ale on the table at this hour turned her stomach. Reed attacked his meal with gusto, and Johanna tried to imagine Olivia's reaction to her love's eating habits.

With a tiny sigh, she pushed her plate away and sipped her acrid coffee instead. She glanced around the public room with its trestle tables, pewter plates and tankards, and dingy whitewashed walls. Her eyes drifted past the fireplace surrounded in rustic local stone. No fire was lit—it might have helped dispel the gloominess of the shuttered room. The brightest thing in the room was her dress, and she felt hopelessly out of place. The innkeeper probably thought she was a strumpet.

Then her eyes lighted on a cutlass and four rapiers hanging upon the wall. She studied them intently as she sipped her coffee. With a sword, she would have the advantage over Reed. She darted a glance his way to see him dabbing a spot of grease from his shirt. She felt sure she could best him in a fencing match.

"Reed, if my husband were here, you know he would call you out."

Reed drained the ale from his tankard then dabbed at his mouth with his fingertips. "But your husband isn't here, Lady Ambersley."

"Indeed he's not," she replied, pleased he was able to deduce this simple fact. "Therefore, I have no one to defend this insult to my honor."

He gave this some thought. "I haven't insulted you."

"You kidnapped me, Reed. Most people would consider that an insult to my honor."

He smiled and wagged a finger at her. "That's your story, Lady Ambersley. If anyone discovers this escapade, I will say you ran away with me willingly."

Johanna quelled the urge to box his ears. *Do you think after announcing you and I ran off together, that Olivia will marry you?* But she held her tongue, for no good could come of giving him that hare to chase. She held true to her course. "I didn't run away with you, Reed. That's a lie, and I demand satisfaction."

She stripped off one then the other of her evening gloves. She, too, could play a part, and playing the helpless lady might give her the element of surprise. "I believe I should cast one of these down before you, but I hate to since the floor looks filthy."

He stared at her for a full second before he burst out laughing. "That's rich, Lady Ambersley. How can you demand satisfaction? Am I to believe you're challenging me?"

"And why not? My challenge is no worse than any man's. We'll use these." She tossed her gloves on a chair and turned to grasp two of the rapiers from the wall. They came out of their holders easily, light and balanced. She felt more secure as soon as her fingers curled around their hilts. She turned back to see him rise from his chair. The pistol on the table lay forgotten as he came toward her with a smile of condescension on his face.

"I couldn't accept a challenge from you. What would I do if you were hurt? Please, Lady Ambersley, put the notion out of your head. Give me the swords."

"I'll not be patronized, Reed. Derek taught me the basics of fencing. I think I can hold my own. As for being hurt, I'm not afraid. Are you?" She raised an eyebrow at him.

Reed flushed to his roots. "Of course not. But these are not foils with safety tips. No doubt Lord Ambersley has convinced you of your own prowess, but I'm an accomplished swordsman and more than your equal."

"If that be the case, than you've nothing to fear. You need only defend yourself to prevent hurting me and to prevent me hurting you. If indeed you are a master, I shall be unable to touch you." She tried a disarming smile. "Come, let us attempt two or three passes. If I'm not your match, I'll openly admit it, surrender my sword and be a good girl. However, if I best you, then you must purchase me that ticket and send me home."

With a huff, Reed ran his hand through his blonde curls, then he accepted one of the swords from her. Johanna gathered her skirt behind her as he pushed the chairs and a table out of their way and doffed his coat. He lectured her throughout. "Very well, Lady Ambersley, I shall allow you three passes to gauge your abilities. *If* you prove you know what you're about, then I shall consider whether to accept your wager."

They took positions in the center of the room a few feet

apart. Johanna saluted him neatly with her rapier.

Reed shook his head. "I feel so silly. Fencing at this hour, and you in a dress. You're a very headstrong female, my lady, and I must say it's not very becoming. I'm so glad Olivia doesn't share these obstinate tendencies. Now, I'll do my best not to harm you. Please take care."

Johanna closed her eyes for a brief moment to fully experience the perspective of his devotion to Olivia. Only a blind man could be ignorant of her willful ways, and then he'd have to be deaf as well. She opened her eyes to see him saluting her, and she looked forward to wiping the condescending smile from his face.

Her first pass, she concentrated on the feel of the rapier in her hand—its weight, its balance, its resiliency. Confident of her weapon, she noted the feel of the floor, the play of the muscles in her arm and thighs, and the rate of her own heart and breathing. The dress was awkward with its rustling silk skirt and the tight sleeves that didn't allow free movement for her shoulders. She longed for her boots, for the thin-shod slippers she wore offered no protection from the uneven floorboards, and she'd stubbed her toe on her first lunge.

Reed met her parries competently but without ingenuity or flair. Johanna suspected his lessons followed the same routine day in and out, and he was most effective if attacked in the precise order of moves he always practiced. He made no aggressive advances, but defended his position with dogged determination. With so little force behind either of their swords, only a soft clink and slide sounded each time the blades touched. In one deft motion, Johanna pierced through his guard, and tapped him on the upper arm with the side of the rapier blade.

"*Touché*," Reed acknowledged. He grinned at her as if she'd done a parlor trick.

They both stepped back to begin anew. Johanna's pulse quickened, and her muscles felt warm and loose. If not for the frustrating fact she was stuck in Dover, she might have enjoyed this—the throbbing toe notwithstanding. "You're being too generous with me, Reed. If you're not careful, I'll tear your shirt."

He scoffed at the implausibility of such a statement.

Johanna couldn't resist baiting him. "You think it impossible? Perhaps you'd care to place a wager upon it—say twenty pounds?"

Reed considered this. "Twenty pounds it is. I can buy Olivia a new outfit once we're wed."

Johanna thought it unlikely twenty pounds would purchase more than a hat for Olivia with her expensive tastes, but it would secure her a way home.

She saluted her captor again, and immediately started her advance. He parried right, and she feinted left. She tried to get past his guard, but he was quicker than she'd credited. Perspiration trickled between her breasts by the time she saw the opening she needed. She swirled the tip of her blade right before his face, stepped forward with her right foot, and as Reed leaned to his left to stop her advance, she flicked her wrist and went directly for his sword arm. The sound of rending fabric was music to her ears as she pierced his sleeve but never scratched his skin.

She stepped back and lowered her blade while hiding her satisfaction. "Do you acknowledge the hit?" Reed was getting just what his foolishness deserved. She felt she'd earned this privilege to teach him a lesson.

"Aye, you tore it neatly, and my best damn shirt—oh, excuse me, my lady. I didn't mean to curse before you."

"Don't give it a thought. My husband has used that word often enough before me. Are you ready for round three?"

He wiped his brow with the back of his wrist and nodded without comment.

Johanna noted a look of determination in his eye. She understood its full meaning when they saluted each other, and Reed launched an attack on her. She retreated neatly, and parried his thrusts. Obviously, it had occurred to him that as long as she defended her position, she couldn't advance on him. She warded off his attack with cool-headed parries. Even pushed against a table, she refused to let him ruffle her. Instead, she tried to make him think she flagged. Her dress clung to her damp skin, and she made no effort to control her panting. Ever the gentleman, Reed pulled back. "Tiring, Lady Ambersley? Are you prepared to give in?"

"No, there's yet one more thing I must do. I'm sorry, but you've given me no choice." Johanna steeled herself, and advanced on him like a whirlwind. Her wrist ached fiercely, but she was determined to make a stand here and now. Aiming directly for his right shoulder, she pierced his shirt and then flesh.

Reed gasped in shock and pain as a brilliant bloom of blood stained his shirt.

Her stomach turned queasy at the sight, but she dropped her sword and rushed forward to help him take a chair. "Here, let me get your coat to staunch the blood." She wadded his superfine coat into a ball.

"You stabbed me! You *purposely* stabbed me!"

"You forced me. I warned you I wouldn't remain here. Put this against the wound." She held the coat out to him,

His eyes grew round with horror. "That coat's by Weston—do you know what it cost me?"

"It could cost you your arm if we don't stop the bleeding," Johanna said with cruel candor.

It worked. With closed eyes, he motioned her to place the treasured coat over the wound.

She did so gently, but asked with firm persistence, "Reed, I'm sorry you became involved in all of this. You must tell me now, what was planned for me? And who made you do this?"

His eyelids fluttered, and Johanna feared he would faint without giving her the information she sought. "Reed, Reed!" His skin color turned papery white, and she cursed herself for allowing frustration to overcome her common sense. She shouldn't have wounded him. She climbed to her feet intent on calling for help when she heard the door open. She spun around, ready to beg the innkeeper for aid.

Lady Vaughan stood in the doorway.

Johanna's shock gave way to dread as her eyes caught sight of a small pistol in the woman's hand. It was the exact mate of Reed's pistol lying on the table.

Reed seemed to recover himself sufficiently to greet his patroness. "Lady Vaughan, I did it. I kept her here."

"So you did, Mr. Barlow, a very good job. It appears you took an injury, and for that I'm sorry. We'll see to it as soon as this business is finished." Lady Vaughan prowled into the room with the rustle of blue silk.

Johanna smoothed the creases from the front of her dress, faintly aware she was no longer the only one overdressed for this hour of the morning. She raised her chin but always kept the gun in the periphery of her vision. "Lady Vaughan, I've been trying to get some answers. What's the meaning of all this? Why have I been brought to Dover?"

The raven-haired woman smiled. "You've been brought to Dover, my dear, because you are taking a special journey, and I couldn't let you go without coming myself to bid you farewell."

A chill ran down Johanna's spine.

Her lips turned a loathsome smile. "You were so good to go into the garden with Worthing. It was the perfect opening to my little play. Now you've even been good enough to injure Reed. I hope you'll like your new life in America."

Johanna raised shaky fingers to her brow. After a long night with almost no food and all the excitement of this morning, she couldn't have heard Lady Vaughan right. "America? What do you mean?"

With a chuckle, Lady Vaughan took stage in the center of the room. "Did Reed not mention it? How kind of him to save the best for me. Johanna, you've left your husband because of your passion for Reed Barlow, and the two of you are sailing for Boston this afternoon. I have your tickets with me right here." She patted her reticule without once letting the gun waver.

"Lady Vaughan," Reed interrupted, "there must be some mistake. I'm not going to America. I'm going back to London to marry Olivia as you promised." He tried to sit up but only succeeded in bringing Johanna back to his side to check his wound.

Lady Vaughan shook her head with mock sorrow. "I'm

sorry to say, Reed, that you've become enamored with Johanna, or more likely her money, and you've cast caution aside to have her. Olivia will be heartbroken, of course, but she'll recover. And one day she'll marry the Marquess of Worthing, as befits her station."

Johanna felt Reed's shock at the older woman's duplicity. She wasn't surprised. She turned her head to glare at Lady Vaughan. "You cannot force me to board a ship. I won't go."

"My dear, the innkeeper believes you're the prisoner of a Bow Street Runner. I've confirmed the story, telling him you've been masquerading the streets of London claiming to be nobility only to rob helpless men. Now you've wounded the man who apprehended you. Lud, Johanna, you've made this too easy for me. If you don't board the ship, I'll see you put in jail."

Staring at the filth-covered floor, Johanna pictured Derek arriving home to hear she'd left with Reed Barlow. Missing without a trace. He already believed she loved another. He would assume the worst and go on with his life, happy to finally be rid of his faithless wife. All she had wanted was to set things right with him. They *loved* each other, she knew. She wouldn't relinquish this newly discovered purpose without a fight.

She looked again at Reed, but his head was lolled back and his eyes closed, from pain or anguish at his burst dreams, she didn't know. How foolish she'd been, believing him to be the enemy she needed to defeat. If she hadn't wounded him, he might have been of some use to her now. She spied Reed's gun still lying beside his breakfast plate. Lady Vaughan hadn't seemed to notice it as yet.

Hope pushed her to regain her feet. She knew not what she would say when she found her way back to Derek, but she'd return to him. "You've gone to all this trouble. It begs me to ask why you hate me so? What have I ever done to you?"

"You exist," Lady Vaughan spat. "You with your generations of Vaughan blood and all your money, you've ruined Olivia's chances this Season. Now, if you provide Derek with an heir, you'll cut Curtis out of his inheritance.

You took money from our pockets and food off our table, and you will never take away from me again."

A catlike smile played about her lips as she appraised Johanna. "You even did your best to turn Olivia against me. I saw your plan. You encouraged her to think this imbecile was worthy of her. Now you see what I've had to do to prove to Olivia I was right all along."

Johanna had been frustrated by Reed's abduction, but now gooseflesh spread up her arms as she tasted the bitterness of fear. She longed to challenge the woman, but needed to proceed with caution. Unlike Reed, her new opponent was crafty and made her own rules. Once joined in battle, the struggle could easily turn to the death. She needed a weapon and a diversion.

"You wanted Johnny out of your lives forever." Johanna sidled across to Reed's other side to check his forehead for signs of fever. She now stood three feet closer to his gun. "You must have hated it when I reappeared."

Eyes narrowed, the woman nodded. "Curtis and I had celebrated destroying Johnny. Not an hour after Curtis dragged you to the barn, Olivia came to me crying that she'd wronged you. I told her the price of going to London for her Season was for her to stand by her story before Derek. She was so distraught, but that only made it more plausible to him. I was positive he'd secretly murdered Johnny and disposed of the body, and I was glad."

A wave of compassion filled Johanna when she recalled those days with Derek. "But he'd always protected me. Even that furious, he couldn't kill me." She braved another step toward the weapon.

"Yes, and when he married you, he thought he could make you happy. Ha! The Vaughan men aren't known for making their wives happy. Reggie made Alicia hateful, and he made me bitter. Oh yes, I fancied myself in love with Reggie when I married him. But there was no room in Reggie's heart for anyone but Derek. He spared no regard for Curtis or even me. The sun rose and set for Derek as far as Reggie was concerned. Derek, the precious son of his precious love, Deborah."

Johanna paused inching forward at these words. "You told me Derek wasn't Reggie's son, but Alicia's—"

Lady Vaughan's laugh had the stark sound of a mockingbird at midnight. "He still believes that. It was my finest moment. I had to find a way to drive a wedge between them and make Reggie love me. But even after Derek left for India, Reggie made no room in his heart for me."

Johanna understood the pain of unrequited love, but not the way Lady Vaughan interpreted it. "Derek went to India, and you hoped he would never return."

"He fought with Wellesley at the battle of Assaye. He had every opportunity to get killed. Instead, he returned and took everything. *Everything.*"

"He inherited an estate on the brink of financial ruin, and he rebuilt it with his own hands," Johanna argued.

"Indeed. The first few years were difficult for all of us. I tried to get rid of him once, you know." Lady Vaughan's eyes had an almost wild gleam in them, and her smile broadened into a mockery.

Johanna felt the bottom drop out of her stomach. "The barn fire," she whispered.

Lady Vaughan nodded with smug satisfaction. "No one ever guessed. He was so engrossed with that horse, he never saw me. I hit him with a pitchfork handle. I hoped the stallion would trample him to death, but the horse escaped."

"You locked me in the harness room."

"Yes, but you escaped. You rescued Derek. To think I could have been rid of you both."

Johanna swallowed. "All this time, I was sure it was Curtis. He and I had such a rivalry then."

"Yes, he showed such promise," Lady Vaughan said with pride. "I thought about seeking his help in bringing you to Dover, but he wouldn't tolerate this kind of interference in Derek's life. Oh yes, he's become quite fond of both you and Derek."

Johanna's eyebrow lifted in disbelief, but she had other more pressing difficulties. "It was never my intention to harm you or your family in any way, Lady Vaughan, you know

AMY ATWELL

that."

"Ever noble." Her eyes narrowed to slits. "Yes, I know. You're just damnably in the way. That's why we must put you on the boat for America."

"I'll only come back. It may take months or years, but I'll return," Johanna warned.

Lady Vaughan chuckled. "I count on it. That's the beauty of the plan. Johanna, you're worth much more to me alive than dead right now. Derek is smitten with you, there's no denying that. Now, he'll be convinced you've betrayed him. He'll never forgive you, never let you come back. He'll also never divorce you. Derek will never have a legitimate heir. Ambersley will fall to Curtis sooner or later."

Johanna followed the far-fetched logic, and wondered if she were talking to Reed. "Possibly it will, but that could be years."

"It could be. Perhaps it will be much sooner than you think."

Any fear Johanna spared for herself washed away in the storm of protectiveness she felt for Derek. She was to be sent to America—undoubtedly, during her absence, Derek would meet with an "accident." She had to make a stand, here and now, even if it cost her everything.

Johanna lunged toward Reed's pistol on the table and grasped it between clammy fingers. She turned and aimed it at her adversary. "I'll not leave here without a fight. I've already bested Reed. Are you willing to meet my challenge?"

Lady Vaughan wavered when she first saw the pistol leveled at her, then she chuckled softly. "You won't kill me, Johanna. I don't think you have it in you to do it."

"Lady Ambersley!" Reed whispered loudly from behind her.

Johanna didn't dare turn to see what he needed. "Not now, Reed," she cautioned. She kept her full attention trained on Lady Vaughan. "You've told me I'm more valuable to you alive than dead. You won't kill me."

"I'd hate to, but then, it might be much simpler to get you on that ship if I wounded you."

"Can you trust your aim is true?"

"Can you?" Lady Vaughan countered.

Johanna smiled. "I've handled guns since childhood. I say we count to three and each take our best shot. I'm willing to live or die with the consequences." She expected the older woman to balk at her ploy.

Lady Vaughan considered her and seemed to measure the distance between them. Finally, she spoke. "Very well, my dear. I believe I'm more than up to your noble challenge."

Reed interrupted again. "Lady Ambersley, I must—"

"In a moment, Reed," Johanna said, cutting him off sharply. The clock over the unlit fireplace started to chime the hour, and Johanna tilted her head toward it. "On the fifth chime, Lady Vaughan?"

The older woman nodded assent.

Johanna heard nothing but the clock chimes as she concentrated on her aim. Even if she killed Lady Vaughan and hung for murder, at least Derek would be safe.

The hour chimes began. *One. Two. Three. Four.* As soon as the fifth one began, Johanna pulled the trigger. She felt the click of the hammer, but nothing else. The clock continued to chime.

Her pistol still aimed, Lady Vaughan smiled. "I applaud your courage. Unfortunately, what I already knew, and I'm sure it's what Reed was trying to tell you, is that your pistol is empty. Reed didn't want to risk any accidents. So you see, while you were being noble and fair, I already knew I would win. That's why you will never best me. You don't understand how to use the element of surprise to your advantage."

Johanna lunged at the older woman, determined to wrestle the pistol from her. She gripped her wrist and tried to take control of the gun, but both Lady Vaughan's hands were already there. The two women tussled with no loss or gain of ground until suddenly a shot rent the air.

Johanna heard the sharp report, smelled the powder, but everything was already pain, blood and blackness.

23

The Ram's Head was the third inn where Derek and his retinue stopped to seek the runaways. Not fancy, The Ram's Head was large and stood close to the docks. If Johanna and Reed planned on boarding a ship, this would be the most convenient place to stay. Derek hopped down from the carriage even as Cushing sawed on the reins to bring the horses to a standstill.

The innkeeper stood in the doorway and squinted. Recognizing members of the Quality, he turned ingratiating in a blink. "My lord, you honor us. How may we be of service? Fresh horses? A room perhaps? Or maybe a meal?" He undid the strings of his greasy apron and whisked it off with a bow as Curtis joined them.

Derek noted the man never gave clearance to allow entry. "I need information. I'm seeking a man and a woman. The man is tall and fair. The woman is wearing a turquoise gown, I believe."

Recognizing the description, the innkeeper smiled knowingly. "Ahh, the Bow Street Runner and his prisoner."

"I beg your pardon?"

"The Runner brought her in at gun point. I hear tell she masquerades as a lady of quality in order to rob gentlemen. Are you one of the gents she robbed? She's a fetching piece, she is," he finished slyly.

Derek stared the smirk down. Frost tinged his voice as he replied, "I believe that *fetching piece* is the Duchess of Ambersley and my wife. Where is she?"

The innkeeper's pudgy bluster faded, and he pointed toward a closed door. "In the coffee room, my lord."

A shot echoed from within the inn.

Derek halted in his tracks only a moment before rushing the portal, Curtis hard upon his heels. Together they burst through the closed door.

In the center of the room, Rosalie Vaughan held a small pistol. The acrid smell of gunpowder permeated the air, its residue lifting in a cloud. Johanna lay sprawled at her feet while blood pooled on the floor beside her.

"You've murdered the duchess," Reed Barlow noted with wonder. It was the first notice Derek took of his supposed rival who stretched oddly across a chair with a wad of superfine fabric bunched up against his shoulder and the sleeve of his shirt torn. Derek's gaze returned to bore at Rosalie.

She stared at him, horror etched on her face. She dropped the spent pistol to the floor with a thud.

He rushed forward, ignoring his stepmother to kneel by Johanna. He lifted her head gently and blanched at her pallor. Thankfully, he saw she still breathed. Blood seeped from two places in her upper left arm, and then he realized the ball from the shot must have passed through her limb. A red lump marred her forehead, showing she must have struck it when she fell.

Whispers of sound made him look up.

"Hold, Mother!" Curtis, his face white, held a small pistol pointed above Derek's head.

Derek realized Rosalie stood over him with a dagger in her hand and fiery hatred ablaze in her eyes. Clearly, she'd meant to stab him in the back.

She cast Curtis a look of contempt. "It's our chance to be rid of them both. Don't be a fool."

"I can't let you do this," Curtis said. His arm shook slightly.

She hesitated. "But I've done all this for you. Ambersley

belongs to you."

"I don't want it. I've never wanted it."

Rosalie glanced down at Derek. "You. You turned him against me."

Derek tensed, prepared to defend his injured wife.

With a wild eye, Rosalie glared at Curtis. "You won't shoot your own mother," she said with disdain as she raised her hand to strike.

Before Derek could spring, Worthing grabbed Rosalie from behind and cocked one of Derek's dueling pistols to her temple. "I, however, should have no such compunction," he said in her ear. "So, don't tempt me."

The dagger fell from Rosalie's hand and clattered to the floor.

Olivia entered the room and squeaked at the scene before her. "Mother!" Then she spied Reed, lolled in a chair. "Reed, you're hurt!" She ran to him.

Derek lifted Johanna in his arms, cradling her to him as if she weighed but a feather. He must have been mad to ever think he could live without her. She was his life, and finally he understood what his father had felt for the maid Deborah. It no longer mattered to Derek why Johanna had left him, or how she had come to be here with Reed Barlow and his stepmother. He only wanted her to wake up, so he could get down on his knees, swear his love and beg her to return home and never again leave his side.

He turned to the slack-jawed innkeeper. "I need a bedroom for the lady, and we must fetch a surgeon immediately."

The innkeeper scratched his head and finally offered a name.

"Curtis!" Derek's command brought his brother immediately. "Send Cushing to find Mr. Carbury of High Street. Bring him here at once."

Curtis looked one last time at his mother before stepping outside. Worthing settled Rosalie into a chair. Seeing her plans in ruins, she'd gone pale and silent.

The innkeeper's wife led Derek up the staircase to the front bedroom where he deposited Johanna gently on the tester bed. He used his handkerchief to bind her arm, grateful that the bleeding had slowed. Lowering himself onto a rickety chair, he leaned his forehead on the mattress beside the woman he loved, his fingers twined through hers. The door opened with a gentle squeak of rusty hinges. Derek rose to meet Curtis at the door.

"I talked with Reed. I think you should know what happened."

Derek glanced back at Johanna's prone form as he listened to Curtis recount Reed's interpretation of the night's events. "Thank you for telling me," he said into the awkward silence that followed.

"Reed said she was determined to return to London today, no matter the cost..." Curtis trailed off with an embarrassed sigh of inadequacy. "I'm sorry, Derek. I never imagined Mother would harm someone. What she did today is indefensible, I admit, but must we call the constable?"

Derek raked a troubled hand through his hair. Full well, he knew the personal cost of a public trial and the ensuing scandal. He wouldn't wish it on anyone. An idea struck him. "Reed says she has a ticket to board a ship for America?"

"Yes, I—" Curtis's eyes lit with understanding. "But won't she return?"

"If she does, she'll face prison for attempted murder. Tell her, if she goes, I'll provide an annual allowance for her."

"After what she's done to you, you'd show her such clemency?"

"Had she killed Johanna, I would have destroyed her. As it is, I'm more concerned with your future, yours and Olivia's. If she'll but stay on the other side of the ocean, an allowance is a small price to pay. I'm only sorry America has to deal with her."

"Then Worthing and I will see to it. Derek—" Curtis faltered but then looked up to meet his brother's eye. "Mother always tried to make me believe I'd be a better duke than you. I only hope one day I prove to be half the man you are."

Derek watched as his brother disappeared down the staircase, then he returned to Johanna's side.

The surgeon arrived minutes later, declared the bone untouched, and made quick work of cleansing the wounds. He recommended a compress for her bruised head, giving his opinion that it looked painful but not dangerous. The duchess, he assured, should make a full recovery. Finished, he repacked his small bag and went to check on the wounded young man downstairs.

Derek brushed his fingers across Johanna's forehead in a gentle caress. The need to hold her became as vital as a heartbeat, and he sat on the edge of the bed to gather her limp form against him. He wanted to pour all his rage and grief into her and have her turn it to love. Something she did so effortlessly. She took all his shortcomings and gave him hope for redemption. Her head cradled against his shoulder, he laid his cheek against her soft curls.

"Could you not hold me so tightly? My arm hurts like the very devil." Johanna's words fell like raindrops on the parched landscape of his soul.

Derek complied, and she lifted her head to consider him. He expected condemnation, guilt, fear, any of a number of emotions to appear on her face, but instead he saw wonder in her regard as she lifted her good arm and traced his unshaven jaw with a trembling fingertip. She met his eyes, and, Lord help him, she *smiled.*

"You followed me. Why?" she asked tremulously.

"Why? I came here after I learned my lovely wife had left town with another man. I should put you over my knee and beat you." He expected her blossoming smile to fade—instead, it opened full bloom, which only annoyed him more. "I've heard most of the story from Reed Barlow, but perhaps you'd be good enough to clarify some points which still make no sense. Such as when you launched yourself at my stepmother while she was holding a gun—had you no concern for your own safety?" He vented all the frustration of the last sixteen hours on her.

He loves me. Jubilation made Johanna lightheaded. When he thought she'd left him, he'd followed immediately. He might believe he followed out of jealousy, hatred, revenge, but they were all ploys to bring her back because he loved her.

She tried to focus her pounding head on his question. "My safety was never the issue. Your stepmother threatened to kill you so Curtis could inherit Ambersley. I had to stop her before she could bring you any harm."

"And why in blazes would you feel the need to protect me?"

"Because I love you," Johanna said simply.

Derek stared at her. The lump in his throat may well have been his heart trying to escape the strictures of his chest. He'd feared he would never hear those words from her again. This woman he loved stated them with straightforward simplicity and left him feeling oddly inadequate. "I feared I'd lost you. There's more you need to know..." he trailed off as Johanna shook her head.

"I know everything about you I need. I only hope one day you will trust me enough to love me."

"Trust was never the issue. Rosalie had me convinced I wasn't my father's son. How could I let you love me, knowing I was nothing but a bastard, a usurper?"

"I loved you knowing all that. I wed you knowing all that. Lady Vaughan told me the night she found us at Ambersley. She hoped by defaming you, she could coerce me into marrying Curtis."

This made no sense to him. "You married me even though I was on the verge of losing the title, Ambersley, everything? It defies reason—you could have wed Worthing."

She stared at him for a moment before shaking her head. "I should never have listened to you when you lectured me about love, for you don't understand it at all." She placed her hands on either side of his face and gazed into his eyes, hoping somehow to get through his very thick head. "I didn't want to wed Worthing. I married you—the one man I love, admire and respect—and who or what your parents were has nothing to do with it."

Derek held her gaze while he slowly absorbed her words. Just as he'd always dreamed and yet dared not hope, here was a woman willing to love him for the man he was, not the title

he bore nor the lands he owned. Yet, if all that were true—
"Then why weren't you happy about marrying me?"

"Because *you* weren't happy about marrying *me*."

He straightened. "I wasn't happy that you were *forced* to marry me. I wanted it to be your choice. There's a difference."

She allowed herself a tiny smile. "You wanted to marry me? Why?" Her lips parted as she waited for his answer.

Derek's heart thundered in his throat. Did he finally dare claim this woman's love? "I couldn't bear to see you wed another."

"And why is that?"

"Without you, my life is empty."

"Is that why you followed me when you believed I'd left you?"

"Not the only reason," he admitted.

She expelled the breath she'd held. "Tell me now," she coaxed with an encouraging smile. "It's much easier said than you think."

"I love you." Derek shared the three words he'd held in his heart too long.

"And I love you, Derek." Johanna leaned up and kissed him.

Only her wounded arm prevented him from clutching her tightly against him as their mouths melded. Speaking words of love gave him a joy he'd never before known.

She reveled as his firm lips caressed away all her doubts, as his fingers framed her face with their delicate touch. The stubble on his chin scratched against her skin as their kiss deepened, but she welcomed the rough awareness of him.

With a ragged breath, Derek tore himself away from her mouth to gaze into her aqua eyes. "You must rest now. You might have died."

"And yet, I've never felt more alive," she said.

A rapping at the door interrupted them.

"One moment." He settled Johanna back against the pillows and covered her with the blankets. Opening the door, he found Cushing, hat in hand.

"Pardon the interruption, Master. Is Lady Johanna…" He

seemed unable to complete the sentence.

"She's going to recover, Cushing." Derek opened the door wider to allow the older man a view of her.

Cushing beamed a smile of relief before clearing his throat. "Lord Curtis and Lord Worthing have taken Lady Vaughan to board her ship."

"Worthing?" Johanna interrupted. "You brought Worthing and Curtis on a hunt for your wayward wife?"

Derek ducked his head. "And Olivia. Is that bad?"

Her eyes twinkled with happiness and approval. "No, I think that's very good."

Emotions he couldn't even name swelled Derek's chest. He turned back to Cushing. "Please inform Curtis and Olivia we'll be staying here until tomorrow. And invite Worthing, if he's at liberty to remain as our guest. I want to assess Johanna's and Mr. Barlow's injuries before we return to London. Book rooms for all of us with the innkeeper, and see what you can do to stem any stories he might tell his friends about this morning's events."

"Aye, Master," Cushing said with a smile. "I can do all that." With a nod to his mistress, he went to his tasks.

Derek returned to sit on the bed and gather Johanna against him once more, content to hold her until she fell asleep. "For one so young, how do you know so much about love?" he asked, his head resting against her hair.

"Perhaps I was born with the knowledge. I've loved you so long, I cannot imagine my life without you."

He cuddled her close. "I almost lost you."

"I won't leave you again," she whispered. He heard her tears.

"God help you if you do, for I'll come after you." He leaned back to look at her. "My love is a selfish, all-consuming thing. I'll need you to help teach me to temper it."

Her eyes glowed with happiness. "That could take a lifetime, my lord."

"I count on it." He lowered his lips to hers.

Epilogue

Johanna had always loved Christmastime at Ambersley, but this year her joy was replete. She'd driven with Derek from house to house to distribute the Christmas geese. She'd stood beside Paget and doled out the rum punch to the tenants during their annual gathering at the stables. They had toasted good will toward men and sung the carols that defined the season.

The Hall was filled with family. Curtis and Olivia had remained in Harley Street until Derek convinced them to come to Ambersley in early November. The days grew shorter and colder, and a fortnight before Christmas, Aunt Bess arrived with Harry and Mr. Minton. Johanna kissed the dapper gentleman on his pate, and congratulated him on his upcoming nuptials. Aunt Bess had decided on a spring wedding, but even without the formality, Johanna announced her intention of referring to Mr. Minton as Uncle Nigel. He blushed and demurred, but she noticed he had no trouble learning to respond to his new name.

Harry and Derek met with a firm handclasp. Harry cast an appraising eye over Derek and Johanna. "You two appear to have settled things. I've never seen you look happier."

Derek nodded his satisfaction. "Marriage is an admirable institution. You should try it."

"Not me. You went through hell to find this happiness. I have yet to find the woman who would make that journey worthwhile." Harry turned as Johanna greeted him with a sisterly hug.

"What about me? What about the hell I went through for him?" she asked with a smile. "You men always believe you fight all the battles. You never consider that a woman meets you halfway."

"True, Johanna. And where am I to find a woman who will face adversity with no complaint? You have few equals, I assure you. I should have taken my mother's advice and married you myself," he quipped.

Johanna grew serious at once. "Harry, you know that if it weren't for Derek, I would have snapped you up in a trice. I would have been a fool not to."

"You would have been a fool if you had. You're very fond of me, but you could never love me as you love Derek." With that, he moved on to kiss Olivia's hand and make her laugh with his droll comments about winter in Bath.

Christmas morning, Derek awoke Johanna with a kiss. Happily, there were no more discussions about where she should sleep.

Johanna opened sleepy eyes, and a smile curled her lips. "Good morning."

"Merry Christmas, sweet." Derek placed a jeweler's box on her breasts.

Johanna sat up and broke into the box with the glee of a child. This was the first year she'd received a present from him. A gold necklace with a large opal flanked by two diamonds lay nestled in white satin. The opal held a fire that dazzled with blue and green flames and brilliant flashes of silver.

"The stone reminded me of your eyes," Derek said. He helped her attach the clasp, and she hopped from the bed to peruse the necklace in the looking glass. Derek smiled as he watched the sway of her hips, her buttocks ripe and inviting as she stood with her back to him. He enjoyed her reflection in the mirror as well. He took little notice of the necklace.

Johanna returned to the bed, ignoring her nudity or how it affected him. "It's beautiful, Derek, thank you. I'm embarrassed to say I have nothing to give to you."

"Nothing?" He tried not to let his disappointment show. After all, it was their first Christmas as man and wife.

"Nothing you can open today. I've placed an order for something, but I don't expect it to arrive for almost six more months."

Derek smiled. "Can you at least tell me what it is?"

She hesitated, suddenly shy. "A baby."

Derek had thought his happiness was complete with Johanna, but this news taught him how much more he had to learn about love.

"Come here." His command was a caress.

She flew to him, and tangled in his arms. "I've wanted to tell you for days, but I wanted to surprise you, too. Can you forgive me?"

"I'll think of some way for you to make it up to me." He trailed kisses down her throat.

"Derek, will it matter to you if it's a boy or a girl?"

He lifted his head to gaze solemnly at his wife. "Not in the least," he assured her.

Johanna smiled. "I'm glad. I think I'd prefer a boy, for he would inherit Ambersley, and I can picture his entire life. But, if it's a girl, there are so many unknowns. Do you suppose it's asking too much if I wish for her to find happiness?"

Derek chuckled. "If she finds happiness the same way her mother has, I shall have to keep a very close eye on her until she is safely wed."

Johanna opened her mouth to say more on the subject, but Derek silenced her with a mesmerizing kiss.

About the Author

Award-winning and bestselling author **Amy Atwell** worked in professional theater for 15 years before turning from the stage to the page to write fiction. She now gives her imagination free rein in both contemporary and historical stories that feature smart women and noble men who find love while managing to mend their meddlesome families. Her manuscripts and books have earned her a Golden Heart® nomination, over 25 other contest finals and *Ambersley* has been featured on the Top 100 Books lists for both Amazon Kindle and Barnes & Noble Nook. An Ohio native, Amy has lived all across the country and now resides on a barrier island in Florida with her husband, two Russian Blues and a demon kitten. She's currently writing the second book in the Lords of London series.

Visit Amy Online:

www.amyatwell.com

୬୶

Other Titles:

The Daughters of Cosmo Fortune:
*Three respectable women find themselves
lying, cheating and stealing their way to love.*
LYING EYES — Available Now

Made in the USA
San Bernardino, CA
13 December 2013